The Drummer
Was the First to Die

Liza Pennywitt Taylor

The Drummer
Was the First to Die

St. Martin's Press
New York

THE DRUMMER WAS THE FIRST TO DIE. Copyright © 1992 by Liza Pennywitt Taylor. All rights reserved. Printed in the United States of America. No part of this book may be used or reproduced in any manner whatsoever without written permission except in the case of brief quotations embodied in critical articles or reviews. For information, address St. Martin's Press, 175 Fifth Avenue, New York, N.Y. 10010.

Design by Tanya M. Pérez

Library of Congress Cataloging-in-Publication Data

Taylor, Liza Pennywitt.
    The drummer was the first to die/Liza Pennywitt Taylor.
      p. cm.
    ISBN 0-312-07738-6
    I. Title.
PS3570.A9435D78 1992   92-143
813'.54—dc20   CIP

First Edition: July 1992

10 9 8 7 6 5 4 3 2 1

For J.M.G.T.

Acknowledgments

Thanks must go to my agent Sandra Dijkstra, my editor Hope Dellon, and my teacher James Krusoe, for making this into a better book. And more thanks to Mary Korns, Erika Taylor, Patrick McCord, Michael Stillwater, Ruth and Eric Taylor, and Dr. Harry Vinters.

I am also grateful to those who helped me at the Biomedical Library of the University of California, The Los Angeles Public Library, The Wellcome Institute of Medicine, The Greenwich Naval Museum Library, The Library of the British Museum, The Victoria and Albert Museum, The Geffrye Museum, The Museum of the City of London, and the John Snow Pub.

Preface

This work of historical fiction is based on the medical discoveries of the British scientist Dr. John Snow. The cholera epidemic and Dr. Snow's research in epidemiology and anesthesiology happened as portrayed. The majority of events in the book, however, and all characters other than John Snow, are inventions of the author.

Book I

1

India, January 1854

The elephant's brass holy ornaments glared in torchlight. They'd
painted his trunk with red and blue flame shapes. Silver bells
hung from the aging tips of his tusks, whose points had long
since worn round and yellow as a monkey's skull.

Most days he spent hauling logs in the jungle behind the
village, but for festival nights, like tonight, they decked him in
sacred trappings and fed him a sedating mixture of betel nuts and
rice. He was the only elephant on the island.

The clearing where he stood formed the hub of a network of
grassy lanes and whitewashed clay walls. Pink mimosas hovered
above the huts at the edge of the clearing. Water burbled on all
sides. Any of the lanes would lead within a few steps to the bay,
except for one, almost a road, which went to the British governor's house a mile to the south.

This fishing village of twelve families had lived for generations
on the islet in the warm waters of southern India's Malabar
Coast. You could get to the mainland by boat in half a morning,
but why bother? A third of the village had never been off the
island other than to course over its surrounding waterways for
fish. By standing on the governor's dock you could see the
mainland; the alien trees, the clove and cardamom warehouses
bigger than life.

The coming of the Dutch colonials in the seventeenth century, and then the British, had hardly disturbed the villagers' lives. Sea breezes, mild and sweet smelling, filled their days and nights.

Tonight was the festival of Shiva the four-armed destroyer. The elephant stood patiently, and occasionally shifted his crusty feet, leaving plate-sized craters in the yellow dust. Lost now in a stupor of betel, he hardly heard the wailing tumult from the festival musicians perched on his back and standing around him.

Their own trance held them. Two drummers, brothers, had sounded out the same sixteen-beat rhythm countless times since sunset. They'd keep it up until dawn. The versatile and sinewy boat maker, cousin to the drummers, played a long reedy *shanai*, like those used to charm cobras from under the brush of ruined buildings. Three sons of the most prosperous farmer swayed to the beat, intoning the same five-note melody over and over, with the whole group joining in as often as their trance allowed.

White *dhotis* around the musicians' waists looked dazzling in the torchlight against their chocolaty skin. The watching women, including the plump wife of the fishing-net maker and her shy, pockmarked sister, set off their dark southern beauty with cotton saris of blue brighter than a kingfisher's wing and of the green of new-sprung rice.

Everyone in the village, even the children, took part. Adults who couldn't make music, or weren't needed to feed the elephant his palm fronds, sat cross-legged on coconut mats by the fire, the men drinking strong *arak* thinned with water. All chewed the special festival sweets made with milk and sugar, delivered that morning by boat from the mainland. The older drummer's small sons played behind the elephant's legs. A rising full moon showed over the edge of the clearing.

The younger drummer, standing in front of the elephant, eased himself out of the rhythm to stop for another drink of *arak*. Only his brother was left hitting the steady sixteen beats against the *shanai* and the singers. He increased his volume, pummeling at the drum he'd fashioned himself out of hide and rosewood. The complex refrain had persisted so long that the whole village had altered their movements, their speech patterns, even their breathing, to synchronize with the plangent beat.

Suddenly, the pulse stopped. All heads, even the elephant's, looked up. The rest of the musicians went on for a few beats before colliding into silence. Every eye fixed on the drummer.

He bent himself double, clutching at his stomach and the

4

drum, and sank to the ground in a grotesque embrace with his instrument. He convulsed in a sudden spasm of vomiting. A puddle, viscous in the firelight, spread from his mouth and widened around him. His face faded to the color of ashes.

For seconds, nobody moved. Then the victim's youngest son peeked out from behind the elephant's leg and toddled over to the writhing man, shouting, "Baba! Baba!" But before he'd gone three steps, he fell, grabbing his belly like his father.

The village scattered in chaos. Three by the fire collapsed like the drummer. The drummer's wife tried to help her husband and their boy, but within minutes she too fell.

The drummer was the first to die. The rich farmer's sons fled the clearing in terror, but shame soon overwhelmed them. In half a mile they turned back to help their neighbors. And they, too, died.

By the time the moon sank behind the coconut trees, all human life in the village was extinguished except for two babies and an ancient grandmother. The matriarch had watched her sons and grandsons die with their faces more colorless and shrunken than her own. She then lay on her mat with crossed arms, waiting for Shiva to take her as he had all the others, but she fell asleep instead. Even though the babies cried through the night they didn't wake her.

At dawn, the hungry elephant, still weighted with festival garb, broke loose from his tether and pushed his way through the tamarind forest to the governor's house. Startled servants came upon him in the east garden. Trailing debris from the swath he'd trampled through the roses and dahlias, he contentedly munched a potted fern whose clay container he gripped with his trunk.

2

London, July 1854

On his rounds Dr. Snow heard stories that never made it into the newspapers. Buckingham Palace was said to be walled off, the Princess Royal dying. Queen Victoria's grim silence was undeniable. By the second week of the epidemic, rumors of cholera ranged from probable truth to the wildest speculation. Hundreds were reported to be dead by the East India docks where the Crimean ships unloaded.

The reports of armed troops blocking the roads out of London seemed dubious. Snow supposed no one else believed them either, for by night one could see a furtive exodus of families heading for greener homesteads. They carried little, afraid that cholera contamination might cling and follow them out of town.

The heat that summer was unlike anything southern England had felt for years. Hay workers in Surrey fainted with sunstroke, dropping from their high rick ladders like shot starlings. Produce sent into London rotted before it reached Covent Garden. Ladies furtively unbuttoned one or many buttons of their constricting dresses. Babies cried continually. And the cholera victims lucky enough to afford it were buried as quickly as a vicar could be found. Most were too poor for that luxury, so back streets held horrifying surprises.

Explanations for the scourge were varied and ingenious. Snow had a hard time with rational answers when people asked him, the expert, about everything they heard. Poisoned wells, poisoned Thames, vile smoke. Was it a foreign plot? An Irish plot? Or a Royal plot to suppress the working man?

Advice flourished. Don't leave your house or let anyone in. Don't eat plums, milk, cockles, hot pies; don't buy from the street stalls. Don't even look at a whore. Sure prevention was promised with rhubarb, opium, or pig urine. You could buy guaranteed charms to hang around your neck on a string. And was it true half of Paris was dead with it?

Despite the nearness of panic, London's main thoroughfares were as busy as ever. The undercurrent of cholera panic wasn't yet strong enough to slow the tenacious business of daily life.

Dr. Snow threaded his way along Oxford Street through carts, horses, sheep, and thousands of afternoon pedestrians. All pushed their way east or west in a fume of coal smoke and river stink. Overhead the tops of rain clouds loomed darker than the sooty London buildings.

Snow fingered in his pocket a note he'd received just that morning, carefully packed in a basket with a dead gray squirrel under the packing straw: "Get back to your godless painkilling and stop working on cholera. They deserve to die." The tufted-ear squirrel stank; it had been far gone. He had tossed it in the covered bucket he kept for dead laboratory hedgehogs and poked through the packing for a clue as to who could have sent it. All he came across was a gritty residue of fine red sand stuck to the shredded straw.

Religious zealots abounded in times like this, and Snow went through the gestures of paying no attention. Even so, he had kept the note.

If anything could make his exhaustion worse, it was brooding over God-crazed threats. His frame was stiff from recent hours in an unlit slum basement too low-ceilinged for him to stand upright. This last place had filled pages of his notebook with data on more than fifty cholera cases, all residents in a penny-a-night lodging. Unfortunately a third were dead by the time he got there, and had no answers for him. The alert ones had been willing enough to talk, and made for useful notes, but in the dark it was hard to write more than a few scratches. He was eager to get home and set things down more thoroughly.

Snow felt one more twinge in his gut, and waited for the first disastrous hints of sickness. He forced himself to slow his pace.

Don't want to put a strain on the body, he thought. Keep things easy. Keep it quiet. A small fear of his own vulnerability reared up, and he quelled it unthinkingly, out of habit.

The fear persisted, though, a familiar and almost comfortable part of his thoughts by now. It twisted through the fragments of a melody which had been stuck in his head for hours. Some street boys had been yawling it to each other earlier, their Cockney a mass of vowels and as foreign to Snow as Urdu.

Though he couldn't make out their words, the tune fingered some lullaby or nursery song from his childhood. Something about playing in the streets by moonlight? At first it had been pleasant, but by now its repetition in his brain had become a queer requiem for all the deaths he'd seen that day. He thought not of children playing and laughing, but of children dying in a cholera stupor. He felt closer to weeping with each new cycle of the tune. Sleep in any lullaby had always seemed to him an equivalent of death.

Without warning, the rain that had been threatening broke in a downpour. Water dripped from Snow's hat and dark beard before he could get his umbrella open. He was fumbling with the fastening, his elbows squeezed awkwardly against his ribs in the crowd, when a blunt-faced woman who barely reached his waist crooked her fingers around Snow's hand and tugged with surprising strength at his medicine bag.

Of course he thought she was trying to steal it. He struggled with both the bag and the half-raised umbrella, the woman hanging like a dead weight on his arm, refusing to let go. By now he was soaked through and trying hard not to poke out someone's eye with his umbrella tip. All this distracted him at first from hearing what she was saying.

"Business. Business for you." She tugged harder, never meeting his eye, her shaky voice hard to hear. "It's your job, ain't it?"

Even in the rain, tobacco smells rolled from her rusty black dress. It didn't seem to bother her that she was getting drenched. She barely blinked the drops from her eyes.

"Is it cholera?" demanded Snow. "Do you want me to see a cholera case?" He dreaded seeing another one, and yet at the same time hoped that was what she had for him.

"God be praised, I hope not." But she must have seen his interest fade because before he could push on she said, "It may be, it may be. How should I know? That's for the doctor to say.

8

Come along, won't you?" She smiled now, showing blackened gums.

Already their blockade annoyed everyone around. A few who'd been close enough to hear the word "cholera" lowered their eyes and pushed at others, hoping to get as far away as they could. Snow saw them and thought of the recent riot caused when one cholera victim collapsed on a Piccadilly sidewalk. Dozens had been hurt. It would be easier to just go with this woman.

She led him through winding alleyways and rookeries, their walls still encrusted with tattered posters from the Grand 1851 Exhibition, now scrawled with obscenities. The two entered a tenement in Pulteney Court. As they climbed up four flights of stairs, the heat increased at every step, as did a stench of sewage and burnt cheese.

Snow went through a door into a windowless attic lit only by a candle. He sensed in himself a rising excitement at the prospect of a room full of cholera cases waiting for help; more notes, more data, maybe an answer. A few inches from his head the roof tiles clattered with the rain.

It turned out to be only one patient after all: an old woman lying on what looked like a heap of straw, or bunched sacks. A disappointment which he knew to be petty made him dump his bag hard on the floor.

"You dragged me up here to see one case? Couldn't the Poor Hospital doctor come?" Snow jerked off his wet hat.

"Please, guvnor, she's terrible sick," she said, the words coming out with a pleading as false as a bad actor's lines. She pulled out a pipe and calmly filled it.

Snow lit his small brass lantern, hoping for a hook to hang it from, but there was none. They'd stripped the room bare, probably even pried the nails from the floorboards.

Now that the woman had settled into her smoke, her questions rushed out in irritating chatter. "Is it true about the cholera, Doctor, that it's the plague pits dug up, from old times, as causes it? And Manchester, is it really mostly gone now? That's what I heard, all of 'em dead. I had a sister tramped to Manchester once, in '32 . . ." Her voice wandered off but then found the thread again. "I'm safe 'cause I had it myself back then. Can't get it twice, I know that. It's true, ain't it, that you cough and then your tongue goes black—"

9

The storm's first full peal of thunder ripped through her words and silenced her. Snow ignored both and knelt to examine the patient.

He pulled in his breath. She wasn't old at all; probably no more than sixteen. Just aged by cholera. One side of the girl's face stood out from the shadows, cradled in its nest of rags. Adolescent down still touched the curve of her collapsed cheek, but cholera had sunk the skin around her eyes into the skull cavities, the way the faces of the very old or the starved will sink in on themselves, as if in self-protection. Her view was fixed with resigned serenity on a dark corner of the room. If Snow hadn't caught the slight rise and fall of her chest, he would have thought she was dead.

Snow lifted her hand and checked the fingertips; blue under the fingernails, and wrinkled as dried winter apricots. He pinched the skin on the back of her hand between his finger and thumb. It stayed there, like biscuit dough, until he smoothed it back into place.

For some reason the street boys' tune drifted into his mind again, as clear as if someone had whistled it in the next room. With it came once more a sense of loss and grief he couldn't explain. It wouldn't be for this girl; she was nothing to him. She could only be a prostitute, judging by the silky rags around her and the old woman's air of possession. Why should he care? Even so, the tears that had been threatening all afternoon rose up. Tears not just for cholera victims, but for the withered babies he'd delivered, for his dead mother, drowned sailors, and the hundreds of dead and dying he'd seen over the years in their dark chambers and sad beds.

He felt as if he could weep for hours. His lower lip quivered once and his vision blurred, but all it took was a quick wipe with his sleeve to fix it. Then his self-control took over and he turned his attention back to the girl.

With no warning other than a quiet belch, her slack mouth opened, and out poured a sluice of thin gray slime, saturating her and the rags beneath her with a quart of watery cholera vomit.

"Damn her!" said the woman. She hustled over to grab the girl's limp foot and jerk it hard. "Damn her! I just finished changing everything. There's nothing clean left now."

The girl moaned once and shut her eyes. A wet gurgle came from beneath her thin skirt and the cholera stink of fish and shit

10

billowed up. Even though he'd been smelling it all day, Snow fought a rush of nausea.

The old woman grunted in exasperation, and went back to her spot against the wall.

Snow took from his bag a square of soft linen, and pulled loose the shoulders of the girl's wet, patched chemise. He wiped off her mouth and the gray skin of her upper body, then tossed the cloth aside.

His eye caught something in the poor light. Lifting his lantern he took a closer look at her chest. The coppery lesions of secondary syphilis covered her torso, random as scattered pennies.

A sudden interest replaced Snow's sadness. He felt almost himself again. He had been wanting to study this aspect of syphilis but rarely saw it. Now was his chance to get all the information he wanted. Taking a notebook from his bag, he turned to a clean page and painstakingly made illustrations of the most prominent lesions and their patterns of distribution, with descriptions of the color variations as well.

The old woman rocked on her heels and smoked her pipe, oblivious to Snow's preoccupation, which was probably no stranger than most things she'd seen. It took Snow a while to get the drawings in the right detail, and the labor of it was the most relaxing thing he'd done in days.

"She probably won't live, you know," he said as he finished the drawing. "Not with this much fluid loss. Not with the pox weakening her."

"Oh, but she's such a beauty, sir. Just look at her. Good years left, plenty of 'em. Just fix her up a bit. I know you can do it." She came over and stroked the girl's cheek in a gesture Snow mistook for tenderness until the girl found enough strength to turn her head away.

Snow knew that if the girl died the woman could just go get another. Despite the rumors, business was brisk these days. There was nothing like fear to give men that need. And he wondered, if by some miracle the young whore survived, how old she'd be before she looked like her mistress. Thirty-five? Forty? He turned to his bag.

"Give her five drops of this, every few hours." It was a solution of opium and would stupefy the girl into a doze too deep for her to notice the woman's cruelty. If she survived, it couldn't

11

hurt her. He pulled out a few shillings. "And if she's still alive tomorrow buy some boiled water. Make her drink."

The old woman's eyes darted under half-closed lids. Even the girl stirred at the clink of the metal.

Snow replaced his tools in the bag, now fighting a dread of the room and aching for light and air. He took the lantern down the stairs, trying not to see the ruinous interiors he passed. In the outer doorway, his feet sloshed through an inch of thick toilet slops from a spilled bucket. He stumbled over the threshold and let the rain's benediction pour over his head and shoulders.

3

India, January 1854

With each breath she took, her French stays pinched her ribs.

Lillian held herself stiff against the rails of the swaying boat, her spine as rigid as the mainland pilings receding behind her. Irritating curls of damp hair escaped her straw bonnet.

She squinted as the Indian sun broke through the clouds in a sudden rush of heat and glare. She ached for skies which she'd only read about. Anything would do, any sky other than India's. A gray mist on Yorkshire moors, or a crisp March blue above Paris housetops. Or snow, drifts and heaps of pure white ice flakes pouring down from clouds above the Alps. But the diffused tropical glare was inescapable.

A black-headed gull swooped across her line of vision. The bird's neat head turned this way and that as if its tiny brain weighed crucial ideas for consideration. Eat fish? Fly home? Head to sea? The bird suddenly folded its wings and plunged into the wavelets, compact and heavy as a plumb bob. It emerged in moments with a glint of fish in its beak.

Lillian envied its capacity for action and sudden choice. It flew, saw dinner, and dived for it. Would she ever be able to carry out such a decisive act? Her movements from one day to the next and across the seasons were governed by her father and stepmother in a way so constant that it took effort even to realize it. Her life felt like a stream of sweetly passive smiles, flowing imperceptibly into loveless old age and a hundred thousand cups of tea.

"Home soon, Bibi," said the oarsman. He balanced on the prow, and pointed one oar at the peaked roof of the governor's house, jutting above the island's bananas and jacarandas.

"Thank you, Naga," said Lillian.

The boat scudded against the beach with a hiss. Pushpa, Lillian's maid, went on sleeping on the floor of the boat where she made a limp and colorful heap in her rumpled sari. Lillian had difficulty waking her. She seemed in a stupor, making Lillian wonder if she had taken some drug to endure the uncomfortable trip. Finally Pushpa shook her head and pushed herself upright, rubbing her eyes, smearing the black kohl. She looked around in a daze. In a tangle of skirts, Lillian clambered onto the dock, and then helped Pushpa, who seemed unsteady on her feet.

Lillian's father's house stood before her, unavoidable, as always, at the end of her journeys. Its enormous roof's barbed turrets cut into the sky like horns. Dog-faced fruit bats roosted in its sloping rafters. One of the winged beasts, bigger than the gull, now circled high over the clearing in its daytime search for insects.

A deep veranda surrounded both stories of the house, darkening its interiors with shadows cast by carved sandalwood screens.

The Governor's Palace was over 250 years old. It was built by Dutch traders before the British came. It was big enough to house fifty guests. The house had lasted so long only by a continual rebuilding of its thick but crumbling mudpack walls, and it stood shaky as a small craft during the periodic battering of typhoons.

Lying under the mosquito nets as a child, Lillian had felt unprotected by the walls, unsure of their strength, for she had assumed that the house held a fearful life and power of its own. Throughout her childhood she had waited for what felt like threats from the house itself to materialize into disaster.

But years ago, this fear had been replaced with more practical anxieties, such as cobras, malaria, and spinsterhood. Now, after her six-week absence, she felt only a familiar unease as she approached through the front courtyard and heard her family's voices raised in anger. What was Henry doing there? Her mouth went dry and she crossed her arms over her breasts, hunching

14

her shoulders. She hadn't been prepared to see her stepbrother, especially after the tiring journey from her aunt's hill estate.

Henry's voice rose in a cadence of self-defense, and her father's answer came, unclear but angry. She knew instantly, as if someone whispered it in her ear, that Henry had somehow muddled his new regiment post. Probably he'd been kicked out. He shouted some accusation; the words were lost but the tone was unmistakable.

She hadn't known him as a boy but she could imagine the screaming matches he must have had with his nurse or governess over things he wanted. If she had heard that tone in his voice when they first met, in her eighteenth year, she never would have let things go as far with him. She would have fought him off, like a tiger, the very first time. But by now his childish fury was as familiar as the feel of her shoe. She sighed and tried to muster some strength against the scene she knew was ahead.

A pulse of headache jagged into Lillian's right temple, linked with a brief surge of nausea, which she tried to quell with a few deep breaths. Both passed. Seasickness, she thought. Or just another family argument. The thought of illness didn't occur to her. She was never ill.

With Pushpa silently trailing behind her, Lillian reached the veranda, and greeted Rajan, Pushpa's father. He bowed and opened the door for her into the subdued light of the drawing room, then murmured a few words to Pushpa in the local dialect. Lillian said to her, "Go upstairs and rest. I won't need you for an hour or two." She stepped into the room.

Before Lillian's eyes could adjust to the cooler shadows, her own father's words sprang into clarity.

"That post with the Bengal Lancers wasn't easy to get for you, Henry. No division will consider you now. Why can't you ever make more of an effort?"

She had a moment to observe the three of them before they saw her.

Lillian's stepbrother Henry stood by a window, his face toward her, his eyes shooting green light. He was as handsome as ever, godlike in the breadth of his shoulders and in the way he planted his feet on the ground. The bones of his face recalled the distant, controlled glance of some noble animal staring over its unquestioned domain—a tiger, a prize racehorse, or even a cherished hunting dog.

15

Seeing him gave her the physical jolt of pleasure she had grown to expect ever since he'd come to live with them.

And yet, looking at him more carefully now, she saw that in recent months something had changed. His expression struck her as off balance, as if he'd stepped out of an asymmetrical portrait by a third-rate artist. He looked at her father with too much attention and too much focus in his green eyes, and at the same time he squinted as though it were hard for him to see the man clearly. His blinks came too often, with a barely noticeable twitch of his head.

And then she noticed, with a small nudge of tenderness, that his hair needed cutting. The red curls were almost touching his shoulders. She could imagine the exact sensation of snipping his curls, the dry squeak it would make, and the dull friction of the scissors against his freckled neck.

"This time you've let it go too far," continued her father, but broke off when he saw his daughter.

"Lillian," he called out, with forced pleasantry. "And a day early, too!"

Lillian stepped over and kissed her father's cheek. His familiar smell of tobacco and sandalwood enveloped her briefly before she bent for a peck at her stepmother's cool jowl, round as a teapot.

Mrs. Aynsworth's plump, ringed hand reached up and stroked dusty hair back from Lillian's face.

"How wonderful to have you back," continued her father. "Is your uncle with you?" And then she wondered if his greeting had been forced after all; he seemed to have forgotten his fury along with whatever argument he'd been having with Henry.

His quick shift from anger to delight struck Lillian as a sign of old age. Had his hair had grown so white in only six weeks? She strove for an image of him before Christmas, when he saw her off at the boat.

But all she could recall for comparison was a scene which suddenly came to her, of her father, then brown haired and taller, kneeling in a red jacket to show her a shiny war medal. His arm was around her. Could it have been her birthday?

Lately, memories like this had been springing out of nowhere; her father leading his horse guard regiment, sword raised high, in a Bombay military parade. Her father about to leave for an inland tiger shoot, standing tall among the hubbub of bearers, elephants, and gun cases, leaning over to kiss her good-bye. Her father, again with a protective arm over her shoulder, teaching her an alphabet rhyme from a small slate board. With this image came the smell of the chalk, even the feel of its dust on her fingers. Could he ever have been as young and strong as he seemed in these scenes?

Some of them she wondered if she was inventing, to compensate for a childhood she had largely forgotten and mainly remembered as lonely. As her girlhood receded farther and farther behind her, she wondered if perhaps some inner voice was trying to hold onto a remnant of imagined happiness.

She cleared her throat, thick with dust. "Uncle George escorted me as far as the mainland docks and onto our boat. He had to stay in town to see about some cardamom sales. That's why I'm early."

She looked across at Henry, who had made no move to join the three of them, but was staring at his reflection in a tall mirror. "Hello, Henry. I hardly expected to see you here."

"Hello, Lillian." Henry turned briefly from his own image but otherwise didn't stir. She searched his face, as well as she could at that distance across the dim room, for some indication of gladness on seeing her. She caught nothing. It had been months since they last met, the July monsoons at least. What is it to me if he's glad or not, she thought.

But that one small touch of resentment brought the memories back and even as she tried to push them away they grew more vivid. Henry, night after night in this very room lit by moonlight or starlight, or with monsoon rains so loud that they could hardly hear each other's whispers. The one single time she had let him finally have his way, her pleasure and her terror of discovery formed a mingled sensation which she could recall as clearly as the smell of the old, mildewed sofa.

From his first, furtive kisses until the final seduction weeks later, it had never occurred to her to protest. Her reaction at the first hesitant caress was an absurd sense that in the dark he had made a mistake and confused her with someone else. In quiet afternoons alone in her room, feeling both guilty and delighted at her thoughts, she had dreamed of Henry touching her. Her daydreams never included any resistance on her part.

Besides, she feared any hostility would help him realize it was

17

not the first time for her, though it seemed that he noticed nothing.

Suddenly Henry's eyes left the mirror to look at her again. He smiled this time, lowering his chin, and she was sure he could read her thoughts. Remembering the way desire had once flooded her, she blushed and looked away.

Her stepmother still held one of Lillian's hands and was stroking it lightly. As always, she looked not into Lillian's eyes but at her cuffs, her cheeks, her linen collar, the brooch on her dress. It was as if she wanted to examine Lillian as closely as possible to see how she looked so well put together. Despite an hour with her maid every morning, Olympia usually had a ribbon untied, some rouge smeared across her earlobe, or a wisp of hair floating free.

"And how are your joints, Olympia?" Lillian gently pulled her hand away and sat across from Mrs. Aynsworth on the sofa, which still released evocative whiffs of mildew. A lizard scuttled out from one of the cushions. Lillian swatted at the spot and made a face. "Your last letter said the pain had been bad. Aunt Flora gave me a tonic for you to try, something new."

Mrs. Aynsworth paid no attention to the lizard. She reclined on a love seat left from Napoleon's day, made for some lost romantic interlude. (It, too, had been there eight years ago, but had been too small for Henry and Lillian.) Even on this hot morning she wore heavy velvet of dark purple. Her face glowed above this somber background, with lips still full and tender and cheeks as fresh as Lillian's had been at eighteen. Though her white collar was ringed with face powder, she still held her head like that of a beautiful woman, with a slightly raised chin and a mild smile stretched over her teeth.

Olympia began a nervous munching of candied violets from a cut-glass dish. One violet slipped through her fingers and she furtively searched for it through the folds of velvet.

"I'm so glad you're back," she sighed between bites. "It's been dull this winter. My rheumatism is gone now, but there's this new pain . . ." She held her ribs in demonstration, then looked across at Lillian, apparently remembering the ongoing quarrel. "Have you heard what's happened?" She lifted the dish of violets again and offered it to Lillian.

"No thank you, Olympia. I'll wait for tea." Lillian shifted on the sofa, trying to ease a spot of prickly heat across her back. She

18

glanced at Henry, who seemed to be paying no attention. "If you mean Henry's gambling debts, Uncle George told me. I can't see why you're both so upset." She looked around at the three of them, waiting to see if she was right about his post. "It's not as if it's the first time. And this was less than before. Only five hundred pounds, Uncle said."

Her father coughed lightly. "It isn't the debts. Henry's been asked to leave his regiment." The words sounded flat and of less interest to him than weather, or tides. "We just found out this morning. A messenger rowed over from the mainland."

And how many days has Henry been here, Lillian thought, not telling them a thing? She looked over at him with anger and fought to keep it as he smiled at her. That smile made all crimes allowable. Henry's smile was like the shade beneath big-leafed palms, or a glimpse of a flock of bright parrots. She could feel the old effect it had on her, draining her anger, as if he had turned some small tap in her throat.

But before she could ask anything, a sudden dimming of the light made them all look out through the carved screens. A huge gray shape loomed slowly past the hibiscus, blocking the sun.

"Rajan, surely that's the elephant from the village out there?" The colonel's voice betrayed relief at one more interruption of the family argument.

"Oh, certainly, sahib. Elephant. He being present in garden at sunrise." Rajan went on setting out the tea table, smoothing over the white cloth with concentration.

"Well, what's he doing there? Why haven't I been told? He can't very well wander in our garden all day."

Rajan gave a short nasal sigh. "Sir, he is most truly no problem. Cook's cousin say he come from last night's Matapundi Festival on island's north side. He escaping festival. Matapundi persons most probably all asleep. I myself know this elephant. He is most genuine pukka goods holy, sacred to Shiva. Because of temple ornaments, I for one may not disturb this elephant." He returned to setting out the teapot and cups. Obviously for him the matter was settled. He mixed a glass of watered whisky and offered it to the colonel on a small tray. Lillian noticed that the tray shook.

"He'll step on my new White Sensation from Bombay," said Olympia.

Olympia's roses. Lillian was sick to death of them. Once a

19

week her stepmother would haul herself out to the garden with a basket and scissors, Lillian at her side. She would cut a few flowers and talk to Lillian endlessly about roses men had sent her, poems they'd written comparing her to a rose, rose-filled scenes from her childhood in England. Then she'd hand her clippings to Pushpa to arrange in a vase.

As far as Lillian was concerned the elephant could trample every rose in the garden.

"Roses quite tip-top, Bibi. None of this worry trouble is necessary for you." As Rajan spoke, there was a tearing crunch of vegetation. The elephant had just pulled up a hibiscus bush, a tree really, in full flower, and bits of earth from the roots spattered against the screen. Some of the earth fell into the room with a dusty rattle.

Colonel Aynsworth pulled out a handkerchief and rubbed a speck of dirt from his cheek. "They should know better than to let him wander like that. Find someone who is allowed to disturb him, Rajan, and have him returned to Matapundi. Until then, chain him somewhere, quickly."

Rajan set down the teapot loudly. He bent his head, hunched his shoulders, and padded from the room on bare feet.

Henry walked over to the window, closer to Olympia, apparently fascinated by the elephant. Henry's face resembled his mother's only in a pleasant softness around his mouth. Even at forty, and with such a heavy build, Olympia's face was lovely, but it was a different look that Henry had. His red hair and fair skin must have been his father's.

Points of yellow light reflected into Henry's eyes from the elephant, who had moved into the sun where its brass ornaments caught the glare.

With a gesture of exhaustion and boredom, Lillian pulled the pins from her hair and let it fall over her shoulders in a tangled heap. She leaned her head back against the sofa cushions and gazed at the high ceiling, where two more lizards clung just above her. From under half-closed eyes, she took a long look at her stepbrother.

"What did you do to get booted?" she asked, trying to sound casual. "They don't do it for gambling debts." By the slight increase in her stepmother's alertness, Lillian knew he hadn't told them yet. Had they even asked? She sometimes felt their complaisance would drive her mad.

Henry turned from the window. The elephant was now more active, and seemed irritated by the two servants who pranced nervously between his feet with a rope and chain. The chain looked too light to hold a pony, let alone an elephant.

"A gambling debt is more important than what *did* happen," he said. "That's an affair between gentlemen, whereas this . . ." He stopped and creased his perfect eyebrows.

Lillian resisted her urge to back away from the questions, to step lightly near this intrusion into the world of men's ethics.

"You'd better tell it and get it over with, Henry," she said.

Her instinct to avoid the violets broke down, and she bit into one. She had forgotten how awful they tasted. The sickly perfume wafted up the back of her throat.

Olympia poured sherry into her teacup and took a sip. "You don't have to tell us, dear, if it makes you uncomfortable. I'm sure they—"

"No. I want to know." Lillian stared at Henry and almost forced him to look at her.

"All right. It doesn't matter, really. He was only a bloody bearer and he acted like the pigs they all are."

"Henry," Lillian whispered. She moved her chin toward Rajan, just returning.

Henry ignored her and continued. "Not especially useful, nor even amusing, as a dog can be. I shot my dog last season because he soiled my bed, and no one objected, so why should this have bothered them?"

Henry picked up one of the room's dozens of crocheted doilies from a tabletop, and absently fingered it as he talked, stretching out the knotted patterns and gradually pulling it to pieces. Shreds of twisted string began to litter the floor as he paced.

"Stop that," said Lillian, more as a routine protest than in real annoyance. "Those things take hours to make." How many afternoons had she sat there with those cruel-looking hooks, turning out useless doilies? And then his words sank in. "Are you saying you shot a servant?"

"Not exactly that. Well, yes. I did shoot *at* him. It was only an accident. I'm not sure if I even hit him. Never know now, of course." Henry absently stuffed the remains of the doily in his pocket.

"It wasn't my gunshot that killed him, you see. He fell into the Bhima River. We were all standing on the dock and he was

21

loading up my kit to go downriver and join the rest of the regiment. It was myself and a few of the other fellows. I was ready to go, and hot. He'd been insufferably slow all morning, as if he just weren't thinking. So we were finally packed up tight and ready to push off, when this dog's bloody wife comes running up. He got out of the boat and actually held it there so I couldn't leave! He started talking to her, and had the cheek to turn around and ask me to wait."

Henry stopped talking, his hands still in his pockets. By now he must have known his storytelling gift was at its best. He paused long enough to make them all restless.

Even Rajan stopped what he was doing, the tea tray in midair.

"You never did learn how to handle your servants," said Olympia. "What did the woman want?"

"Oh, nothing much. One of their brats was dead, or sick, or something. She looked sick herself. The man wouldn't let go of the boat, but kept talking to her, even when I shouted at him. So I shot at his foot just to scare him; that was all I meant, really. And he fell in the river. A crocodile nipped over in a moment and had him. It got a good grip on the leg and he was pulled under. Never surfaced again. I hope it was quick, for his sake. Bloody monsters."

Henry glanced around for some other hand-sized toy, and grabbed a small clay monkey the cook's boy had left on a table. He started rolling it between his palms.

"At any rate, something about this man's face as he fell, and all the ridiculous fuss after, I don't know. You had to be there, I suppose. Well, it set me off laughing. The fellows with me, they didn't like it. The laughing. Bad attitude, they said. So when we got downriver they had a quick trial and kicked me out. Sods."

By now, he had somehow cracked the monkey in two. He looked down at the pieces in surprise and returned them to the table, then walked over to sit next to Lillian.

He smiled. "So you see, it really wasn't my fault at all."

Lillian couldn't decide if his expression was earnest or skillfully sarcastic. Above her own travel staleness, she inhaled his nervous sweat.

He playfully picked up a curl of her hair and pulled it, hard enough to hurt, then wound it around his hand.

"Don't, Henry," said Lillian. She pulled her hair free and moved a few inches away on the sofa, not meeting his eyes.

Then he grasped her wrist, as if trying to take her pulse, and with one finger began to draw on the inner curve of her elbow a heart with an arrow through it.

The action froze her. It was an old game they had played on the long hot afternoons when they wanted to touch but had to observe propriety until night when the rest of the house was asleep.

They had used the game to signal each other for a late-night meeting, but also as an acceptable adult parlor game, with the two of them spelling words or drawing simple pictures on the arm of a closed-eyed partner. Each would seriously try to guess the other's intent with a clumsy house, a palm tree, a buffalo, or a short poetic phrase. Sometimes the colonel or Olympia would even play along.

For Lillian it had always been difficult to guess the figures; aside from the distraction of the occasional meeting-signal from Henry, so many letters were indistinguishable through her silk or heavy cotton sleeves. On the hottest days, when she wore short sleeves and he worked on her bare skin, she succeeded. Henry, however, had been an expert at deciphering all Lillian and everyone else wrote or drew.

The game had ended after the rainy night when Henry forced their sofa meetings to their inevitable conclusion. The next day when he picked up her arm she gently pulled away and pretended not to know what he was doing.

She should have known better, though; he was good at reading her thoughts. After days of her evasion, an afternoon came when Henry confronted her. With the rest of the house resting, he grabbed at her wrist as if to play the game but instead forced her onto the sofa and began pulling up her skirts, smashing her mouth under his.

She fought him off more easily than she expected, though he kept a painful grip on her wrist while the two panted and glared at each other.

"We have to stop, Henry. You know that." Despite her panic and anger, she spoke gently, as if reasoning with a playmate.

"You think you're so pure." His voice almost broke. She felt his pain and also sensed something threatening she'd never seen in him before. "You think I never noticed, Miss Lily-White. I know what a virgin's supposed to feel like."

She yanked her wrist free and ran from the room. They never

23

once spoke of what had happened, and the game was abandoned forever. Soon after that, Henry went off to Bombay to continue the law studies he'd begun in England. Even though he did poorly and quit in a year, he never returned to the palace to live.

Now, all these years later, he went into the old drawing gestures without even seeming to think about it, and shivers went up Lillian's arms. For one instant, obedience took hold and she began to think how she could keep herself awake until midnight, and if her best nightgown was clean enough to wear. Then she forced herself to pull her arm free.

Olympia stared at them with narrowed eyes as she went on munching violets. She suddenly stopped chewing.

"It won't do, Henry." Olympia's voice was almost too soft to hear, but it was firm, allowing for no interruption. "All that money for the law tutoring. The gambling." Her hand groped for the dish, but stopped halfway. "And now this."

Lillian wasn't sure if Olympia meant the shooting or this finger play with her arm.

"They just don't appreciate me." Henry laughed at his stale joke.

"You'll have to go."

"Go? Where do you expect me to go?" For a moment his peevishness almost made him ugly.

"It doesn't matter. You can't stay here."

Henry glanced at the colonel, but Olympia raised a hand toward her husband before he could answer.

"It's not your stepfather's decision. I know he'd give you another chance. He's too kind."

Lillian watched, unconsciously holding her breath. The colonel took a long drink from his glass.

Olympia continued talking to Henry as if no one else were present. "I see what will happen if you stay. I know, you think I'm slow. But I do see. At every visit we become more used to your ways. Especially Lillian. Look at her."

On cue, the two men turned their eyes that way. Lillian lowered her head, embarrassed, only partly unsure of what Olympia meant.

"She heard your story without a blush, as if murder were part of the breakfast service. It's intolerable." The creamy voice stayed level but a sudden jerk of Olympia's knee sent the glass dish to the floor. She ignored it. "And that's not all of it. You know what I mean."

"But, Mother, be a sport." said Henry. His smile was back. "What can a fellow like me do for a living? You know I'm useless. I have as much talent as one of your rose bushes. Crimson Sentinel, you know."

The colonel stepped forward, but again the hand came up to bar him.

"It's out of the question that my husband support you. Some of the funds from your father's estate were always left in case I had another child. That seems unlikely." She smiled a short, dry smile. "I'll sign it over to you. With careful habits you can do well on the income."

"What a joke. There's less than a thousand pounds in that account."

Olympia's eyebrows went up on hearing that he knew the sum, but she only said, "I want you to leave by the end of the week."

Henry started to exit the room, but turned at the door.

"You're wrong if you think my going will have any effect on *her*." He tossed his head at Lillian, but didn't take his eyes off his mother. "It's disgusting, the delicate way you treat her, a woman of close to thirty. She'll never marry, you know. I think you'll find the harm's been done; ask her some day." He looked the colonel in the face. "Blame it on me if it suits you. But it won't change anything."

He shoved open the door and ran down the veranda steps.

4

London, July 1854

It wasn't a long walk back to Snow's house in Sackville Street. Even though the rain slowed almost immediately, Snow avoided the busier streets leading to Piccadilly Circus, which would be awash in mud. He decided to take a chance that the sewer construction in Golden Square would have stopped for the day.

The site was quiet and empty. He could go straight through the center path without getting jokingly cursed by drain diggers or having red clay spattered on his boots.

Halfway across, he saw his mistake. The square wasn't deserted after all; a dozen men hovered at the edge of one of the open trenches. As Snow approached he couldn't help edging in for a curious glance down, along with the rest of them. A slow drizzle still fell.

Pressing against a man who was probably one of the drain workers, judging by the mud caking his clothes, Snow peered over the heads in front of him. All he could see were two booted feet, lying in the trench. The rough leather looked fairly new, and the feet were bent inward at an angle, flattened, and limp. Ropes and the depth of the ditch obscured the rest of the body. A white splotch in the shadows marked the face. Snow's eyes went back to the dead man's boots; white stains around the toes reminded him of something he'd seen that day and couldn't quite place.

"What's happened?" Snow asked the worker next to him. He turned as he spoke, and found that the man was staring straight at him, studying him. Their faces were only inches apart.

"Murdered," the fellow answered. His eyes were wide set and pale green, as pretty as a girl's. Mutton clouded his breath. "Can you believe it? They just found 'im. 'Ead bashed in." The man kept his head averted from the body, either to avoid the sight or to keep scrutinizing Snow. The doctor couldn't tell.

"One of the workers?"

"That's right, sir. 'E was diggin' 'ere just this afternoon."

A waft of fresh earth smells came up from the red clay pit.

"Was there no one to help him?" asked Snow. Even as he spoke a surprising self-pity and isolation engulfed him, as if the question were for himself. No help. Got to handle it alone. He suddenly felt abandoned and resentful that not one other doctor had offered to help him today.

For a long moment the feeling flooded him. Then, with a second breath of that clay odor from the pit, he knew where the self-pity came from. He could recall a similar earth smell of an uprooted pine tree felled by a summer storm and lying in a field, its black splayed roots groping, witchlike, into the sky.

It was when he had begun his first village medical practice, twenty-two years ago. The tree had fallen in his third week. That same week, cholera broke out in nearby Kellingsworth coal mine, and he had passed the dying tree daily on his way to see the stricken miners in their cottages.

He had tried everything in his brand-new medical text to help them. Smoke inhalation, cold baths, rosemary ointment. Leeches, even, as a last resort, though he suspected they were useless.

After seven deaths Snow grew desperate and frightened. He had never felt so helpless before. As a last measure he sent for the district medical man from York, the nearest city. Nobody ever came, not even a reply. When it was all over, forty had died.

From the beginning he had tried to determine how they caught it from each other, and why the miners sickened and died while, paradoxically, the farm workers, exposed to animal wastes and the foul air from Yorkshire pig yards, stayed healthy.

He suspected the reason then, and now he was sure of it. Those miners helped form the earliest of his theories. Down in their pits for fourteen hours a day, the men lived, ate, and

27

washed in their own excretions. They gave the cholera to each other with every bite of black bread and onions eaten with wet and filthy hands, with each jar of cold tea that they diluted with the water dipper and drank in the darkness. Cholera was in every sip they took.

But all those years ago, to prove anything about his ideas was impossible. It had been beyond him to do more than keep up with the useless treatments. Back then, a theory like his would have been laughed at. After all, the authorities were convinced that cholera was a moral disease, a disorder of air and poor life habits. More church was the answer.

He hadn't dared to even suggest his opinion. He'd only begged for help. Even now, staring into this ditch, Snow could find the resentment he still carried with him. Months afterwards, they'd sent him a letter; nothing but a series of questions on the spiritual fiber of the miners. "Did they go to services once on Sundays, or twice?" "Were prayers said at each meal?" "Were their children properly taught the catechism?" On reading it, Snow had thought of the children he saw emerging daily from the coal shafts with coal dust tattooed into their cheeks and eyelids. He had crumpled the paper and burned it.

He swore to himself, back then, that one day he'd prove they were wrong about cholera.

"Nobody will care who did it," said the muddy man, bringing Snow back to Golden Square and the present.

The bitterness in his voice made Snow ask, "Did you know him?"

"I was 'is chief. I'm the foreman of these works. It'll fall on my 'ead, you'll see. 'E was a good man. Aside from the grief of it, I got to find a new one. Not so easy with this plague all around." He gazed ahead, chewing on the inside of his cheek.

Just then there was a disturbance at the other end of the pit and a short, well-dressed man in a bowler pushed his way to the edge. He stared down at the body and then glared at the crowd.

"I'm the inspector for this case. You there!" He jerked a forefinger at the man by Snow. "They say you're the foreman."

"That's right, guvnor. Matt Canty."

"Why was this man working so late today, Canty?"

"That's just it. 'E weren't. I sent 'em all home at six sharp. 'Im too."

The inspector narrowed his eyes at the foreman and said

nothing. Then his glance fell on Snow's bag. "You, sir, you're a medical man?"

Snow cleared his throat. "Well, yes, but I—"

"You two men, get this body out." The inspector grabbed the two gawkers closest to him. "And you, I want you to examine him."

"Now see here, Inspector . . ." Snow pulled out his watch and glanced at it. "I haven't time—"

"McGowan. Chief Inspector McGowan, Scotland Yard. Just step right over here, it won't take a moment." The crowd stirred and Snow found himself pushed to where the dead man had been hauled out onto the wet grass. Someone shoved a box forward and Snow sat next to the body.

The man had been killed with a single, powerful blow to the skull. His face was intact, but just above the eyebrows, where the forehead should have risen up, his skull was smashed into the same concave shape as the bent tin colander Snow's mother had used for shelling summer peas. There was surprisingly little blood.

"Well? Is it a clear-cut bludgeoning?" The inspector fidgeted at the edge of the ditch.

The dead man's eyes were open and Snow ran a hand down the face to shut them.

"There's no doubt this injury is what killed him," said Snow, without looking up. "As to what they used, I would guess the back of a shovel. The shape is right." He pulled at one stiff hand. The long, ragged nails, as well as the cracks and callouses, were dark red with a mix of mud, sand, and blood. "It looks like he fought back," said Snow. Had the victim had any more chance than that dead squirrel in the basket? Snow looked up at McGowan, and saw that the foreman was near them now, and seemed to be about to speak to the inspector. Snow waited. But the man stayed silent.

"I really must get back to—"

"Of course, Mr.—"

"Doctor. Dr. John Snow." He was no apothecary; he was entitled to be called doctor. He had his medical degree from the University of London and he wouldn't let anyone forget it.

"Yes, Dr. Snow. I do appreciate your help."

Snow got to his feet and took one more look at the dead man below him. His eyes fell again on the boots and he knew where

29

he'd seen those white stains today; salt stains on the boots of a dying workhouse man who'd tramped up from the salt flats of Epsom. But why should this London ditch digger have salt on his boots? Snow forgot the question almost as soon as it came to him. A better death than cholera, he thought. He headed again on his way.

5

India, January 1854

1

After Henry left the house, Lillian went straight upstairs to her room and lay flat on the bed. She was oblivious to her rank sweat and dust and thankful just to be alone.

She gazed at the cotton canopy over her head, the same dingy canvas which had been up there forever. Its stains from damp and mildew spread in familiar continent-shaped spots that were as comforting as a nursery rhyme.

The room had been only partially cleaned, and a vase of orchids she'd placed on her writing desk a week before leaving was still there. If she hadn't known that the objects it contained had once been flowers, she would hardly have recognized them, fused to the side of the glass in limp decay. A bit of slime remained in the bottom of the vase; she could smell it.

"Pushpa!" she called. There was no answer. "Pushpa, come quickly!"

And then another thing caught her eye. Her music cabinet, full of her song books and opera scores, was open and disordered. A drawer in the cabinet gaped unshut and had obviously been gone through.

Her heartbeat sped up and her headache came back. She sat up and hurried over to look in. There was dust on the open drawer, so it must have been like that at least a week. After a quick scan of the letters and papers she was sure that something was missing, but it was hard to know exactly what; she looked through them so rarely.

Just then Pushpa appeared, her eyes cast down. She didn't look well. She still hadn't changed out of the creased green sari she had traveled in. Her face was sunken and had turned the color of cheap paper. Probably another bout of malaria, thought Lillian. She didn't want to say anything. The last time, Pushpa had denied all her symptoms so strongly that she'd finally fainted while putting up Lillian's hair.

Lillian decided to watch her and order her to rest when it got really bad. "Take those away." She gestured to the vase. "And bring my wash water. It should have been here by now." There was no point in asking about the open drawer. Later tonight she'd go through the old papers. It was time to destroy them.

When Pushpa returned with the water, Lillian stood by the bed and let her unhook and unbutton her dress, and then begin the slow process of removing the corset. Each unloosed eyelet allowed a fraction more relief. When the lowest was undone, the garment had to be peeled off Lillian's white skin like rind off a fruit. Red marks burned at her waist and under her breasts, where the corset had chafed, but Lillian knew better than to scratch them, and instead reached for a bottle of rosewater to rub over the area. In this climate, the slightest break of skin could turn overnight into a suppurating wound.

She looked down at her flat stomach and at the small silvery streaks on either side of her navel. She rubbed rosewater over them, too, but she knew it wouldn't help. They were part of her forever.

The whole time at her aunt's, with so little time alone, she hadn't remembered much or thought about her weeks with Henry, or the more distant past. But here, in her old room, with innocent but painful reminders all around her, the little thoughts crept back.

It was before Henry. Before her father had married Olympia. On the day that her maid (long before Pushpa, and her name wouldn't come to Lillian now) could no longer hook the waist of Lillian's skirt, she'd told her father. Until then, she had waited, every morning and night, for a letter which never came. All that ever arrived was a packet of her own letters that she'd written to the man, with no message from him, no markings. She spent endless afternoons pacing under the mango tree by the dock, dizzy and nauseated and looking for the daily mail boat to come from the mainland. It might bring a note; maybe even a passenger.

Her father hadn't mentioned it for years now. Today, in the drawing room, when Henry said what he said, she'd looked over at the colonel to see his response. But there was nothing. Maybe he had forgotten, as even she did at times.

The child was born dead. They said it had been a boy. Scrutinizing her reflection now in the spotted glass—the straight, long nose, the too-heavy brows—Lillian wondered, once more, what he would have looked like. Would he have had his father's high forehead and dark eyes? His morbid tendency to self-examination? Would he have been tall? She wondered if she could ever think of the infant's death without a thick feeling at the bottom of her throat. It was little more than a shadow of weeping, but still there after ten years.

She had made a quick and secretive journey inland, with concealing shawls wrapped around her despite the searing heat. With her own mother dead, and Henry and Olympia not yet part of their lives, there was nobody to ask questions. The house in the Nilgiri Hills with its two bare rooms became her entire world for a few months. A dusty plain was her only view from the narrow windows. The servants chattered at her in English and Telagu. It was nothing to them where a memsahib chose to have her baby.

At first, the worst part of the waiting was trying to hide from herself a feeling that totally confused her at the time, a feeling which she recognized now as relief. Relief that the boring cycle of days had been broken, that something would finally *happen* to her. Her bowed head, her silence, her tears (of anger, not repentance, but all tears look alike) were a pretense of the expected worthlessness and shame.

But as she got nearer to her time, and too big to move easily, her feelings grew softer. Her tears came, instead, over the little blankets and shirts the women had taught her to sew. There was an oddly pleasant metallic taste in her mouth that even now she could recall and associate with a sense of cherishing those fluttering kicks.

No one had prepared her for the pain of giving birth. In the first hours the pains were predictable and small. She thought that the birth would be simple; just wait until the pain ends and a baby appears. But the pains grew and began to have a life and character of their own. Rounded, almost globe-shaped, the huge pains rolled through her body in unstoppable orbits, and seemed indifferent to her survival or the baby's.

She had sometimes wondered about the mortal pain one might feel dying in battle of sword thrusts, or dying of some cankerous disease; this pain was just as deadly. After endless hours or days of it, when she was using up the last of her strength in screaming, the pain grew unthinkably worse, then suddenly vanished into a silent, wet, red infant sliding out from between her legs. Moments later she fell unconscious.

But just before the people around her faded into darkness, through the midwife's shouted commands there had been a confusing disturbance of someone arriving and a scuffle outside her room. She was sure she heard her lover's voice but she was too weak to even raise her head. Later, everyone who had been there insisted she'd imagined it. She finally stopped asking.

Then came a time of fever, confusion, and sweats that seemed to last for years. The only real sensation she remembered was of a terrible ache in her breasts, which continually saturated her bedclothes with leaking milk. Afterwards she discovered that she'd lain sick with puerperal fever for an entire month. They told her that the boy was dead, and that she herself had barely survived. That she should forget.

But the concept of the baby's death couldn't be absorbed all at once. The ideas she'd formed so slowly and carefully over the long months by herself had to topple one by one, in their own time.

The impression of a nursery hung with white lace and full of light; that had to darken. The guessed-at sensations of the baby sucking at her breasts had to fade. There would be no rocking horse in the corner, no toy drums or trumpets cluttering the stairs. The personality she'd already had a mysterious inkling of; a peaceful, introspective child who would stare at leaf shadows and listen to songs; where was that child's soul now?

One piece at a time, the world she'd imagined for herself dimmed and changed back to the world she knew.

She came home to the island to find a new set of house servants and fresh decor in her room. There were days when she could do nothing but weep. She couldn't eat, and within months her old dresses fit easily. But with no one to talk to about it, soon enough it really was as if it had never happened. Only her father knew—her father, and whoever had been outside the door shouting, if she hadn't imagined it.

Half a year later she happened to hear the news about Jampur. She could remember the words accurately even now.

She had been reading at a table in the garden, and her father had passed with one of the clerks.

"The entire Fifteenth Regiment, Tippu? Is it possible?" His voice had been low, secretive.

"It is without doubt, sir. Fort Munro, on the edge of the Thar desert. All those young men from last winter. The Afghan people are fierce."

"And the mutilations?"

"As always, sir. Most of them washed down the Indus afterwards, so the burials were not easy. The flag was rescued, though. That was a good thing. They retrieved the flag near Jampur."

If she hadn't overheard their words she would never have known; no one ever mentioned the battle at Fort Munro again. She might have spent years waiting for him to come back. As it was, her actual sense of loss was less than when the baby died. She'd already lost this man. But for a long time her dreams at night were spliced with terrible visions of blood on dusty mountain rocks.

Yearly visits to her aunt punctuated the cycle of tea parties on the mainland and the music lessons with Signor Bastini who was rowed over once a week from town. For the first year she went through the motions of all these events without feeling much more than the daily need to eat and sleep.

Then her father married Mrs. Bince while on a short trip to Bombay, and brought the lady and her son Henry back to live on the island.

Lillian had few memories of her own mother, dead of yellow fever at twenty-one, when Lillian was four. A portrait still hung in one of the guest rooms of a smiling blonde with a frizz of short curls and a high-waisted white dress. She held a tiny spaniel. The image of the dog had always been more vivid in Lillian's memory than that of her mother's face.

She wasn't unhappy about Mrs. Bince, a wealthy widow who was easy to get along with. To this day, Lillian could only assume that her father had never told Olympia what Lillian had done. She also knew, without his saying a word, that he had married to give his daughter some protection. To give her a guard.

The second Mrs. Aynsworth must have felt grateful toward Lillian for pretending not to notice occasional slips of grammar, and for avoiding all references to her previous husband's glue profits. In return for this acceptance she gave affection without judgment, and even now coddled Lillian as if she were a fragile innocent still in her teens, with a miraculous musical talent.

If it hadn't been for her music, and perhaps what happened with Henry, Lillian wouldn't have forgotten the past so soon.

She'd always sung well. She had been singing at the piano the first night she had met her lover, and his strong baritone voice accompanying her was the first reason he'd stood out from the rest. But afterwards, she tried not to remember that, and threw herself into musical study to escape her loneliness.

Most of the music on the shelf in her room was from that period, seven and eight years ago, when Signor Bastini's weekly visits marked her activities as nothing else could. How he had praised her voice! Such a rich alto, he'd said, perfect for Schubert lieder. He'd even tried to get up an amateur production of a Donizetti opera on the mainland, but her father hadn't approved, so she sang the parts only in private.

But her fervor for singing wore off. There was no one to listen, at least no one who understood the music. Her father had heard everything countless times, and Olympia just nodded and smiled, saying, "Lovely, dear, just lovely." Lillian tested her with wrong notes, sometimes singing an entire song a whole step higher than the piano part, but the response was always "Lovely."

If Henry were home he would stare at her as if mesmerized while she sang. He would move closer and closer to the piano, sometimes onto the bench itself, as if he wanted to breathe the air coming from her lungs. From the very beginning, she cringed at it and was sure he would give the two of them away. His mother must know he cared nothing for music. He never said a word, unless it were to whisper, "Sing another one." Soon she made an effort not to sing when he was home. And then she stopped singing completely.

Now Lillian left her seat in front of the mirror and walked over to the music cabinet to leaf through the crumbling pages. One of the thicker books, a Schumann song cycle, still bore old instructions in Signor Bastini's shaky hand: "next lesson March second," or "open upper register more. Think of a swan's neck." She touched the letters with her fingertip. There was a raised pucker where the ink had wet the paper.

2

Dinner was usually served at eight o'clock, but they waited tonight for Henry. Nine passed, and then nine-thirty, without a sign of him, so they went ahead with the meal. None of them spoke about him or about what had happened earlier.

"They say the rains will be late this year," said Olympia, as she beckoned to Rajan for a serving of mutton.

The colonel didn't answer. He poured himself another glass of claret.

Olympia spoke up again. "The mango tree in the side garden is producing well. That's usually a sign of rain, isn't it?"

"I wouldn't say it was producing well, dear. There were only a dozen over the last week."

"There were three on the ground today," said Olympia.

"No, dear. Only two." The colonel didn't raise his eyes from his food.

"Three. I counted them."

"I expect what you took as the third was a dead leaf."

"You must be right. At any rate, it will be a relief if the rains are good."

The elephant wasn't referred to, though they could all hear the animal, trumpeting occasionally, from the spot where he had been chained. It seemed no one had yet taken him back to the village.

The food was poorly cooked tonight; apparently the head cook was ill. The spices were too strong and bit at Lillian's throat. She toyed with the bits of chicken curry and cabbage on

37

her plate until she and Olympia left the colonel to his bottle of port. The women returned to the drawing room, resuming the same seats as always; the faded love seat, the musty sofa.

Earlier she had pulled the book of Schumann songs from her music shelf and brought it down to the piano, thinking she might try them again someday. She was too restless to sit and do nothing, so she wandered over to the piano bench.

Dampness kept the instrument perpetually out of tune, but long ago Lillian had forced herself to endure its sour notes rather than have no music at all. She struck the opening bars of the first song, with hesitation at first, and then with more confidence she sang through it. After all this time, the German was difficult to pronounce.

"Lovely, dear. What is it called? I've never heard you sing that before."

It was true; she hadn't opened the book for eight years; but she was surprised that her stepmother knew one song from another.

"It's called *Frauenliebe und Leben*, Olympia. 'A woman's love and life.' A song cycle by Robert Schumann."

"What a title! I hope it's nothing you shouldn't be singing, dear." Olympia gave Lillian an indulgent smile, with her head to one side, and shook her finger at her.

"It's not what you think." Lillian wondered what exactly Olympia did think; that the lyrics were about some Teutonic den of vice or prostitution? "It's about marriage and children." She left out the other subjects of most of the songs: betrayal, disillusionment, loss, and the inevitable fading of love.

She started the next song. The cycle had eight in all, but tonight she wanted to hear only the first few, before the darker ones ended the woman's story. As she sang, the colonel entered the room and stood listening at the door, his head to one side, a slight frown on his face.

When she finished the song he walked over and gently shut the book. "Don't sing any more of that, Lillian. I'll send to Bombay tomorrow for some new music."

Lillian looked up, surprised. "I don't need any new music. I have plenty, you know."

"My dear, I don't like to think that you . . ." He put a hand to his head and stopped.

"What is it, Father?"

Olympia's gentle snore came from her chair. She would sleep heavily for some time.

"Nothing," her father answered. "Just a bit of headache. That song. You used to sing it before—before your life was so changed."

Lillian's heartbeat sped up and her hands began to sweat. At first she was too surprised to answer him. He hadn't mentioned her pregnancy for years. Like him, she had no language for it. She said the first thing that came into her head.

"How awkward it must have been for you." The moment she said it she was sorry; it sounded accusatory, as if he had diminished the importance of her feelings and worried only about his own. She looked at him, quickly. He met her eyes for a moment and looked away.

"Oh, sweetheart, no, no. It was an unpleasant time, but it's so long ago, and doesn't matter now."

Did he really think that? She suspected he had other thoughts he wasn't saying. "It doesn't matter? You heard what Henry said about me before he left."

"He meant nothing. He was trying to wound your stepmother and me with any vicious invention. How could he know anything?"

The open drawer in her room came to mind. "It was an odd thing to invent." She waited, hoping and dreading that he'd explain more, perhaps reveal that he had guessed about her and Henry as well. But he said nothing.

She aimlessly turned the pages of her music. "I wondered sometimes if you'd forgotten about it."

At first her father didn't answer. Had she said too much? Maybe now he'd drop it.

"Forgotten! Dear God, Lillian, how could you think such a thing? I will never forgive myself. I think of it every day."

She thought it was herself, Lillian, he couldn't forgive. "But you never speak of it."

"And what should I say? I can hardly discuss it over dinner. I thought you yourself would prefer it this way. Some things are too bad to talk about."

She thought of all the things they never mentioned in the family. Henry's uselessness, his gambling and violence. Olympia's love of sherry. The way that the colonel's hands and

39

chin had begun to shake last year. The way he forgot things. All too bad to talk about.

In a burst of frustration she said, "Why can't we talk about it, ever? I still feel ashamed and foolish when I think of it, even though it's so long ago. If I could have talked about it back then—"

"Lillian, the man who—"

"I don't mean that kind of talk. Please. We should forget him. I beg you, don't ask me again." Her face was averted from him now but when she stole a look at him she caught his expression of relief. They were both silent for a minute.

"I do think, sometimes, what he might have been like," he said. "By now the boy would be nine years old."

"You sound as if you're sorry he didn't live. It would have made it even worse, don't you think?"

Her father didn't answer.

She knew she was wrong. It would have been a blessing if the baby had lived. It would have changed her life in a wonderful way.

Lillian's throat tightened and tears filled her eyes. She hoped her father wouldn't see. She couldn't tell why she was crying. She wiped tears with the back of one hand while the other nervously stroked the keyboard.

"Hush, hush, child. I'll make it up to you, somehow." He sat next to her on the piano bench and awkwardly put an arm around her.

This is my future, she thought. I'll live with my father and play piano for him to sooth his troubles, while Olympia dozes in her chair. Once every few years, we'll talk secretly, like this, until we've both forgotten or it's too much effort to bring it up. One day I'll wake up and I'll be old.

She looked at the backs of her hands where they lay on the keys, and saw, for the first time, how prominent were the veins and how her skin was beginning to look like expensive silk crepe. I'm old already, she thought.

A breeze came through the window and made a dry clacking in the palms outside. The perfume of plumaria was strong in the room, but along with it came in a darker, sweeter stink of decay. Lillian noticed it at once but said nothing. Probably a dead animal in the garden.

Olympia stirred and raised her head.

40

The colonel took his arm from around Lillian's shoulders with as much awkwardness as he had embraced her, and they didn't speak again except to say good night.

As Lillian finally left the room, her father was still sitting at the piano bench, leaning forward with his hands on his knees, staring into space.

6

London, July 1854

When Snow reached home, he was so exhausted that he didn't even wash. He collapsed in an armchair and stared fixedly at the curving glass tubes of his laboratory equipment. Even the effort of moving his eyes seemed too great. The hedgehogs in their cages rustled nervously. One of them started to run on its wheel.

He made a mental note to have the red leather cover of the chair wiped down with carbolic acid in case any contamination had stuck to his clothes. He tried to think of his data, but his mind didn't go forward. His thoughts revolved on the combination of carbolic and red leather; what would the carbolic do to the leather, get up and wash, what would the carbolic do to his skin. Then he woke from his doze with a start.

An ugly shrieking came from the colony of starlings in the ivy on the front of the house. No epidemic could affect their routine, and their lives would be unchanged if all London died of this plague.

A vague picture rose before him, like a child's drawing, of a gravestone and flowers, with himself dead of cholera. His work would be unfinished but his mind finally at rest; the street abandoned, and the starlings still jammering away sunset after sunset. With relief, he felt his detachment return, and with it his ability to shut out any response to the cholera cases. They were sources of information for him, nothing more.

42

But a new anxiety crept in, and he realized that what he'd been smelling for some minutes was not his own house's signature but the odor of the slum with the prostitute, and those stairs on the way out. Was it on his shoes? He forced himself to his feet and tugged off his boots.

In the bedroom, he stripped off his damp clothes and washed in cold water. Already the abuse of the past weeks showed. Sleepless nights had made rusty patches under his eyes and his beard couldn't hide the skin flaking around one corner of his mouth. New wrinkles marked his high forehead and his hair seemed even grayer. Was his bald spot really bigger? A bruise from a forgotten collision with furniture or a doorway showed on his forearm.

He put on his home uniform, an old smoking jacket he'd bought second-hand his first year at medical school. It still held an aura of that initial taste of freedom, away from home and his father's rigid rules. Twenty years had added to his waistline and tonight Snow didn't even try to button the jacket.

Already more comfortable and protected from feeling in its worn velvet, he returned to the front room. His housekeeper, Mrs. Jarrett, was in there, leaning over a tea tray crammed with small cakes and dry biscuits. She'd pushed aside a jumble of chemistry apparatus to set the tray on the table. He didn't realize until then how hungry he was. She was already in the midst of a rambling sentence which must have begun the moment she heard him leave the bedroom.

"—no more cinnamon anywhere, it's just not to be had, so I couldn't do those biscuits you like so much, even though it *is* baking day and I thought I'd go ahead despite all this heat. So terribly sorry, but I had to do pork pies instead, thought the butter for the pastry looked bad. From Brand's shop you see, it was all we could get."

It was all addressed to the tray; she never looked at his face. With her left hand she held out a plate and she poured his tea with her right.

He took a pie and went to the window. Munching the greasy pastry (she was right about the butter; a faintly rancid taste lingered behind his teeth), he looked down into the dark street. Few people were visible and half the houses had no lights at all. Their owners must have left town. It was just a matter of time before the looting would start.

How differently the street had looked a month ago! This was an easy route through Soho and the foot and horse traffic had always been abundant. Housemaids would steal a chat on their employers' front stairs. Cabs waited at all hours.

Snow remembered the night he'd stood at the window four weeks ago, after coming home from seeing his first cholera case in five years.

Mrs. Jarrett had been busy then, as now, setting out the tea as if he were some duke waiting to be fed. And he had tried to warn her of what would happen.

"There was a cholera case today, Mrs. Jarrett." He'd waited for some response but she had continued to fuss over the tray. He went on. "Not far from here, actually. Broad Street."

She still didn't answer, but tightened her mouth into deeper than usual lines of disapproval. As if he'd mentioned sex, or toilets.

"There will be more. You may want to consider going down to Yorkshire for part of the summer."

"What, pick up and change house for a few upset stomachs? I'm sure you'll find that it's just some summer flux, like Mrs. Grant had two houses down. Too many peaches, it was. Two days of misery and she was right again. That's the trouble with all this summer fruit."

She shifted to a mechanical dusting of Snow's books and kept talking under her breath.

"Cholera, I'm sure." As if *he'd* seen cholera. These striplings don't know what disease is. Oxford in the thirties, now *that* was cholera.

Snow had to raise his voice to get her attention. "It was most definite. A three-month-old infant died of it this afternoon." His throat tightened briefly with the memory of the still body of the baby boy, which was large for its age and must have been healthy and thriving until it fell ill. The mother had been crying so hard she couldn't answer his probing questions.

She stopped dusting for a moment. "Poor mite. Probably fed off one of those new bottle and tube contraptions, mother too sluttish to do her duty right. I know how they live over on Broad Street. If it was fed at all. That's the trouble with girls, they go off and—well, there's justice, that's all I can say."

She started to straighten papers on his desk, which he'd repeatedly asked her not to do, but this didn't seem a good moment to stop her. "All that fruit," she went on. "Unhealthy stuff. It's peaches now, and green grapes—"

"Whatever you choose to think, be sure you boil all the water for cooking—"

"—in all the stalls. Fruit. Everyone will be sick, you'll see. We'd better put an extra chair in your consulting room, you'll be busy with it, I can tell. No restraint with these people, that's the problem."

"—and even washing." Snow noticed his voice rising and felt like a fool. He still hadn't tasted his tea. He wanted to throw the cup at her. "This water was fully boiled, I assume?"

"What? Me serve you tea made with tepid water? Of course it was boiled. The idea! You needn't tell me how to run my kitchen."

With a disgusted look at the three cages of hedgehogs, she had left the room, which was still in a mess. All her fussing never did seem to clean it.

And now, weeks into the epidemic, she behaved no differently. Snow knew she admitted to the existence of the disease, forced by the death of Lady Sowerby's groom next door. But even when he told her this she'd sniffed and reminded him of the groom's drinking habits. Struck down by God, she'd pronounced. When Lady Sowerby herself died the next day Mrs. Jarrett said nothing.

As she left the room, Snow finished the last bite of the pork pie then downed a few cups of black Darjeeling. No milk for the tea; there hadn't been for days, and he missed it. Yesterday Mrs. Jarrett managed to get a bucketful. Even after boiling it tasted so sour that Snow refused to touch it and ordered her to throw out the whole lot.

He went over to the laboratory bucket and peered in; the dead squirrel was gone, of course, or he would have smelled it the moment he had entered the room.

The front bell rang. Snow hastily wiped pie grease from his fingers and pulled a stack of notebooks from his bag by the desk. He was leafing through the day's notes when his friend Caleb Beersdon walked in, unannounced.

Dropping his small bony body into the chair next to Snow's, Caleb pulled some papers from his jacket. Sweat blotched his white shirt where it wasn't already marked by printer's ink.

"Sorry I'm late."

45

"Quite all right. I'm late myself. Stopped in Golden Square. There'd been a murder." He thought briefly of telling Caleb about the letter that morning and the sandy dead squirrel, then decided against it. He didn't want his friends to start thinking he was imagining things.

"That fellow in the pit?"

"What, you knew already?"

"About an hour ago. I couldn't get out of the newspaper office until seven so I was there when the messenger came. You should find a better neighborhood to walk through." He paused for a moment. "I have to get back sooner than I'd planned. Deborah's out of sorts from the heat."

An image rose to Snow's mind of Deborah Beersdon, red nosed and steely as a scalpel. When was she ever in sorts? Since his marriage ten years ago, Caleb seemed not to notice that his narrow shoulders had drooped farther every year, and his posture was more like that of a man twice his age. His hair had thinned much more than Snow's.

Caleb tugged at his mustache now with inky fingers as he glanced over Snow's shoulder. The man twisted, restless as always.

"What's that you're looking at?" he asked Snow.

Snow had come on the drawings of the prostitute's syphilis lesions. He found himself wondering about her. What would her laugh have sounded like? How had she spent her tenth birthday? As if to find an answer, he held the drawings up to the lamp for examination, and turned one so Caleb could see.

"Horrid stuff," muttered Caleb, turning his face away. He went over to poke a finger into one of the cages.

"Secondary syphilis." Snow glanced at Caleb's back. "Careful. They bite. I wouldn't want to have to give you any painkiller afterwards."

Caleb turned back to Snow and scanned the bottles of drugs on Snow's shelves. "You still don't trust me? It's been eight years since I've touched any opium."

"It's not you, Caleb. A man has so little control over those things. I've seen patients, the most upright of churchgoers, addicted for life after a bad broken leg." Snow cleared his throat. "Do the drawings bother you? You shouldn't let yourself get so affected." The girl's face came to mind and he tried to dismiss it. "I've got plenty of numbers for you tonight," he said.

"You aren't the only one anymore." Caleb turned from the animals. His voice was back to normal. "Farr's collecting deaths for us now. He dropped a list by *The Times* today." Caleb pulled out more papers.

"He'd been in Southwark all day," he went on. "His total is seventy-six. They're all by parish at time of death; no origins given. There are three poor hospitals in Newington parish alone. It looks like all he did was hop from one to the next and sweep up the figures."

Even though he had longed for help, Snow tried not to show his jealousy, knowing that someone else was on his ground. Not that Farr would have found anything meaningful; he was as narrow-minded a survey worker as you could find.

"God," he said. "How can we figure anything accurately with idiots like Farr out there making notes? We may as well jumble all the cases together. Let's throw in deaths from railway accidents and French duels while we're at it."

Snow took the creased pages from Caleb's hands. "Look at this trash." He proceeded to read aloud. " 'Deaths and Morbidity. London. June.' I like the precision of his title. 'Seventy-six deaths. Addresses unknown. Names unknown. Ages unknown. Half from unknown cause or suspected Asiatic Cholera.' " Snow tossed the pages on the floor.

Caleb didn't pick the papers up. "Farr's launched a new plan, you know. Determined to prove that a miasma of bad air causes cholera; that it isn't actually spread from one person to another."

Snow sat up straight. "What? That old theory of his again? He couldn't make it stick five years ago. How's he going to prove it this time?"

"Some project, I don't know. He was explaining it to me, I didn't really listen. Laboratory analysis of the bottled atmosphere of cholera neighborhoods."

Something dawned on Snow. "And who's paying for all this?"

"Well, I didn't want to tell you, but he was awarded money yesterday by the Board of Health. It was Sir Philip Constable's idea, the Deputy Minister of Public Health. An emergency fund for disasters like cholera and typhus. Five hundred pounds."

"No. For miasma? And through Constable?" Sir Philip Constable, whom Snow scarcely knew, had talked to him, months ago, about a possible nomination for The Royal Surgical Society. He hadn't heard from the man since. Everyone's theory but his was getting attention. "Listen, Beersdon, I *know* it's carried by water. I just can't prove it yet. All the others, they're on the right track with these miasmas and dust clouds. If I could just get enough figures—"

"Why don't you join in with Farr? He's offered, I know. You could share his project."

Snow turned his head aside, gazing at the wall. A craving for medical companionship, even Farr's, came over him. What a relief it would be, to let out some of the stabs of loss and defeat he'd had that day to another doctor who could understand it. He almost agreed to Caleb's suggestion.

But then he remembered that he would have to share any discoveries as well. "No," he answered. "It's out of the question. That theory's hogwash. And even if I could persuade him to go along with me, I could never adapt to his methods."

"He's good at the money side of it, you know," Caleb persisted. "Able to get backing from big people. And are you so very sure that you're right about your water theory? The chief at the paper thinks that contagion may not be—"

"No amount of money can prove that cholera is spread by air." Snow smiled in mock, patronizing patience. But even as he spoke he wondered how he would ever be able to prove that it was spread by water. He hadn't been able to show anything yet; it was just a theory, like any other.

"All right, all right." Caleb stirred in the hard seat. "If you're so critical, let's see what you've got. I can't stay here all night."

"Wait a moment." On impulse, Snow changed his mind and reached into his pocket, then handed to Caleb the note from that morning. "Tell me what you think of this."

Caleb read it and then started laughing. "What do they think you'll do, stop your life's research so you can avoid damnation?" He fingered the paper. "It's dirty enough."

"That's from what it was packed with. A dead squirrel, nested in a basket like a prize fillet of pork. But they do concern me, Caleb. You, of all people, should know what religion can do to a man's sense of proportion." Deborah spent her Saturdays and Sundays at Methodist prayer meetings, dragging Caleb along whenever she could.

Caleb cleared his throat. "If they want to think that cholera's from immorality, fine. What on earth can they really do to you? I wouldn't give it another thought."

"Well. Let's get to work, then." Snow ran his eyes along the list he'd compiled from the workhouses and lodgings that afternoon. He could hardly read his own crabbed writing. " 'Lodging, 15 Longacre Alley. Fifty-seven cases, twenty-nine deaths.' Here's the list of deaths, first: 'Abel Carter, twenty-eight, unemployed laborer. Cholera, seventeen hours. Miriam Hart, twenty-one, basket maker. Cholera, seven hours. Infant Hart, two months. Cholera, three hours. Sam Worth, forty-six, hatter, cholera, twelve hours.' "

"Wait a bit, will you? I can't write that fast." Caleb wiped sweat from his forehead and slowly copied it all down. In his years as an editor he'd lost the fast hand of a Fleet Street reporter.

"Now here's an interesting one," continued Snow. "This woman was still coherent when I reached her, said she'd been in a sick household up north in mid-May but swore she'd had no contact since then, had been out tramping where not a case was to be found. Such a long incubation—"

"Just give me the numbers, Snow. I can't print all this in the paper. Certainly not their names, you should know that." Caleb pushed damp hair back from his eyes. "Better yet, just hand me the list. I'll copy out what I want."

Snow felt an embarrassing reluctance to let anyone, even Caleb, see his notes. They were the work of so many days on the street and nights at his desk. You never knew these days what people would do, who they talked to. He didn't hand them over.

"All right, I'll slow down and abbreviate it. Sorry. It's so rare that I get a chance to talk about these things. I can hardly expect my housekeeper to be interested."

Caleb didn't seem to notice that Snow had covered the notes with his hand. They hurried through the rest and finished in half an hour.

When they were almost done Caleb interrupted.

"Listen, Snow. This is a bore. I know we have to print it in the Public Health section, but couldn't you give me something spicier? How about a description of the lodging where you found all these cases? Think what a story it would make."

"What? Nobody wants to read about that, any more than you wanted to look at pictures of those lesions."

"No, no, you're wrong. Didn't you read the paper this week? They're doing a series on the trial of an abortionist, who not only committed the act, but overcharged the girl and didn't do it properly. The going rate is only eight pounds. He asked ten. God knows where she got the money. He botched it and she had the child anyway. A clergyman was the father. It's sensational, but it'll be finished in a day or two. We need new material."

Snow wondered how far the pregnancy had progressed. Did the man use ether, or chloroform? Or did he just tie the girl down and do it cold? Snow had been doing work in anesthesiology for years now, and he knew that the paralyzing effect of the chloroform could have had an interesting effect on curtailing post-abortion bleeding. Of course, if the abortion didn't work, that didn't apply. Whatever tools the abortionist had used with such ineptitude must have scarred the girl's organs terribly. It was amazing that she and the child survived.

Then came a brief and agonizing memory of his mother, bleeding to death in childbirth when Snow was eight. Years later he had asked the ancient local doctor who attended the birth what exactly had gone wrong. "Her womb burst, boy. The child's head was too big to descend. A girl. We had to take the child out with a knife, but it was dead. In among her intestines by then."

Snow by then was no stranger to grim details; he had used chloroform to anesthetize dozens of leg amputations and to ease some terrible, fatal childbirths, but even so he had turned white and had to sit down. "Sorry," the old country doctor continued. "You shouldn't have asked. At least her suffering was short."

Now Snow thought of the exact pain, however short, his mother must have felt when the walls of her uterus burst. And the pain of the girl in the newspaper story, who had gone on to give birth through a canal lacerated by the botched abortion. She probably couldn't afford a doctor in attendance, let alone the relief of chloroform. All Snow said to Caleb was, "What smut. Did you write it?"

"God no. I don't have to do that sort of thing anymore. But I edited some of it. The men who write those things aren't always as discreet we might like. There were details one couldn't put into print. But really, I think it would make a good story if you could tell me where you went today."

"No, no, I don't think so." He felt an unexpected aversion to broadcasting the details of these folks' last hours. Their deaths

50

had been so undignified, so public. Besides, he didn't want Farr and everyone else heading over there tomorrow.

"Why do you go to these places, anyway? You could get the deaths somewhere else less nasty."

"Don't you see? I'm asking them where they drank, what they drank, what they ate. It's pretty much the nasty places, as you put it, where the problems come up. If I can prove that all these cases got their water from the same spot, I'm clear."

Caleb didn't seem to listen to this. He was too heated about his own story. "Can't you at least tell me what the place looked like?"

"Well, it was in a cellar. You had to go down stairs to reach it."

"What neighborhood?"

"Not far from here, actually. North of Seven Dials. I'd rather you didn't give the address, if you're going to print this. And especially don't use my name. Just say 'a doctor.'"

"Cholera's not the best way to attract the Grosvenor Square patients, is it? I can hardly blame you."

"No, that's not it. I just don't want anyone getting notions about what I'm doing until I finish." For some reason the muddy face of the green-eyed drain worker, staring at him, came back to Snow.

Caleb looked closely at the doctor, who was reading his papers. "Quite. Not necessary at all. And what were your impressions when you first went in?" Now that he had started the interview Caleb's voice changed, he spoke faster.

"The details are hardly discreet, as you put it."

"Oh, that doesn't matter in this case. No abortions here. We can say what we like."

"Well, there was a smell, first, of cesspools and damp. But then you noticed the cholera smell."

"What? You can smell it?" Caleb's eyes narrowed and he dropped his jaw in disgust.

"Oh, certainly. Sweetish, fishy." Snow looked at a corner of the ceiling, trying to remember the room. "I think the floor was wet with all the excretions. You know, they can lose half their plasma volume in the first few hours from the diarrhea alone?" He wished he hadn't agreed to tell Caleb the details. He felt the tune coming back, and the sense of grief and loss from before creeping up on him. Suddenly his friend's zeal was distasteful.

Caleb cleared his throat. "I thought cholera just made you weak. You faded away." A slight tremor shook his words. The zeal had apparently faded.

Snow laughed, not a real laugh, but a snort of mock disbelief. "You mean you don't know?"

"No. One reads of such and such a number of people dying, but I've never seen it."

"Here's how it works, then. Every bit of fluid in your body goes out one end or the other. One vomits and one shits until there is nothing left. Excuse me for my bluntness."

Caleb didn't answer. He looked disgusted and fascinated at the same time.

"They simply dry out," continued Snow. "After a few hours, if they're lucky enough to live that long, it's just gray water coming out. Even the diarrhea is just water, as if every drop of fluid is getting squeezed through their tissues. For the fools who still believe in bleeding their patients, the blood comes out thick and gluey, like old molasses. It slows down autopsies. And of course there's the loss of turgor."

"I probably don't want to know, but what's turgor?"

"Pinch your wrist." Caleb was obedient. "Then let go. See? Your skin goes back, of course. In cholera so much body water is lost that the skin has no elasticity. If you pinch up a man's flesh on his arm, it stays there. Like clay." The girl's weak hand hovered before him in his mind, along with the glaze over her blue eyes.

"And after they lose all that fluid, what happens?"

"Death." The word had repeated itself in Snow's mind so many times that day that it had lost meaning, and was simply a sound associated with an end point on a graph. It had nothing to do with sadness or loss or the girl in the attic. "Or recovery. It's a fifty percent chance either way, unless the cholera is malignant. Then the chance of recovery is much smaller."

Caleb swallowed once. "All right, let's get back to this place, the basement. Where were the people?" he asked. "On the floor?"

"No, not exactly. In boxes. Rows of boxes with small corridors down between them."

"Boxes? What do you mean?" Caleb's pencil stopped again.

"Boxes. Like coffins. That's where they sleep in those places.

The penny lodgings. You should go some time, just to see. There's a wretched sort of padding lining them."

Caleb's pencil was going fast enough now. "And it was dark down there, of course. Hard to see. There was a darker area where they'd piled the bodies. They were short of staff to take them out. I went from box to box and checked on them. Some were already dead, and I informed the caretakers. It was pretty hopeless. And so filthy." Snow remembered a young blond mother and her blond, one-year-old girl, lying squeezed together in a box. Both dead.

"Couldn't you have done anything to help them?" Caleb's voice sounded desperate and demanding. "Surely there is some drug, some treatment?"

"Well . . . hydration injections. Replace the lost body fluids. If there had been clean water, that is. It's worked occasionally, if the situation is spotless and the patient isn't too far gone."

"If it works why didn't you try it? Why not do something?"

Snow laughed, harshly, feeling pie crust caught in his throat.

"Granted, it might work. But that's when you've got one cholera case in a clean, well-lit bedroom off Park Lane, and you can sit there for twelve hours repeating the treatment while they possibly recover. A lady's maid or two to fetch the fresh linen and keep boiling the water. In that cellar it would have been a joke." He paused and was silent for half a minute. "I was just there to take notes, anyway. There's no point in trying to save them."

"Good God, you mean there's really nothing else you can do?"

"What do you expect? All this talk of cures, essence of this or that; it's all lies. Swaine's Revivifying Drops. Opium water is a popular one this year. Yes, it's just as easy to get as it always was. Useless. The only hope is in prevention."

"How many people were down there?"

"I told you, in the list. Fifty-seven. Two to a box. It was crowded. And more brought in while I was there, from a nearby workhouse. But I couldn't stay to count them, or I would have stayed all night."

Caleb stopped writing and both men fell silent.

Snow finally asked, "Do you want the rest of the cases too? The ones still alive this afternoon?"

Caleb pulled a watch from his pocket and checked it unhappily. "God, is it that late? I can't get into any worse trouble than I already am. Might as well stay and finish."

Snow read out the rest of the figures. Their monotonous repetition sent his mind wandering to another time when he and Caleb had sat with their heads hunched over a desk like this. Years ago it must have been, in the York Technical Secondary School they had both worked so hard to qualify for, getting their figures ready for the Presentation Day. Everyone was going to come; parents, sisters, sweethearts. The students' one day to show their talents and the fruit of this expensive learning.

As a chemistry student he had prepared, with Caleb as his assistant, a delicate reaction of crystallized sulphur with magnesium salts to be acted out for the small audience in the lecture theater. How well he could see it now; the glass tubes and polished brass calipers mounted in precisely cut oak. He was supposed to create a swirling green vapor in a clear tube, with a cloud that would glow and fade slowly.

His father had sat in the first row, his sunburned face tense with doubt and suspicion under the unaccustomed tall hat. He hated Snow's scientific bent. When Snow had told him he wanted to study medicine, his only response had been to snarl, "How do you expect to pay for it, boy?"

Snow had measured wrong, something, he still didn't know quite what. Too much magnesium, not enough sulphur. Or perhaps the little oil lamp was too hot. At any rate, he bungled it. A foul brown fountain splashed into the audience over the gauzy dresses and the stovepipe hats. There was a sulphurous stink like old turkey eggs from the poultry coop behind his father's barn.

People had rushed from the room, handkerchiefs over their faces, while Snow frantically tried to explain. Caleb's arm was badly burned and he had to wear a bandage for weeks. The district medical man, the same one Snow wrote to for help three years later, started Caleb on opium drops for the pain. Even now Snow could remember the broad, peaceful smile on his friend's face as he showed off his recovering burn.

His father's mistrust of science, a farmer's self-righteous conviction, never budged after that. And when it came time to pay the exorbitant license for Snow's first London practice, his father hadn't handed over a penny. Not to mention the transport.

Snow had walked the three hundred miles from York to London.

Snow's resentment mingled with the memory of that first remote practice when they'd let him handle the Kellingsworth mine epidemic alone. It was nothing to them how many miners died. There were always more. It was nothing if he himself died, a cheap doctor working for almost as little as the miners themselves.

Surely his father could have done something back then to help him into a better post. His whole body became tense just thinking about it.

"Are you all right?" asked Caleb.

Snow found he'd stopped reading the numbers and was breathing in short, sharp breaths, clutching his pen tightly. Caleb was looking at him, brows drawn together.

The image of Snow's father faded and most of the anger faded with it.

"Yes, yes. We're done, anyway." They really were at the last of the data. After a minute or two of yawning conversation Snow got up to see Caleb out. Mrs. Jarrett had gone to sleep hours ago.

"Same time tomorrow night?" asked Snow.

"If I can. You know how it is with Deborah." Caleb shrugged and went down the front steps. The clip of his small boots on the pavement faded down the street. Snow went back upstairs.

It was well past midnight. He opened his laboratory notebook to the spot where he had stopped a few days ago, and went to get the bottled carbonic acid, hydrocyanic acid, and ammonia. The hedgehogs, quiet until now, began to stir again, and the one who favored the wheel started running.

As he adjusted the burners, the tubes, and the heights of the bottles, fumes began to bubble into vials and flasks. He reached for the first cage and opened the small door.

Toward three A.M. shouts came from the street and Snow raised his head from the inert animal. The window was wide open, letting in a hot breeze of roses and horse manure. Snow dimmed his lamp and went to look.

Below him, to the right, two men struggled, locked in a wrestler's grip. Now the only noise was the scrape of their boots on the pavement and their loud grunts as they pushed at each other. One of them finally yanked himself free and stood, panting, staring at the other.

"I won't have it," he said, anger making him loud. "Do your own fuckin' dirty work."

The voice sounded familiar, but Snow couldn't place it.

"Suit yourself," said the other. "Don't come cryin' to me when your wage dries up."

Suddenly a crash of shattering glass came from a few doors down. The two men looked into the darkness and ran off in the opposite direction, toward Piccadilly, still together. Then, from the same spot as the glass, came the splintering groan of a wood door being forced.

The empty houses were fair enough prey for looters. Snow just hoped they didn't start to attack the occupied ones. He went back to his experiment and forgot about both incidents in minutes.

When dawn broke at four-thirty, it was still hot. The hedgehog, its limbs spread-eagled by cotton string and pinned to a board, was beginning to recover from a measured dose of chloroform. It tugged with growing strength at its ties. Before it could hurt itself by pulling too hard, Snow carefully untied the animal and restored it to its cage. It scuffled over to a corner and stared out at him with mistrust. Still doped, its eyes kept falling shut, but then they would jerk open again, glaring at Snow.

He felt a fleeting stab of pity, even though the animal would feel fine in a few hours. Apprehensive scuffling sounds came from the other two in their cages.

Snow closed his notebooks and tossed a few empty test tubes off the sofa onto the carpet. He lay down in his clothes and instantly fell asleep.

7

India, January 1854

1

That night Lillian dreamed that the moon fell out of the sky. It didn't just drop like a ball, but it warped and melted out of shape, growing oblong and yellow as a mango before plunging into the sea. And then she was in the water herself, buffeted by waves off a barren and rocky coast. A rowboat bobbed beyond the breakers, and perched in its stern was her lover, the dead soldier who had fathered her child. His face was pale and beautiful. His hair was shorter than she ever remembered seeing it in real life, and there was a difference to his features which even in the dream wasn't easy to define at first, and then she knew; he had shaved his military mustache. Clean lipped, he seemed more vulnerable and already wounded.

Slowly, luxuriously even, he tossed perfect stones into the water, one after the other, following their descent with his eyes. His supply seemed inexhaustible.

Afraid for some imagined danger which could fall on him, and guilty both at keeping him waiting, and at the fall of the moon, which was her fault, Lillian felt herself sink through broad-leafed seaweed.

She awoke breathless and panting. The moon, still safely in the sky, was setting through her window. It was just before dawn. Guilt from the dream stayed with her and for a groggy moment she thought she'd missed a meeting with Henry, until she remembered that there was no meeting, and she was old now.

A racket came from the part of the house just below her room; yells, a table falling, a breaking plate. Familiar resentment swelled at her bad luck in having the room closest to the servants' quarters. She should have changed it years ago.

Calls for Pushpa brought no answer, so she got up and groped for her slippers. They wouldn't help if she stepped on a cobra, but scorpions couldn't strike through the thick leather. One slipper was missing. Her annoyance sharpened. Barefoot and feeling sullen and as sorry for herself as a cranky spinster, she followed the sounds down the moonlit stairs. A night's sleep wasn't so much to ask for, she thought.

The commotion came from the servants' common room, on the way to the outdoor kitchens. A bar of yellow light from under the closed door fanned across the corridor.

Lillian yanked open the door and found herself in a scene of bright lanterns, colors, and powerful stench. A freshly butchered sheep's carcass in a corner seeped blood over the floor and into rivulets around three prone women. The blood stained their saris as they tossed in agony. Vomit slicked the packed earth.

In a moment, she took in the piles of cut onions, the polished brass bowls, the red and pink mutton, all interrupted preparations for today's meals. In a dark corner lay a motionless older woman and Pushpa, who was just able to lift one hand toward her mistress.

Lillian picked her way over the wet floor, resisting the urge to shake her bare feet, catlike, after each step. She reached Pushpa and knelt beside her. The white cotton of her nightgown was immediately soaked with sheep's blood.

"Pushpa, what is it? What's the matter?"

Pushpa gasped a few words through blue lips. Lillian knew little Telagu, but this she recognized. The purging and fainting disease—cholera.

She gripped Pushpa's shoulders, fragile as small antelope bones under her sari.

58

Lillian had heard stories of other colonial settlements. Entire households could be wiped out in hours, masters and servants alike. Two winters ago, her cousin Rose died of cholera up in the hills, and soon after that, a few mild cases broke out here in the house among the servants. Her family left the island that day and didn't return for a month. But it was too late for anything like that now.

With shock Lillian realized that the grandmother by Pushpa must be dead. The flesh on her face was so sunken that the eyes bulged from the withered face.

Lillian hadn't seen any of the faces of the dead in her life; her mother, her baby, her lover. Suddenly she wondered if their deaths might have been easier for her if she had seen this expression of removal. No suffering showed on the old woman's face.

Around her, the rest of the house seemed to be waking. Lights and shouts came from down the halls, and through a window she could see a light flickering in the administration cottage where the clerks lived, separately from the rest of the Indian staff.

Lillian still held Pushpa. The girl's slight weight felt comforting against Lillian's lap, and part of her wished she could have sat, without action, waiting for someone else to come and take care of everything.

At the same time she racked her brains trying to remember the home remedies she'd heard of, and if any of them were here in the house. Rhubarb? Opium? She vaguely remembered that treatments for natives were guaranteed fatal to whites. Somewhere in the house was an old army medical kit.

Her father would know. He could send to the mainland for help.

"Pushpa, stay here." She realized how ridiculous the warning sounded and almost began to giggle, feeling a bubble of hysteria rising like gas. "You'll be fine. I'm going to get help." She grabbed a nearby pile of dish cloths and laid them under the girl's head, then left the room, this time avoiding the bloody puddles.

Her feet left dark spots on the matting as she rushed back down the corridor and up the stairs toward her father's rooms. Halfway there she met Olympia coming from her own bedroom with a candle.

"Lillian, what's the matter? What's all the fuss? I wish they'd be quiet. I called Lakshmi but there's no answer. I'm not feeling at all well."

Her stepmother's hands returned over and over again to her stomach in stroking, pressing movements which Lillian found repulsive.

Lillian took a deep breath and tried not to look at the hands. "The servants are ill. It's probably nothing. You should try to rest." She felt like shoving Olympia back in her heavily draped bedroom where she'd be insulated from everything, but all she did was gently push her by the upper arm. But Olympia wouldn't budge.

"Ill? Did Pushpa tell you? Maybe we should go check." She frowned, skeptical. Olympia had labeled Pushpa as a malingerer. Even in her distress, she looked carefully at Lillian's ears, her neck, the buttons of the nightdress. She didn't seem to notice the mess of stains below her knees.

But Lillian's face must have given her away, because Olympia suddenly gripped her wrist and said, in a tense voice, "What is it?"

Lillian looked away and answered in a monotone. "Cholera. One of the kitchen women is dead. Three are dying. So is Pushpa."

"You were in there with them? Dear God, Lillian, you may have caught it—" Her hold on Lillian's wrist became sharper, her fingernails digging into the skin.

"Hush, don't worry. They say it's not infectious." She pulled her hand free from Olympia's grip and tried once more to steer her back to bed. Olympia brushed her away with impatience.

"We've got to leave the island. Immediately. Are there enough clean sheets, and are the water tanks full? Is Henry back yet? Go wake your father and—" Olympia stopped short and lurched forward, gagging, a hand cupped over her mouth.

Her vomit gushed over Lillian's ruined nightgown. Olympia staggered to a basin in her room and kept retching until she was too weak to walk the few steps to her bed. Lillian, her own legs suddenly shaking and uncertain, had to help her to lie down. She fought an urge to gag as the stinking vomit cooled against her skin.

"We've got to leave," gasped Olympia from the bed. Her hair, wet now and glued into little points, tangled as she tossed her head from side to side.

"Just try to rest. I'll go wake Father. He'll know what we should do." Lillian set another basin on the bed beside Olympia, and ran down the hallway to the colonel's room.

He was always good at emergencies. The time monkeys had attacked her when she was twelve, a whole biting troop of them clinging to her skirts and hair, his one gunshot in the air had frightened them off. And when that fire broke out on the ground floor two years ago, he cleared the household in minutes and organized fifteen men with water vessels. She'd never seen him at a loss.

In just the few paces it took for Lillian to reach her father's room, she already felt less panicked. Besides, dawn was approaching. The coming day made things seem less catastrophic.

There was no answer to her knock so she pushed open the door and entered.

Colonel Aynsworth always slept on a camp bed in the middle of the room. It kept him from getting soft, he said. Rajan had a spot on the floor close by, between the colonel and the door. They kept these military habits even though the colonel hadn't seen active duty for years.

As Lillian crossed the threshold, from the garden there came a raucous shrieking of peacocks, backed by the caws of dozens of crows. This harsh bird song had started most mornings of Lillian's life, and she rarely noticed it anymore. But today it drummed into her ears and seemed inseparable from what lay before her in the room.

Rajan struggled to pull himself up the side of his master's cot to help him, but even as Lillian watched he fell backward and didn't move again. Her father was soaked with vomit, his sheets twisted into a sodden mass, and liquid excrement covered his bed and the floor around him.

Three steps brought Lillian to the camp bed. She raised her father's head but he looked right through her. She ran back to the door and shouted for help; her voice sounded weak and puny so she shouted again. Maybe the clerks were awake and could come. Or the rest of the kitchen staff, the ones that weren't in the room with Pushpa. But only the crows answered.

The old wooden medicine chest that she remembered sat

among the neat military trunks against a wall. She pried open its rusty lid and lifted out the tin trays of bottles, scanning the labels for anything about cholera. In the second tray was "Tincture of Cream of Tartar and Rhubarb, Guaranteed for Headache and Cholera." Half the liquid remained, dark and sluggish in the old brown glass. At first the lid was stuck fast and she wrenched it, cutting her palm on the rusty metal. Finally it twisted open.

She was able to force some down her father's throat but he immediately vomited it up again. Rajan by now was unconscious, and she was afraid it would choke him.

She was torn with indecision and let precious seconds pass trying to think what to do. Should she leave her father and go around the house to search for help? Run the mile to Matapundi? Or stay here and try to get him to take more of the medicine?

Then she remembered Henry. Maybe he had returned in the night. She ran down the corridor to his room, but, as she expected, the bed was empty and unslept in.

She went to look in again on Olympia. A quick glance showed her deeply asleep. She had vomited again in the basin, but she was still without any of the terrible signs; the blue skin, the loose flesh. Her fingers were pink and her breathing was even and deep.

A feeling of disbelief began to rise in Lillian, with a suspicion that this was all happening to someone else, or that she was in the middle of a dream. It couldn't be real.

She knew the feeling. She'd had it before at times when her own actions were beyond belief; after the first time she had given in to her own desires with her lover, then again with Henry. But this was the first time events outside her own control had been unbelievable to her.

She found that she had been standing in Olympia's doorway for ten minutes, doing nothing, hardly thinking. Then a desperate sound of retching from her father's room made it real again.

She rushed back to find him barely conscious but still vomiting incredible amounts of thin gray fluid. She gave up any attempt to catch it in a basin, and simply sat by him, holding his head. The spurts of diarrhea stopped smelling foul and became as gray and neutral as the vomit.

I'll just clean it up later, she thought. Rajan might help me. If the laundry servants are gone, I can wash out the sheets myself. I don't mind. They'll be dry by sundown. Or by tomorrow at the latest. Father will be more comfortable then.

Even though Rajan remained unconscious, she found herself repeatedly planning on what tasks his caste would allow him to help her with. The room would need to be scrubbed down; he'd refuse that chore, but she could do it herself. And her father would need to be tended to and fed for a few days until he was himself again. Rajan was good at that sort of thing.

2

The sun rose unclouded by yesterday's haze, and beat into the room. Lillian realized at one point that she couldn't hear the elephant. They must have taken him back after all, she thought. Throughout the morning, shrieks and running feet came from outside, always dashing away from the house, but Lillian paid no attention. Eventually the noise faded and the house fell silent. Even the crows stopped.

The hours passed. In her father's room, Lillian stared for minutes at a time at the maps and etchings showing famous battle scenes from around the British empire and from her father's career in India. A large scene from the field at Waterloo dominated one wall. Queen Victoria surveyed it all from a print made in the year of her coronation.

A small voice in her mind told her that she should do something, not just sit here looking at pictures: get up, run to Matapundi, anything. She couldn't envision a walk to Matapundi; it was always a headlong run down the chalky road under coconut trees, out of breath and her hand held to a cramp in her side.

She repeatedly dragged herself back to Olympia's room, where the woman still slept and seemed no sicker.

Finally Lillian returned to her father's room to find that Rajan had changed his position and now lay on his side with one arm stretched out.

"Rajan," she said. "Here's what we need to do." She stepped over to him. His eyes gaped at the ceiling, and a fly crawled across his cheek. The insect paused at the moist crust around the man's mouth, then flew up and buzzed over to the colonel's head, where it landed on his lower lip and settled, rubbing its back legs against its wings.

3

Lillian sat with the bodies for an hour. How could she be sure they were dead? Maybe she should stay and wait—if a doctor were to check them . . . But another voice told her this was foolish. One had only to look.

Her disbelief came and went like a breeze. The feeling of watching it all in a play was so strong that she had to physically shake herself to admit what had happened, even when she forced herself to look at the dead faces.

Her father's features had aged twenty years in the past hours. The angles of his cheekbones pushed up behind the gray skin so tightly that you could see the curved facets of the bone beneath. Wrinkles scored his bluish fingertips, as though he'd been bathing for a day.

Because of the flies, she finally had to act. She dragged the sheets from her own bed to cover the men. Then she left the room, pulling the door shut behind her.

Her stepmother was still unconscious, but her skin glowed pink and she didn't seem nearly as sick as the others. Lillian wiped her face with a cool cloth and left her.

Swaying now with exhaustion, she made her way downstairs, looking into all the rooms, and calling out names, the syllables sounding like nonsense and ringing in her ears. "Lakshmi? Narajan? Pushpa? Rajan? Naga? Gita? Mehta?" She knew that Rajan was dead upstairs, that Pushpa was almost certainly dead in the kitchen, but even so, she repeated the roll call in the same insistent voice, going from room to room, down the corridors, up and down the stairs.

She headed to the outbuildings, the clerks' cottage, the tool house, the stables where the elephant's droppings still lay by the post where he'd been chained. Out of a staff of thirty a soul must be left. But there was no one.

The clerks lay dead in their beds. Three of the grounds work-

64

ers were dead too. A look into the huts beyond the stables showed more bodies, hard to see in the dim interiors.

Everyone else had vanished. One look at the dock told her how. All the boats were gone. Not just the ferry she had arrived on yesterday, but the fishing dugouts, the sailing skiffs, even the two rafts. She scanned the waters, which were empty all the way to the mainland.

Finally, under a low tree branch, she spotted a half-rotten skiff that would probably make it across the bay. It even had an oar in it. She stood for a minute, imagining the hundreds of yards from Olympia's upstairs room to the shore, wondering how she could drag the heavy, sleeping body so far. Or, if she managed to wake her, if the boat could even carry the extra weight. Only a fool would try it. And only a fool would stay here for one sick woman who wasn't even a blood relation.

Lillian actually had a foot in the boat, and was ready to make off alone for the mainland, before she turned around and slowly headed back to the house.

She dragged her feet up the stairs to check on Olympia, who slept solidly, looking peaceful and totally unconcerned. Then she made her way to her own room and sat on the edge of the bare mattress, staring into space, her hands limp in her lap.

After an hour or more she noticed the missing slipper. Its toe poked out from under the dressing table, the gilt embroidery catching the afternoon light.

The ticking of a small gold clock on the mantel broke through her thoughts. It showed three o'clock. A mail boat was due in two days. It wasn't that long to wait.

After it grew dark and she still hadn't moved, she realized she had never changed out of her nightgown. That put her into action; she tore it off, literally ripping the thin, filthy, cotton, and then washed herself with clumsy, slow movements. It seemed to take a long time. Then she caught herself staring into her wardrobe, trying to decide what to wear. As if she were going to a tea party. In self-disgust she grabbed the first thing her hand touched, a plain gray cotton afternoon dress that had never fit well at the waist, and put it on.

Without Pushpa it was hard work doing up the buttons in back.

The next day passed in giving cold tea to a recovered Olympia and in trying to hide from her the source of the terrible smells. Lillian herself ate nothing and only felt a little lightheaded. Olympia seemed to have no memory of the previous night.

Lillian forced herself to avoid looking down the hall toward her father's room, and to think only of immediate needs, such as her struggle to keep the fire going in the drawing room so as to boil water for the tea (which she had to find in the kitchens, cringing as she stepped over the bodies of Pushpa and the others). The servants had always done everything. It was even a mystery where to put the contents of Olympia's and her own chamber pot. She might have eaten some bread or fruit, but aside from her total ignorance of where food was kept, the entire house seemed contaminated and she was afraid.

On the second morning, she went down to the dock and paced in the sun, quickly at first and then more slowly as time passed. At last the mail boat appeared as a dark fleck on the horizon which separated itself from the mainland harbor. Lillian tried to focus on it, but small swimming dots like golden gnats hovered in her vision. Icy cold swept from her temples and over her scalp.

She took deep breaths and fought to remain standing. A tree to lean on would have helped, but only a stump remained of the mango that used to shade the dock in the days when she waited here before, years ago, for a message from the father of her son.

As the mail boat grew close enough to see the men on board, Lillian's knees started to buckle and the few steps she took toward the water wavered askew. She tried to shout, but instead she crumpled onto the rough boards of the dock.

8

London, July 1854

1

Snow stood at an attic window, his hand flat against one pane, with St. Paul's dome looming against the mauve summer twilight. The girl locked the door behind him. Water gurgled from a jug and a match scratched as she lit a candle. After the street din, it was so quiet he could hear the wick's gentle hiss when it caught.

The room was so hot that Snow couldn't think. His chief sensations were of the heat, his headache, and a throbbing erection.

The girl's dress fell to the floor in a shabby heap. She stooped for it and laid it over a chair. She stood in a dirty white petticoat and a corset too large for her. Her boots, scuffed blue ones with short heels, were still on.

"Do you want the petticoat off too?" She lifted her arms in a pantomime of pulling up the garment.

"What?"

"Some likes it on, some likes it off. What about you?"

Snow didn't answer. His eyes stayed on her bare white arms. Though she was so blond, the hair in her armpits was dark. He couldn't believe how much his head ached.

Her mouth lifted in a patient one-sided smile, tired, but still willing to please.

"Well then," she said, "if it's all the same to you I'd sooner take it off. Keeps the laundry bills down." This was in the tone of a casual housekeeping tip, something he might want to remember for future occasions.

Snow sat like a nervous suitor on the edge of the bed while she unlaced the corset and stripped off the petticoat. The triangle between her legs was as dark as her armpit hair. She sat on the bed next to him and started unbuttoning his trousers. The blue boots stayed on.

He remembered the dying girl in the house off Pulteney Court the other day. How many men had touched this pillow, the grubby counterpane? Visions of hell and his future as a syphilis-ridden idiot passed through his mind, but only fleetingly. As she leaned back and spread her legs, her adolescent breasts fell sideways, ever so slightly. She just looked at him and waited.

Even as he finished pulling off his trousers he wondered if it was too late for him to get out of it. He'd never intended to be in a situation like this; it was a complete accident.

He'd spent the day in cholera houses, collecting water samples and asking questions. Dazed and exhausted, lost in Eastcheap, Snow had encountered the girl when she blocked his way in an alley off Drury Lane.

"Ey guvnor," she had asked, "kee' a lass comp'ny tonigh'?" Her cockney was so heavy he could hardly understand her.

Prostitutes rarely stirred Snow. Except for medical cases like that girl in the attic he'd never exchanged a word with one. But tonight his weariness led him to an indulgence. He slowed his pace and looked at her eyes. He stopped.

She had smiled and raised her brows in imitation of some arch look she must have thought was sophisticated. She was no more than fifteen. Adolescent baby fat still plumped her cheeks. Blond hair without a curl in it, pulled back tight behind her cheap bonnet. Her eyes, though small, were slanted and of an odd seawater blue, a blue he had seen somewhere . . . a smell of hay. A bowl, roses painted on it, holding a few peaches? Sun through a window.

And the first line of a tune came into his head, a silly baby's rhyme he hadn't thought of for years,

Oranges and lemons,
say the bells of St. Clement's.

He heard it as clearly as if the girl had sung him the song
herself. She reached out and ran her finger lightly down the lapel
of his coat. For the briefest moment her smile faded. She bit her
lower lip, took a quick breath and turned on her heel to saunter
down Dudley Street. Grime splotched the pink satin of her dress
over her wide crinoline. She held her back straight, and below
her waist she swayed like a sapling in a breeze.

Now it was too late to get out of it. His headache fit over his
skull like a black cap. As the girl leaned back on the bed with
such patience, a great urgency rushed him forward. It was hardly
a feeling of passion, or even desire; just a sense that this was a
procedure he must go through before he would be allowed to
leave.

As he entered her he was filled with aversion at his own
detachment. He climaxed in seconds. The aversion didn't fade
for a moment.

After he caught his breath he felt her shaking and at first
thought she was crying; but no, it was laughter. She was softly
giggling to herself with her eyes shut.

The sound spun like a dart into some spot in his memory.
Clover. A bowl with flowers. He hung onto the memory as long
as he could but it faded in seconds to shame and caution returned. Was she ill? The pox? Clap? Nits?

He pulled himself out and staggered to the basin, wanting only
to wash and be gone. She began to laugh again.

"I always love it with the clergy."

He turned, covering himself with his hand. "You're mistaken.
I'm not a clergyman." It was then that he realized the headache
was gone.

"No?" She frowned in disappointment, and laughed again,
this time at herself. "Well, you sure looks like one, with your
frowning mug. I could tell, when you saw us on Dudley Street.
A messenger from Satan, that's what you thought. See where it
got you!" She held out her palm, smiling. "Two shillings." It was
as if they'd had a small joking bet, and he'd lost.

Snow paid and avoided her eyes. He quickly began to dress.
God, what time was it? The window panes were black now. He
pulled his shirt over his head, then pulled his watch out. Mid-

night. He groped for his jacket and couldn't remember where he'd put it.

The girl picked it off a coat rack, offered it to him, and then pulled it back playfully.

"No 'urry, guvnor. Half a crown'll get you the whole night. It'll be light in a few hours. With this cholera everywhere like it is, yer safer in than out. Sit yourself."

She sat down again and patted the bed. "I'll send out for vittles. You got that pinched look. I know all about it. What do you like? Taters? Northern folks always does."

Snow decided it wouldn't hurt to wait a moment. "Can you hear it? My accent? Most people don't."

"Oh, enough to tell. Besides, me mum came from Yorkshire, afore she was like me."

"Like you? How?"

"On the street, I mean."

Snow couldn't think of any polite comment to make on this, so he stayed silent.

In the end, it was the thought of food which kept him there. They spent more time in the bed. The gray sheets seemed less foul. And it got cooler in the room, cool enough that the girl's warmth was good to lie against.

She fell asleep within a minute, but sleep was beyond him. He thought of sneaking out, but it was pleasant lying there, and for the first time in hours he could stop and think. It had been a long day.

That morning seemed as if it was a week ago. Still asleep on the sofa after his late-night hedgehog experiment, Snow had been awakened at ten by Mrs. Jarrett, saying there was a boy to see him.

Snow had followed the messenger through the hot, brick-shaded gloom of the alleys off Drury Lane. The day before, the thermometer had stood at one hundred and two degrees according to *The Times*.

By now cholera was all over the poorer parts of London. The epidemic thrived on the heat. There were over three hundred cases, starting with that first baby Snow had seen four weeks ago.

Doubt had begun to erode at Snow's theories. What if Farr were right, and miasmatic fumes from the river could carry the disease? Or if it thrived in the gray street dust which coated his clothes and clung to his teeth? It was easy enough in his cool

70

library in Sackville Street to believe in his own ideas of water transmission. Out here any truth seemed likely.

He'd had little time to worry, though. Word had quickly got around that the doctor in Sackville Street would come to see cholera houses and maybe help.

The boy came for Snow saying his entire household was sick. Snow had seen four houses like that the day before, large families all sick and dying. The two reached their destination and Snow stepped up to the door of the building. It was then that the stone fell.

Just as they were about to enter a house, a dark object rushed past Snow faster than a lunging hawk and smashed against the pavement beside him. Chips of broken stone flew up. The boy jumped back, as startled as Snow. Snow's pulse raced. Both looked up to the roof above, ready to dodge again.

It was a crumbling roof cornice the size of Snow's medical bag. After they caught their breath both of them scrutinized the top of the four-storied row house. There was a snaggle-toothed gap in the broken masonry.

"Are you hurt, boy?" asked Snow. It was impossible for him not to think of the note, the dead squirrel. He made a physical effort not to go over to the stone and examine it for traces of red sand.

The boy shook his head while crouching over the fallen stone. He poked it with a grubby finger and turned his face once more to the roof.

Snow glanced at his watch. "Come on, let me in. I hope the rest of this place is more solid." His heartbeat slowed to normal in a few seconds. The collapse must have been an accident.

The boy didn't move. Scabbed knees showed through holes in his pants. He turned a finger in one ear and looked at Snow. "Don't you want to wait for the other, then?"

"What other?"

"That short fellow as was with you down the street."

"You're mistaken. No one is with me." Snow frowned and turned to glance down the street. He saw only intent pedestrians.

The boy gave a last look to the stone on the pavement and opened the door.

Snow entered the first room on the ground floor to the right of the stairs. The bodies of an older man and a young girl were laid out on the floor with crossed hands. This house had nothing like shrouds or sheets to spare for their dead. The wrinkled cadavers wore only the rags they'd died in. The room stank.

Snow stalked around the room once and turned to the boy, who eyed the corpses with mistrust, as though they might spring to dangerous life any moment. "You said there were cholera cases here. Is this all?"

"No, sir, these as was died last night. Come upstairs to see the rest." The boy averted his head from the corpses and preceded Snow up the stairs.

In the room at the top a woman in black, looking like a prison matron, stepped among moaning adults and children. She redistributed basins and chamber pots as each was filled. Her head down, she droned a string of words that Snow could barely make out.

". . . pestilence that stalks in the darkness, and the plague that destroys at mid-day, for adulterers and sodomites and perjurers . . ." She trailed off into silence. "Boy, where's that doctor?" she shouted suddenly, before seeing Snow. "And get these emptied, outside." She gestured at the full pots.

Her eyes were big as a grouper's behind thick spectacles, her hair wild and bushy. She grabbed at a cross around her neck and ran her tongue along dry lips. With an arm full of dirty towels she waved at the bed and the floor.

"It's about time you're here. Too late for them sinners downstairs."

The woman went back to her distorted Bible quotes as Snow first picked his way over the people to try to open the window. It was so marked with years of soot and grime that the room was too dark to see more than the white faces of the victims. The heat felt as encompassing as a brick kiln.

The window was hopelessly stuck. His attempt to open it left him nauseated and even hotter, with a bleeding finger. The smell in the room was terrible. But blended with the sickly sweet cholera evacuations was another, less unpleasant odor which filled his mind with sadness. Apples.

With the apple smell came a clear memory of the last sight he had of his mother, heavily pregnant and sleepy, smiling at him the night before she went into labor. It had been early autumn, at the peak of the apple harvest, and apples were piled in the kitchen.

He must have been staring, sightless, at the thick window for a long moment before he turned and saw that under the bed and stacked up to the edge of the overflowing chamberpots were baskets and piles of apples. This was a house of fruit-selling costermongers. Time to get to work, he thought.

Snow checked the victims but none was coherent enough to answer his questions. He told the woman to give them as much boiled water as they would swallow.

"Where's the medicine for me to give 'em, then? The Methodists what sent me here said you'd bring medicine."

"What medicine? There's no medicine for cholera."

She stroked a mole on her cheek with shaking fingers before returning to her tasks. Snow couldn't tell if the shaking was palsy or anger.

It was unlikely that any of them would survive. "Where do they usually get their water?" he asked her.

She looked up as if in surprise that he was still there.

"Wine is a mocker and beer a brawler, whoever—"

"Water, I said, water."

"They buys it off Buckingham Palace, as they does their apples." She broke into a cackle, close to hysteria.

"No, please, it's important." He tossed her a shilling and was startled at how deftly her hand shot out. "Does it come from a well? Or a tap?"

"It's Bill there as fetches it. Some days from the river. Some from the ditch. There's no taps for them that lives in this hole."

"Can you spare him? Bill? I want him to show me the ditch."

"If you can catch him, take him where you likes." She limped to the head of the stairs. "Bill! You devil's imp! Where're you off to, then?" Bill appeared at the doorway below, scratching his head. He ran up the steps.

"Bill, take this gennmun round to the ditch. He wants a look. But here, take these too." She shoved more brimming pots at him, and he left the house. Once outside he dumped their contents in the gutter, then beckoned to Snow to follow.

"Is that lady a relation of yours?"

The boy mouthed his disgust. "I got no relations. But she's no relation of nobody. The Methodist Sisters sent her over for the sickness. I wish it'd take her and her preachin' with it."

Snow could smell the waterway before he could see it. It was an amplification of the room he'd just left. A handkerchief over his nose did nothing to stifle it. He and the boy reached an

73

unsteady wood bridge spanning the ten-foot-wide channel. Rotting steps led down to the water. On the opposite side was the crazed back wall of a brick tenement, propped up by rotting timbers and ready to crash into the murk.

Snow descended the steps. The water lapped at the toes of his boots and washed the street dust away. A bloated dead cat floated past.

"Is it always like this?" he asked.

"Oh, no. When the tide's low it ain't nearly so nice as now. You can't swim then, nor drink. Too much mud. And the smell is awful. But now it's fine. This where I meet my mates to swim." Without warning Bill pinched his nose shut and jumped in the canal.

Snow grabbed with an instinct to stop him and then felt foolish.

Bill resurfaced. He filled his cheeks with water and almost spat it out at Snow, but remembered just in time the doctor's honored position. Instead he spouted it straight up in the air and back onto his own head.

"Come out of there, boy. You'll get ill."

"If it was beer I'd be well, I know that." The boy clambered out and dripped on the steps. He held out his wet hand palm up. "Give us a flatch, guvnor."

Snow put a halfpenny in his hand, then another. "Don't drink this water, boy. It's poison."

The boy's blue eyes narrowed at Snow. He opened his mouth to speak but his glance moved a fraction to the left and widened at something at the back of the alleyway.

Snow turned and caught a glimpse of someone scuttling around the corner. At the same time the boy pushed past him and darted down the alley.

"Hey! What was . . ." Snow's voice trailed off. He stared a moment at the trail of wet footprints. Then he took three glass vials from his pocket and stooped to fill them with water from the canal.

He was a few steps out of the alley when he heard the rapid approach from behind of a brisk clicking and panting. He didn't turn fast enough to see the dog before it had him, a snarling streak of white fur gnawing his leg.

"Hoi! Get off!" Snow tried to shake off the dirty bull dog but it seemed furious and wouldn't budge. Although it only had the

74

skin of his leg in a pinching grip, at any moment it could bite deeper. Snow tried to lurch down the street with the animal clinging to him. It was impossible. A few street boys stopped to watch the show.

He finally had to beat the dog with the top of his medical bag so it would let go. It stayed on the pavement barking at him while he walked off with his trousers in shreds and blood dripping into his shoe.

Would Methodists have been so violent? That stone falling from the roof could have killed him, and the dog—it made no sense. Perhaps even this girl lying next to him was part of a plot. He laughed at the idea of that cross-clutching, fish-eyed nurse paying a whore to trail him.

The girl sighed in her sleep and muttered something about mangoes. Dreaming of tropical fruit, thought Snow. He raised himself on one elbow to study her face. In sleep the childish lines shone out. She smiled once, then her features were again blank. A sense of his own good luck at meeting up with her took him by surprise.

He found himself remembering her face earlier that evening, as her pale eyebrows had frowned in the childish concentration of unlacing the back of her dress, her hands in an awkward position behind her. A familiarity flooded over him. Singing games in a hay field came to his mind, and a puppy, a slice of bread. And more of the song.

> Kettles and pans
> Say the bells of St. Anne's

Sleepiness, like his sense of luck, took him by surprise.

When he woke the next morning she was gone, but she'd set out a teapot with a chipped spout and a small loaf on a cracked plate. There was a scrawled note beside the tray.

"you come back, an aks for Sofy. dudley strete. dont forgit to et yer taters."

Maybe it was the spelling that called him to his senses. This cholera work must be driving me mad, he thought. I could have caught anything from her. Pox. Clap, lice.

In daylight it wasn't hard to get his bearings and he made his way back to Soho with his head down, praying no one would remember him in the girl's neighborhood.

It was clear he'd been working too hard. He needed a change. There were other subjects besides cholera.

He needed more work to develop his theory of stages of unconsciousness and pain; he suspected that the occasional deaths from chloroform and other agents used in surgery were due to overuse of the substance, or a descent into sleep which was far too rapid and deep.

The notebook was still where he had left it the night before. He had stopped at timed inhalations of three percent chloroform. Last night it had worked on one hedgehog, leaving the animal limp and compliant during a needle probe, yet perfectly healthy an hour later. But a week or two before, in an experiment with twice the dose, another animal had died in five minutes. It was smaller than the first, and female.

Rather than use an animal this time, Snow thought he'd try it on himself as he had many times before. Anything he found out with these animals was really not very useful until it had been demonstrated on humans. He checked his notes from his last try at this; half a dram of diluted chloroform had rendered him confused in twenty seconds. He knew he had lost weight since the last time he had used himself as a subject, so today it would have to be a little less.

He made sure everything was ready by the sofa, so the fall, if it came, would be short. No real danger threatened him; the lethal amount for a human was a hundred times that for an undersized hedgehog.

Even so, he felt nervous while he laid the marked needles on the tray, and arranged the clock with its large numbers, the mask and its attached tubes.

An absolute scale for pain was impossible. Snow had decided years ago to abandon all subjective measures and instead calibrate external things only. Externals were easy. The exact depth of the needle under the skin, the length of time, the ability to hold the arm still under repeated jabs.

His own will power was, of course, a large factor, and he calculated that as well, using a scale he'd invented of age, sex, and whether or not the patient had been through childbearing or unanesthetized surgery. The scale went from one to ten. Because he'd never had surgery, he rated a seven. He wished he had the nerve to ask Mrs. Jarrett to volunteer for an experiment. She'd had two children, so she would have rated a nine.

When everything was quite ready he began the deep breaths into the mask. A dreamy state floated over him. His hands felt disconnected from his body. Being careful not to breathe too deeply, he counted to twenty by the clock and began the slow jabs with the needle.

2

Two days later, Snow's mind felt clearer and ready again for some hard work. His moment of madness with the prostitute he tried to put out of his mind. Whatever had caused it, he had got it out of his system now. A good day for work lay ahead of him; Caleb had sent word to cancel their evening exchange of notes, so he had no deadline for his return.

He considered walking over the Vauxhall Bridge, but he decided to risk the traffic and get a cab on Oxford Street instead. If there really was someone after him, he'd be harder to follow that way. The hansom rattled west and then south to the Embankment, at a slower and slower pace as the street grew more jammed.

He felt more tired than he'd been for days. He'd ended up spending most of the previous night checking the case lists against his ordnance survey map of Lambeth. This time he arranged the cases by address instead of date. It was a terrible task, without any interest other than the one goal: to be able to walk down a street and up the next and knock on the door of every cholera case without skipping one.

Staying up all night was usually nothing to Snow. He couldn't figure out why he was so much more tired today. Perhaps, he thought, it was the weight of the lists themselves, the awesome power of death after death. The names and addresses receded from real souls into meaningless numbers and then back into people again, so that for each name on the list he had an image, a life, in mind.

Hamish McFarland, 38, wife Betsy, daughter Ann. He hadn't been able to go on reading; the couple was there before him in his study, with their smocks, their dusty boots, their stringy undernourished hair. Ann, age six, had circles under her eyes and a checkered apron. He would admonish himself and go on, but it happened again and again.

He hadn't been able to finish the work but he had enough streets catalogued to make the day worthwhile. He held the lists folded like a testament inside his old lab notebook and stared at its mottled cover. The design of these laboratory notebooks hadn't changed since he was a schoolboy.

The traffic on the bridge came to a standstill. Snow stayed in the cab, breathing the horse smells and feeling sleepy. There seemed no point in getting out; the houses would stay there. He fingered the frayed cardboard edge of his book.

He could remember holding just such a notebook, walking through the university courtyard with Caleb. What had been folded in it that day? Not data, that was for certain. Tracts. Thin tracts, poorly printed, and full of fundamentalist Christian bunk. He and Caleb had been on the way to the Methodist chapel to hear a new preacher. They had stopped briefly in Snow's rooms for Caleb's opium dose. That was when Snow was just beginning to try to get him down to ten drops a day.

They'd heard that the preacher was charismatic and profound, that just listening to him you could receive a literal vision of the plague of locusts and the burning bush flaming in desert heat. No figurative interpretations sufficed for this man.

At the University of London, variations on the Church of England formed a large part of the amusement for country boys like Snow and Beersdon. It gave them something to do if they weren't up to the alcoholic binges and betting sprees that were the other options for fun. It was like a social club where the main entertainer was God.

If they hadn't gone to this particular sermon Caleb might still be a single man. That was where he met Deborah. Her father was the preacher. She had latched on to Caleb instantly. Probably she sensed his vulnerability. Snow remembered the way she sat in her pew next to the young men, and looked up at the speaker with such filial devotion, but had still managed to look sideways at Caleb and sneak in a smile. They were introduced after the church service and from that time Snow and Beersdon were weekly sheep in the pastor's flock.

The cabby's voice from above jolted him back to the present. "Queen Street, sir. Two shillings."

Snow paid and stepped down, suddenly feeling a dizziness so

powerful he had to grab onto the vehicle until it passed, and a sharp pain in his lower back. Not the gut, thank God.

When it was over he felt fine. He wondered if it was his kidneys again, or if it could be from the chloroform experiments. It was impossible to judge how harmful these things were when done more than once or twice in a lifetime. By now Snow had experimented on himself countless times. Maybe he would just use hedgehogs for a while, though he felt uncomfortable when they died. Even if the animals had no souls they surely would rather be running on a wheel in a cage than not existing at all. God must have made the animal for some purpose, though Snow doubted if Caleb and Deborah's God could have told any of them what the purpose was.

All these years later, and Caleb still couldn't escape frequent attendance at religious meetings. Snow knew what Caleb's congregation would have said about Snow's experiments in deadening sensation with chloroform. To them pain was an act of God, and to escape from it was a sin as deadly as intemperance or adultery, punishable with unimaginable torments.

It was Deborah's vision of hell which finally scared Snow off the religious life in those old days. She knew the height of the blaze and even the temperature that God would use to incinerate workers drinking rum on a Sunday. Some exacting Methodist had figured the fire's dimensions out in cubits, using certain obscure texts in the Old Testament. Deborah had compared it to one of the pottery ovens at Stoke.

Surely none of those imagined pains could equal the real pain of the child last year whose entire right eye had to be removed without chloroform because of her parents' religious fervor. That they had hesitated to agree to the surgery, to save her life from the deadly tumor behind her eye socket, was amazing to Snow, but then when he understood that they were refusing chloroform he had been appalled. They said her pain would teach her the strength of God's power.

Though Snow didn't do the surgery himself he had stayed in the operating theater with his chloroform kit the entire time, in case the parents changed their minds. But the girl's moans didn't sway them. She had been a brave creature; the surgeon only needed two assistants to hold her down. The last Snow heard she was doing well, and had kept full sight out of the remaining eye. He doubted that she'd keep much in the way of religious enthusiasm.

And that was hardly Snow's first encounter with religious resistance to pain relief, and even resistance to saving a life. He remembered his summons to a recent childbirth that could have ended in an all too typical disaster. The woman's husband had sent a note begging Snow to come. By the time he arrived with his equipment, two other doctors had been there for some time, and the husband was weeping in a chair outside the room. One doctor glanced at Snow with resentment, and the other gave him a quick, sullen summing up.

"Been in hard labor for thirty hours. Fully dilated. It's obvious the head's too big to come down. The mother has reached the danger stage: low pulse, delirious, a fever raging. If we do a craniotomy right away there's a chance of saving her." The man picked up a long forceps with jagged teeth, tipped with points.

Snow had flinched. A craniotomy. He had seen enough of those to last him his entire life. When the fetus's head was too large the only way to save the mother was to reach in through the cervix and cut through the baby's skull, killing the baby of course, and withdraw the crushed head and dismembered body parts through the mother's tortured vagina. The physical pain the mother would undergo was unthinkable, aside from the chance of infection, which was enormous, as well as likely laceration from bone fragments. He'd seen a case last year of gangrene following a craniotomy delivery. It had resulted in the mother's vagina, bladder, and colon, putrefying and turning into one fused channel before she died.

"You're certain the child is dead?" asked Snow.

"No, in fact there was a distinct kick a moment ago. But the mother will surely die. You can't want to risk a cesarian."

Snow knew the recovery rate from a cesarian section was barely ten percent. Such surgery was only worth the risk when the mother was dying anyway, but the infant had a chance. "I'd like to try to chloroform her and bring down the child manually."

The other doctor shook the craniotomy forceps in impatience. "It's impossible. We already gave her opium, but the uterus is so clamped down we can't do a thing. And we can't hold the woman still, she won't tolerate it."

"But you didn't have chloroform then." As he spoke, Snow

was rapidly opening his case and assembling his tubing apparatus, carefully measuring the minimal dose.

The third medical man finally spoke up. "I don't like this. It's unnatural. You'll kill her anyway, likely as not. Women were meant to suffer with childbirth. They have for thousands of years."

Snow ignored him and held the mask over the face of the wretched woman, who was beyond speech but seemed to agree, with her eyes, to his treatment. In ten seconds her eyes closed. In fifteen seconds she made no response to a pinprick.

Snow rolled up his sleeve and slowly inserted his hand into the woman's vagina, then attempted to pass the resisting cervix. A contraction came, and when it ended he was able to move his hand in and around the infant's skull. When he pressed against the carotid artery there pulsed a distinct, rapid heartbeat.

"The child's still alive," Snow called out. "I think we can bring it down. One of you, when the next contraction comes, push against her abdomen." The woman didn't stir.

"It'll never work," said the attending doctor. "The uterus is too spasmodic and rigid. You're wasting our chance to save her."

The other said, "The Church should put a stop to this sort of thing. The child obviously was not meant to live."

Another contraction came and Snow pulled gently at the base of the infant's skull, actually moving it down another half inch. The next contraction, and the next, kept sending the child further out. Because the chloroform had relaxed her involuntary muscles so thoroughly, the woman's uterus ceased the irregular spasm which seemed to be gripping it, and her now unconscious body worked with Snow's hand to release its burden.

Finally the first of the other doctors stepped over and began to push against her abdomen as Snow had instructed.

In ten contractions the child was delivered. A boy. It gasped, choked, arched its back, and did all the things an infant was supposed to. Snow handed it, still attached to the umbilical cord, to one of the other doctors, and bent to check the woman's face. Her eyelids fluttered open.

"Did you do it?" she murmured. "Did you have to destroy the child?" Snow could barely hear her.

"No, madam. You have a healthy son. Your pain is over."

As Snow left, the other doctor had been carefully packing

81

away the unused craniotomy forceps, shaking his head in either disbelief, disgust, or stunned relief; Snow couldn't tell.

Heading down Queen Street with his cholera notes, Snow tried to bring his mind back to the present task, but couldn't. If the zealots had had their way that time, the child would be dead and the woman probably too mutilated to ever have another. How long could the world resist the relieving of such dreadful suffering?

He reached the first house on his list, and tried again to put religion, pain, and its relief out of his mind for a while.

A slum.

Eight deaths, ages two to sixty-three. He went through the questions, memorized and pat: where does the house get water? Was it treated before drinking it? Could he see the source? What company provided the pipe line? Snow filled yet another bottle and labeled it. His plan was to ask the questions for every house and collect specimens from one house out of ten.

At the next house on his list lived a laundress with one living child. Two weeks ago there had been four children, a husband, and a grandmother, but cholera had blasted them all. The laundress had lived and lay pale and weak, hardly understanding the disaster. A neighbor came in to watch the surviving baby who crawled through the dust and scraps on the floor.

Tomorrow was a Sunday, and Snow doubted that attending a morning and evening sermon was part of the household's plan. According to Deborah, missing church alone would condemn the woman, and the baby, to those Stoke pottery ovens.

He didn't think Deborah knew about the years of Caleb's opium addiction and Snow's fight to wrench him out of it. She only saw Snow as a bad influence on her husband. Even worse was his counsel to Caleb to pursue journalism instead of the church.

Snow's notebook was getting fat. By four o'clock he finished the street. He was crossing the opening of an alleyway when out of the corner of his eye a white shape moved. Suddenly he felt both his arms grabbed from behind. His papers scattered around him. Before he could shout, a hand clapped itself over his mouth. A strong smell of dog came up from the skin on the back of the hand.

They shoved him forward, into the alley, the grip behind him still strong. Once he was farther into the shadows, he was pushed roughly to his knees. The hand stayed over his mouth.

"Lay off, see?" A kick landed on his lower spine, bringing back the pains he had felt earlier, and the dizziness too.

"Do as you're told. This is just a gentle warning. We gets worse fast." The voice was generic. It could have been any poor man on the street.

Snow felt himself being pushed forward until his face pressed the packed dirt of the alley. The spat-out shell of a sunflower seed was under his eye.

He tensed his muscles to yank his arms free. But just as he was about to do it, he was kicked once more, harder, and suddenly released. Footsteps ran back toward the street.

He scrambled to his feet. Too slow. He saw no one. Cautiously he stepped into the sunlight at the edge of the alley. No one.

His papers and notebooks littered the pavement and he self-consciously stooped to gather them, looking on both sides at the pedestrians, who ignored him.

3

A day later he found himself checking a house on the street where he'd met Sophie. He never once consciously intended to try to see her again. Even so, he chose this house out of a list of fifteen, and he saved it for the end of the day, when dusk was falling.

She was there, talking to someone, perhaps a child. It was too far to tell, with the street crowd in between. By the time Snow reached her she was alone again.

Confusion clouded her face, but lifted immediately.

"Hey, it's the vicar," she cried, looking pleased to see him. "Ready for another go?" she asked, pulling at his arm.

Once more there was a fleeting echo of eyebrow, and this time a turn of the head as well, a line of the nose. Oranges and lemons. Then it was gone, swallowed up in the present and forgotten. But the smell was real enough; not of hay this time. Of wet dog.

The suspicion rushed over him like a bad taste in his mouth. "Wait a moment. Who was that you were just talking to?"

"Nobody. Just a friend."

"You have children for friends? Are you the best person to be their friend?"

She gave him a hurt look and he immediately felt guilty for suspecting her.

"What are you so worried about, anyway? No one would know you in this part of town."

Snow rubbed his leg, where the dog bites from three days ago were healing, and looked uncomfortably to either side, even though his chat with a whore was no more noticeable on this street than if he'd been buying turnips. The dog smell didn't fade, but no dog was in sight.

"I . . . I can't go with you, Sophie. I have my work . . ." The regret in his voice surprised him.

Her small eyes crinkled in amusement at the weakness of his excuse. "Look, guvnor, I know you're busy now, but I'll be here around ten. Come and see us."

She turned away and took off without waiting for a reply. Snow kept walking, as though she had merely asked him the time, or begged a coin. He knew he'd be there.

After that, every few nights he would turn up at her corner after eleven. They would go to her attic and make love, then she would cook him a supper over a spirit lamp. Then they would do it again. Snow's quick way in bed soon changed, as Sophie persuaded him that there were better methods of doing it. She turned out to be surprisingly strong and resisted his impatience in creative and maddening positions.

His suspicions of Sophie faded along with his distaste for her gray sheets. As long as she didn't expect him to drink unboiled water, or eat raw foods, he was content.

When Sophie first suggested that they go out instead of staying in her hot attic, he had refused absolutely, out of fear of recognition, contagion, and just plain stubbornness. But her laughter and a guarantee of a disguise for him finally changed his mind.

They left one night after midnight, she almost drunk on rum and he intoxicated simply at the mild danger of what he was doing. She had never been able to persuade him to have a drink with her.

They stuck to the alleyways close to the river. Smells shifted from sewer stench to the mossy breeze a lily pond might have, and gave Snow no clue where they were. When they finally stopped he knew they'd reached the East India Docks, judging by the ships' masts which swayed and clanked, making spears of dark against the lit London sky. The murmurs of shifting rope and chain mixed with squeaks of countless river rats scurrying over the cobblestones.

Snow and Sophie descended into a cellar. Snow had to stoop to pass under the low door and once inside, the ceiling brushed the top of his head. Rough men packed the room, a hollowed space under two or three of the old houses. In the poor light it was hard to see how big the place was. At least a hundred people were pressed together.

The crowd's anticipation was high. Everyone's attention was fixed on a circular pit in the room's center, about two feet deep and ten in diameter. River damp glistened on the walls and shone in the clay floor of the pit.

Snow's height gave him a good view, but most had to jostle for priority, pushing and shifting against each other. If Sophie hadn't kept such a strong hold around his waist they would have been pulled apart.

Snow guessed a fight of some sort was ready, dogs or cocks, but even so, the crowd's fevered eagerness confused him. So did the shining eyes of the few women present, as if this place were forbidden and sexual. It reminded him of crowds outside the public hangings. He overheard a few remarks.

"I hear he's something powerful, this one. Done in two dogs last week. They're talking of setting him at rats next."

"Rats! Jesus! Not while I'm in the room. He'd be nothing but bones after. The dogs is bad enough."

"It's all one to me, so long as the man comes through on the bets. I got a shilling on him tonight."

The announcer came to the edge of the pit dressed in an old frock coat and top hat. His hair was dyed black and clung to his head in an oily glob. At first the crowd noise obscured his voice.

"—and as was said before, all bets is now placed. Any ladies like to faint, better leave now before it starts."

No one stirred.

"Here we have the renowned beast Rumbler, prize rat killer and blue ribbon fighter." A small pit bull dog was carried in over the heads of the crowd. The dog's wide studded collar and two-foot chain were then bolted, with ceremony, to a ring in the wall of the pit. Those who had edged close now backed off as far as they could.

Gray splotched the dog's white coat and pink gums matched his pink rheumy eyes. His huge lower jaw displayed yellow teeth. He slavered and pulled at his chain. No barks or even growls came out; just the clank of the chain.

"And for your special entertainment tonight, ladies and gentlemen, against this brave beast, we have Monsyoor Mango, just back from his renowned tour on the continent. May the best win!"

At the name, a light flashed in Snow's mind and then faded. He tried to see what they were bringing in, and in his first shock he couldn't recognize it. Another dog? A pig? But no, it was a dwarf, a male dwarf, dressed only in short leather pants and a leather collar. Snow felt sick.

"Sophie, why didn't you tell me what this was? I can't watch this. The man will be killed."

A tremor went through Sophie where Snow held her waist.

"Aw, don't be such a pansy. I told you this'd be good fun, and so it will. It ain't like he's human. It's all fixed, anyway. Besides, you can't leave. It's too crowded. They'd think you're a copper."

She was right. They were both pushed up to the edge of the pit and retreat was impossible. And he realized too that his accent had given him away. Mistrustful glances flicked in their direction.

"It's all right. He's straight. Just out for a lark." Snow's rough disguise hadn't succeeded.

"See? Shut up now. It makes 'em nervous. Just watch."

So Snow watched. The dwarf was being chained, by a ring in his collar, opposite the dog, and two men held the dog back. Some ointment hateful to the dog must have been rubbed on the dwarf. The animal went wild. Snow thought it would pull loose from the restraining hands.

The dwarf's long square skull and bridgeless nose quivered once in and out of human vulnerability, and then set itself in a hard bestial fix. He raised his arms into a mock boxing position.

Snow thought about stopping the fight. A second too long. A bell clanged and the dog was released.

In half a second the dog had its teeth buried in the dwarf's right forearm. The dwarf used his left hand to partially strangle the animal, forcing it to release its jaws. This worked, and the dwarf began to pummel the dog's tender nose. It snapped and clawed, too busy for another attack, but held its ground. And it was clear that the dwarf's wounded right arm was already weakening. As he punched at the pink nose his blood spattered the walls of the pit and spotted the feet of the closest spectators.

The dog got a tooth grip again, this time on the dwarf's leg, and sent him sprawling in the mud. The dwarf was able to get his hands around the dog's neck. The veins in his muscular arms bulged in blue streaks under the muddy white skin. For three long seconds they struggled, equal in strength, without motion. The shouts of the bettors turned to a roar.

The dwarf quit his stranglehold on the dog and reached his unhurt arm around to grab the animal's hind leg. Bracing it against the mud floor, he wrenched it up at an angle and dislocated it at the hip joint.

Snow winced. He knew what it should have sounded like, that dislocation. The crowd was too loud to hear it.

The dog loosed his jaws for a moment to yelp in agony, and the dwarf lurched free. But a foot slipped in the mud, and the dog was instantly on top of him. His jaws were at the dwarf's throat. The dwarf thrashed from side to side, trying to throw off the beast, pulling at the animal's mauled leg and battering it around the eyes and nose with his good fist. His blood soaked the dog's hide. He was weakening fast.

Snow, unable to look away, began to calculate blood loss and system shock. The dwarf's jugular vein was half an inch from the dog's teeth.

Sophie, at Snow's side, began to breathe noisily. Does she know this man? Snow suddenly wondered. It was not, however, the time to ask questions.

Finally, in a last effort, the dwarf strained his thumbs up to the dog's eyes and in one spasmodic thrust dislodged both eyeballs. Dog blood gushed over the dirt, and although the canine jaws still held, they weakened for a second. The dwarf was able to prize them open, grab the beast around the throat, and pull himself to his feet. He snapped back the spine and the animal was dead.

The crowd roared with glee or chagrin, depending on their bets. Sophie looked shaken and relieved. Her words were obviously a lie. "I had sixpence on the dog. Ten to one, too."

The dwarf was carried out above the heads of the screaming audience, his face white as a cheese and his right arm dripping blood. He pushed past Snow and Sophie.

Snow met the man's glance. The shocking blue of the eyes held Snow's for a moment in a surprised recognition. The dwarf had time for one quick, questioning look at Sophie before he was borne away.

All of Snow's suspicions flooded back, much stronger this time. Then it flashed back in his mind; tropical fruits. In Sophie's sleep that first night together she had murmured "mango." What a fool he had been.

He turned to Sophie. "That man knows you. He knew *me*. What are you up to here?"

Sophie tried to push ahead of Snow through the crowd, acting as if she hadn't heard.

Snow grabbed her arm from behind, jerking her around to face him. "Wait. Answer my question, I tell you."

A few men in the crowd looked at them hard. Sophie said, "Fine. I'll tell you when we get outside. Come on, then."

They stood in a dark doorway while the crowd filed past. Harbor smells enveloped them.

Sophie wouldn't look at him at first. He waited a long time for her to speak.

"All right, then. It's true. But it ain't like you think. I do know him." At Snow's gesture of impatience she changed this to, "He was my lover. He asked me to do you. Someone hired him."

"Do you mean to tell me that you approached me on purpose, that first night?"

She almost smiled. "Yup. He followed you, all the way, signaled me when to stop you."

For all Snow's suspicions, he was stunned. Why would anyone bother? It couldn't be Methodists, not this.

"I don't know why, but he was plannin' to catch you in the act, with another fellow along as witness. Make you look bad." Her expression was earnest now. "You got to believe somethin'. Except for those first few minutes before we talked, I weren't going to do it. I couldn't, not after I knew what you was like. And I didn't do it, neither. Since that first night Mango's been at me to come with him and tell all about you so they could catch you in the act, ruin your name. But I kept sayin' him the wrong times, the wrong day. He almost had us once or twice."

"Yet you kept seeing me."

"Yeah." She hung her head. "I got feelings for you. You were good to me. And you needed feeding." Now she laughed, lightly, and raised her chin, looking almost defiant. "Besides, after I stopped doin' him, Mango cut me off. I needed your cash."

"But couldn't you—get other business?"

"Don't you understand? He cut off *all* my business. He's got ways." She looked to one side now, nervous.

"There's more you're not telling me."

Her glance held his. "That's right, guvnor." She swallowed. "Mango wants you now. Himself."

Snow's head was reeling. "Wait a moment. Who hired him in the first place? Why? I don't understand you."

"I don't know who hired him, or why. You should know that better than me. But first all he was hired for is to 'get you off the cholera,' he kept saying. Now he's livid. Jealous. He wants you dead."

Snow laughed in a broken voice. It was all mad. "I don't believe a word of this. And why did you bring me here tonight if you thought he might see you?"

"I dunno. I thought you might like it. And maybe he wouldn't see us."

Snow suspected that she had been wanting to tell him and she had brought him half on purpose. He said nothing.

"You believe what you want, guvnor. But one thing I know, I ain't goin back with 'im again." She shuddered, crossing her arms over her small chest.

She looked so vulnerable. Maybe she was telling the truth. That attack in the street was real enough. The bites on his leg were still raw.

They walked back to her place in Dudley Street without talking. When they reached her door, Snow said, "I can't come up, Sophie. I'll come by again soon."

"Sure."

He pressed a five-pound note into her hand. She must have known it was a final gift. To his surprise, she didn't try to refuse it.

89

4

In the days Snow had spent with Sophie, cholera increased all over London to thousands of cases and deaths. Soon after he stopped meeting her, Snow gave up hope of attempting to see patients in his office. Instead he spent his days going from house to house where the outbreaks had occurred. For a few days he had braced himself for other attacks or threats, but nothing happened. Her warning must have been a hoax, or a fanciful invention. Because he was so absorbed in his work, he soon forgot.

At the houses he asked the same question, over and over, repeating like a sedge-warbler's call: *"Where do you get your water? Where do you get your water? Where do you get your water?"* At first the incanted inquiry, with Snow's voice quick and sure, gave the same tactile pleasure as snapping the ends off fresh green beans. But after two mornings of it the tediousness of the work was beyond belief. The notebooks grew thick.

His bottles filled a wall of shelves in his library. He hadn't yet decided what to do with them, what tests he could possibly run in the little basement laboratory, and they waited in accusing, shining rows. His notes on the cases and conditions and locations were stacked in teetering piles. His desk, the sofa, armchairs, the little tables, every surface, all were buried under paper. Paper had spread itself over most of the floor, except for a narrow path from the door to the desk. Mrs. Jarrett stayed out.

He began missing his nights with Sophie. Caleb, without explanation, had completely stopped coming by to get the cholera counts for *The Times*, so Snow's evenings were empty. To distract himself he would sit up almost until dawn, leafing through the sheets, reading all the data and coming to no conclusions at all.

It was such a contradictory mess. If water carried the organism causing cholera, then diseased water supplies should affect everyone and be easy to pinpoint. But no patterns existed. Sick households got their water from a paradoxical variety of sources; some obviously polluted, such as the Thames or that ditch, and others proven clean and pure, piping systems run by respected companies and repeatedly checked by the city.

There were neighborhoods where half the houses were sick and half as untouched as if they stood in some other city.

Some sick houses were near the river, others a mile or more inland. Some were low, others were at one or two hundred feet above sea level. And not all were poor; several houses on Grosvenor Square were hit. Lady Hardwick lost her three children, and she was famous enough to have her tragedy singled out in an article in *The Times,* along with the name of her "society physician," Dr. Phineas Greeley. Greeley, Snow's old teacher from Westminster Hospital, held that cholera was caused by fumes and fogs. Snow wasn't surprised to see him mentioned. He tried to decide if he was jealous. He was.

Snow had a map of London over his desk. He spent hours at a time looking at it, thinking of the areas hardest hit and what they could have in common. The dotted black lines separating the parishes etched themselves into Snow's mind. The shapes of their borders spread across his vision like a badly done patchwork quilt.

One day it rained and he couldn't face another trek through the slums. With the map before him he sat once more at his desk, determined to come up with something, some solution to try to work on. His mind felt blank. Nothing made sense. And a sexual urge crept over him, along with memories he couldn't erase, of Sophie's white legs and her dark triangle. To annoy him even further, that song, stuck in his head ever since the first night he met her, wouldn't stop jingling away.

> Brickbats and tiles
> say the bells of St. Giles.
> You owe me five farthings
> Say the bells of St. Martin's.

He idly began drawing zigzag marks around the churches in the song. St. Martin's, St. Margaret's, St. Clement's, St. Mary-le-Bow. The distances looked so small from one parish to the next, though he knew how many hot exhausting minutes it had taken him that morning to walk from St. Ann's near his street, past St. Paul's, over to Drury Lane. His pencil point lightly traced his day's route.

Here comes a candle to light you to bed
And here comes a chopper to chop off your head.

Then it came to him. He couldn't believe how he had forgotten it, all these years. A smell of hay, and the song, were completely mingled with a sense of adoration for a little girl. What was her name? Her face came to him as clearly as a daguerreotype. Blond, with small sea-water blue eyes.

The memories came back in a rush. He was five or six, before his mother died, and it was a perfect day in June, around haying time. Out in the field between his house and Hazelhangar Farm, playing with the daughter of a hay worker. She'd been there with her mother every day that week, for the harvest, and would stay another ten days or more.

He and the girl were both too young to help with the haying, and to his child mind she seemed a permanent addition to his life. She knew games. Circle games, string games, riddles. And a game of London parishes with a head chopping ritual at the end of it. At the end she would catch him and his neck would be nipped gently by her grubby hands held out straight to simulate a giant scissors. That brief touch was thrilling to him and even now he remembered the shock it sent down his spine, like sparks from a carpet in winter.

She was from Haversham, a village over five miles away, and she seemed so exotic. He struggled once more for her name.

The following summer, he remembered, when haying time approached he waited every day for her and her mother to come. They never did. After his disappointment faded, he had forgotten her until this night.

On one of those endless June days she had explained the song to him.

"It's the parishes, you see. In London."

"There's more than one parish there?" he had asked. In his village, one church served every neighbor he knew.

"Like the fields here, with walls between. And a church for each one."

"How do you know?"

"I know all about London. I asked me mum. I'm going there when I grow up."

And they had gone back to the game.

He gave up trying to remember her name. Now that her face

92

was so clear, though, he knew that she looked nothing like Sophie. It was just the eyes. His thoughts moved to parishes. The parishes, the parishes . . . it could work.

A map of the case concentrations. Something one could actually see, rather than numbers to analyze.

He took the nearest pile of paper and began to scribble on the map with a red pencil. By dawn he had drawn in the total cases in each of the central parishes, grading the areas with different colors. Red was for the highest number, green the lowest, and five colors ranged in between. He hoped the colors would emerge in a pattern, something meaningful to make sense of all his collected details. It would be so exciting if something would finally be clear.

When he finished he scrutinized his work.

It proved nothing. It was still a crazy patchwork. He knew no more than before. Another night's work wasted.

9

India, January 1854

The small mainland cathedral was poorly lit by one east-facing rose window, whose tinted glass had been smashed in spots by aggressive birds, or boys with rocks. Despite the brilliant January sky outside, shadows, spooky as sleepwalkers, pooled behind the altar.

Lillian felt that she'd been sitting on the hard cane chair next to Olympia for hours. The funeral service and thoughts of her father drifted in and out of her mind. One thing bothered her terribly; she couldn't remember her father's hands. It had only been seven days since he died, but every time she tried to picture them she would see Rajan's hands, or her uncle's, or Henry's. Hands of the men she had known waved themselves across the altar screen and down the vacant miserere seats of the choir.

A closed-mouth yawn flared her nostrils. It was from exhaustion, not boredom. She and Olympia were now staying in the mainland city with Olympia's brother, the cardamom merchant. In the strange surroundings and damp, poorly aired bed linen, Lillian had slept badly and had waked long before dawn. She stayed in bed until the morning came, listening to Olympia's heavy breathing in the other bed.

Just as she had decided to get up, a surprise summons came for her and Olympia, from her uncle, asking them to come to the drawing room as soon as they could. She knew Olympia would take forever to rise and dress, so she headed out to the garden by herself for a few minutes.

A high stone wall separated the house from the hectic wharf, but in working hours it couldn't block out the earth-shaking thumps of huge bales as they fell from the loading cranes, or the yells of the foremen. Now only an occasional rooster broke through the quiet.

Once, when the grandmother whom she had never met died in England, her father told her that death wasn't as complicated as it was made out to be. She had wondered then if he meant for the person who died or for everybody else. This morning, in the garden, she decided he must have meant for the dead.

Voices floated to her from an open window in her uncle's study. His tone was unmistakable, hoarse from years of cigars. The other voice she didn't know.

"We thought you would want to be told as soon as possible, sir. In the bay."

"Yes, quite. And you say there's no chance of a mistake?"

"Well, the body was badly decomposed. He'd been caught in the tree roots around the other side of the island. I know it was only three days, at most, but with this heat . . . And the vultures had been at the part of him that was out of the water." They mentioned no name, but she found herself thinking, Henry's face. Pushpa's name for him in Telagu had been "He Who Loves Mirrors."

Lillian hurried inside, to find Olympia in the drawing room, with her uncle and a military doctor. From over the wall came a metallic crash and some shouts, the first of the day.

Her uncle looked over at the two women, and then asked, "But the identification is certain?"

Outside, a pile of crates fell over.

"Oh, no doubt there. All his papers were still in the pockets." The dock noise fell for a moment and there was a sodden thud as the doctor laid a bundle of papers on the table. "Something about a discharge?"

Her uncle had cleared his throat. "Yes, we won't go into that now."

"And a notice of withdrawal of a thousand pounds on account. No bank notes, though. They must have washed away."

Lillian and Olympia caught each other's eye. It's not Henry, Lillian thought. She couldn't think why, but an inner voice told

95

her Henry was not dead. She suspected Olympia was thinking exactly the same thing.

"And it was cholera, of course?" asked Olympia. Her voice was flat. It could have been grief.

"Pretty sure. I'm so sorry, ma'am."

Olympia swallowed and looked once more at Lillian, then said, "Thank you. You're very kind."

The cathedral organ started up, whistling and creaking in four-part harmony, bringing Lillian back to the funeral. It was time to sing another hymn. She thought of Henry. It was possible, no, quite probable actually, that the man in Henry's clothes was a man Henry had killed for some purpose. She once again tried to understand why she didn't feel shocked or frightened. It seemed that anything was possible now. All the old rules had been broken.

The short trip on the mail boat from the island to the mainland was the last time she had felt relaxed or relieved. It was a brief rest, when she could allow herself to believe in a life without cholera, and it ended the moment she stepped off the boat with a staggering Olympia.

Cholera was everywhere in Cochin. The Indian part of the city was completely in quarantine by now.

Though Europeans could come and go as they pleased, less than half a dozen people occupied cathedral chairs, and everyone but Lillian and Olympia breathed through handkerchiefs. The bishop's wife had died the day before, yet he read the funeral service all the same.

"Lillian," whispered Olympia, "you don't think it was Henry, do you?" She lifted her black-bordered handkerchief to dab at her upper lip.

A shred of smoke wafted through the window, bringing a smell of cooking meat. For a moment it made Lillian remember her hunger; she hadn't eaten breakfast. Then, with a rise of nausea, she realized that it was another pyre from the Indian neighborhood. Or perhaps, in this scorching heat, a pyre had spread and set fire to some rooftops. Luckily, small canals flowed everywhere, between the neighborhoods.

Her black wool dress was unbearable. Sweat stung her forehead and trickled between her breasts.

"Do you know what I think?" Lillian whispered. "Not only was it not Henry, but Henry might have killed—"

Olympia's quick pull of breath was too loud, but no heads turned. A widow was allowed anything at a funeral. "Perhaps the man wasn't a European," Olympia whispered, more quietly.

"I don't know. They said no features were recognizable. And it's just as bad either way, isn't it?"

"Don't be a fool, Lillian. They wouldn't prosecute for a murdered native." This was the most clearheaded thing Olympia had said for days.

It was only yesterday that Olympia recovered from her cholera. Her actions were still slow and she had hardly spoken since regaining her health, so until now Lillian hadn't been sure how well her stepmother understood what had happened.

Olympia had lost weight, and it wasn't becoming to her. Her face wore the look of inward crumbling that shows up in the deathly ill, even weeks after recovery. Loose skin hung in folds at her jawline. Her measurements, when taken for her mourning clothes, had decreased by inches.

The woman sighed slowly, settling into the small hard chair like a sack of rice shifting its center of gravity. After a moment the handkerchief went once more to her upper lip.

Lillian stared straight ahead at the worn prayer book in the bishop's hands. Age spots mottled the skin over his knuckles, which looked swollen with rheumatism. His voice shook as he read the service, maybe from grief, or it could just be fever. Lillian wasn't a churchgoer and she hadn't seen him for years, but she remembered her romantic longing for him when she was ten. His hair had been a pale blond then. She almost smiled thinking of it now.

"Lillian," Olympia whispered again. "What are we going to do now?"

Do? The question had hardly occurred to her. She hadn't thought much beyond the end of the funeral or getting back to Uncle George's house. If she didn't answer, maybe Olympia would drop it. She kept her eyes fixed on the bishop.

How much did he believe in his life of devotion? Did he keep track of Indian conversions with notches on his English walnut walking stick? Or was it enough for him just to maintain faith in this place? Lillian scrutinized him as he finished the service. She caught a hint of white under his closed, fluttering eyelids as he read the last words. He believed, she decided. Perhaps her father's rule applied to him as well.

97

"Lillian, think. Where should we go? We can't stay with my brother forever."

This whisper was so soft that she could pretend not to hear. But Olympia's hand found hers and held it, clinging like a limpet. She longed to pull it away but didn't.

"Don't worry," she finally answered. "You can go wherever you like. There's no hurry."

With a final hymn the service ended. Lillian stood and held the back of the chair to steady herself. Ever since fainting by the dock she had felt constantly light-headed, her knees uncertain. But nothing worse than that. In a moment she was all right.

The few mourners left at an artificially slow pace, as if trying to endow the moldy place with a Canterbury-sized nave. Two pale scorpions scuttled past Lillian's feet to hiding spots under fifteenth-century burial plaques.

The last time she'd been here, for a church bazaar a year ago, she had glimpsed the Hindu caretaker's sacred cobra coiled by its bowl of milk near the baptismal font. There was no sign of the creature now.

The group made their way to the burial plot in the churchyard. In deep shade cast by a huge fig tree and clustered palms, the coffin stood ready by the open grave. Flies clouded around it; seven days was too long to wait. During the bishop's few words, Lillian's uncle stepped to her side and took her arm. His sudden sympathy moved her. He had never been the least bit affectionate before.

He leaned toward her to whisper something and she readied herself for the condolences. "A little bit of a surprise for you, dear."

Lillian dropped her polite, sad smile. "What are you talking about?"

"I had a chat with the solicitors. I thought you'd want to know right away. A substantial figure, much more than expected. And the bulk of it in your name alone. My sister will have to make do." His breath smelled of curry and garlic.

Lillian pulled her arm free. "Hadn't we better wait to talk of these things?"

"If you like. But fifty thousand pounds, at four percent, comes to over four shillings an hour in interest. You'll be needing advice very soon."

Despite herself, Lillian paid attention. Fifty thousand! She

98

knew his fortune was large, but not that large. It should have gone to Olympia, not to her. And, ashamed, she did a quick mental calculation. Two thousand pounds a year. She could do anything she wanted.

"But—what about my stepmother?"

"A small sum for my sister, enough to be comfortable. He left it entirely up to your judgment. 'To provide for my dear wife, and give her a home, as she sees fit, and as guided by her friends and family.' I think that was how he worded it. But don't you worry. We'll manage all that for you."

The burial verses were over. The coffin had been lowered, and Lillian realized that the long silence was because the bishop had been waiting for her to join Olympia and cast her handful of earth.

She gathered up a scoop of the red soil, thinking, is it enough? Is it too much? Am I doing it right? It hit the coffin with a dusty splatter. She stood, silently looking down and rubbing her gritty fingers.

As she left the cool churchyard and stepped through the gateway into the full city heat, she felt her father behind her, staying on in the shadows under the palms. And she finally remembered his hands; at least the right one. Large, with an old ungainly callous on the trigger side of the forefinger. The nails grooved. A slight tremor. A yellow snuff stain on the thumb.

It was the snuff stain that did it. A deep ache tightened her throat and her eyes spilled over. The tears blurred her view of the horde of inquisitive Indians grouped around the church gate. She could feel their survivors' curiosity boring into her, dissecting every detail of her appearance; the tears on her face, the grim black dress.

Olympia suddenly gripped Lillian's upper arm, so tightly that it hurt. "You're all I have left," she said, still whispering.

She hardly knows how right she is, thought Lillian. She knew if she spoke she would break into childish, squeaking sobs. Or even worse, begin to laugh. So she clenched her jaw even tighter and took shallow breaths.

With fifty thousand pounds they could go anywhere, couldn't they. Russia. Paris. The United States. London.

An image of London came into focus in her imagination, drawn mainly from newspaper prints and outdated fashion magazines. A picture of breezy, tree-lined cobblestoned streets and polished brass door knockers. Of smart carriages drawn by perfectly groomed horses and filled with ladies in bright silk dresses, heading for fascinating dinner parties. Opera houses, theaters, concerts of the latest music.

That's what they would do. They would go back to the home she'd never seen, to a place without lizards, or cobras, or scorpions. To a place without cholera.

10

London, August 1854

An hour before dawn, Ralph Bucks, wearing a new check suit and only slightly drunk, opened the door to The Drowning Man. It was one of a hundred pubs at the edge of the East India Docks, where the Thames sent up a marshy fog and the water glowed in reflection of a sky never completely dark. The place was crammed with a crowd of drinkers. Tobacco, foul lamp oil, and opium clouded the air.

Bucks was in a bad mood and had been so for weeks. The cholera was making him nervous. That job in the Golden Square works two weeks ago didn't help. He hated knowing the murder was going to be done in a public place like that, where anyone might have seen. And it turned out to be much messier than he had thought. Not in terms of blood, the men knew their work too well for that. But the fellow had pleaded with them, convinced of his own special reasons for living. He was bawling like a child when they finally hit him. They'd had to bash him twice; the first blow only sent him to his knees, screaming, his hands to his head.

Today was the day Bucks had told the men they'd be paid. The two of them turned up at the appointed spot, regular as sheep, holding out their palms. After paying them off and putting the rest in his pocket, he'd gone to his rooms off Drury Lane. He'd waited until night when he could join the rooftop rum drinkers who climbed up to escape the heat and carry out the standard prescription against getting this new plague. Their noise made sleep impossible, so it was easier to go up with them.

Tonight, three more had died in the rooms below him. Bucks coughed and wondered once again if he should leave London. But where could he go? He had a decent job now, contracting for these street works, and then anything extra on the side. Picking up a legal wage in some dead market town was no life for him. Nights like tonight, and quick work like today's, were what kept him going.

Inside the pub he finally spotted who he wanted, alone at a greasy table against the wall.

Bucks's quarry was hard to miss; a dwarf, with stiff red hair and freckled skin, whose light blue eyes pulsed sweet as meadow lupines. Scars crossed the cheekbones of his elongated skull, and one freckled ear was scabbed over from a recent wound. The dwarf sat with a pint of beer before him, along with a few finished mugs, carefully lined up, their handles all pointing the same way.

In places like this, the owners, always fearful of an evil eye, filled the dwarf's glass as soon as it was needed. Ralph Bucks saw the dwarf's row of empties and felt the remaining coins in his pocket. He made his way through the tables.

"Damn you, Mango. You said you'd be at The Wheatsheaf. I've been looking for an hour. Took three pubs and had to buy two blokes a pint each before they'd say they'd seen you."

"The George, The Raven, The Wheatsheaf. It's all the same," answered the dwarf. "I said you could find me tonight, and so you did. Now what do you want?"

"I need a drink before we talk." Bucks raised a hand to the woman behind the bar. She looked straight through him as if he were a hat rack. He wasn't a regular at this place. He waved again. She finally came over, her hands dripping soap suds, her cheeks looking boiled.

"Two gins," said Bucks.

"Not for me," said Mango. "You can rot your guts on that swill if you like. I'm for beer. Aren't I right, my darling?" The dwarf batted his thick lashes at the woman and grabbed at one of her breasts. She swayed out of his reach and eyed Bucks with curiosity.

102

"You're a brave one if you sit to drinks with him," she said. She wouldn't look at the dwarf at all, but dealt only with Bucks. "Men say as he's one to give you these cholera vapors."

"Just bring the drinks. I didn't come here to chat with a barmaid."

"Barmaid yourself. I own this place."

Bucks jerked his chin at her and she went off. He watched her retreat until she was out of earshot, and turned to the dwarf.

"He says you're going too strong," said Bucks. "Out of your line."

"Who said I had a line?"

"Don't play the fool with me, Mango. I know it ain't just the dogs as keeps you going. You don't want to lose this one. He's got money to spend. In the government, he says."

A surprisingly delicate frown creased the dwarf's brow and he fingered one of the scars across his cheek. "Well, maybe I'll listen. Talk."

The woman returned, slammed the drinks down, and stood with crossed arms until Bucks paid. He took the gin in one shot. Mango ignored his beer, except to straighten the mug's handle and line it up with the rest. He then kept his fist clenched like a barnacle on the sticky table.

Bucks wiped the back of his hand across his mouth. "The toff says you're not to kill him off. The money's good only if he looks bad and quits, not if he's dead."

"That's not what you said last time. You said two bob a day."

"Right-o. But the big one, the thirty guineas; that's only if he quits."

"I suppose there's money in it for you too?"

"I never said that. Just doing my job is all. And besides, you never ask, or so I was told."

"And isn't it true we're very respectable these days? Works foreman, something like it, I heard."

"Better than that. The foreman, he works under me. And I still keep a hand in, you know. It's the only way to turn a decent sum. Now what about this number?"

"What if the bloke has an accident?"

"Like I said, no pay. Why're you so taken against him?"

"I got my reasons."

Bucks's breathing grew heavy. His hand grabbed his empty glass. "Listen, you little—I don't give a bloody damn for your

103

reasons. If you blow this one for me I'll see you back in the hulks again."

The dwarf laughed. A few men at the other tables nervously glanced his way and quickly went back to their drinks. "If I rot away in a prison ship, Bucks, you come with me this time." He nodded his head, smiling. "With this plague everywhere you wouldn't last a month." He reached to pat Bucks's hand where it lay on the table and Bucks snatched it out of the way.

"I'll pull back," said the dwarf. "But I want double pay."

Bucks's forehead reddened and he raised his glass. It was empty. He paused for a moment and fingered a gold watch chain at his waist. "You're a tight bastard, you know that? I don't have the final word, but I know you only get half 'til it's done. And where can I find you? You'll have to report, regular like. I can't be searching every pub by the river."

Mango moved his eyes to a ladder against a wall which led to a sleeping loft above. "I kip here for now," he said in a low voice. "Between you and me." He finally took a pull at his beer.

11

Haxby, Yorkshire, August 1854

Snow stared through the glass out at the green oaks twisting in the wind. Rain ran off their trunks and poured into moats at their bases. It was chilly enough here in Yorkshire that his father had a fire in the grate. He wished the North Country summer weather could be packaged and sent to London, where the thermometer had stood at ninety degrees two days ago.

His father snored in his chair by the fire. For all his urgency in summoning Snow here from London in the middle of the cholera epidemic, he seemed to have little to say. Snow found himself resenting the miserable eight-hour train ride that had filled his Friday, and would now take up his entire Monday. Four days of research wasted for his father's false sentimentality.

Duncan Snow stirred himself and irritably grabbed at the plaid blanket around his legs. "Damn thing never stays on. Cold as a vault in this room."

John Snow went over to the already blazing fire and poked at it.

"Stop that!" barked the old man. "You'll only make it worse."

Snow returned to his chair, then picked up his *Times* and tried to finish the article he'd been reading.

*The Times' Bombay correspondent reports that the severe
epidemic of Asiatic Cholera which broke out last January
in southern India has not abated. Over ten thousand natives are presumed to have died so far.*

For all Snow's absorption with cholera in London, he had
thought very little about its source. It seemed probable that a
boat from India must have brought the first case.

"Since you won't talk to me, John, you might as well tell me
what you are reading."

Snow answered with his head still buried in the paper. "A
reference to the cholera epidemic in India. Rather severe. Thousands have died so far."

"From what I hear, cholera is a just punishment for their sins.
All those black heathen souls. As they sow so shall they reap."

Snow felt an urge to debate and at the same time a silencing
shame that he, too, had once almost become as self-righteous
about religion. His voice betrayed more irritation than he
wished.

"Father, that area of India has a large Christian population.
Indians there were converted by the Portuguese before 1600.
And besides, white people died too. The governor of one of the
smaller provinces. Listen to this." Snow read out loud.

This is the same epidemic that in its early stages in
January carried away Her Majesty's governor of the
province, Colonel Augustus Aynsworth, along
with his stepson, Mr. Henry Bince. The governor's
wife and daughter survived the scourge. As the contagious aspects of this dreadful disease are not yet
agreed upon, Sir Philip Constable, the Deputy Minister of Public Health, advises that all cargo entering
any British port from that part of the world should
be treated with caution.

"I suppose you can't accuse a colonial governor of pagan
idolatry."

"Who knows, boy, with the way the upper classes live these
days. The man could have fallen into some foreign temptation."

He brushed the blanket on his lap with impatience, as if dusting off contagion from tropical immorality, worse than any plague. "I suppose there's no chance the disease will come here, to England?"

"Don't you realize that it's already in London? That thousands are dying? And hasn't anything of what I've told you about my work sunk in?"

His father look away, apathetic, and stared at the fields beyond the wet oaks. He obviously cared as little about Snow's medical search as Snow did for breeds of dairy cattle, or weights of flax seed. Then he turned back to his son. "John, why can't you see reason and give up this fool practice of medicine? We could get the farm going again, the way it was meant to be. The south meadow could be drained next spring . . ."

Snow sighed in exasperation. "Is this what you summoned me up here for? I should have known. I've told you a hundred times before, I would fail at farming. My heart's not in it. You'd do better to hire some young man from the area. Leave the place to him in your will, if you like. I won't mind."

"But John, it's not too late. You can still get out of that practice in London. You know you'd like to."

"Can't you understand? Medicine is my profession now. It's not as though I'm a failure at it, either." Snow paused and pulled at a loose thread in his waistcoat. "I don't think you realize. People come to my lectures. I've sent you the articles I've published. And that medical society that I wrote you about, I'm their orator now."

"Orator? Don't try to impress me with fancy titles. What is it?"

"I make speeches. But never mind, it's not important. The main thing, as far as you're concerned, is that the practice is more profitable every year."

"What rubbish! As if the pennies you bring in from that consulting room could ever equal the income of a prosperous farm."

"Seven hundred pounds last year, Father. From the anesthesia."

The old man raised his brows and went on. "But it's not respectable. The idea, you with your hands all over those sick people. Just anybody." The old man blew the breath from his mouth in exasperation. "And another thing. This anesthesia,

107

you call it. It's against everything in the Bible. Pain was created for a reason, boy. To go against it is a devilish thing."

"A devilish thing? Would you have said that when Mother was dying in labor, screaming in agony with the dead child still inside her? You thought I didn't understand at that age, but believe me, even then, I couldn't fathom how God would let such a thing happen." Snow saw the grief pass over his father's face but he refused to relent. He had to make his point even if it were for the last time. "Who knows if Mother might not still be with us if someone could have helped her with the kind of surgery we do now?"

"No moral family would submit to such a thing," muttered his father.

"You seem to forget that I assisted at Her Majesty's lying-in when Prince Leopold was born last spring. She asked for the chloroform herself. Or are you just irritated because I made you swear not to discuss it with anyone? You lost your bit of village gossip, didn't you?"

"The queen, God bless her, should have shown a better example."

Snow opened his mouth for a rational answer, but all he said was, "We won't talk about it, Father. We can't agree." He stalked out of the room, heading into the hallway and out the front door, slamming it behind him.

The rain had stopped. Snow walked ahead, unseeing. Every time he came to visit it was the same; there would be a few hours or days of bland talk about nothing, and then the two of them would explode in anger at each other. Each incident felt worse than the one before it, and every time he swore he wouldn't let it happen again.

Snow decided to walk off his anger. A cold wet wind whipped cow smells from the barn while he crossed over a field of summer cabbages, saturating his shoes with mud and manure. Once he reached the only road, he began to walk quickly and soon found himself at the Norman church tower with its adjoining cemetery.

He thought he would look at his mother's grave. He hadn't seen it for a year now.

Snow opened the lich-gate of the churchyard and passed through a gap in the mossy stone walls. Immediately the wind died down, kept out by a border of pines and the church wall.

In the new quiet a mild bird song came from the hedges. He picked his way over the graveled paths and sodden leaves to the graves of his mother and infant sister.

Although his mother had died when he was eight, these stones still looked new compared to the surrounding ones, many of which dated from over two hundred years before.

Snow tried to pray, as he always tried when he came here, but he hardly knew what to pray for. Surely his mother's soul was safely lifted to heaven by now? And if not, what could his feeble pleas do to change it? His mind routinely went through an "Our Father" and an inane rhyme about Jesus he'd learned as a child. He was thinking that he'd stayed long enough when a shabby gentleman approached him from the main path.

His receding chin and bald head gave him the look of a turtle, and he spoke so softly that Snow had to bend to hear him.

"Excuse me, my good man," he said. "Would it disturb you if I were to take some notes from this stone? A departed spouse?" He looked at Snow with sympathy. "You see, I'm collecting historical information for the County Record Society, and it's important to keep track of locations in the churchyard."

As explanation he held out a simple map of the graveyard, with boxes drawn for each grave, filled in with names and dates. "Some of the names have quite worn away on the stones, you see, and I had to go through the parish records. But this one here is still sharp. Good Oxford stonework." He ran an appreciative finger over the precisely cut letters of the Snow family memorial.

"Of course," answered Snow, "please go ahead." Snow took the proffered map. It held for him a macabre fascination. All those deaths! The names of his ancestors and his neighbors' forebears showed in a spidery handwriting. What had they all died of?

How much more engrossing it would have been if each coffin-shaped box included that fact; ague, dropsy, smallpox, scarlet fever, and on the seventeenth-century stones the many bubonic plague deaths. Those details were lost. Anyone was lucky if after all these generations even their names remained.

He handed the map back and watched while the man carefully transcribed the details from the Snow tomb into the empty box on his map. Snow was so lost in his vision of a map of diseases that he almost shook the man by the shoulder and said of his mother, "Uterine rupture. She died in childbirth in terrible pain. And the infant died before it ever saw light, before it could breathe, before it could cry." But instead he simply accepted the researcher's thanks.

Early the next morning he took the train back to London.

12

The Indian Ocean, February 1854

1

In the starlight the metal pole wasn't hard to see where it jutted from the side of the ship. Seawater made it slippery, and Lillian's left hand clung to it so tightly that her fingers ached. She needed it for support to lean so far out from the side of the ship.

She'd already untied the bundle of letters. Now she pulled papers from the stack one by one and dropped them over the edge. The starlight was so bright, it was hard not to read a word here and there before letting them float down.

Her writing had changed since she wrote them. The perfect governess-trained loops of the "l's" and "p's" had long since been replaced by a more abrupt scrawl.

It looked as if the letters were drifting onto the whitecaps of the phosphorescent sea. She lost sight of them below the edges of the lower decks, but could imagine them littering its surface with pale scraps until they were swallowed in the glowing wake of the steamer. Then followed the dozen little shirts she'd sewed for the baby. They unfolded as they fell.

Only one shirt remained. This one she'd keep; who could conjecture anything from one cotton baby shirt? No one would see it, anyway. She could always make something up; a friend's christening, or even her own childhood memento.

Then she heard a noise, right behind her. She jerked around and knocked her hand against the rail, losing her grip for an instant. Catching herself just in time, she stared through the night, trying to silence her breathing. Her arm throbbed in pain the way she was hanging there. She was afraid to stir. In her black dress she prayed she'd be invisible.

Four men's sailor uniforms shone through the darkness. They carried a long white bundle, heavy and swinging. The four of them approached the rails close to where she stood; only the ropes and masts separated them from her. She could see as clear as morning.

"Heave ho, boys, and send her away," called one of them in a harsh whisper. They swung the body three times and flung it into space. It turned twice before hitting the swell. The men brushed their hands and headed back to the hatchways.

"There's two more down below," said the leader in a harsh mutter. "Be sure to use that tar water after, like the captain said." He spat over the rail. Their shadows faded behind the masts.

Lillian loosed her grip and stretched her fingers with pain. It was only then that she realized the last shirt was gone. It had fallen over the rail after the rest when she slipped. She shut her eyes, and waited to see if the heaviness would leave her throat. Perhaps with all physical reminders gone she could finally forget. But the sadness didn't change. She turned and picked her way toward the stairs.

Her mind had registered the sight of the bodies going overboard, but she didn't think about it at all. It was as if she had seen nothing. She didn't want to think about who they were or why they had died. She wanted her mind to be as empty as the carved box which had held her letters and the shirts.

She looked up at the sky, where a thin cloud cover was drifting over the stars. Just then her foot hit a projecting cable and she stumbled forward over her skirts. Her knee landed hard against a spar and it caused a clink of metal. A deep ache pulsed through her leg.

"What's that?" a sharp voice called from the starboard side.

Lillian didn't move.

"Who goes there? Answer, I say!"

Lillian let out her breath, which she'd been holding, and took another before calling, "It's Miss Aynsworth, a passenger. I meant no harm." She tried to make her voice sound as casual as she could.

A figure came into view through the rigging. From his trim figure and slight limp Lillian recognized the ship's captain, Mr. Trevelyan.

"Miss Aynsworth?" He peered at her and frowned. "What are you doing? Do you realize what time it is?"

She hesitated a moment before saying, "I needed air. I hardly meant to disturb anyone." She thought of the bags going overboard. "It's so . . . close below decks."

Voices emerged from below. The sailors were coming back with their second burden. The captain glanced over his shoulder, then reached a hand toward Lillian.

"Let me escort you downstairs, ma'am. I'll speak to the purser tomorrow about the ventilation in your suite. For now it's best that you go below." He took Lillian's arm above her elbow and steered her to the stairs.

His palms sweated. She could feel it through the thin silk of her sleeve.

Two sailors came up from behind with another shrouded bag.

"What about this one sir, should we—oh, beg pardon, miss." The man's glance went from the captain to Lillian and back to the captain again. He moved away two steps and stood with his body bent slightly forward, his hands still gripping the bag behind him. His partner lingered in the shadows.

"Yes, all of them," barked Trevelyan. He turned back to Lillian and his grip on her arm tightened.

"A few crewmen fought over some bets. These incidents will happen aboard a ship. Nothing to concern yourself with." He stepped toward the entry again and they descended the steep stairs, both of them stiff and embarrassed.

In her cramped stateroom Lillian undressed quietly so as not to wake Olympia in the lower bunk. Her hands were shaking slightly. Other than a decision to believe the captain, she refused to think about what she had seen. Fighting over some bets; it made perfect sense.

She swallowed three of the tablets that the military doctor had given her after the funeral, and climbed to the upper bunk. She found she still needed them to sleep, though she had started with ten at a time, and over the days had reduced the dose. Gradually the drug took effect and she relaxed. Her fate was out of her hands. Her breathing slowed a little.

The first few days of the trip had been miserable. All the preparations for the departure from India were beyond Olympia, and eventually Lillian had to make every decision without asking. The day they left, Olympia had allowed herself to be led onto the deck of the steamer as a little child would. So far on the voyage Olympia had only left her room for meals, and even those she ate in private. She rarely spoke.

Lillian had been seasick from her first hour at sea. Her nausea was compounded with an ailment of the soul, a kind of dread of everything around her. Now that the efforts of packing and directing were over and there were no more distractions, she slipped into a state of mental paralysis.

Her thoughts had been fixed in a cloud of fear and confusion. The very wood grain of the beams over her head, the shape of the waves outside her porthole, the flying fish, all held menace in their movement and color. Olympia's rare words sounded threatening, even though she knew rationally that couldn't be so. Lillian tried to wrench herself from the grip of the mental weakness, telling herself it was absurd, that the shape of a cloud or the smell of her tea couldn't be sinister.

Every time she slept, which wasn't often with the seasickness, as she slipped into drugged unconsciousness she prayed that on waking, her thoughts would be clear again. And she would slide into nightmares of that terrible dawn as she stood at the door to her father's room, with the shrieking peacocks outside.

Sometimes she woke from these, sweating and with a scream stuck in her throat, and the sound was still there—or was it the shrill wail of sea gulls? No gulls flew to the middle of the ocean. She tried to listen and decide where it came from, but every time the creak of the ship overpowered all else.

Then one morning, two weeks into the voyage, she woke later than usual. The fear had disappeared. Lillian turned her head cautiously, as if the dread were a headache that could return, and took in the details of her room. The furniture, though shabby, was only furniture. No evils leered from the corners. The light was like lemons and she felt happy for the first time in ages.

Throughout that day she handled herself prudently, pacing out her strength and holding her euphoria in check. She felt as if she were recovering from a long illness, and she experienced the recovering invalid's delight in the ring of the ship's bell, the taste of her salt bacon, and the slip of clothes against her skin.

That night, and many nights that followed, it wasn't seasickness, but her thoughts, which kept her awake. The starlight and phosphorescence through her porthole added to her trancelike state of mind. Nothing seemed to really matter except what she was feeling right at that moment. The voyage seemed like a dream to her, as if past, present, and future had merged into a timeless stream as she floated west.

Henry's disappearance still made no sense to her. Of one thing she was certain; the body they found was not Henry's. She and Olympia had still never discussed it, in fact they had hardly spoken at all. There had been a few awkward times when the two women received condolences for father and son, and Lillian and Olympia had exchanged glances and said as little as possible.

Whatever his reasons for wanting to disappear, she felt a definite sense of relief that he was out of her life. He knew too much about her past. In some people that might be a blessing. But Henry wasn't to be trusted. And it wasn't just his knowledge; that last morning together, before cholera had struck the house, he had looked at her with a green light in his eyes that she found disturbing. She was no longer sure of his sanity. Things were better this way, with Henry probably settled as a merchant somewhere in the Far East. She could imagine him in Bombay, or Hong Kong, slowly increasing his thousand-pound inheritance until it became a solid fortune. He would find a docile, middle-class wife who would never have to know about his many failures or his complicated relationship with a stepsister she would never meet. It was better this way.

Other ideas drifted into her mind as reassuring talismans to turn over idly. As time removed her from her father's death, she now occasionally felt a flicker of perverse gratitude at events; no one else could know her true history. She was safe. And she could afford to set up her own household in London with her stepmother.

No saris anywhere, no lepers, no cobras, but streets full of gentlemen and ladies, and a pure white snowfall every night in winter.

After a few days of this sort of careless meditation the carved box with its old letters and the shirts began to weigh on her mind. She should have destroyed them years ago, or never kept them at all. It seemed like another lifetime now, that day before the cholera came, when she had come home from Aunt Flora's and found her things opened up. She had vowed then to destroy everything. Of course she hadn't. Nor had she ever checked to see what might be gone.

Lying in the bunk now, still sleepless, the bruise ached on her knee and the place where she'd smashed her arm throbbed. She thought about the letters which were lost forever to fish and seaweed.

There used to be fifteen in the pack. Ten from him and the five of hers that she'd asked him to return. Had she dropped fifteen into the water?

Through all her thoughts pulsed the image of the sacks of dead men, turning over as they fell heavily into the waves. In her heart she knew they had died of cholera, that cholera was on the ship, and that it would still be a part of her life. But somehow she couldn't bring the thought to the surface, and she let it stay buried too deeply to do more than give a slight uneasiness, like the recurring throb of pain in her knee.

Sleep washed over her and she settled more comfortably into the bunk. The raucous cry of peacocks broke once again into her ears. She couldn't be imagining it. But, like the image of the falling sacks, she pushed it to the bottom of her mind.

2

The animals for the London Zoo weren't loose below the third deck, but once you were down there it sounded as if they were. Hoots, cries, barking, wails, roars, and a constant twitter rumbled from the hold day and night.

Besides an elephant, there were a two-humped Bactrian camel whose dehydrated humps sagged piteously, three dozen long-tailed langur monkeys, and a flock of mynas and lorikeets whose feathers gleamed like jewels in the dark. A dainty-hoofed onager shared his cage with three muntjac deer. A pair of leopards flicked their tails at the continual sight of a box of long emerald-colored snakes. And there were a half dozen dholes or wild dogs,

116

their tongues lolling in the heat. Other unnamed creatures lurked in the shadows of their cages.

The animals' undersized bamboo and brass cages were filthy, overcrowded, and barely gave most of them enough room to turn. The monkeys had some vertical space they could climb, but they were the lucky ones. The peacocks had lost most of their tail feathers. Many of the smaller birds had died. To open the cages and retrieve the dead ones would risk the escape of the others. So their limp bodies were left, the feathers still brilliant and falling in clumps from the decaying flesh.

Only the elephant was uncaged. A chain bound his rear leg and tethered it to a pile of waste iron, which lay buried under a thick litter of wet and rotten straw. The top of his head brushed the ceiling. A few weeks into the voyage, he started a habit of banging his skull upwards against the boards, gently and repeatedly. Perhaps it eased some itch or nightmare memory of his journey.

The passengers in steerage were shocked at first that they were expected to share a living space with this menagerie. Their objections were laughed at. The owner of the troop paid well for his passage and the ship's captain wasn't about to lose the money, more than all the third-deck payers combined.

When the cholera broke out, the worst place was down here in the hold. The foot soldiers and fortune seekers slept four to a bunk, packed tight as coiled rope. Those who weren't sick tried to force their way to the upper decks, so that the hatchways were kept locked.

It killed twenty-six of the forty in steerage. But only three of the first-class passengers fell ill, and none died. Most hardly sensed any problem, and no one questioned the captain's announcement to stay below decks after dark. Mosquito danger, he said.

The bodies later washed up on the west coast of Madagascar where they were seen only by sea tortoises and giant crabs.

The owner of the animals stayed healthy. Although he had booked first-class accommodations, he never showed himself above. Tonight, as usual, he spent his hours in the unchanging gloom of the only private room on the third deck; first looking over his contracts with the London Zoo, and then lying in his bunk scrutinizing the rough ceiling beams and restlessly pulling at his fingers. The smaller beasts had cost him almost a thousand

117

pounds. The elephant had fallen into his hands, without cost, at the beginning of his journey from Cochin, though its transport to Bombay hadn't been cheap. But even if only a third of the animals survived the trip, he'd be rich.

When the lady's letters drifted onto the wet third-class deck the other night it was a delightful bonus, completely unexpected. He recognized the handwriting instantly. If he'd been sleeping in first class, instead of pacing the slippery third-class deck, he would never have seen them. The paper dried out in a few hours, with the ink clear and even the ribbon still attached to the thick one.

He wasn't surprised at what was in them. Or that she had tried to destroy them so inefficiently. He had expected all along she might do something like that. *Some day she'll appreciate how carefully I've watched her, and followed her,* he thought. *Why, anyone could have got hold of those letters if I hadn't been here. She's lucky.* And he smiled to himself.

He spent day after day gazing out of his dirty porthole and making plans.

3

On a freezing March day, with a sharp wind biting through the thickest overcoat, the steamer finally reached London's East India Docks. Captain Trevelyan was more relieved than he had been at the end of any other voyage for years. He had achieved his goal; the cholera was still a secret and no quarantine was placed. He left the unloading supervision to the first mate and he limped over to The Drowning Man for a pint. He chose a window seat, his eye on the ship, so that he could get back in a moment if any problems arose.

"Trevelyan!" A rough hand clapped him on the back. "Returned from the climes of paradise!"

"You too, Wentworth? I thought you'd shipped for a year to Rangoon." Trevelyan signaled to the owner for another pint.

Wentworth, a short, nervous-looking man, sipped at his drink. "So I did, so I did. But the winds changed early this year and we had word of a big indigo cargo in Ceylon." His voice dropped. "Cholera on the ship."

118

"You too?" Trevelyan found that he had joined the other man in whispering. "Did you unload?"

"Had to, man. I'd be out five thousand pounds if that cargo was quarantined; indigo can't be washed. They'd have dumped it in the Thames and turned the river blue." He laughed, but it was without humor.

Both men drank in silence for a minute.

"Besides," began Trevelyan, "they say it's not catching."

"Of course not," Wentworth rushed to agree. "It'd make no difference what we did with our cargo. Anyone would have done the same. And the passengers, well, that's their own look out."

"Were many sick?"

"Just a few. And it was steerage, anyhow." Trevelyan nodded in agreement. "It could have been anything, really."

The two men sighed with partial relief, finished their beers, and headed back to their ships. They shouted directions and abuse at the laboring dock workers as they watched them guide the passengers down the gangplank, unload the various cargo and animals, and pour hundreds of barrels of stale drinking water into the Thames.

Within five hours the passengers were scattered all over London.

Within five days captains Trevelyan and Wentworth, sharing a rooming house near the river, were dead of cholera.

119

13

London, August 1854

1

Snow looked up from his papers, surprised to hear the bell so late at night. He wasn't unhappy to be distracted. His concentration was gone. For the past fifteen minutes he'd been staring at figures while dreaming first of Sophie's thighs, then of sleep.

Mrs. Jarrett knocked sharply on his study door in one of her most eloquent raps. He heard it all too clearly. "See what I have to put up with? And just going to bed, too." Her hair was in papers under a bursting cap. Carpet slippers, down in the heels, jutted out from under her skirt. She was in a fit of annoyance. Snow paid no attention. He reserved all his interest for the guest.

It was Sir Philip Constable, the deputy minister of public health. The same man who'd hinted at an invitation to the Royal Society last winter. Snow had almost forgotten. Almost, but not enough to want to tell his father that the offer hadn't come through after all. His father thankfully hadn't asked about it in his few letters since last January.

Snow turned his eyes back to his notes for the briefest moment before rising, long enough to allow him to enjoy the gratification of finally getting his invitation. Why else would the man have come?

"Good evening, Sir Philip." He tried to sound surprised, puzzled, modest; all the things he was not.

The man stood in the center of the room holding his hat and gloves, looking dazed, as if he had stumbled off an omnibus in the wrong part of the city.

"Can I offer you something?"

Constable stirred himself and looked around. "No, nothing, thank you."

His smooth dark hair had receded farther since the one time Snow saw him, and his hands swelled around gold rings. There was a marzipan look to him of too many cigars and long days in soft chairs. His gliding brown eyes could have been sinister but were merely withdrawn. Under his arm was a copy of *The Times*.

We're probably the same age, thought Snow.

He seemed to recollect himself. "Snow, I must speak to you about these letters." Sir Philip held out the paper in explanation.

Snow pulled his shoulders back and flared his nostrils. The man talked as if he were addressing his groom. Snow couldn't fool himself; this was no preamble to any invitation.

"What letters do you mean?" Snow pulled out a chair and gestured for his guest to sit.

"Surely you've read the paper today?" Seeing Snow's bewildered look, he opened the paper and turned it back to the correspondence section.

"Here, see for yourself." Snow made no move to take it. "Shall I read one to you then?"

Snow was still angry and now confused, too, so he simply nodded.

Sir Philip's eyes scanned the sheet. "Ah, here it is."

> *If a certain doctor would spend more time seeing patients and less spending the crown's money on the useless daily annoyance of private citizens, we could all rest easier. His ridiculous questioning of bereaved families is a public insult.*
>
> Unsigned

Snow had no idea whether Constable was in sympathy with the writer or not. Why on earth come here to read these things?

He held his head to one side, eyebrows drawn together. A suspicion was beginning to dawn on him.

"And here's another," continued Constable:

> Dr. John Snow should give up. The cause of cholera is too varied and treacherous for any one scientist to define. It were a far better thing for us to return to the public religious fasts of a decade ago, with the queen's support, than to rely on this claptrap they call the study of medicine.

A Devoted Member of the Presbyterian Church

"Are you beginning to see?" said Sir Philip. "At the House of Commons tonight the minister of health expressed concern about the letters. I've just come from a night session." At this his eyes looked away from Snow's for a moment, then back. He shifted the gloves in his hand.

It was a moment before Snow could speak. "Well now, Sir Philip. The minister isn't always so solicitous. You are the deputy minister now, I understand."

Constable bowed slightly.

"You must thank him for me. I appreciate his sympathy, Sir Philip, but public service is often open to hostility. I wouldn't give the letters another thought." Snow carefully moved a list of cholera addresses on his desk from one pile to another.

Sir Philip's eyebrows contracted like the wings of a crow thinking of flying off. His right hand squeezed tightly around the lavender suede of the gloves. It was then that Snow noticed the man's fingernails; each had been eaten away by fungus to the size of a grape seed. Onychomycosis. Snow restrained himself from peering over for a closer look. The man must have been in the tropics.

Constable saw his stare and self-consciously put his hands in his lap. "Perhaps you're not aware, Dr. Snow, that the minister has appointed an officer and a committee to look into these very matters?"

"What?" asked Snow, opening his eyes wide in mock innocence. "To look into the letters? Very kind of him, but—"

"Not the letters. The water supplies. The cholera. The disease rates."

Snow still looked at him, face blank, refusing to become defensive.

Constable was forced to go on. "I'll be blunt. The minister is distressed that you've made allegations against his reform policies. He doesn't believe such connections can be possible. They've begun their own cholera inquiries, similar to yours but on a much larger scale, of course."

What allegations? What reform policies? Snow knew he'd never said anything of the kind. He rose and walked to the window, put his hands flat against the glass. "Yes, I read that such a plan had been made. But that was weeks ago. I looked for the survey workers around the sicker areas. Have they finished? Did you bring a copy of the report for me to read?" He turned back to Constable.

"The surveys haven't started yet. There are—complications to work through." The lower lid of Constable's right eye began a tiny quiver that only a doctor would have noticed.

"Then they'll be wasting their time and the public funds." Snow snatched up a piece of scrap paper and crumpled it. "People forget, records are lost. A worker who loses his family will hardly remember in two weeks what they ate ten days before they died. Assuming you can find him, of course."

"The minister is aware of all the details, Dr. Snow. I must be plain about the reason for my visit. He has asked that you return to your practice and cease your survey efforts. You must get requests for chloroform treatment every day. Surely it is enough to keep you busy."

Snow couldn't believe what he heard. "But that's impossible, Sir Philip. These house-to-house questions provide the details essential for my project."

"You don't understand. Your project interferes with that of the minister, who has a Royal Sanction for Dr. Farr. The man's miasma theories are proving to be sound."

"The queen has asked him to do the work, specifically?" Memories flashed across Snow's mind, of the queen's exophthalmic eyes turned up in agony while he prepared the chloroform for her labor pains. The expensive beeswax and fresh flowers hadn't been able to overpower the smell of blood and amniotic fluid. She had asked that Snow refrain from using his chloroform mask, and that he use instead a few drops of the fluid on a handkerchief. It seemed less a violation of God's will, she had said. Snow knew her descent into unconsciousness was less controllable with the soaked handkerchief, and therefore more dangerous, but he didn't want to enter into a debate with her. The handkerchief, despite all Snow's publications and efforts, was still more fashionable than his invented inhalation apparatus. Ladies said the apparatus left a mark on their face. Within an hour of Snow's arrival, the royal doctors had easily and safely delivered her of Prince Leopold, despite her tiny frame.

Constable went on. "Not exactly. The queen didn't ask him herself; Her Majesty hasn't been well and it wasn't the time to disturb her. But her closest advisors—"

"It's out of the question that I should stop. You don't know much about how a scientist works if you even suggest it."

Should he confront Constable with the threats? Who could they be from if not from this source? But caution made Snow silent; he didn't want Sophie thrown at him as an accusation.

Besides, if he were mistaken, he would sound like a madman. Who would threaten a London doctor with bodily harm, just for doing his research? He said nothing.

Both were standing now, facing each other and as close to a fight as men with clean cuffs and gold watches could get. Snow found that his fists were clenched.

Constable was the first to break the locked stare. He sighed. "Dr. Snow, believe me, it would be in your best interests to listen to me. I was commissioned to make certain, well—offers, if you were to comply. That appointment to the Royal Society. I didn't forget it, you know. It could be made certain. They could use a man like you."

Snow's anger kept him from speaking. Forget the invitation, he thought. He walked to the library door and opened it hard enough to hit one of the bookshelves and set all the bottles of Thames water rattling. Sir Philip had no option but to go.

When his footsteps died away, Snow turned back to his lists, figures he'd gotten just that morning from a back office at the Registrar General, in the Board of Health's own building. He had the address of every cholera case reported to the board in the past seven days, all two thousand of them. If the director really wanted to keep Snow away from the data, he should have talked to his clerks. They'd been most helpful, and offered Snow everything he wanted, even copied out some of the things he was too busy to do himself.

Snow didn't sleep well. The bedclothes seemed heated. Even after throwing them to the floor he felt as if he'd been running a foot race and losing, gasping to keep up. He tried mental exercises to get his mind off Sir Philip's warning. Nothing helped. He would imagine a field of barley in Yorkshire, or a stream falling over tumbled rocks, and almost before he was aware of it Constable would be there too, crushing the foliage, admonishing Snow, cramping his thoughts, fueling his anger.

It was the anger that kept him awake. He had decided that Sir Philip must be behind the scheme, after all. How dare they? Sneaking after him with cheap threats, like a bunch of American gamblers. His entire being felt dirtied by it. It wasn't as if he were an unknown medical student pursuing a ridiculous notion. He was John Snow, he'd published articles, he'd given chloroform to the queen. It just didn't make sense.

And he wondered about those reforms Constable was so anxious about—the man must have meant sewer reforms. That's why they were digging up Golden Square.

The next morning he woke at seven after three hours' sleep. His knees were weak. He wobbled like an old man to the window and looked out, checking the sky, checking the wind, looking for any hope of a cooler day. But what he saw made him forget the weather. Across the street, leaning on a lamppost and reading a paper, stood a man with the posture of a laborer, wearing a plaid suit and a stiff shiny hat. The man turned a page of the paper and glanced at the front of Snow's house, then pulled out a watch.

They must have decided that the dwarf was too conspicuous. The questions returned to his mind—why would the Board of Health waste a shilling of their funds to bother with John Snow? Well, they'd have to do better than that. He smiled to himself.

Lately he had left his house at eight every morning, but today it was a quarter to when he went through the untidy kitchen into the area back of the house. He ripped out the side seam of his jacket climbing over a wall into the alley. When he reached the corner of Sackville Street he looked down toward his address and sure enough, the man was still there.

Eight o'clock and it was already hot. His lack of sleep sat on his shoulders like an organ grinder's monkey, making his thoughts weave drunkenly from sense, to memory, to excited new ideas. A thread of anger against Constable and the Board of Health was woven throughout.

He hadn't gone two streets before he caught the sounds of yelling crowds. He turned a corner and saw that the street was full of workmen running toward Golden Square. They carried shovels and picks. One snatched up a piece of broken cobblestone and hurled it randomly at a house window, and glass shattered loudly.

Snow felt the damage personally, as if the man had spit at him. But he also had an adventurer's urge to chase the crowd, see the commotion, the fire, the murder, whatever small catastrophe it was they joined. He gave in to the craving and followed them.

The mob was yelling under the plane trees in Golden Square, around the digging site where he had seen the dead man so many weeks ago. It was a strike. Workers from all around the neighborhood had heard of it and joined in. Red clay caked the shoes of a few who stood in the ditch, still shoveling away at their task, stolidly ignoring the strikers. They stood like grave diggers, waist deep in the earth.

Shouting voices rained down on them like stones.

"Yah, you're digging up the plague pits. Pulling up old bones. Killing us all!"

"See how you feel when your wife and brats die of this thing. Stirring up these plague pits, it's shameful!"

One by one the diggers lost their nerve and stopped, climbing out over stacked pipes and equipment and slinking off through the crowd. Finally only one still kept at it.

He was a few inches taller than most and looked vaguely familiar to Snow. The only thing Snow could focus on was a faint sense of unease on seeing his face.

The man's persistence infuriated the strikers. One with mud-caked hair and the narrow and powerful shoulders of an ape leapt into the hole and grabbed the man's shovel. The digger struggled to keep on, straight-faced, almost holy, as if he were laying the foundations for a new chapel.

"Let me get on with my work, man." He spoke from the side of his mouth. Sweat dripped from his chin and caught the sun.

The bully yanked the man's shovel free and hit him lightly, almost in play, on the side of the head. The digger staggered, one hand to his head, then took back the shovel and resumed digging.

"Good work, ain't it, filling the air with disease and muck."

Just then the crowd parted like a small Red Sea to let through a gentleman in a top hat. Snow was astonished to see it was Sir Philip. Constable stood at the edge of the pit with the bullish authority of a slave owner.

"What's the trouble here? Why aren't you working?" His question was bellowed rather than asked. Snow hadn't known he had anything to do with these works.

The man in the pit jammed his shovel into the earth. "We're digging for new sewer lines, sir. Some folks think it's here what the plague bodies was buried, long ago. Stirring up bad air. Bringing on the cholera."

"Anyone who believes that is a fool. It's nonsense. All those facts were investigated long ago, when they planned the lines. You were hired to do a job here, so get on with it. Leave such things to higher minds." Sir Philip's shout faded a bit and he slipped a look at the angry crowd and then back to their spokesman, the monkey-shouldered one. "All of you, get back to work immediately or you'll be sacked."

"It's easy for you to say, as hasn't got your family and friends dying around you. Go to work yourself. We'll give you work."

The man shoved Sir Philip, who stumbled and fell into the ditch. Two of the rioters closed in on him with their fists. His tall hat fell off and served as a football for others.

Snow's suspicions faded as he rushed forward. After all, Constable was a government official. He couldn't have anything to do with those rough minutes in the alley.

"Stop it, leave the man alone." Snow's voice startled himself, as well as the aggressors, who backed off. No one looked as surprised as Constable.

Snow kept up the heroics. "Someone, run for the police," he shouted. At the word "police" most of the crowd began to back off and within a minute Snow and Constable were left alone except for a few stragglers.

Snow extended a hand to Sir Philip and helped him out of the ditch. Once again he noticed the man's fungus-eaten fingernails. The only other case of onychomycosis Snow had ever seen had been on the feet of an assistant to an explorer up the Nile, whose nails had disappeared entirely. He ignored it this time and helped

127

Constable up and tried to brush off some of the mud. It was hopeless.

"Are you at all hurt?" asked Snow.

"No, no, it's nothing." Constable fingered his bruised cheek. "I'm afraid my coat is rather battered, though. What ruffians! How lucky you were here."

Didn't Constable remember that Snow lived near here? He was acting as though last night never happened. Snow decided to say nothing. Sir Philip began again to have the distracted look he'd had the night before, as if he'd already forgotten that he was knocked into a ditch. His argument with Snow last night seemed completely abandoned.

"I live just a few houses away, if you remember. Would you like to come to my house and wash?" Snow hardly thought Constable would accept, and he didn't relish the thought of more time with the man. But it was hard to truly resent anyone covered in mud. Pedestrians returning to the street began to stare.

Snow thought he'd give Constable a way out of having to come to his house. "On second thought, I suppose you ought to wait for the police?"

"I suppose I could, but I don't think I'll enjoy reading about myself in the papers tomorrow. 'Mud-spattered MP found off Oxford Street.' Perhaps we should leave while I'm still anonymous."

Snow shot Constable a quick look, trying to detect some reason for the change of attitude. He saw only a polite mask. They headed for Sackville Street. There was an awkward silence which Snow finally broke.

"You spent time in the colonies, I take it?"

Constable glanced up in complete surprise. He didn't look happy to be asked this question. "Yes, in the Indian Army. When I was much younger. That's all behind me now." He frowned and was silent for a moment. "You noticed my fingernails, then?"

"A doctor does tend to see these things. I hope it's not too uncomfortable?"

Constable cleared his throat. "Only in the early stages, years ago. Now I never notice it."

Snow thought he had better change the subject. "Is there any truth, Sir Philip, in this plague pit theory?"

"I'd have thought that to be more in your line, Dr. Snow."

"I don't mean the question of exhumed corpses causing the disease. That's not possible, I know. But the location; where were the bodies buried? Near here?"

"A historian worked on it when it came up before. Along with Dr. Phineas Greeley—you know him?"

Old Green Eyes Greeley from Guy's. Snow wasn't surprised to hear him come into this. All Snow said was, "Yes, he was my teacher at Westminster Hospital."

"Well, he suggested there might be reason to fear, so we had it looked into. The site was far from here, nowhere near any of the new pipe lines."

"Is Greeley a consultant on the project, then?"

"Oh, yes, we were lucky to get him. Eminent in his field of contagion theories. Or so I'm told."

"I know he came up with some useful work before my time. But I haven't seen his recent writing. We travel in different circles." The truth was, Snow thought Greeley a charlatan. He could believe that Greeley might cure society ladies, but he was shocked to hear of his connection with the board. Dr. Farr's work on cholera, though Snow disagreed with it, was at least the result of hard work. But Greeley had no idea of any kind of scientific method.

The two men reached the house and Snow got Constable settled with a wash basin and a stack of his own clothes. He also changed his own jacket, whose torn seam Constable didn't seem to have noticed. While he waited for Constable to finish, thoughts of Greeley took over Snow's memory.

The first thing that came to mind was Greeley's walk, the way he'd enter lecture theaters with a peculiar bounce of the toes, as though small springs were concealed in his boots. He was a small man; maybe he bounced as an excuse to get up on his toes and look taller.

The main memory, though, was an affair with botched laboratory experiments. As he remembered it now, Greeley never did withdraw his paper from *The Lancet*. It was some nonsense to do with spontaneous generation, growing amoebas from a jar of water struck by lightning. Greeley's experiment had been funded by one of the new churches, Baptists most likely. When the fallacy had been exposed there had been a touchy year for Greeley and he had almost lost his post at the hospital.

Splashing noises came from the bedroom. What was taking the man so long?

And Greeley thought the plague pits could contain cholera. What trash! Even though Greeley wasn't alone in his theory it was easier to think that one little pink-cheeked man was responsible for such worthless ideas.

The previous night's conversation filtered into Snow's mind. How much did Greeley have to do with all Constable's orders? Was Greeley working on the "official" investigation? If so, no wonder they weren't getting anywhere. Snow remembered Greeley's lecture technique at Westminster; loose papers drifting from the podium, talks canceled a third of the time, and trains of thought drifting off to nowhere.

How much longer would Constable take? Snow was anxious to be off for the day. Now that he had to be careful he wasn't followed, things took longer.

Constable emerged from the bedroom wearing a pair of Snow's trousers which clearly showed the difference in their heights. Cloth wrapped his ankles like loose elephant skin.

"I'm afraid I'll have to send for my man to bring some clothes. I can't walk down the street in these, can I?" He looked down at the rumpled cuffs in folds around his ankles and began to laugh. Snow had forgotten to have the trousers cleaned since he last wore them; he caught sight of mud on the cuffs. Not the red clay of Golden Square, but a dry gray sediment. From the house by the river, with the dog pit.

Constable saw his gaze and lifted a leg to see. "Ah, I see your daily work takes you into the less scrubbed parts of London. You must not have looked much better than me the day you came home in these!" He laughed, but it sounded forced.

This threw Snow off. Just as before, he couldn't tell if Constable knew something. There was no more time, though, to wait. He had to be gone. He decided he didn't need any excuse to leave; the man must know he had to work.

Constable held his muddy shoes at arm's length with a questioning look. "By the door," said Snow. "The housekeeper will see to them. I'll have them sent to you."

As Snow tucked a stack of notebooks under his arm, he continued, "I've got to go. Mrs. Jarrett will see to your needs until your man arrives. I hope you've quite recovered."

"It was nothing. Thank you for your help."

"Good morning, then." Hate would have been so simplifying. It would have wrapped up all his uncomfortable emotions into a package as easy to take in as a pork bun from a street stall. But he found himself liking the man, and, even more troublesome, wanting his approval.

On his way out the door, Snow glanced down at Sir Philip's shoes. The tip of each one was white with dried salt.

3

The fresh early light was gone and now the day was bronzed and hot. Snow pulled the list from his pocket and out of habit looked over his shoulder. It was then that he remembered where he'd seen the man digging in the ditch. The day he'd passed the murdered man in Golden Square, the same man had been there, talking to that Inspector McGowan. He'd said he was the foreman.

And Snow remembered another thing that had struck him at the time but that he had forgotten because immediately after he'd seen Sir Philip at the riot. Behind the ditch, fenced off and roofed over, was a hole which hadn't been there before, with the top of a ladder poking out. A narrow hole, like something leading down into a tunnel. Snow had crossed the square hundreds of times in the past years and had never known a sewer entrance to be there.

For the first time it occurred to him that close examination of a sewer might tell him something about the water supply and cholera. He decided to go see the spot again. It was on his way. By now the crowds would probably be dispersed.

The tin roof and ladder were gone, and the hole was freshly turfed over with grass sod. Only the thin line of earth around the square edges gave it away. By the end of the day, when the earth dried out, it would be no different from the rest of the grass in the square. The work would have taken a man almost two hours, he thought. They must have started the moment the riot began.

Snow tentatively poked at the edge of the sod with his boot, until one of the diggers, back at work now, called out to him.

" 'Ey, guvnor, that area's off limits. You could 'urt yourself."

It wasn't the man who had been digging before. Snow looked at his watch and reluctantly left.

14

London, August 1854

As Lillian rang the bell for the maid it happened again, like a hiccup. She felt yet another moment of disorientation where in the middle of a simple act, such as lighting a candle, or putting on stockings, she lost all sense of where she was. She recited in her head the schoolroom litany she'd relied on before: eight o'clock, south window, front room, second floor, Brook Street, Grosvenor Square, London, Middlesex, England. Earth. Solar system, universe. By the end she was placed.

When she first arrived in London in late March she felt as if she were hovering in one of the hundreds of glass fishing floats her steamer had passed throughout the Mediterranean. She was walled off and immune, invulnerable, separated from all the filth that had been that last month in India. Her rented London house seemed as immaculate as a royal nursery. The servants gave her no sense of hidden disasters, and for the initial busy time all she saw was organized and elegant.

And there was another immunity as well, a sense of release from expectations and routine. Olympia would probably never ask her to finish that satin stitch altar cloth she'd started last year, or to complete the series of hideous shell boxes she'd begun as a gift for Aunt Flora, in another lifetime. Everything that had happened in the past six months was better than any excuse she could have dreamed of to avoid the boredom of her old life. She had a sense of fresh beginnings.

But within days of her arrival, Olympia's cousin, Dr. Greeley, told Lillian of cholera in London. Her initial response was to believe he was wrong. Some ignorant person must have made a mistake. After all, what could *they* know of cholera, here in civilization? It was as if she had forgotten what she saw on the boat. She didn't want to remember it. She wanted to feel surprised. The bubble still floated around her.

When the cases increased, she conceded that there might be cholera in London. Of course, it's a human disease. But not near me, she thought, not where people like us live.

Then, just yesterday, she had spotted a black rag on the knocker of Number Six, two doors up. She asked the butler. Cholera, the whole house dead.

Now everything felt dirty; her skin, the air, the flecks of street straw on her boots. Her eyes wandered to where the candle reflected off rich tapestries on her bed, curtains with gold weave, the ornate crystal jars on her dressing table. She wished she had bare floors and a military cot like her father's old room, things plain and easy to scrub. Who could tell in Olympia's tasteless opulence where disease might be hiding?

What a waste it all seemed. Lillian had allowed her stepmother full indulgence in the decor of the entire house, using Lillian's money. At first she was appalled at what the workmen were doing but it gave Olympia so much pleasure that it seemed cruel to make her change it. Lillian had come upon her stepmother fingering the gilded wallpaper with delight, or turning back the bed in her room just to see once more the high quality of the French-hemmed sheets. It seemed to ease a lingering resentment Olympia harbored against her now-wealthy stepdaughter.

And what did waste matter, anyway? It was likely that cholera would kill them all whether the walls were covered with maroon velvet or peacock blue enamel.

It wasn't just cholera that shattered her protective glass globe as if it had been tossed on a barnacled rock. Cholera was only the first in a chain of three calamities. Soon after they arrived, the second shock came to her: when they were still staying at Dr. Greeley's house, a plain letter had arrived for her, not with the regular mail, but delivered by a messenger whose looks the housemaid was unable or unwilling to remember. It was short, but long enough to ruin her day.

I am waiting for you. Soon I will be rich and then I claim
you as my bride. God speaks through me and he names you
as the false harlot; but all will be forgiven if you bend to
my wishes. I was on the ship with you and my mother. I will
be everywhere you turn. I have all your letters. I know every
detail of your life. I know your heart.

As she had read the note in disbelief, then read it again, she
remembered so clearly the image of her letters washing into the
sea, but on forcefully recalling the scene in her mind, she had to
see them pulled in by the backdraft of the boat's forward motion, so that they fluttered onto some inner deck instead of the
water. What had tossed on the whitecaps that night was only sea
foam.

It was impossible not to see before her the music cupboard in
her room in India, and her own hands as the smooth white hands
of an eighteen-year-old, on the day she decided to save the letters. At least once a year since then she had tried to destroy
them, and couldn't. Even now she couldn't tell herself why she
had waited so long. The man was dead, the boy was dead. She
would never marry. She would have no children to teasingly
reveal them to when she was a dying old woman, as her only
romantic secret. Yet they held some meaning for her; perhaps a
proof that love could happen, if only for a short time. And she
knew that whatever the man had chosen to do in the end, for
whatever reason, he had certainly loved her. For a time. His
hands and the way they touched her; his mouth, the very breaths
he took when close to her; all spoke an unmistakable language.
She had seen it since then, rarely, in other couples, but never for
herself.

After the day at Dr. Greeley's when the message came from
Henry, there was no sign of him and no more letters arrived. For
all she knew his letter could have been posted from Bangkok,
not London.

The maid had arrived behind Lillian, appearing in the mirror
in a limp black dress, impatient and hot, holding out a few slim
cases. "Which necklace, ma'am?"

Lillian almost heard instead, Which life? Which purpose?
Which solitude? and didn't answer but went on staring at her
reflection in the gilt mirror.

She had changed. Her face was thinner now, her cheekbones

more visible. French lacquer and combs weighed down her hair. Her colonial tanned skin a thing of the past, her cheeks and shoulders were now as white as the blancmange she'd had at lunch.

"Ma'am, the carriage will be here in ten minutes." The maid's voice rose in irritation. Lillian still hadn't been able to think about necklaces.

Olympia, dressed in full formal mourning and ready an hour ago, entered the room. In her widow's black she had the image of a charred but still edible wedding cake, all black frills, black puffs, black ribbons and ruffles.

"The messenger just got back from the opera house. The performance is still on. The party afterwards, too."

Olympia's voice had a girl's delight in it. There had been rumors of cancellations because of cholera. Then she saw what Lillian was wearing. Her hands went up in protest.

"Lillian, my dear. I can understand you might end your mourning so quickly. But not with *that* dress."

"It's been six months." Lillian smiled, ready to humor her.

"For the opera? It's just not, well, *enough*."

Lillian looked up in a moment of doubt. It was so hard to sort out Olympia's judgment. She was from London, it was true, and knew with accuracy a certain limited type of social behavior. But most of it was from twenty years ago. Not only was there the old and the new for Lillian to sort through, but there were odd notions of Olympia's own, personal ideas such as "don't use words with 'k' sounds in them," or "don't eat stewed figs if they're offered for dessert, it's too suggestive."

On top of that, Lillian had to discern between the social rules she herself didn't care about and the ones she did. She hardly wanted to do something that would put a tea party in an uproar, or make someone lose their appetite for dinner, but a mere raised eyebrow didn't bother her in the least.

Just when she thought she had the table manners learned, the subtly different things, she would make some terrible mistake. There was a recent dinner at Dr. Greeley's that she cringed to remember.

She had been tense the entire time, thinking that Henry might soon contact Dr. Greeley, whom he had known years ago during his two-year stay in London, for money, or help. It might have been Lillian's unease which had caused her mistake at dinner that night.

The dessert included ripe fresh pears, which were new to her. She'd eaten them chutneyed, preserved, dried, and pickled, but had never seen them fresh. She covertly watched the others and the way they held the fruit with a fork while they carefully peeled it and speared pieces into their mouths.

"These cholera theories of Dr. Snow's are quite interesting for a young unknown, Olympia," Dr. Greeley had been saying.

Lillian had tried to listen but was also concentrating on her fruit technique. At her first attempt she flipped pieces of pear sideways, knocking over a glass and smearing Dr. Greeley's dinner jacket with pear juice.

It was then that she noticed one thing no different from the colonial British life; the controlled nonreaction. Just as at home, no one turned around or even looked.

Dr. Greeley had simply removed the pear slices from his lap and dabbed once at the front of his coat, before going on with what he was saying. "This Dr. Snow seems to be close to a proof that water carries cholera. It won't go over well with the Deputy Minister of Health, I can tell you that. I asked Sir Philip to come tonight, so he could meet you. A late session of Parliament prevented him." And Olympia had yawned, trying to look interested. It was as if nothing had happened.

After that Lillian snuck fruit up to her room and practiced secretly until she could do it with her eyes shut.

Whatever her own failings, tonight's dress, she decided, was perfect for the first stage out of mourning, and she was well in the bounds of the half-year minimum for a father's death. Using thirty yards of watered gray silk, the dress had cost more to make than a year's wardrobe in India. Black Belgian lace trimmed its plain skirt and low neckline. The lace was even more exorbitant than the silk.

After the cheap labor in India, Lillian had been shocked to find how expensive life was here. Her income was two thousand pounds a year, but it took almost all of it to keep them in style. Their cook charged twice as much as they had paid an Indian family of eight to work in the kitchens.

The high prices affected more than just her wardrobe. After the heaped tables and four meals a day at the Governor's house, the meagerness of the food here astonished her. At Dr. Greeley's the same dwindling leg of mutton was brought out cold for lunch four days in a row. He carved small bits off as jealously as if it were suckling pig. And at breakfast, when she was always hungry, he watched the table like a thrifty farmer's wife.

"Here, let me get these out of your way," he had said one morning in reference to three sausages she had been about to serve herself. He had handed the plate back to the sideboard.

"Your necklace, ma'am?" The maid had reached a fury of impatience. This was another thing Lillian still wasn't comfortable with, that servants wouldn't stand and wait for an hour in silence while you chose a dress or wrote a letter. They had schedules of their own.

"The pearls, I suppose."

Olympia drew nearer.

"Lillian, not those boring old pearls. They need to be cleaned and restrung."

Lillian's grandmother's jewels had been pulled out of a strong box at the bank when she first arrived from India. These pearls were yellowed and still in the plain Empire style which probably copied something Empress Josephine had worn. They were impressive, though; six strands of five hundred shining drops, with the full parure of earrings, bracelet, brooch, and even a belt.

"You're right, Olympia," Lillian started to say, and began to reach for a different box, but the impatient maid had already put the necklace around her neck and fastened the catch. It was heavy and cool against her skin. The maid's fingers brushed lightly across the nape of her neck and sent a shiver down her back. Lillian looked in the mirror.

She was beautiful. Her reflection in the old pearls and the heavy silk was of someone else. The old Lillian who had swatted at lizards, watched her father die, and sailed naively to England no longer existed. And as she stared at her reflection, she remembered that it wasn't just her looks that were changed.

The third thing which had happened, besides the cholera in London, and besides the letters from Henry, had altered her entire view of the world.

Three nights ago she had been sitting like this, before the mirror, letting Olympia brush out her hair before going to sleep. They had been talking of their plans for the next day and Lillian had hardly been listening.

"We must try to have you meet more people. I can understand that you might need to rest sometimes, but try to make an effort, my dear."

Lillian had been depressed that afternoon, sunk into despondency by the heat and the news of cholera close by. She'd spent two hours lying on her bed, staring at the ceiling.

"I meant to tell you. Another colonial lady came for tea. So elegant, so kind. One of my dearest friends, really, in Bombay before I met your poor father. Mrs. Fanner? Booner? Connor?" Olympia paused in her brush strokes, her eyes on the ceiling.

"We were speaking of our old times together. And she talked of that terrible day at Jampur, and all those nice young men who had been quartered in Cochin the year before I arrived to marry your dear father. You probably didn't know about Jampur, though; I can tell you India wasn't all tea parties, believe me."

Jampur. Across Lillian's vision flashed sheets of blood, a blur of flies, skulls hacked like coconuts. No, she hadn't seen it. But Henry had heard about it and described it to her with typical, yet insane, relish, and she'd never forgotten. Could he have known what agony it caused her? One of those skulls . . . she repressed a sudden wave of nausea and asked, surprised at how controlled her voice was, "What did you say? Her son was at Jampur?"

"Yes, that's right. Fancy your remembering a name like that. You have such a way with those languages, dear." She began brushing again, pulling at a tangled section.

Lillian gently shook her head to pull the lock from her stepmother's hands.

"How sad for her. Her son."

"Oh no, her son was with her. Today, while you were resting. There were some survivors, you know," continued Olympia.

"No, I didn't know." Lillian couldn't understand why the room seemed to be revolving around her, the lights moving, everything in motion the way vultures might circle in the sky over a battlefield. She put a hand on the edge of the table.

Olympia put down the brush. "My dear, I can see you getting paler by the minute. Your stays today must have been too tight." She started to rummage among Lillian's cast-off underclothes to check the laces of her corset. Lillian watched her intently.

"But no one survived. No one." Lillian spoke as if the complete slaughter of the regiment were a thing promised to a child, a treat or an outing, suddenly snatched away. Her knowledge had been so sure and had explained everything for her these last ten years. And the familiar, sad thought of the dead baby rose slowly in her senses, like a loose water weed floating to the surface.

"Calm yourself, dear." Olympia began adjusting the laces while Lillian sat rigidly, hardly breathing, waiting.

"Apparently, according to this lady, you know I just can't remember her name. Was it Mrs. Bonning? Or Donning? So sweet, too, and her sister was so—"

"Olympia, please. What did she say?"

"You must learn not to interrupt, dear. Her son was with the Fifteenth regiment. And just between us, a few of them got out. Decamped. Retreated. Scattered. I don't know all those words they use."

"Deserted?"

"Yes, that was it."

"Are you sure that's what she said? Deserted, not reversed or restricted, or . . . regrouped?"

"No, dear, that was it. Deserted. And sounds sensible to me, too."

Sensible. Olympia wasn't so far off the mark. He wasn't a man to turn down an opportunity that came up. It came back to her, those weeks she had watched him before she fell in love. He had been out of place. Not from the upper classes. But at Aunt Flora's no one could tell, or maybe they didn't care.

He played piano well enough for those musical afternoons of Flora's. Only a snob would have sniffed about having him there. Aunt Flora certainly didn't; she was glad enough to have one more handsome young officer in her salon. And he sang in a good, solid baritone. That was how Lillian had started watching him so closely in the first place.

At their third afternoon party together she had heard him announce, "Poems. I'm reading a lot of them lately. It takes so much less time than a novel."

A guest, an older, established poet who knew Byron in his youth, had laughed loudly. Lillian knew the young man hadn't meant it as a joke, and was surprised to see him start to laugh too. Along with her sense of being coolly observant of his secret embarrassment, she felt a moment of obscure intimacy from knowing how his mind worked. She shared a secret with him. From this secret, one-sided intimacy, it was only a small step to love.

"So you'll wear the pearls, ma'am?" The maid's voice was less grating, almost admiring. It brought her back to the present.

Lillian looked at her reflection once more. In this necklace, it was as if she were looking into another time, some other person's past, or her own cloudy future. She saw a woman glowing with a private fire.

The first time they had been alone together she probably had looked like this, she thought, only young. And happy.

He had found her on one of her solitary walks and she knew without him telling her that he had searched for her, hoped to find her. When he took her arm she didn't feel her usual indignant resentment, but a relaxed sinking into his strength. After a mile or so, when he kissed her behind a screen of young banana trees, she knew she had no more control. She would do whatever he asked.

When she went back to Cochin and her father's house a month later, by luck the man's regiment went as well. Good luck or bad, even now it was hard to say. At any rate, two months after that, she knew she would have a child, and she never saw him again.

The pearl necklace warm around her throat, she kept staring at herself in the mirror. How would he feel if he saw her again? "I think I will wear these pearls after all," she said. "We can take them to the jeweler's tomorrow." The maid nodded an approval Lillian would never have admitted she was anxious for.

It could be that dirty pearls were another false step she didn't know about. At least they weren't paste. No one would see them, anyway. Lillian didn't believe the messenger's answer. The opera house would be empty, the party deserted. Cholera was everywhere. They were fools to go out.

"Ma'am, the carriage is downstairs." The maid, her brows down again in annoyance, held out Lillian's pumps and knelt to slip them on. Lillian looked down at the back of the woman's head, the neck muscles taut with displeasure. Probably she would give notice tomorrow. So far no servant had lasted more than two weeks.

140

At the opera house, gaps showed in the private boxes. The orchestra seats were half empty, but the upper galleries where you could buy a seat for a half crown were packed, as always.

The company was doing Mozart's *The Magic Flute*. Lillian loved Mozart. She owned the scores to several of his symphonies and operas, including this one. She had never heard *The Magic Flute* performed, and it had been years since she had tried working out the various vocal parts of the opera on the piano. She remembered most clearly the occasional appearances of the three celestial boys, who sang their innocent encouragement in exquisite three-part harmony.

Once the performance began she felt swept up in its fairy-tale charm and hymnlike chorales. Then, during the scene when the supposedly evil Sarastro reveals himself to the heroine as her kind and all-knowing father, Lillian looked up to a box across the theater. A shock went through her, an actual stinging sensation pulsing down her bare arms and into her fingertips.

He was there.

She took a deep breath, and another. Swallowed. She picked up the opera glasses from Olympia's lap and looked again.

There was no doubt. He was older, heavier, and his hair had receded, but it was the same man. His skin was white rather than the campaigner's brown she had known, and his face looked as if he had lost interest in everything in his life. Or maybe it was just that his face wasn't interested in her anymore.

An old dream came back to her. It had been the turning point. Until she dreamed it she had watched him in the drawing room with pity. In the dream, he had been throwing stones into a pond. Round, translucent, the stones were alike and symmetrical, yet each was preciously different. And each stone was just for her, the thrust of his arm as he tossed it gently into space, the arc of the thing as it fell onto the glassy surface. It was as if she had heard him sing to her, with a soaring voice like this man on the stage. Each toss had its own phrase, its own melody and cadence. It was a passion in stones.

She had always remembered that dream, because when she woke up from it she was in love with the man. And now that she thought about it, at no point in their passion was any sensation as wonderful as the dream had been.

She wanted to tell herself that it was the cowardice that appalled her, his desertion of the battle and of her, that a man who could do such a thing was worthless. But an inner voice taunted with the truth. That these things didn't matter at all. If he had still been as handsome as he was in the dream of the stones, she would have gone through the door of her box, trotted down the corridors, and burst in on him, claiming him back.

Her pain, which she'd cherished like an heirloom for ten years, seemed to float up to the domed gold roof of the opera house, where it vaporized and disappeared. Lillian stared, unseeing, at the final act of the opera, and fingered her necklace.

She hadn't been aware of how tightly she was pulling at the pearls until they broke. She let out the quiet, embarrassed mutter of someone slipping on a wet floor.

The pearls fell like slow hailstones, all five hundred of them, running down the folds of her skirt, over the velvet seat cover, onto the sloped floor of the box seats. She pulled up a lapful of satin to save the few she could but in her confusion, as she stooped to gather more, the ones in her lap spilled out too. They splashed over the lower edge of the box. A few landed on the heads of the surprised audience five feet below and the rest bounced silently down the banked floor of the opera house and were lost among shoes, dust balls, umbrellas, and the bassoon cases and music stands of the orchestra pit.

The strings hung limp around Lillian's neck, rotted with damp and age. Olympia had dozed off, her head slumped to one side and her hair arrangement askew, and when the audience's final applause woke her she had missed the breaking of the necklace as well as most of the opera.

"I'm afraid Mozart is a little dry for me, dear." She yawned and licked her lips, trying with one hand to rearrange her falling hair. "Shall we get an ice before we attempt to push through the crowd?"

For answer Lillian held out two pearls that she'd been able to retrieve from the front of her dress.

Olympia sought out the house manager and explained, in the hopes that a few might be returned. Lillian put the broken strings in her bag. Her neck felt naked and vulnerable. After struggling through the crowds they left for Lady Tewksbury's party.

15

Snow climbed the grand stairway to Lady Tewksbury's ballroom and wondered for the tenth time what he was doing at this party. He should be home, working. The opera had been indulgence enough. If Caleb, whom he hadn't seen for days now, hadn't sent a note reminding him of the invitation, he wouldn't have even thought of it. He suffered without protest the butler's mispronunciation of his name as Tonker James Gnome and entered the huge room in a daze.

It took him a moment to register that he was hearing not the expected party sounds of violins filtering through a tipsy ringing of crystal, but a pounding, hammering rhythm of incredibly loud drums.

Squeezed into the fern-framed alcove where one would normally find a discreet string quartet or small brass band was a cluster of ten black-skinned Nubians in leopard robes, swaying like a Welsh chorus, pounding at their waist-high drums. Snow's mouth fell open.

He looked around and realized that no one was paying much attention to the din. The hundreds of guests chattered and shoved their way through the crush for more champagne, calling out over high hair and jewelled tiaras as if nothing were out of the ordinary.

The room looked like an imagined forest grove, or a walled

garden. Live greenery covered most of the walls, hanging not in traditional festoons but in wild profusion as if it had grown up overnight. It must have been five hundred guineas' worth of ivy. A stirring in hanging moss near the ceiling made Snow realize there were birds flying through the room; long-tailed parrots, green budgerigars, doves. One landed on a lady's shoulder and she broke into hysterical shrieks and laughter.

More Nubians, naked to the waist and looking depressed and chilly, squeezed through with trays of food high over their heads; piled grapes, chunks of lamb, a whole roast calf. It was as if some opium dream of King Solomon's palace had come to life.

Then Snow remembered; Lady Tewksbury had provided forty thousand pounds for an exploration up the Nile five years ago and the leaders had just returned. She was showing off her spoils.

The party was well under way, with everyone's face showing the delighted look of the fourth glass of champagne, as if nothing could bother them, and this wild troop of dazed and homesick Africans was just one more fling to pass the time. You would never guess that a plague was speeding along outside the door.

Snow had stayed until the very end of the opera. When it had been time to leave and push through all those departing hordes he found himself shrinking from touch. Behind the communal scent of ambergris and expensive face powder lingered a base of sweat and wet dog. In the first corridor his arm wedged against a lady's back, his face almost in her gray hair. Her damp heat pulsed through the thin silk of her dress. He suppressed an urge to push, shout "fire," scream at the limit of his lungs, anything to get the placid look of post-show contentment off their faces. Instead he groped to the edge of the crowd and grabbed a chair to wait it out.

When the corridors were nearly empty he had left the building and walked the mile and a half to Lady Tewksbury's, gulping the stale Thames vapors, which seemed fresh by comparison. He kept looking to all sides of him along the way, but saw nothing suspicious.

Now that he was here at the party the crowd was just as dense, always shifting, moving on, seeing something prettier on the other side of the room. Caught in the flow, Snow found it hard to look away from the famous faces he spotted, in the same way it's hard to look away from a deformity or an open wound. He had to keep himself from gawking like a yokel at personalities he recognized from caricatures in *Punch* and *The Times*.

To his surprise he caught sight of a few men he knew from Westminster Hospital or Guy's Hospital; professors, squirrelish characters, faces he'd never thought to see out of the surgery theater or anatomy laboratory, certainly not in this opulent room.

One of them talked with Lady Tewksbury herself. She was smiling without respite, her dress cut low enough to hint at the nipples of her breasts, and cuddling her inevitable terrier with its diamond collar. She was glowing, celestial, and leading a physicist by the pinky for yet another introduction. Perfume hovered over her like a cloud of gnats.

Suddenly Snow realized how he had merited an invitation to this event; Lady Tewksbury wanted to surround herself with "men of science" and make a trend, a name for herself. Forget the opera stars and the minor lords, ignore the fashionable ladies who collected sheiks and unknown eastern European kings. She would go for the scientists. She was collecting them the way people keep drawers full of lengths of string. In case they came in handy.

Snow smiled to himself at his childish disappointment. And he thought she'd heard of his work! She must have got his name off some list. Another scientist for her collection. He wondered if she had illusions of contributing her own ideas to some discovery or development; a new treatment for consumption, or a revised measurement of the circumference of the earth.

This was no more a scientific gathering than shaking the hand of the Princess Alberta at a fête was getting to know the royal family.

The drumming was getting out of hand, so loud that one had to shout to be heard. Now he recognized Crooksworth and Gump, the leaders of the expedition. They sat on mock thrones at the head of the room, under gilt palm trees. Crooksworth's face was deep yellow with fever and he looked about to fall over. Gump's hand shook as he raised his glass to his mouth. The tropics ruined a man in a year. Snow shuddered. He'd take a London slum any day, even in this cholera epidemic.

Snow still hadn't been able to reach the end of the room where the refreshments were. He could see light glinting off a giant ice sculpture of a hippopotamus, and a punch bowl the size of a cathedral's baptismal font. He assumed it had water lilies floating in it from the crushed ones all over the floor, staining the wood boards with their slime. He gave up trying to get there, found a pillar, and pressed his back against it.

Directly across the room from him he saw a woman doing just the same thing, clutching the pillar behind her with a kind of amused desperation. At least she'd been able to get a glass of champagne. She saw him and smiled at their mutual predicament, then raised her glass to him with a gentle swoop. It was clear she'd had more than this one glass to drink. She seemed to have no escort.

Snow couldn't look away from her. It wasn't that her face was symmetrical, or delicate, or even dramatic. It was the way she looked at everyone, enjoying it, as if watching a play. Eating it up. Taking mental notes. She was actually listening to the drummers, moving her head in time. A mist of sweat on her upper lip caught the light from the chandeliers.

She wore something gray. Wisps of light brown hair escaped her elaborate arrangement and curled in front of her ears. And there was something odd about her appearance, but he couldn't quite place it; then it came to him. She had pearls on her wrists, in her ears, even at her waist in a narrow belt. But she wore no necklace. Her white throat was bare above the low neckline of the dress.

A couple squeezed past him and he let go of the pillar a moment to make room, then had to step a bit to one side for a footman with a tray. In half a minute he lost his spot. When he looked up to see her again she was gone.

He hadn't forgotten about her, but was beginning to think of leaving when he recognized Sir Philip Constable five yards away, looking just as ill at ease as Snow felt. It took minutes for Snow to push his way over. They shook hands.

"Ah, Dr. Snow. Good evening." The man was shouting over the drums. "How is your work going?"

By now Snow was getting used to Constable's vagueness, his air of never having remembered their last exchange. At first he tried to understand if Sir Philip was referring to the objectionable survey work, or Snow's medical practice, his laboratory work, or even some other imagined work such as furthering his knowledge of South Sea island languages.

Snow decided to fight vagueness with more vagueness. "The

patients keep coming in, and that's what pays the rent." This, of course, was untrue; Snow hadn't seen a patient for weeks. And he owned his house.

"You must drop by my office soon so we can discuss that membership in the Royal Academy."

But he hadn't agreed to anything! For a second Snow wondered if he'd imagined the late night visit, the threats, the strange offer. No, he couldn't have. This man made no sense.

Luckily the drums and jostling of the crowd allowed Snow to avoid answering, and then they were interrupted by the minister of finance, who began a long and technical election discussion with Constable. Snow tried to maintain a politely interested expression on his face but gave up after five minutes. It was clear they had nothing more to say to him. He excused himself.

Within two steps he recognized Deborah Beersdon. Her gleaming bird eyes shone even more than usual at her triumph of being at this great party of the season. She stood out from the other ladies in her drab rust-colored dress, its severity barely softened by a few inches of revealed skin at her upper chest. Snow wished she hadn't revealed it. Of all the hues she could have chosen, this burnt red made her skin look the yellowest.

Deborah looked straight at him with a blank smile, as if he were a stranger. Of course. As the wife of a prominent editor, who could report on the party tomorrow with all the glory it deserved, her status was higher than a mere doctor. Snow decided to aggravate her.

"Why, Mrs. Beersdon, what a surprise. I never thought to see *you* at Lady Tewksbury's."

Her eyes narrowed in annoyance, which she turned into a pretense of trying to place him. "It's Dr. Snow, isn't it? How nice that you are able to come to these little things. I know that evening clothes are so expensive."

"And where is Caleb? Unable to introduce you to the heavenly bodies?" He had to yell over the drums, which seemed to be getting louder.

Deborah said something he couldn't hear and gestured to the top of the room, where he saw Caleb talking to the explorers and Lady Tewksbury, along with the owner of *The Times.* Deborah started chattering again, apparently having given up trying to snub him and preferring to talk to him rather than nobody.

When Deborah spoke, the tip of her long nose moved down

toward her upper lip, in time with whatever syllables she used. It had always been hard for Snow to look her in her eyes instead of watching the antics of that bit of flesh, and this time he stopped even trying to listen.

The drumming grew louder and even more frenetic until, in a dazzlingly orchestrated unison, all of the drummers stopped short. The silence left Deborah's words audible everywhere.

"—Dr. David Livingstone over there? They say he was intimate with native women all through the Congo, and now his syphilis—" She caught herself up with a cough as sleekly as a stumbling cat.

Violins began tuning up. After the drumming they sounded whiny and feeble, like insect music. The clearing of the center of the room for the dancing resulted in a worse crush along the walls. Snow and Deborah swayed like deckhands until they were pushed apart and separated. Snow caught sight of Caleb again, closer this time and still deep in conversation with *The Times*'s chief. Snow tried to reach him, and immediately Caleb walked off, his arm on that of the other man. Snow could hardly believe Caleb would avoid him, but that was how it looked.

The dancing began. They started with old-fashioned country dances, the lines of couples moving through strictly ruled formations, but after a few selections the orchestra broke into a waltz.

One of Snow's first arguments with Caleb's wife had been over waltzing. She thought the new dance was indecent and he had been foolish enough to debate the point with her. Of course, *she* never danced at all, it was a sinful waste of energy, but she could allow that some less devoted souls might occasionally indulge in a chaste prance across the floor. But waltzing, where you actually held on to each other's waists, was little better than public fornication, she said. She used the word probably not even knowing what it meant.

Snow stood wistfully gazing at the dancers. He felt his life draining away into middle age, his youth wasted. He had never danced at an affair like this, not once. He spotted the woman he'd seen by the pillar, dancing now, looking happy, her head thrown back in the pleasure of her turns.

Snow could see she didn't care about her partner. She would have danced with anyone just to be out there. It wasn't until he came to this conclusion that he realized how hard he'd been staring at the two of them. He forced himself to look away. But

"I'm afraid so, Lady Tewksbury," continued Snow, his heart beating faster. "It's fairly clear."

"If water carries the sickness, young man, then why isn't all of London dead with it?" asked Greeley, bristling like a shuttlecock. "We all drink water, every day."

Snow was afraid someone would ask that. It was the weak point in his whole theory. He fumbled for an answer.

"There must be different sources, different pools of contamination. The water does flow, after all. It changes. The poisons, or cholera organisms, could move their location, from one day to the—"

"I never heard such nonsense. That could only be true if the water was actually separated. But it's all from the same place, all from the same place. The Board of Health, Sir Philip Constable over there, they all agree." Greeley looked smug.

Was it? Snow had never stopped to wonder about this before. It could make all the difference. What if there were actually two, or even more, sources of piped-in water, that were truly separated? Not the ditches and ponds, or the water straight from the river. He knew that stuff was deadly. But the supposedly pure water that the companies provided.

Greeley, probably sure he had won the argument, wandered off. Snow was trying to fend off the cholera questions of the clamoring hangers-on near Lady Tewksbury when he saw her. Ten feet off, the woman in gray, the waltzer, was talking to Greeley. Snow winced when Greeley touched her bare arm. With her was an older, fat woman in black. As soon as he could escape the questioners, he edged beside Greeley.

Snow forgot his debate. He felt a rise of all his old student's misgivings, as if an examination were about to take place. He was afraid to look at the woman, and with a desperate churlishness acted as if she weren't even there. She became a very important gray luminosity in the corner of his eye.

He plunged his hands in his pockets like a schoolboy. Feeling the bits of pocket lint and a pencil stub he came upon something he couldn't believe he'd forgotten about until now.

Two pearls. At the end of the opera he'd felt a slight tapping at his heels, a small rodent kind of sound, and he'd shifted his feet over what felt like pebbles until he'd stooped to retrieve them. Good ones, from the little he knew about pearls, though yellowed.

Now he rolled them, warm from the body heat in his pocket, between his fingers and thumb. For something to say, he pulled them out.

"The most extraordinary thing, really. At Covent Garden, the end of *The Magic Flute*. These pearls. I suppose they're quite valuable." Snow held them out to Greeley, a student offering, like an odd bug he'd found, or a bright agate from the beach.

Greeley leaned over, frowning, to peer at the shining globes.

Lillian spoke. "I believe you've got two of my pearls there."

The tone of her voice was half cross, half flirting, so that his first thought was that he was standing on the train of her dress. It took him a long moment to connect what she said with the pearls in his hand. They matched the drops in her ears and the ropes wound around her wrists. Close up like this her bare neck looked as inviting as if she had pulled up all the silk and hoops under her costume to expose the white inner skin of her thighs.

With great seriousness he dropped the two pearls onto her outstretched palm. When she smiled at him he felt as if he'd been blessed by one of the lesser saints.

Greeley was halfway through the grumpy introduction before Snow heard him.

"Dr. John Snow, Miss Aynsworth, Mrs. Colonel Aynsworth."

Mrs. Colonel Aynsworth? he thought. She's married? Oh, no, that must be the mother, the fat one.

"The Aynsworths arrived here a few months ago from India. Old family connection."

Snow had a dim recollection of the name Aynsworth. Cholera. That was it, the outbreak in India. In the paper, just last week when he was in Yorkshire. The governor had died. Her father? And a son. He felt he should give something in the way of a condolence, and opened his mouth, but instead heard himself say,

"You waltz beautifully, Miss Aynsworth. May I have the pleasure of the next dance?"

Snow could hardly believe his own words, or that she was assenting as casually as if he'd handed her tea. The orchestra started up and they curved together onto the dance floor.

He was hopeless as a dancer. He stepped on her feet three times before she whispered to him, sending goose bumps down into his collar, "Just let me show you."

Their steps meshed. He winced to think that she'd probably done the same with the other man ten minutes ago.

"They were part of my necklace. It broke at the opera."

"How unfortunate." Snow saw a confusing expression of sadness, then relief, cross her features. "Were you able to find most of the pearls?"

"Oh, no. Yours were the only ones." She gave him a smile of gratitude, but mocking, as if he'd picked for her one meadow poppy when there were thousands on all sides.

"Of course the theater manager can recover them."

"Yes. Perhaps."

He couldn't understand why she seemed so unperturbed by the loss.

"Have you known Dr. Greeley long, Dr. Snow?"

"He was my teacher in medical school." Greeley was the last thing he wanted to talk about.

"I don't think you like him very much," she said. "Neither do I." After another few bars of music she said, "We don't need to talk."

The joy of holding her overpowered everything else. He could feel her abdominal muscles twist through the turns, and the pulse in her left hand was strong and slow. His fingers were only three inches from her breasts. Her breath smelled of strawberries, her skin smelled of sandalwood. Snow felt far from reality, as if he'd been drinking champagne the whole night.

When the long dance ended gloom suddenly descended on him. He'd actually forgotten for a few minutes that he wouldn't be able to spend the rest of the evening with her, the rest of the night, and all the days after that. In miserable silence he returned her to the large woman in black.

Just as he was leaving them, Sir Philip Constable caught up with him. "Ah, Snow. So sorry to have to interrupt our talk back there. The minister is persistent. As I was saying about that membership—"

Sir Philip's glance fell on the woman and the two stared at each other. Their eyes locked like those of nervous wrestlers. Her hand, still on Snow's arm, began to shake. He was astonished to feel from her an almost telepathic sense of distress and shame. It was nearly visible, like a green cloud flowing out of her and into his mind. He had never known anything like it.

His clinical side took over and ignored such impossible sensations; she must be about to faint, he thought. He stepped closer to support her, but then he looked at Constable. The man's face had gone bright burning red, even up to the large bald patch.

She didn't faint, and Snow's sense of being invaded by her distress disappeared instantly. He suddenly remembered the salt on the man's shoes, and stole a glance at the toes of his polished opera pumps. They were spotless, of course.

Constable finally pulled his eyes from Lillian and turned back to Snow. "As I said, you must come to see me this week." His voice shook. He abruptly bowed to Miss Aynsworth and left. She said nothing.

The stepmother spoke up. "Lillian, dear, you don't look well. I'm afraid all this dancing has been too much. Please come sit down." Mrs. Aynsworth shot a look at Snow, as if he were to blame for her sudden exhaustion, and led the young woman away. She stumbled once as she went off.

A moment after she passed him he inhaled the air deeply, an old trick he'd taught himself, and smelled her; sandalwood again, and a faintly athletic tinge of fresh sweat.

So her name is Lillian, thought Snow. And she knows Sir Philip Constable. He laughed at himself at his own use of the word. "Knows" was putting it a bit lightly. Seeing their eyes lock like that he had felt more intrusive than during the most intimate medical exam.

He stood in a daze for a moment or two, letting the crowd push past him. He hadn't known how physical the sense of jealousy could be. It had a shape to it, like some sharp metal object ready to burst from his chest. Of course a woman like that would be taken, he thought. But why should he have the terrible luck for it to be Constable?

Another dance, not a waltz, began. It was time for Snow to leave. He'd wasted enough of the night in this place.

He didn't get to the door. A rising murmur of voices grew to shouts and screams, all directed at the center of the dance floor. One of the dancers lay writhing in a puddle of silk and vomit at the center of the floor. The rest backed slowly away from her with white faces and covered mouths. Cholera. From several points around the room came sounds of coughing and retching. A woman screamed.

A frantic surge for the door began. The stairs clogged as more and more guests pushed their way out. One woman fell, then another. The table with its vast buffet of a dozen lobsters and the ice-sculpted hippo crashed to the floor, as well as what remained of the punch. The floor was awash. The anonymous victim still lay in the center of the ballroom. Snow couldn't have reached her if he tried.

Craning his head over the crowd, he scanned all sides for brown hair and gray silk. He finally spotted Lillian and her stepmother near the outer door, Greeley leading them out with an arm over her shoulder. Lillian turned her face back into the ballroom for one long, searching look before she was forced out by her escorts. Snow knew she searched for him. As the panic increased on all sides, so did Snow's trembling euphoria. He understood that for the first time in his life he was in love.

16

"Bince! Where the devil are you in this murk!" Greeley peered into the darkness of the brick elephant house. A strong smell of elephant droppings compounded his nausea and headache from all the champagne at Lady Tewksbury's the night before. He fought to keep from vomiting and wondered briefly if it was cholera. No headache with cholera, he remembered with relief. Just alcohol poisoning.

"Bince!" Damn the boy. What was he, Greeley, doing in a foul place like this? No other prominent scientist would be caught dead in the elephant exhibit of Regent's Park Zoo. Self-pity, habitual to him as a nun's rosary, filled his mind. Almost sixty and not much to show for it. No knighthood in sight. Hadn't published an article in almost five years. Everyone else made all the discoveries, got all the credit.

Greeley stepped back into the intolerable sun, squinting, and spotted Henry on the other side of the elephants' enclosure, talking to an Indian man who must have been the elephant keeper. He made his way over and caught their words before they realized he was there.

"Ah, sir," the keeper was saying to Henry, "I see you wait for me. I am so very glad you have received me to your home to ask after my worthy and humble information. All my apologies and grief for the lateness of this my reply."

156

"All right, quit groveling."

They didn't seem to notice him. Greeley decided to wait behind a brick pillar and listen.

"Tell me what you have, fast," Henry continued to the keeper. "And don't expect too much pay, either. Things have been short."

"With certainty, oh worthy one. Here is my news. The boy you ask after, or a boy just like him, has been found. The boy lives. Ten years in age, all the description you asked about."

"Where? Where is he, you fool?"

Greeley didn't try to make sense out of what he heard, but stored it carefully for later thought.

He hadn't seen Henry since the boy's arrival in London, four months earlier. Not a boy anymore, he remembered. Man, then. The man didn't look well. Haggard, with some streaks of gray in his once flaming red hair.

"Please, sir, lose no distress over this matter. You may see the boy this very night if you wish. Here in London, England. He is here." He handed to Henry a scrap of clean and carefully folded paper.

Henry glanced at it and stuffed it into his pocket. He dug into another pocket, and threw a few coins on the ground. Then he caught sight of Greeley. "Ah, you've finally found me!" The keeper backed away and disappeared behind the elephant house.

Greeley waved and picked his way over elephant droppings to where Henry stood. It was a complete mystery to him what Olympia's son was doing here. Greeley should have refused to come; he had never liked the boy. But he had limited choices. Twelve years ago, when Henry was here reading for the bar at Lincoln's Inn, the two had spent time together. Out of bad luck Henry had walked in on Greeley one night, while the doctor entertained one of his more aristocratic patients. She had been just to the old doctor's taste; blonde, obese, a loud laugh, and naked except for a pair of gloves. A modest sum had kept Henry silent, but now Greeley was afraid to refuse this bizarre request to meet him here at the zoo.

Just as he joined Henry, the elephant finally appeared from behind the building and slowly lumbered toward them.

"I say, Bince, hadn't we better—" Greeley headed for the gate in alarm, but Henry put an arm around his shoulders and steered him to a small building in the enclosure. They went through a low door into a spartan room.

The room held a camp bed, two cages of nervously chattering monkeys, and a rough table.

"Not exactly Grosvenor Square, is it, Doctor?"

"I can't understand why you won't contact your family, Bince."

"Absolutely not. They know I'm alive, and that's enough. They'll see plenty of me one day."

"Perhaps if I could give some assistance . . ." Greeley reached into his pocket, trying to decide how to make it clear that this would be a loan, not a gift.

"No. All I want from you is this: let me know if my mother and stepsister leave London. Or if they're planning any other major changes. And keep my whereabouts a secret."

"What kind of changes do you mean?"

"Oh, anything. Marriage, perhaps." Henry fiddled with some papers on his table.

Greeley flushed. He had been thinking the very same thing himself. Lillian, close to thirty, would make a perfect older man's wife. Her fortune was just the thing he needed to boost what remained of his career. She was too thin and her looks were faded, but he didn't care about that.

"Have your eye on the old girl, eh, Doctor? The merry widow? My mother didn't inherit the estate, you know."

Greeley didn't answer.

"Our Miss Lily has every penny." Henry tossed a packet of papers into the air and caught it without looking. "Just let us know, Doctor. I'll be contacting you again soon."

Greeley, no less nauseated, made his way out of the zoo. He took a hansom cab home, where he lay down in his darkened bedroom with a cold cloth on his head for the rest of the day.

158

Book II

17

1

"There's another letter," said Caleb, holding *The Times* at arm's length. His voice hummed with the small satisfaction of seeing a predicted catastrophe come to pass.

Beersdon and Snow sat in the library of Snow's house two mornings after the party at Lady Tewksbury's. It had been days since the two had talked. Snow slouched in an armchair, his legs stretched out before him, a cup of tea perched at an angle on his thigh. He'd summoned his friend in the hope that Caleb would send Snow's mind back to work. It was almost ten and he should have left for his street rounds two hours ago. But since waking he had felt leaden and unable to concentrate. And even worse, uninterested. If he had been asked at that moment about the cause of cholera his honest answer would have been, I don't give a bloody damn.

All he could think about with any concentration was Lillian Aynsworth, and the sweat on her upper lip as they had danced together. It was impossible to think of her without thinking of Constable. It caused him an almost physical pain.

Caleb rustled the pages of the newspaper. Without waiting for

161

a response from Snow he read the letter out loud in mock oratory, one hand on his chest.

> If a certain doctor is to continue with his illicit surveys in Soho and Lambeth the authorities must assume he has no faith in the sovereign management of the Public Health. He implies that any number of impurities are being sanctioned by those in authority when in fact major reforms on the public waterworks of the areas in question are nearing completion. Is this man so concerned with his own advancement through artificial publicity that he refuses to see the illogical nature of his pursuit? We advise him to discontinue his persecution of the bereaved families of cholera victims, and encourage his return to private practice.

He ended with a flourish worthy of Hamlet's soliloquy.

Snow kept his eyes on his tea. "I expect they're right." He took a sip. "I may as well quit." He said the words just to see how they would sound.

Caleb touched one of the deeper pockmarks on his cheek and said quietly, "Perhaps you should. If you stop now there's still a hope of putting your practice back together."

"You don't mean that, do you? I wasn't serious." Snow jerked his arm and his cup hit the arm of the chair, breaking with a surprisingly melodious crack. His finger and thumb still gripped the delicate handle, and he felt the missing weight of the cup as one might feel the drop of a suddenly severed finger, before the pain throbbed up.

Caleb looked startled, and defensive.

"Surely you don't expect me to quit my research because of crank letters in the paper!" continued Snow. "All that data. I've just got to think of a way to use it." He tried to think of himself as an ordinary doctor, with no papers in print, no reputation, and how it would sound to Lillian if he ever had a chance to be alone with her. He began to pace.

"Besides," he went on, "at this point so many people want me to quit that I want to go on just to spite them." Then he told Caleb about the meetings with Constable, and the attack in the alley. He said nothing about Mango and the prostitute, or the falling cornice and the dog bite. He was afraid he would begin to sound obsessed.

162

As it was, he wished he had said less.

"You want me to believe the Board of Health is trying to threaten you? That's absurd." Caleb's voice was flat under his protest. "It must be coincidence. London is full of thugs." He shook his head and went back to reading the paper.

Snow decided not to pursue it. "You know, maybe you're right," he finally said. "Not that I should quit, but that I can't prove anything with this data."

The data, all the data. The lists, the papers, the hundreds of brown bottles lined up against the wall above his microscope. If only he could *see* the body causing the disease, he could have found it in those bottles, at least when he first collected the water.

Ignoring Caleb now, he went for the hundredth time to the microscope and took out a clean slide, took one of the bottles from the shelf and put a drop of water on the slide. With a short stab of guilt the memory of Sophie came up; that first night with her, when he had those bottles in his pocket. He hadn't thought of her once since meeting Lillian. He bent his head to the eyepiece.

"Could I have a look?" Caleb had stepped over.

"By all means, waste your time if you like. There's nothing. As always."

Caleb bent over for a minute. "Nothing?" he asked. "There's stuff floating all through here!"

"Protozoa. Dead ones. Harmless. They're in everything we drink. They mean nothing."

Snow had examined the water from every single bottle on the shelf. There was never a difference between that from healthy households and the sick ones.

Maybe he was looking too hard, with too much intention. Maybe he expected something so specific that he was blinded to easier facts. Blinded like a cab horse, with every view but the one straight ahead shut out. Moving forward with brute purpose was useful enough in its place, but he needed to see sideways, up, down, he needed to look in some other direction.

"Caleb, here's what I want you to do. Go down to my storage room, to the big pile of notebooks, I showed it to you once." Snow saw Caleb's short flash of resentment and decided to ignore it. "Without looking at the covers, or anything like that,

163

flip through the pile and pick up, say, twenty. From different points in the pile."

"You could do that just as well yourself!"

"I'm not so sure of that. I need someone to make a random choice. Please, just do as I say." Caleb was obviously not going to refuse at this point.

"I'll confuse your system. I know you had them ordered in a certain way."

"That's the point. My system has to go."

In a few minutes Caleb returned with the stack. He set them in front of Snow and waited calmly, looking a little detached from it all. In the meantime Snow had laid out several large sheets of paper and a stack of pens.

"Read them, please," he said.

"What! All these notes? In your terrible writing?"

"It won't be so bad. Just read them out loud, and I'll take new notes. But you listen too, to see if you notice the slightest detail, anything different about the cholera houses."

Caleb read through a hundred cholera cases, from dozens of different houses. The notes gave the numbers, deaths, average income, age, time from first symptom until death, proximity to the river, source of water for the house ranging from piped in water to straight from the river.

Snow drew orderly columns and separated everything out into categories.

After three hours they were finished and Caleb's voice was hoarse. They had produced a huge chart the size of a tabletop, covered in tiny but legible writing. It showed nothing, except that if you were poor your chances of dying were higher. As they had always been.

"Are you sure you've read everything out?" Snow felt powerless with frustration.

"No, I didn't read everything." Caleb sounded angry now. "You noted some pretty silly details, you know, like the color of their wallpaper and if they were cheerful or not. How long a girl's hair was. What kind of accent they had. We'd be sitting here until midnight if I read out all of it."

Something nagged at Snow's memory when Caleb mentioned wallpaper.

"I remember that house where I noted the paper." He said it almost to himself. "It was only one," he added accusingly. "The

164

neighbors didn't have paper, none of the houses on that street did except . . . can you find it?"

"Good Lord, do you expect me to keep track of a hundred entries of someone else's notes!"

"No, no. Of course. Let's stop. I'm terribly hungry. Shall we see if Mrs. Jarrett can fix up something?"

"It's fine for you to sit around all day, but I have to get to my office." He took out his watch. "You can't expect me to always be available like this. Hire a lab assistant or something." Caleb looked directly at Snow. "And think about quitting. It might be the best solution. I don't say it just because of the letters."

2

Snow never did go out on his survey work that day. Minutes after Caleb's departure the bell rang again. It was with a sense of total disbelief that Snow saw Lillian Aynsworth enter the room.

Mrs. Jarrett held the door aside, her back rigid with disapproval.

"A *lady* to see you, sir." Her mouth pinched off the word "lady" in a way that made it clear what she thought of a woman coming to see a man in his house.

Snow couldn't take his eyes off her. Every fact from Caleb's reluctant list immediately went out of his head. She looked even more beautiful than she had at the ball; paler, in an ordinary gray walking dress, and the intensity of her personality shone out more distinctly now.

He finally realized he was expected to speak. "That will be all, Mrs. Jarrett—no, wait." He turned to Lillian. "Will you have some tea, Miss Aynsworth?"

Mrs. Jarrett gave a short snort. "The kitchen's being turned out for a scrub. Can't get no hot water for an hour."

"I don't really need any—" began Lillian.

But Mrs. Jarrett gave another snort, and she was out of the room. She slammed the door.

To Snow, the heat of the room suddenly seemed stifling. The grainy urine smell from the hedgehog cages rushed to Snow's senses, along with rotten egg from a recent experiment with sulphur, smells he had ignored for years. As much as he craved to be alone with Lillian, this room, stinking and layered with anxieties about his work and Caleb's hostility, was all wrong.

"I'm so glad you've come to see me," he said to her. "But it's awfully close in here. Shall we go out and walk toward Hyde Park?"

She nodded, as if in relief. Despite the logic of it Snow felt a twinge of rebuff. How foolish of him to imagine she could be interested in his smelly work.

Once out on the street she seemed to relax. "I see I'm not the only one in London with servant problems," said Lillian with a short laugh. "I thought we could talk more easily out here, too. I came because—I wanted to ask you about cholera. I hope you'll forgive this intrusion on your work."

Disappointment hit Snow like a punch in the stomach. So it was a formal call. He had hoped that she, too, could not forget their dance. But after all, what lady would ever visit like this unless it were for a purely impersonal reason?

"What can I tell you?" he asked, his voice almost sullen. "Surely your friend Dr. Greeley is an easier person to ask."

She frowned. "But I don't agree with him. He says cholera can't be spread by water." Her voice had changed, softened, as if Snow's small jab about Greeley had launched them into intimacy. His hope returned and he slowed their steps, fearful of reaching some destination where they would have to sit on a bench and be proper again. As they crossed Bond Street he took her arm, and he didn't release it after they reached the curb. Even the rough linen of her sleeve was a delight to touch.

"He says it's spread by bad air, but that makes no sense to me. If it were true, why aren't more people sick? We all breathe the same air. I think your water idea makes so much more sense. Listen." She turned to him and stopped walking, her face earnest and almost beseeching. "After I heard what you were saying the other night I started to think about the cholera in India. The afternoon before my father died he drank water with his whiskey. I drank only tea, as well as my stepmother. With a little sherry, that is," she added in an undertone. "And the servants drink copious amounts of water all day, as they work. Only my stepmother and I survived. I thought you should know, it might help your proof."

Snow lost track of what she was saying for a moment as he was jostled from behind, only slightly, but enough to arouse his suspicions. He whipped around but saw no one behind him. The sidewalk crowd was as busy as ever. He had been a fool to go out with her like this, he thought. Even though Mango had abandoned his attacks for a week, that meant nothing. There was still a risk. He turned back to Lillian.

"What's the matter?"

"Nothing, nothing. Please, go on. But let's head back to my house. I just remembered something I must finish." He looked ahead of them, unable to disguise his sense of caution.

She paused, stubborn, and obviously aware of his fear. "You act like a man who think's he's being followed. What—"

Snow never heard the rest of her sentence. From the shadows of an alley off Albemarle Street rushed the same white dog as before, who this time leaped at Snow's throat with the agility of a Spanish dancer. Luckily the dog's first snap missed, and its teeth closed around Snow's collarbone instead of his jugular. A frantic, high-pitched growl came from its throat, as if it were in pain. Its short legs scrabbled at Snow's coat, ripping the fabric.

Pedestrians backed off, shrieking. Snow grappled with the animal, trying to pull it off. Blood ran down his arm as the dog's teeth broke skin. Snow remembered the fight in the pit and closed his hands around the dog's throat. It weakened, and let go.

With a curse Snow flung the animal from him against a brick wall. It didn't pause, and within half a second it had thrown itself on Snow again, this time glancing its teeth off Snow's forehead and then dropping down, trying to tear a chunk out of Snow's right pectoral muscle, just below his armpit. Even in his panic, Snow searched the shadows for Mango. He was ready to bargain. He tried again to close his hands around the dog's throat. The dwarf's final method of self-protection was still too much for Snow. Blood dripping from his torn scalp began to blind him.

"He smells something," Snow heard Lillian shout, through the frantic growls. "Get your clothes off. Someone has smeared something on your jacket. I can see it."

She's still with me, he thought. Blind now with blood from his forehead, and with waves of cold sweat washing over him, he felt her hands grasp his jacket by the collar.

"Get your left arm out of the sleeve," she shouted. "Don't touch the outside." He pulled as best as he could, keeping up a one-handed throttling of the dog's thick neck. His left arm was useless now, anyway. She yanked at the rest of the garment. As before, the animal loosed his jaw's grip and fell to the ground, letting Lillian pull away the rest of the right sleeve.

She tossed the jacket away, and the dog leaped after it, pouncing on the ripped wool as if it were some prize rabbit. Its jaws were frothing now, its growls more like gasps. Snow was forgotten.

Lillian, breathless, said, "There was something smeared on your coat. It drove the dog mad. The man who jostled you must have done it."

Snow stumbled over to a wall, where he sank to the pavement, his head between his knees. He was afraid he would faint. He still could hardly see for the blood in his eyes. Speaking was beyond him. For a minute he wondered if Lillian had lost courage and left him, but then he heard her again.

"I've got some water from a street vendor." She sloshed a bucket beside him, and he reached for it with cupped hands, without thinking. Her strong hand grabbed his wrist. "Stop it!" she cried out. "Are you out of your senses?"

The realization of what he had nearly done made him almost as weak as his wounds. Within a day or two, he could have been one more cholera statistic for Caleb's lists. "Close your mouth," she said. As he obeyed, cold water splashed over his face and he could see again. But he kept his eyes closed, savoring the feel of her fingers, even the pain they caused, as she washed his various gashes. He finally opened them and looked at her crouching before him, her dress and face splattered with his blood.

Mango, he thought. "Did you see a dwarf?" he asked.

"Don't talk. Let me finish, and then we can get back to your house and send for the police."

"No. It's no use." The idea of explaining it all to her exhausted him. His dizziness returned.

"Do you think you can walk?" His protest against the police didn't seem to bother her. She stood beside him and held out a hand, which he used to pull himself up. Both eyed the dog, still slavering over Snow's coat.

A short wave of nausea, and then he was fine. "Yes. Did you see anyone who might have done it? A dwarf?"

She looked at him, frowning, and shook her head.

"Let's go, then."

They didn't exchange a word the entire way back to Sackville

Street, but endured in shared silence the stares of passersby. At his door Mrs. Jarrett's shocked, hoarse scream got no reaction from either of them.

Snow dragged himself up the stairs. He shouted down, "A large can of boiled water, please, Mrs. Jarrett." Then he shut the door.

Lillian leaned against his desk, her hands behind her on his papers. Snow was stirred even by the way she touched his things. Against her fingers they seemed to take on a new, animate life of their own.

"Perhaps, Dr. Snow, you had better explain to me what this is all about."

3

It was dark outside before he finished his story. During her questions and his explanations, he had probed, cleaned, and bandaged the two main gashes on his collar bone and chest. The damage was far less than he thought. He wouldn't need stitches, and strength was coming back to his left arm.

They sat by candlelight and waited for Mrs. Jarrett to bring them supper. Lillian had sent a message to Olympia saying she was delayed.

"Someone is after you, that's certain," said Lillian. "But I still don't see why you are so sure Sir Philip is involved. It seems incredible."

She mentioned Sir Philip's name as if he were merely a social acquaintance. Snow hadn't yet had the nerve to ask her any questions about herself, especially about her scene with Constable at the party two nights ago.

"The salt on his shoes, don't you see? Like that man in the ditch. There has to be a connection, it's just too much of a coincidence. At first, as I said, I thought it was some fanatic religious group. But they would hardly be so—" Snow broke off, remembering that he had been vague about Mango, and hadn't said a word about Sophie. "They would hardly be so violent," he ended, knowing it sounded lame.

"And what about your friend, Mr. Beersdon? What does he think? Did he ever see the dwarf?"

169

Snow sighed. "No. I hardly know about Caleb anymore. I used to think he was on my side, but this morning, just before you arrived . . ." It was then that Snow remembered Caleb's complaint about the wallpaper: a housewife in a house with fancy, colored wallpaper, where three children and the housemaid died of cholera, had proudly added the detail that their piped-in water came from the Southwark and Vauxhall Water Company.

"What is it?" asked Lillian.

Snow sat up straight, leafing, with one hand, through the notes he had been taking with Caleb. "I just remembered something that I almost figured out this morning, just before . . ." He found the list, and started searching. Then he stopped. "But this will bore you. I can wait." This was the moment he had dreaded ever since she arrived; there was no further excuse for her to stay. Her clothes were clean, his story was told. He braced himself for his final question of "When can I see you again?"

"No, no. I don't mind," she was saying. "But if I'd be in your way . . ."

In his way! With her there he'd work even harder. He explained to her, quickly, what he was looking for, and then sat with the notebooks on his desk until he found the right entry. It was number 356. He then went to the shelf, found bottle number 356, and held it up to a candle. Of course it looked just like all the others. He decanted it into a clear test tube. "A proven example of water from the Southwark and Vauxhall Water Company."

"What can you do with it?" she asked.

"Well, it would be stupid to try once more to isolate organisms from the water. Those got me nowhere so far. In fact, a few years ago another doctor, Farr, tried to find a difference between the two water companies and found nothing. Or at least nothing to fit in with his theories, which are quite different from mine."

"Couldn't there be some test neither of you has tried yet? That's what I always imagined men doing in medical school; fiddling with vials and smoking tubes, testing things."

Snow laughed. "All right. There are tests I haven't done, and others I have done but perhaps didn't do perfectly last time. But I'll need a control, a normal sample."

Just then Mrs. Jarrett appeared with a steaming kettle and a

170

tray full of sandwiches. Lillian gestured to the kettle. "What about your own water?" she asked. "Southwark and Vauxhall?"

"No, Lambeth." He had paid their bills often enough, but he still boiled it. "Just the thing. I didn't want any tea, anyway. It's too hot tonight." He poured half the kettle into a clean glass flask and placed it back on the tray.

"Waste of all that firewood," muttered Mrs. Jarrett. "You should ha' said something before I boiled it up." She swished out with a poisonous look at Lillian.

Lead content? Arsenic level? Alkalinity? Acidity? His mind ran through these and other tests, unsure of what he was even seeking. He knew of only one limitation; he had exactly four ounces of water to use. Any tests had to take less than that.

He took off one ounce and boiled it dry, scraped up the white residue and weighed it. He put it in a hand-wound centrifuge and spun it for twenty minutes, pulled out the sediment with a dropper, tried to burn it, dye it, melt it with phosphates. Nothing happened.

Lillian watched, not speaking.

With another ounce he gave one last try at the microscope and cursed the dead protozoa that floated across the visual field, and the antennae of a brown cockroach which must have been in the pipes. He filtered it and filtered it again, ran it through tubes, boiled more dry, shone candlelight through it, gaslight, light from burning sulphur. Foul smells rose into the air, but nothing happened.

Lillian watched.

With the third ounce he tried reactions with magnesium, sodium carbonate, crystals of naphtha, bile syrups. He even got out a magnet and examined any possible reaction with it.

Lillian watched, silent, breathing more heavily now.

There was one ounce left.

Snow wondered how long it would be before he was ready to take it into a church and have it exorcised. His arm and shoulder suddenly began throbbing. He knew he was getting close to being too tired to do any useful work. He was ready to weep with frustration. He paced the room and felt more irritated every minute. He wondered if he could think more clearly with Lillian gone.

She looked restless, and no longer stared at his experiments with such intensity. Instead she was looking around the room, perhaps musing on its owner, he liked to think. He, too, looked around, and his eyes fell on the wilted-looking dinner tray that Mrs. Jarrett had neglected to clear. Lately she had become more lax in her methods. The house seemed a mess. He couldn't remember when his sheets had last been changed, or when hot water had been delivered to his room. And the food had got less edible every day, tasteless, dull. Tonight he'd had to send her back for the salt.

"Salt," he said out loud, so unexpectedly that Lillian jumped. He picked up the salt cellar and held it in the palm of his hand, its absurd feet shaped like animal paws, the tiny spoon jutting out. Salt on a dead man's shoes. Sea salt. He raced to the bookshelf and pulled out his old chemistry text.

"What is it?" she asked. "What have you found?"

He shook his head for silence. He had to make an effort to keep his hands from shaking. He found the experiment he was looking for, and quickly scanned his shelves for the correct reagents. Thank God they were all there.

Lillian was standing now, leaning over him as he worked.

To the last ounce of water from the bottle he began to add a solution of silver nitrate. He sensed her impatience.

"You see," he explained, "this silver nitrate will cause any salt in the water to bind with the silver and form a heavy silver chloride. It should make a precipitate and form a deposit at the bottom of the tube."

"But if there were salt in the water wouldn't we taste it?"

"No, not in a trace amount."

He watched, holding his breath, as the silver solution went in by drops. The contents of the test tube became cloudy. He swirled it, and a light dust appeared on the bottom. In another minute the dust was half an inch deep.

Neither of them spoke.

He repeated the experiment with water from his kettle. This time the deposit appeared again, but hardly a fraction the size of the first. He poured off the liquid, extracted the deposit, and weighed the two amounts.

The water from the sick household had twenty times as much deposit as the boiled water from his kettle.

"What does it mean?" she asked.

"The salt in the water? In this one bottle, nothing. If it's in all those bottles," he said, waving his arm at shelves of collections

172

from all over the city, "it means that we can separate out one type of water from another. Perhaps Southwark and Vauxhall."

"But why would it be salty? I don't understand. And salt doesn't cause cholera, does it?"

"Wait, and you'll see." Snow took a deep breath. "Can you stay longer, and help me? It's very late."

Without a moment's thought, she said, "Yes, of course."

"We'll have to test every single one of those bottles."

4

It took the rest of the night. Once Snow showed her how, Lillian began measuring into empty vials the proper amounts of silver nitrate, and arranging them, ready for Snow to drip into the water samples. After each experiment, he read out the results while she noted them in a book.

By the end they both had bloodshot eyes and stiff backs. Snow's muscles were throbbing terribly with the trauma of the dog attack. The cut on his forehead started slowly bleeding again.

And they both were avoiding each other's glance, embarrassed beyond words by this incredible breach of propriety they were both committing.

Their time, though, hadn't been wasted. Seventy percent of the bottles with high salt content had come from a house with a cholera case. And when they studied the few records that Snow had on water companies, what they found didn't surprise him.

Each house with the modern, pure, filtered, guaranteed water piped by the Southwark and Vauxhall Company had produced a salty bottle.

Hardly able to speak, Lillian said, once more, "I still don't see it."

Feeling drunk with tiredness, triumph, and unspoken passion, Snow sat on his sofa and laughed. "It's easy. Listen. The Thames is an estuary. From the sea. The only source of salt in the water around London is the tidal flow of the Thames itself. That river receives all the sewage, the refuse, and pollution of two million inhabitants. If you pay for water from the Southwark and Vauxhall Company, that's what you get. They call it filtered, but it must be untreated, cholera-ridden water straight from the Thames."

"Now I understand. You were right all along." She sat next to him. After a long silence she let her head fall on his uninjured shoulder, and he realized she had fallen asleep.

He may have been right, he thought, but this discovery didn't get him that much farther along. Even if water from these bottles caused cholera, what about all the cholera in houses with no piped-in water, where the costermongers had lived, the work-houses, the households which took their water from the corner street pumps? And what about the thirty percent of bottles with salty water from houses whose residents had been perfectly healthy? There were still so many questions to answer.

Studying Lillian's sleeping face, though, he forgot his questions and his worry. Bliss washed over him. For a moment he was afraid to breathe and wake her up. Then he cautiously lifted his right hand and laid it on her hair. A childhood memory of a reverence for softness came back to him, almost a cult of worshipping the rich fluff on a cat's belly, the surface of whipped cream, new grass sprung up in the hay field, or the corner of his worn flannel blanket that he used to comfort himself to sleep. Lillian's hair, loose and falling from its pins, now joined the list.

He savored it for a full ten minutes. Then, hating to do it, he shook her gently. "Miss Aynsworth. Wake up."

She opened her eyes and sat up. She seemed suddenly apprehensive.

"It's all right. You fell asleep. It's very late, almost dawn. I must get you home."

She cleared her throat and smoothed her dress. "Of course. I'm terribly sorry."

"Do you live far from here? I'm afraid it will be difficult to find a cab. I can walk with you and see that you're safe."

"No, not at all. I can manage. It's you they want, not me." She was already gathering up her jacket, and the bag she had been carrying. She seemed brusque and tense. In a moment of wild fantasy, Snow wondered if she had expected him to try to seduce her. She was heading down the stairs.

"Of course not, Miss Aynsworth. I insist—"

By now she had reached the bottom of the stairs. Before opening the street door she turned back to him, suddenly pulled his head toward hers, and kissed him on the mouth. The smell of her breath and skin, still of strawberries as it had been at the dance, flooded over him. His knees felt weak.

Before he could stop her, she was down the front steps and gone. He thought of running after her, but changed his mind. The woman would be more than a match for anyone she happened to meet.

18

1

The waves were bigger than any he'd seen at an English seashore. And bobbing like gulls, floating on the crests, were dark imps with barbs popping from their skin like fishhooks. One of them ran out of the surf, faster than a sandpiper, and straight up Snow's leg. The tips of its little claws sent shivering currents up his thigh. He shouted and jerked his leg out, then woke up.

Mrs. Jarrett was knocking loudly, and calling his name. He untangled his legs from sweat-damp sheets. His muscles were miserably stiff and painful. He checked the bite on his shoulder and saw to his relief that it wasn't going to fester.

Light coming in strips under the heavy curtains showed that it was well past noon. Suddenly he remembered the water in the jars. Southwark and Vauxhall. Lillian. He had gone to sleep the night before without coming to any decision about what to do next. He must get to work immediately.

Mrs. Jarrett's voice reached him again as he sat up, the sounds muffled from the thick door and bed curtains.

"Dr. Snow, wake up. Your father is here. He's been waiting almost half an hour and he's not pleased. You'd better hurry." Her voice held a smug anticipation at a potential conflict.

He dragged himself out of bed and drew the curtains, letting in a midday glare. Pulling on the dressing gown he strode barefoot into the library. His father was ready for him.

"Good morning, John. Or perhaps I should say afternoon. The doctor is keeping virtuous hours, I see."

Old Snow sat glaring in the armchair, his thin legs crossed, a few lingering strands of silver hair combed across the scalp. One strand had escaped and hung long beside his ear, and this unknowing disarray saddened Snow. His father's dry spotted hands fingered a copy of the morning paper.

"Hello, Father. I was up late last night, the entire night actually. Experiments."

The man slowly nodded his head, as if to say, "I know all about that devil's work." Then he cleared his throat and spoke again. "While you've been wasting your morning sleeping off your foolish laboratory messes, I've been to the City, to our bankers. Investment opportunity, enormous potential." His eyes brightened.

Mrs. Jarrett appeared with a tray full of tea, toast, and fruit, and lingered as long as she could, dusting books, straightening tubes and jars. She even started to feed the hedgehogs until the old man's glare chased her out.

Snow poured two cups of tea. He was hungry and wanted toast but was embarrassed to eat in front of his father, who had always considered any food between sunrise and two P.M. to be a slothful indulgence. "What investments, Father? I thought there was nothing left to invest. Other than what we have in the funds. You wouldn't touch that." He handed a cup to his father, who thrust out his lower lip and shook his head. Snow set it down as quietly as he could.

"Wouldn't I?" said his father. "That lump sitting there all those years, earning just enough to keep me in pipe tobacco and mend the fences? It could be earning ten times that!" He picked up the paper and swatted it, as if the letters were solid proof of his words. "The Great Western Gravel Company. Expansion. Five hundred shares, that's what I bought."

Snow tried not to show his panic. He took a sip of tea and burned his tongue. His father's financial instincts were terrible. The last time he had tried an investment scheme was when Snow was still at school, and there was such a loss that Snow had to come home for the rest of the term.

Maybe it wasn't too late to stop him. "Have you discussed this with the solicitors, Father?"

"Damn the solicitors! If they had their way no one would ever buy anything and trade would collapse in a week."

"But, Father—"

"Don't argue with me about this, John. Your poorly informed objections have no weight. If you'd spent some time learning about important things instead of all this piddle we might have got somewhere by now." He looked calmly at the disorder around him, the bottles, the piled papers, chemical equipment, spilled solutions in puddles just as Snow had left them at dawn.

"I'll ask you one last time. Isn't it time you abandoned all this and did something worthwhile? You could get the farm functional again. Your being there would change everything for me."

Snow had been trying to sneak in some toast but he had to put it down. He felt too upset to swallow. He cautiously took another sip of tea to avoid choking on the dry crumbs.

"Father, let me try to explain. I've been working so hard on this cholera thing and I'm just on the verge of finding a cause for it. I was awake all night, and just this morning I pinpointed something. Look, I'll show you."

A remote hope that he could get his father to share his fervor prompted Snow to pull out the salinity notes and bring them over. He spread one of the maps on his father's knees and traced the districts of London with a forefinger. He tried to outline the facts slowly but by the time he reached the part about the water companies his words stumbled with enthusiasm. He could feel his father's impatience, but he persisted despite a warning inner voice.

"You see, these lists show the cases and water supply strongly linked, here, in this area I've colored in, and especially here, where they had indoor plumbing. And if you look—"

"Are you saying that the Southwark and Vauxhall water is polluted?"

"Yes, that's exactly it!"

"Oh, no. They filter their water. I read all about it in the newspaper last year. A new method; through sand beds up beyond Teddington Weir."

"But don't you hear me saying that—"

"The idea, that a water company would knowingly pollute water for houses." The old man swept the papers off his lap, tearing one of the maps, and stood up. "You'd better come up with something stronger than that if you expect anyone to listen to you." He started for the door but stopped halfway, turned around. "Besides, what if it is? How does that prove anything about your precious cholera?"

"But if the water has sewage—"

"Think about it. You say yourself that half the houses in those neighborhoods were healthy. Where's your logic, John?" Snow's father shook his head slowly. "Your trouble is, you think you know what's right and then try to prove it, instead of the other way around. I read the paper, too, you know, even up there in the wilds of Yorkshire."

The door opened and Mrs. Jarrett ushered in Lillian. She smiled at him, glowing, and then stopped short when she saw his father. Snow turned to his father to introduce her, but the man went on talking as if she weren't there. He didn't even look at her, but focused on the retreating figure of Mrs. Jarrett.

Snow's father gestured with the paper which now jutted from his clenched hand like a scepter. "I've read all those letters about you. I know what real scientists, like that Phineas Greeley, think of your work."

He pointed at Snow with the rolled paper. "Johnny, I don't *want* to see you fail at what you're doing. But at this point I don't see how you can do anything else. What makes you think you have what it takes to do science, even if there were any sense to it? Come back to the farm while you still can."

He turned and left, ignoring Lillian.

Snow stood for a moment, not looking at her, his bare feet feeling the gritty dust in the unswept carpet, and his dressing gown growing hotter by the minute. He glanced down at the page of lists he'd been trying to show his father. To his deep embarrassment, tears began welling in his eyes. He frowned and went to a mirror to wipe them away as though a speck of dirt had fallen in.

Lillian came to his side. "He's completely wrong, you know. Parents can't see their children clearly, even when the parents have good hearts. And your father—"

"His heart's rotten," Snow said, afraid to look at her.

"Maybe it is." She was silent for a long time. "I don't know that love for one's child is a given fact. But I *do* know that you are a real scientist, and your work is good, and will get you somewhere."

He finally looked at her. Her face was turned up to him. Her eyes had dark circles under them, but they glowed. She was so beautiful that he found it hard to listen to what she was saying.

"And I know another thing. Whatever your father thinks, you are worthy of love."

This he heard. He put his arms around her and pulled her to him, just holding her. Her breathing rose and fell against his chest. Like that moment at the party, he felt himself invaded by her soul; only this time it wasn't distress that reached him, but an overpowering, enveloping sense of her love. It was far more intimate than kissing or even sex had ever been for him. He felt naked and godlike. He wanted to shout.

She pulled away and looked up at him. He kissed her; desperately trying to hold on to his sense of communion with her, though he knew it was a feeling no one could experience for long without going mad. It faded, but not completely, leaving a warm glow like the last ember of a candle wick. The strawberry smell of her breath replaced it.

She pulled away and smiled at him. "I came here today to tell you that. Even if your father hadn't been here."

"Thank you." He was reluctant to let go of her. "You changed my life." And he meant it; even if she disappeared tomorrow, he would always know how it felt to be loved.

"I also came to say I want to help you more. You said last night that Caleb wasn't happy. Let me do what he used to do." She disengaged herself completely now, and sat on a chair. She looked businesslike and very serious.

"What did you have in mind, exactly?" Part of him loved the idea; but maybe she would distract him. Maybe the work would disgust her.

"Today, for example. Shouldn't we start to do something about all that salinity information? Talk to someone?"

Snow heard the "we" and it sounded right. "You're right. I know just where to begin, too. The Registrar General Office has the history of all the major utility companies. We'll start there. Just let me get dressed."

An hour later Snow and Lillian sat with Caleb in a dingy, high-ceilinged back room of the Fleet Street office of *The Times*. The Registrar General Office had said that all their files on Southwark and Vauxhall had been released to *The Times* the previous week.

Caleb eyed Lillian with mixed interest and distrust. He was still grumpy but had agreed to help Snow find the files he needed. "But what does the salt prove?" asked Caleb. "I still don't quite connect." He leaned with one hand on the door frame, trying to leave but obviously too interested to head back to his desk.

Snow had said nothing to Caleb of the dog attack. His cuts and bruises from the dog fight he had attributed to a fall on a tenement stairway.

"The filtration systems they use should pull out most of the salt. Like the Lambeth water. Either Southwark and Vauxhall's system is useless or they aren't filtering it at all."

"And what do you think you'll find, digging through all that?" Caleb finally left.

Snow turned more pages. It was so dull. Prices of shares, details of the '51 sewer renovations, records of public donations for reconstruction, areas supplied.

"Look at this, Lillian." Snow unfolded a map. "It's the streets they supply, the actual water lines."

On the map the Southwark and Vauxhall Water Company lines were red, the Lambeth lines were green. They crisscrossed on top of each other, tangled like a poorly done tapestry. On a given street, one house might have Southwark water piped in, the next Lambeth, the next Southwark, and so on.

"Do you see this?" Snow's finger traced the colored lines. "It explains everything."

"It looks like a tangled mess to me."

"No, look at it. One of my biggest problems has been that the cases seemed so arbitrary from one street to the next. I thought an entire street would have the same water company. But they don't at all."

Lillian peered over Snow's shoulder. "I see what you mean.

But what about all the cholera cases in this neighborhood?" She pointed to an area of Soho where there was no piped-in water at all. "And I know there's cholera here, too." Her hand covered the East End, Seven Dials, the whole dock neighborhood where thousands were dying. No red or green lines ran through there. Their water could come from anywhere.

"Well it's obvious, isn't it? Most houses there get water straight from the Thames, or a ditch. Even if they get it from a street pump I can't believe that pump water is consistently pure." Despite his confident voice, Snow felt his enthusiasm fade. The only thing he knew for sure was that Southwark and Vauxhall water was salty, not that it caused cholera.

Lillian sat quietly leafing through papers while Snow stayed at the desk, unable to come up with any new ideas. He might as well go home and start looking at the data again. But since he'd gone to all the trouble to get them, he would finish going through the last pile of records.

"Look at this," Lillian said suddenly.

She handed him a folder labeled "Trustees." He leafed through it once, bored, not paying much attention. "You missed it," she said, "Look here." She pointed to a section in print so fine it made his eyes burn to focus on it, but it was worth the pain. Southwark and Vauxhall Water Company was a subsidiary of the Great Western Gravel Company. And the president of the board of trustees for both was Sir Philip Constable.

Snow looked up at her. "Great Western. That's the company my father—"

"Said you should invest in? I heard him, but I only noticed because my stepmother said the same thing. Dr. Greeley was talking about it."

"And Constable—" He looked up at her, suddenly wary. "Hadn't you better tell me about him?"

She lowered her head and pulled her shoulders up. "You mean about the other night, don't you?"

"Of course."

She was silent for a long time. Finally she said, "John." She stopped. It was the first time she had said his name. "John, I can't tell you yet. I need some time to understand. My past is, well, complicated. I promise you, I'll tell you everything as soon as I can."

182

She looked at him then with such earnestness and love that he hadn't the heart to question her.

Snow had already put an explanation together in his mind: most probably, Sir Philip had heard of the water company's poor methods, and had managed to install himself on their board of supervisors, an easy task for an MP. Constable must be planning to expose them. As deputy minister he wanted all the credit for himself, perhaps to boost a fading political career. Why should he want Snow honing in on his discovery? Of course he would ask him to stop investigating.

But even as he thought it out, it seemed absurd, and explained nothing; none of the violence, or that trace of salt on the man's shoes.

Snow felt confused and discouraged. The elation of being in love was already spotted with complications and questions. He forced himself to copy down a few pages of data, and the two left the office.

19

The Ministry of Public Health, housed in a second-rate building from the 1820s, overlooked an unpicturesque curve of the Thames. The opposite side of the river held a soldierly rank of smokestacks from the Lambeth pottery works. From his window, Sir Philip Constable could see ships passing. If he let go of dignity enough to squash his face to the glass he could get a glimpse of fellow members of Parliament hurrying along Whitehall Place.

Since Parliament had closed for the season Constable had spent more and more time in this office. Something about its high, discolored ceiling and the late summer quiet of the nearly deserted building was soothing. He sat for hours at his bare desk, doing nothing, just pressing his hands to the wood surface, his face blank.

He didn't quite do nothing; he counted his heartbeats. They had held a sickly fascination for him as they gradually increased in speed over the course of the drawn-out hot season. Looking at his watch he would count them again. Another minute passed. One hundred fifteen. Another minute. One twenty. Sometimes they skipped, with a tiny jolt in his throat as though a mouse had jumped.

He kept track of the beats on scraps of paper, scrawling the figures in tiny writing, always planning to average them at the end of an hour or the end of the day. But they ended up in his jacket and trouser pockets, turning up when he fished for coins or a pencil. Then he would throw them out and plan to start fresh the next day, more carefully.

He had started the counting at the beginning of the summer when he would only do it once or twice a day, as a curiosity. He began to do it more often. It became a fixed habit, something he would fit in between his sessions in the House, letters, and meetings. And then it took over, so that the reports he had to write and the briefs were done in between the counting. He did less and less work, and would sit at his desk an entire afternoon, silent, unmoving. Counting.

Lawes, his secretary, would stick a head around the door in hourly inquiry, amazed that Sir Philip wasn't shouting out orders and letters to be sent. After a while, Lawes gave up and took long naps instead.

Today it was a morning like the rest; hot, of course, overcast, and sticky. Constable found himself unable to remember what day it was. He took his engagement book from a drawer and turned the page. Thursday. That was right. Yesterday he had met with Bucks. The bench in St. James's. It had been a stupid choice; Bucks stood out in that park like bare feet in a dining room. After talking to the man Constable always felt as if he needed to go home and have a bath.

Constable had been late. His guilt at planning to go out like this had pushed him to actually write two letters and he lost track of time.

Bucks was fuming. "It won't do to keep me waiting like this, sir. I was stared at."

"I'll bet you were."

"Someone might remember the two of us. There's another shipment ready for hauling down to the works."

"Why in the devil's name do you need to bother me about that?" Constable tried to ignore his heartbeats for once.

"I can't ask just anybody, sir. You know that. You know what happened to the last one as didn't hold his tongue." Bucks spit out of the side of his mouth, then looked to see how far it had gone.

Constable felt sick. "Yes, you don't have to remind me." He had never seen the body, but Bucks told him how a fight had been engineered, so it would look like one ditch worker against another. "I wish you could solve these things with less—" He groped for the word.

"I can't," Bucks answered in a flat tone. "Them as I hire have their own ways. Including silence."

"I still don't see why we had to meet."

"No. I don't expect you do. I don't expect you realize the expense of hiring men like the ones we need, who'll do their work, not ask questions, not even wonder about it. I don't expect you do see how much it costs to avoid mistakes like last time."

"I believe that was your mistake, my man, not mine."

"How was anyone to know the fellow came from bloody Yarmouth? And he'd know about salt sand? He never looked like any fisherman to me."

"Never mind that now." Constable took out paper and pencil. "How much this time?"

"Five hundred."

Constable's hand had started to shake so badly that it was hard to write the draft to his banker's, but he hadn't protested.

Now, safe in his office, he knew it wouldn't be long before Bucks would turn up for more. But not today. Today, at least, could be his own. He could spend hours yet, motionless, no decision expected of him, no action. The page in the date book would be blank.

But it wasn't blank. Eleven o'clock, Dr. Phineas Greeley. Damn, he thought. Why isn't he off in Scotland shooting grouse, like the rest of the world? He looked at his watch. Five minutes from now.

Greeley was the last person Constable wanted to see. For Greeley he couldn't put on the frozen mask and stick to the official protocol. He would have to smile. Constable had known him for years, but when they had met last week at Lady Tewksbury's party it was the first time they had spoken in months. And Lillian had been with Greeley.

Lillian. Every time Constable thought of Lillian he had to start again from the beginning of the story, in the simple words you would use to explain an adult dilemma to a child. He thought, Oh yes, Lillian. That one. Remember? From the time before. Here in London. You could see her, now, if you like. And, then, invariably, his thoughts would turn to other things; reports, Bucks, the sewer problem. Like an insomniac, who tries so hard to dream of trees and fields but within three thoughts returns to an image of himself in a coffin.

He knew that when one received a great shock it always took a little time to absorb the idea; a declaration of a war, for example, or the loss of a leg. But it had been well over a week since he'd seen her and his thoughts still circled like a simpleton's. He wondered if his heart condition was affecting his mind. Perhaps it was Lillian's surprising connection with Greeley that put him off.

Eight years ago, when Constable first arrived in London from India, Greeley had been something of a celebrity for his theory about spontaneous regeneration of life. He was at all the parties. He had been presented to the queen on the same day Constable had been knighted five years ago.

Constable's own rise in rank took him by surprise. Until recently, before he became so entangled in this horrid waterworks business, and then felt so ill, there were days when he woke and for long moments couldn't remember who he really was or how he got his title.

Upon his return from India, two years after the massacre near Jampur, he had tried to keep a low profile without actually changing his name. But there had been some unbelievable mix-up in the lists of survivors, and he was named as the missing hero who had been responsible for retrieving the flag. Constable decided later that the government must have needed a figurehead for a few weeks to boost national morale about colonial concerns.

At any rate, within days he found himself eased into a vacant spot in the Foreign Office, and then a year later voted into the Ministry of Public Health. His knighthood, at the minimal level which allowed him to be called 'Sir Philip,' but with no hereditary rank passing on to his children, was supposedly for both his heroism at Jampur and his authorship of a half dozen health reform bills he had written and seen passed in the House of Parliament. In fact, they were the very bills which allowed him to finance the reconstruction of the sewers. On the day of his knighting ceremony, Constable had shared the floor with a host of second-rate bureaucrats receiving smaller medals and honors, including Greeley, and Greeley clearly resented being bunched with such a crowd.

It wasn't long before Constable understood that Greeley was

a man on his way down. There was a paper in *The Lancet* he had been forced to retract. A highly publicized paid lecture series he was scheduled to give was canceled and then Greeley left England for a year. By the time he returned he was a figure from the past, no longer of interest to the newspapers or the medical journals. He kept up a small private practice and published occasional insignificant case studies, or letters to editors that were more gripes than scholarly notes.

Constable, however, quickly started to rise. He saw less of Greeley. But he had always been drawn to the man for some reason. Unless one feels absolute contempt, he thought, it's hard to dislike a man who likes you.

Lawes, stifling a yawn, ushered Greeley into the office. The doctor looked older and pinker in daylight than he had by the gaslight in Lady Tewksbury's ballroom. His suit needed brushing. He was thinner. Constable felt a faint rush of guilt that he didn't look up Greeley now and then. Take him for supper.

"Greeley! Good of you to come by. Wish I could spare more time." Sir Philip's practiced diplomatic chat was intended to leave no doubt with Greeley that he had no more than six minutes.

"Sir Philip." Greeley leaned across the desk to shake hands.

The doctor's hand was sweaty and surprisingly cold for such a hot day.

Greeley said, "It was good to see you last week. That cholera outbreak at the party was terrible."

Constable felt a sinking in his gut. Greeley must know about the sewer scheme. Why else would he be here? Why else would the man be so nervous? "Yes, yes. Tragic." He paused to write down 'one thirty.' "I hear that ten guests died."

"Not really? So many? You'll find the report's exaggerated, I'm sure. None of the people I met. You'll be glad to hear that Mrs. Aynsworth and her daughter are fine."

Constable fought an urge to tell Greeley the whole story, about Lillian, that instant. Her supposed death. Fort Munro. Jampur. Instead, he roused himself to an appropriate response. "Perhaps they should leave the city for a time."

Greeley smiled. "No need for it. If cholera were a contagious disease I would agree with you. But as long as they take proper precautions they are quite safe."

Constable felt an odd surge of hope at hearing this again. If the thing weren't contagious, perhaps he could sleep more easily. "Not contagious? But surely—"

"Not from person to person. If it were contagious quarantines would prevent its spread. But look at East Worthington."

"Where's that?"

"A village in Surrey. Last month half of the village fell ill and they cordoned off the place. Not a soul left the area, they all swore. Yet within a week two of the neighboring villages down the river were just as bad."

"So you would say, for example, that a leak of some sort into the water supply here in London—"

"Not healthful, definitely not. But not a cause of cholera." Greeley smiled with closed lips. "You have nothing to worry about, Sir Philip."

"Why, no, it never occurred to me to worry for myself. I feel safe in my neighborhood. And if the thing hasn't got me by now . . ." He laughed a friendly, meaningless chuckle. "Now, what can I do for you this morning?"

"Ah, yes. A little matter I thought you might be concerned in. I hardly know how to begin." Greeley picked at the cloth of his cuffs and fell silent.

Constable felt it would be a better tactic to keep asking the questions, to retain a small amount of control. "Is something troubling you, Greeley?"

"To tell the truth, Constable, things are not going as well as one could hope. As you know, I used to enjoy somewhat of a reputation for my scientific work."

"Yes, of course. I don't know why you put it in the past tense like that." The lie was like the delicate touch of a fencing foil at the beginning of a match.

"Please. Let's both be honest. You know my story as well as I do. No wing of Guy's Hospital will ever be named after me. You won't ever see my name in a medical dictionary followed by 'disease,' 'sign,' or 'suture.' "

Constable was unable to reply. To say "you're wrong" would be ridiculous. Greeley glanced at the piece of paper where he had just written his last heartbeat count. Greeley seemed to take it for granted that Constable was making notes for some governmental purpose.

"Have you published any research papers recently?" Constable finally asked this just to say something.

"Papers? One must have ideas to write papers. I used to have ideas. Where did they all go?"

Greeley pushed his chair back and became lost in what he was saying, in a way that made Constable think perhaps he knew nothing after all and was simply here for some favor.

"Your mind is still functioning as far as I can tell," said Constable with a slight laugh.

"No. You don't understand. Back in the twenties my brain felt so full it was hard to write it down fast enough. Theories considered brilliant at the time. But all I hear now when I propose anything is, 'Where's the proof?' That's all they want to know. 'Can we reproduce it?' All they seem to want is a description of an experiment and its results; any interpretations or possibilities are apparently beyond their understanding."

Greeley took out a handkerchief and touched at his forehead, a gesture so melodramatic and calculated to show distress that Constable's doubts returned.

Greeley clenched the handkerchief in his fist. "Confound their infernal nitpicking! What happened to the days when the impeccable logic and elegant prose of a theory was enough to guarantee publication?"

Constable decided to play it safe. Greeley was clever and could hide his intentions. It was better to take no risks. "It's a shame to see your work go unrecognized, Greeley. I have some influence in these matters. Perhaps, as soon as we are in session again, you could have a little ceremony with the queen that would at least leave you as Sir Phineas."

Greeley acted as if he hadn't heard, but Constable spotted a faint flush on each cheek.

Greeley went on speaking. "And with all this cholera madness everywhere, it's such an opportunity to find out interesting material. There's this fellow Snow. What do you think of him?"

Snow. That clinched it. Greeley must know it all. Constable felt his heart rate soar. He stalled while he counted. "Snow? John Snow? Surely no one is really taking him seriously?" He finished. One thirty. He pulled another scrap from under his blotter.

"Some people are taking him seriously. He seems to think there's something wrong with the water supply. All nonsense, of course. You'd be the best person for him to talk to about that."

"Yes. Of course. We did have a little talk."

At times Constable wished Snow would move faster, finish

190

finding out whatever he could, tomorrow, today even. It would take so much of the aching load off Constable's back. He would welcome a chance to confess. His heart did the little mouse jump again and he breathed heavily for a moment. There was a pain, too, a new one, shooting across his chest. It was gone almost before he noticed it.

"Are you feeling quite well? You look a bit gray. All this sickness about . . ." Greeley pulled out his handkerchief again.

"No, it's nothing. Just some mild palpitations. I've had them before. Perhaps you have noticed. I know I don't look as healthy as I used to."

"Oh, no, Sir Philip. Not at all. Quite fit. Trim. Working too hard, if anything."

Constable didn't listen. He had only to look in the mirror. There was a dark flush on either side of his nose, a hollow at his jawline. The swelling under his eyes grew deeper every week. And a puffiness had started about a month ago in his hands and feet. He could no longer remove the gold ring from his first finger. At this moment it was cutting into the flesh, throbbing with the heartbeats. One hundred and fifty.

"Overwork? Possibly. I am quite busy; perhaps you already know. I stand a chance to take over the Ministry of Health at the next election. At any rate, Greeley, I will try to put your name forward in two weeks' time for at least an O.B.E., if not more. But I can't promise anything, you understand."

"No, no. Of course. It's most kind of you, Sir Philip. Most kind. As a matter of fact, it is exactly what I was going to ask you about. So difficult to begin that sort of thing. You're the only member I know well enough. If there's anything I can do to—"

"No, please, don't mention it. We are all here to help one another, right?" He again gave that generic chuckle, and this time Greeley chuckled back.

20

The neighborhood always looked worse in summer than in winter, thought Constable. But never a slum, not quite that. Nothing like that, really. As Constable let himself in, the piano music floated over him. If he hadn't been so wrapped in his worries he would have heard it two streets away. All the windows were open because of the heat.

He probably should have spent more on the house, bought something in a better area. But he just didn't have that kind of cash. Aside from this separate, secret establishment for the boy, he had his official household near Buckingham Palace to maintain as well, dinner parties to give. And there was all the entertaining at his club.

The boy's piano playing was improving, there was no doubt about that. The easy Mozart sonata rose above mere notes into a perfectly executed miniature. He measured phrases with a subtle ear, using just enough rubato on the minor cadences to show he heard every change of key and felt it.

The boy probably didn't care where he lived, anyway. As long as he had a piano he was oblivious to his surroundings. Too serious for a child of nine.

If it hadn't been for Paul, Constable wouldn't have worried so much. For himself he didn't care. It was Paul's future that tormented him.

The illegitimacy was nothing, that made little difference these days. As long as Constable stayed safe and beyond reproach, the boy was safe too. But if Constable should go under? He still hadn't quite given up hope, still tried to think of a way out. Even if it meant coming forward with some of the truth. Anything to keep it all from surfacing.

It all started a year after Constable managed to pass the sewer reform bills, just when Great Western Gravel merged with Southwark and Vauxhall. Great Western was contracted to do most of the sewer reconstruction work under the streets.

When he really thought about it, the turning point must have been the day he saw Bucks for the first time. God, if only he'd been elsewhere that morning.

The man had been so respectful, then. Obsequious, but not oily. He had approached Constable after a meeting with the shareholders of Great Western Gravel.

"Sir, might I have a word with you?" Bucks had asked, hat in hand. "I know you're looking for a works manager."

"I don't handle that sort of thing, my man. If you inquire at the office they'll tell you with whom to speak." He had kept walking, but Bucks walked with him.

"Yes, I know that. But you're the only one who might understand a system I know about, from engineering before, in Manchester. To save money. Lots of money."

Constable had kept on walking, so quickly that Bucks's breaths came short through the explanation. Bucks assured him that the shortcuts Constable had the power to enact would have no effect on the purity of the water. Simply minor adjustments to too-strict regulations.

The first "adjustment" saved a thousand pounds, most of which went to lease this house and furnish it for the boy. The rest went to Bucks.

Constable had tried to make a few trips down into the works, to see exactly where the alterations and shortcuts were happening. He found that the dripping, glistening underground passageways were unbearably claustrophobic. He couldn't concentrate on any of the foreman's complicated explanations and would emerge into daylight more confused than before.

The money came in a regular way, and Constable found himself spending it as soon as it appeared. Soon Bucks became more secretive and less inclined to answer Constable's questions.

Just as Constable had determined to rid himself of the whole loathsome project somehow, cholera had broken out in London. And this John Snow had turned up, nosing into things, stumbling along like a fool and to Constable's amazement actually finding something. Fine, he thought. Find what you can. Do it soon.

It made sense, Greeley's noncontagion theory. It made perfect sense. Constable clung to the thought tenaciously, willing all other suspicions out of his mind.

Paul had come halfway down the stairs to meet Constable.

"I've learned a new piece!" he called out. Too impatient to wait he turned and ran back up the stairs and started playing again. Constable followed him.

At the top of the stairs he felt a rush of blood to his head, a sudden weakness so debilitating he had to grip the rails to keep from swaying. His heartbeats skipped erratically and pulsed with violence. This was more than a mouse in his heart. A weasel. Or a toad. He stood until the beats were steady again, waited a full minute while he counted. One forty-four. The boy didn't notice the delay.

Paul finished the Mozart again. "Wasn't it good?"

Constable heard Paul's voice through a roaring in his head, and had to wipe chill sweat from his forehead. "Well done, Paul," he managed to call out, then walked into the room. "Where is Mr. Romney?

"Practicing violin." Paul sounded impatient. The feeble and flat scratching was so soft Constable hadn't heard it before.

He had placed the boy with this relative of an old servant. An aging violinist who used to play with the Covent Garden Opera House orchestra, it was he who had discovered the boy's music.

"Here, listen, I wrote this one myself." Paul pushed a creased sheet of manuscript paper onto the music rack.

The boy's feet dangled from the bench, too short to reach the pedals. He began to play again without a trace of either shyness or precocious showing-off.

Constable recognized the melody, a simple Bach chorale he himself had sung to the boy when he was just a toddler. But now it was strangely altered, so that its minor intervals were emphasized. Paul had written out a set of six variations alternating in a minor and major key. They were intricate, sober, and mature.

Paul was a pale child. His thin hair, very straight, was cut in a line across his forehead. He looks just like me, thought Constable. I wonder that he's never noticed it before. The boy's only resemblance to Lillian was in a wide bridge to his nose, a tendency to get freckles, and a reddish highlight to his dark brown hair. And of course, the music.

It was impossible for Constable to look at him without imagining where the boy might be now if things had turned out otherwise; a street rat in Calcutta, eaten by disease, worn to a skeleton. Living in some hole, treated like a dog for his white skin and Indian talk. If Constable hadn't rescued him—perhaps he would have been better off, after all.

When he stopped playing his face smiled with the same enthusiasm a normal boy might have for a game of cricket.

"Did you like it?"

"A very grown-up piece. What about your school work?" He finished another count. One sixty.

Paul began to pick at a loose chip of ivory on one of the piano keys. "Oh, it's all right, I suppose. I just don't like reading much. Aren't there any schools where they do only music?" The restless scratching at the ivory irritated Constable, who didn't answer.

"Where is my mother?" Paul asked, looking up, casually, a little nervous, and smiling in an adult way. A planned smile. He must have been brooding for days on the right moment to ask this question.

Constable was as taken aback as if the boy had struck him. He hadn't asked about a mother for years. Constable had a vision of Lillian at Lady Tewksbury's, holding on to Snow's arm and staring at him, white faced. It was the first he had been able to focus on her since that night.

"Your mother is in heaven, Paul." He immediately regretted the answer. It was just the sort of lie he hated. And what if things turned out differently?

"Oh, I see. With the rabbits?" Paul didn't wait for an answer, but began to fiddle with a tune as if he had only asked about a toy or plans for supper. He broke into a Mozart sonata and paid no more attention to Constable. It was impossible to tell if the answer satisfied him.

The lyrical tune and mathematical perfection of the Mozart formed an easy background to Constable's thoughts. He poured himself a sherry and sat by the piano in a worn armchair. He was

195

finally able to concentrate on Lillian. It was all so simple. He would ask her to marry him. Tomorrow. He would tell her about Paul. They could marry in two weeks, in any registry office.

He would tell her everything. The struggle he'd had to try to see her, when they said she was lying dead in the other room, with a dead child. The escape across the desert from Jampur. Well, perhaps not all of that. The wet and screaming boy delivered to him, two years later in Calcutta, as he was waiting to ship out. With an unsigned letter in illiterate Hindi, which wandered, begged for money, and really explained nothing.

The child had been dressed in shreds of fabric so filthy it was only as he went to burn them that he recognized Lillian's initials on the cloth, a piece of a bed sheet. The boy had been painfully thin, with bruises around his eyes, burn marks on his feet. He would touch nothing to eat except a weak rice gruel.

The day the boat left, when Constable heard the first long wail from the harbor, there had been a moment when he thought of leaving the boy with the childless woman who ran a seamen's boarding house; she had offered, happily. It was a thought long enough to plan details, money arrangements. She would have raised him well enough. No one would ever have known.

The moment passed. He kept the child.

And if the worst came to pass, if he was caught and tried, at least the boy would be back with his mother.

One twenty. Not bad. He tried to imagine sitting in the parlor in his Portland Square house, Lillian across from him, sewing, Paul playing the piano in the next room. For the first time in weeks he felt relaxed and calm. He believed it could all happen.

21

Greeley parted the canvas flap which served as a door and peered inside the tent.

The elephant keeper sat in the dust while Henry hunched in a chair in front of a cracked mirror. A candle shone on his white face as he slowly rubbed in a salve to darken his skin.

They were surrounded by the dark canvas walls of a makeshift circus which Henry had persuaded the authorities to let him maintain at the zoo. As before, Greeley had reluctantly agreed to meet Henry here. Greeley was in a worse mood than last time. At least he hadn't spent the previous night drinking champagne. He had just come from his meeting with Constable, and the man's promise to help him toward a knighthood seemed unreliable. Doubt gnawed at him like an ulcer. Also, he was trying to get up his nerve to propose to Lillian.

To procrastinate, he had come here, even though the note from Henry had said, "Come by any afternoon this week. The show starts at six."

Henry caught sight of Greeley. "Ah, you've come. Good. I'll be right with you; just let me finish this face job." He then ignored Greeley and continued with his makeup as if he were some transcendent opera star. "Ajit, how are the ticket sales tonight?" he asked the dark man.

"Sir, yes. No sales."

"Damn you. Were there sales or not?"

"No crowd comes anymore. Less each night. Wounded monkey died today." Ajit went over to the elephant and started painting the tips of its tusks with a blue wash. The elephant held its head very still.

"I suppose the whole bloody city will be dead of cholera before long, eh Greeley? Then we can have it to ourselves. You, me and the elephant. We didn't need so many monkeys, anyway. Shooting them was well worth the sport."

Ajit didn't answer, nor did Greeley.

"Did you make it to Brook Street today?" asked Henry. Greeley almost answered, then he realized the question was addressed not to him but to Ajit. Brook Street was where Lillian and Olympia lived.

"Sir, yes." The dark man splashed some of the blue water by mistake and it trickled down the elephant's trunk, dripping into the dust.

"Well? Did you watch?"

"Of course. The older lady not going out. The young lady went out. Went to house of the doctor again."

Henry seemed unaffected by this news, but it interested Greeley. He hadn't known Lillian was ill.

"And, sir, a man walked by three times. He waited but did not go in."

Henry stopped the face work and sat up. "The devil. What man? What time? This is just the kind of thing I wanted you to tell me straight away, and here it is eight o'clock at night!"

"You were not here. A plain man, Britain man. Less hair. Rich man. Morning time."

Henry pulled open a drawer in the table and took out a packet of paper, bound up with thin pink ribbon. He flipped through the letters, peeled one off, and tossed it at Greeley, who had to retrieve it from the floor.

"Take a look at that, Greeley. But wait; perhaps you didn't know that our Lillian had taken up the cause of that Dr. Snow?"

"That's who the doctor is?" Greeley felt confused and vaguely jealous. "What's she doing with him?"

Henry was apparently still too agitated by Ajit's news to finish his face job. He paced around in the small space. "God only knows. Probably some social work. Or it may be that the poor

198

devil is in love with her. He hasn't a chance. She's above his level. But that's not important, and it has nothing to do with what you've got in your hand."

"Sir, there is more. Please. I followed this man, as you asked." Ajit sounded hurt. "He pondered a thing."

"How do you know that?"

"Not difficult. His hands went like so." Ajit worked his hands in exaggerated tension, the fingers pulling each other like thick rope. "And he muttered, he sweated, he wiped his brow and his bare head."

"Did you follow him home?"

"Sir, not home. He received to office. To the House of Westminster. Tomorrow I show you."

Henry turned his face up to the ceiling, gazing at nothing with an ecstatic smile. "Tonight, the plan can begin. Finally."

Then, more sober, he went back to the table and finished his face oils. "That's who I'm worried about, Greeley. Sir Philip Constable's after her." He looked brown and bizarre. Only a dim-witted child would take him for anything but an Englishman with face paint. "But I'll throw a cog in his works. One look at these letters and he'll throw her over in an instant." He faced Greeley full-on now, his eyes too wide and very white. "And it's *me* she'll turn to, you'll see."

Soon it would be time for the show to start. The elephant waved his trunk gently. Ajit sighed and picked up the brush.

Greeley still hadn't opened the letter. It was crisp and yellowed at the edges.

"Go on," said Henry. "Read it." He smiled, his teeth too white in the brown, smeared face.

Greeley unfolded the thing.

September 5, 1843

Dearest Lily,

Meet me under the mango tree when the moon rises, and I will have a boat. I can get you back to the house well before dawn. I have a place we can go.

Philip

At first it meant nothing to Greeley. His only response was a vague distaste that Henry should show him such a thing. Then the realization hit him.

Philip. Constable and Lillian. Greeley had seen their meeting at Lady Tewksbury's. And Greeley knew something Henry probably didn't; that Constable had spent time in India. It took Greeley a long moment to believe it, but it must be true. And then he realized that Henry didn't know yet; Henry thought it was a coincidence that both men were named Philip.

Henry started laughing. "Yes, that's right. Our young lady." He reached out and deftly snatched back the letter.

"But Bince, don't you realize . . ." Greeley couldn't believe Henry hadn't made the connection. "These letters can't help you at all." Even as he said it, Greeley realized that the letters could, on the other hand, help *him* a great deal.

"What the devil do you mean?"

"If you wanted to blackmail Constable they might get you somewhere. But you can hardly make the man spit on the girl by showing him his own love letters to her."

Henry stared at Greeley, his mouth open slightly. "You mean—this 'Philip'—Constable—"

"You didn't know the fellow was in India for five years? These are *his* letters. They must have been doing it on the sly."

Henry didn't answer. The muscles of his face were slack. Greeley had never seen a man, sane or not, look so disappointed. "You have no idea how long I'd planned—these letters were like gold to me." To Greeley's horror, Henry began to cry, his face twisting out of its handsome lines.

Despite his distaste, Greeley went and sat next to the other man, put an arm around him. "Buck up, old fellow. Things will look up," he said, forcing himself to stroke Henry's shoulder. "Besides, I have a plan."

22

1

There was too much furniture in the room. In this stifling mid-day heat, Lillian felt suffocated by the sofas with their down cushions, the Louis XIV bergère chairs, the thick purple drapes and carpets. The air smelled dusty. The drapes were tightly closed, to keep out cholera vapors and the sun.

She already forgot the name of the woman who'd asked her to perform at this hastily arranged salon concert. A distraction from the cholera, the woman had said. Lillian and Olympia arrived so late that there were only two seats, near the front and too close to the piano.

She was late because she had waited until the last possible minute to leave the house, hoping to get a note from John Snow. After their session in the office of *The Times* their parting had been cool, and she already regretted not telling him everything about Constable. There was no word from him, though. She ached to see him today, and had a wild hope that he'd be here at the recital, though it seemed completely unlikely.

She looked around as well as she could, but didn't spot him, and gave up. The salon was very crowded. Obviously the epidemic wasn't keeping the upper classes from enjoying their bit of music.

She had missed the introduction so she didn't know who the boy was. He played well. His dark head swayed and trembled above his sailor collar and the eyebrows frowned in concentration.

Lillian was on next. She wasn't nervous. In fact, she was washed over by elation at the prospect of performing. She always loved it. At home when she practiced she felt self-conscious, afraid of making as much volume as she liked, afraid the neighbors would complain. But here, where she was supposed to be heard, her voice could rise to a true swelling ring of sound.

The boy finished and stood shyly waiting for the polite applause to end.

The audience doesn't realize how good he is, thought Lillian. He probably doesn't know, either. I hope he gets some decent training. She forgot him as she made her way to the piano, settled her music, and readied herself to sing.

She knew the Schumann songs so well by now that she could sing and think of other things at the same time. Her eyes wandered around the room and scrutinized the audience, careful to make no eye contact. She assessed them. The music lovers' bodies were relaxed, their heads alert, looking straight at her. There were the bored ones with the crossed legs, the tight smile, the inward glance. And the ones engaged in blatant conversation, just using her music as a backdrop. She searched again, half-heartedly for John Snow's face. It was unlikely, but still—

Then she spotted Philip Constable and the boy sitting together, the man's hand protectively cupping the small shoulder, the boy sucking on a candy and listening to her singing. Her first sense was a childish disappointment that it should be him and not John Snow. An image came to her of Snow's bleeding shoulder and chest after the dog attack. Could this really be who had done it? It seemed impossible. She stole another look at him, and the boy on his lap.

Then she realized.

For a moment it was as though the lamps in the room flared up for a second or two, and the volume of her singing even went up in her ears. The lies she had been told broke on her. The baby wasn't dead. He was here in front of her with his father's eyes and chin. Her father's mouth. And her own musical gift.

202

Her father had told her the baby died. Her father must have lied. The song faltered for a measure but she caught it again. She knew the notes so well that she functioned on some inner mechanism which pushed her along.

And if her father had known about the baby all along, perhaps he had known about Philip, too, that he was alive, where to reach him. That must be why he had left her so much money. "I'll make it up to you," he had said.

A suspicion began to grow as counterpoint to the expanding melody of the song. What if she were wrong? What if the boy were just some distant relation to Sir Philip?

A second doubt hit her, much worse than the first. What if Sir Philip himself was not the soldier she'd known? What if at Lady Tewksbury's she had imagined his glances and his embarrassment? The name wasn't uncommon. And what if Snow himself were mad, accusing this innocent official of wild threats and impossible plans?

The most disturbing thought of all, surfacing repeatedly through the bars of the Schumann, was the possibility that there was no young officer at all, never had been. She could have imagined the whole thing in a fever. No lover, no pregnancy, no dead child. There was no proof. Even the handwriting on the music, this very copy in front of her, was smudged. It could have been anyone's. The silver lines on her abdomen could have been from a pox, or some terrible rash when she was too young to remember.

And those little shirts that had lain in her box on the top shelf of the wardrobe? They could have belonged to a servant's baby. Or no baby, they could have been just shirts made for a doll, or for a sewing exercise. They were gone now and could prove nothing for her.

She was now on the sixth song of the cycle. Her concentration was failing. She smudged a string of notes on the piano and missed an entrance, hoping no one would notice. She looked at the boy. His eyebrows had gone up in childish derision, without malice. He noticed.

She didn't want to sing any longer. The notes started to sound like croaks to her, her voice harsh and ugly. She finally reached the end of the last song and somehow made her way to her seat amidst loud clapping.

"So polished, my dear," said Olympia. "In a different life you could have been a professional."

"Thank you. It was nothing, really." Lillian found that her voice was shaking so she just smiled at people. She kept looking over at Constable, and every time, she found his eyes on her. The boy, unconcerned, played with a cat that had wandered in from another part of the house, stroking its back and apparently telling it some story, for he looked as though he was chattering.

Two more performers went to the piano and began a Beethoven sonata for violin and piano. The violin whined in and out of pitch, and the cadences were overly dramatic. Lillian tried hard to block her mind from listening, so that she could think.

At Lady Tewksbury's she hadn't been surprised to see him, just mortified. The surprise was all at the opera. She never did recover any more of the pearls; just the two that John Snow had given her.

Even in the swell of her disorientation, her love for Snow didn't change shape or lessen one bit. It was like a live thing she carried inside her, a warm and dangerous animal hidden in her soul. The feelings she'd had for Constable ten years ago were nothing compared to this; this was based on no vaporish dream, but on the way the man's whole being shone through his eyes. It began almost the moment she saw him, at the party, and it was a feeling so new and unknown that for a moment she thought she was going mad, or had the first touch of cholera. After they danced she knew she wasn't mad. Only the terrible luck of running into Philip, and then the stampede afterward, had kept her from saying something to Snow that very night.

Constable still sat behind her, probably with the boy, but she stared straight ahead. At the end of the party, during the cholera panic, he had grabbed her arm so hard it hurt and pushed her toward the top of the stairs violently, apparently not hearing her protests. When Dr. Greeley joined her on the other side with Olympia, she felt cornered and wanted to pull free but the crowd was too tight to do anything but move toward the door.

"What happened?" she had whispered to him. "How are you here? I thought—"

"Don't talk," he had said. Or that's what she thought he said. Maybe he didn't hear her, maybe he had said "Don't fall." Maybe he hadn't spoken. The noise had been overwhelming, of crashing glassware and ripping silk. Men bellowed directions. As

204

she went through the door she had heard the drums starting up again.

And then they had all been in a carriage together: Greeley, Olympia, Philip. All were silent except for Olympia.

"I knew it. I just knew it as soon as the lady fell. Dear Lord, first India and now this. I told you, Lillian, we shouldn't have gone. Not one foot out of the house from now on, dear, that's my advice. I knew it."

No one answered her. Lillian had looked hard at Philip but he stared rigidly out the window. Her knees bumped his as the carriage jolted over holes in the cobblestones.

The wailing violin broke in again, playing a fast movement of the sonata, missing a quarter of the notes. The man took false dramatic breaths and swayed from his waist.

Lillian finally looked over at Philip. The hostess's cat was in his lap now and he gazed, blankly, at the performers. Had those hands really unbuttoned her dresses, stroked her legs, taken the pins from her hair? She searched herself and found only the faintest stirring of desire and remote affection. The dream of stones was merely an image now, and evoked no more response in her than would a picturesque view seen too many times.

The boy was apparently restless. He kicked his heels against the chair legs. He didn't look like her at all, she thought. He whispered something to Philip, slipped out of his chair, and left the room. The cat followed him.

It could have been a stranger's child. She tried hard to dig up some love. What came instead was curiosity. Who had trained him on the piano? What did his voice sound like? What sweets did he like best? What were his dreams? What story had been told to him about his mother, his life?

And what was his name?

Even though her fascination increased every moment, if she had found out that the boy was struck down by a carriage outside the house, she would have felt shocked, and horrified, but not grieved. In this stifling room, she felt cold as an icehouse. How could this be her child and she feel so unmoved? Something must be terribly wrong with her. She must be making a mistake. It couldn't be hers; her father lying to her like that, it was impossible. She must have dreamed it all, even

205

the pregnancy and the room in the hills and the view from the window.

This Constable was a stranger to her. And if she were wrong about everything—again there was the effect of shifting and changing light, with shadows appearing in midair, shadows of nothing, the lamps flaring up and dimming. If she were wrong about everything then nothing could be solid. The gilded chair in front of her could melt away or her skin could change color.

Then she remembered the look her father had given her that last night, his eyes uncertain, his mouth gentler than she had ever seen it. Of course the boy looked just like him. There could be no doubt.

The bad violinist finally stopped and Lillian breathed an automatic sigh of relief, then changed it to a polite cough. She looked again to Constable's corner but he and her son had left.

2

After all the performances were over a few of the guests wandered out into the hostess's walled garden, braving the August heat, flaunting the deadly vapors, hoping for an illusion of coolness in all the greenery. Lillian followed, blindly, still smiling vaguely to the compliments. She found a shaded bench under a mulberry tree and brushed off two pieces of bruised fruit. It would be a good place to think, alone, for half an hour.

A skirt rustled and she looked up to see a woman holding out her hand.

"Good afternoon, Miss Aynsworth. I'm Mrs. Beersdon. Perhaps you don't remember me after such a thrilling performance." Mrs. Beersdon didn't smile. "I met you at Lady Tewksbury's two weeks ago, when those poor souls fell ill."

"I remember you perfectly." The woman had been with John Snow. Lillian smiled broadly, not unhappy to have her thoughts pushed aside. The other's face remained stiff.

"Sit down," said Lillian. "Please."

Deborah lowered her skinny frame onto the bench. "You must feel terribly exposed standing in front of everyone like that." Disapproval trickled from her like drops of bitter medicine.

"I don't think about it that way at all. I just think of the music." Lillian felt dislike rising.

"I hope you haven't been unwell since that night, Miss Aynsworth."

She can't be much older than me, thought Lillian. Yet her face was dragged down, with lines leading from the corners of the mouth to her chin. Her long nose wouldn't have been so ugly on a kinder face.

"Quite well." Lillian clipped her words and gave up trying to be pleasant. She remembered what it was that had put her on guard with the woman in the first place. John Snow. When she had stood with him after the dance, before she saw Philip, this woman had given her such a look. As if she claimed the man for her own. But she was married herself.

"It was Dr. Snow who introduced us, wasn't it?" asked Lillian, smiling slightly. She tried to keep the love out of her pronunciation of his name. "Have you seen him since then?"

"We never see him. Never." Mrs. Beersdon's sudden anger was inappropriate and puzzling. "He spends all his time working on this dreadful cholera. And going into such houses! It's not just the dirt in these places but the moral decay which is so repellent. These people bring their downfall on themselves."

As she finished she began to swat the air around her face, clumsily, and she looked crazy to Lillian, unbalanced. Lillian spotted a hovering gnat, which explained the gesture, but the impression of irrationality remained.

Lillian found herself leaning forward and she could hear her heart beat. This woman was awful to have to talk to. But she wanted to hear more of John Snow, and to say his name again.

And even as she thought of Snow, a picture of Philip with the cat in his lap crossed her mind. He would probably seek her out. A short sense of exhaustion passed over her, and her thoughts reverted again to Snow.

"Has Dr. Snow been making progress, then?"

"Progress? You could hardly call it that. He certainly doesn't see patients in Sackville Street. He goes to the worst neighborhoods and takes notes. He has some wild idea about the source of the disease. Just spreading panic, if you ask me."

Lillian smiled to herself. It was obviously hopeless to get anywhere with this woman.

"He was explaining some of it to me—at Lady Tewksbury's. Fascinating."

"If you don't mind my saying so, young lady, it would be better that you occupy your mind with more suitable subjects."

Lillian couldn't think of any answer to this.

Deborah went on. "The people who suffer this scourge live in the lowest degradation imaginable. Information about them shouldn't be passed out to corrupt decent folk. It's all that John Snow's doing."

By now Lillian felt removed from the scene, as if she were watching it in a play. She knew the woman expected no response, and she stared as Mrs. Beersdon sailed out of the garden, her huge skirt blowing in a sudden hot wind.

3

A few hours later, Lillian was home, reading a volume of Wordsworth in the drawing room while Olympia slept. The maid opened the door without knocking and announced, "Sir Philip Constable."

He was in the room before she had a moment to think about seeing him or not. He sat down without speaking, first pulling at the knees of his gray trousers and nervously fiddling with his gloves but not taking them off. Sweat beaded up on his forehead and she could hear his breathing, as if he had climbed a steep hill and was trying to hide his exertion.

"Miss Aynsworth, although we have met several times since your arrival in London, this is our first session with no others present. It is awkward for me to begin. I hardly know what to say." He stopped to recover his breath.

His manner was so formal and distant that Lillian remembered her notion of having imagined the whole thing. That was nonsense, of course. She sat flipping through the poems.

"Miss Aynsworth—Lillian—for weeks I tried to get in to see you, before your—confinement—but they kept me out. Then your father told me you died."

"It seems it was convenient for you to believe that," she said. Her anger was on Snow's behalf; for Constable's desertion ten years ago she felt nothing. Her heart began racing. She drummed her fingers on the book, and pretended to still be reading. "You could easily have come to see for yourself."

Constable swallowed and toyed with a pencil from his pocket. "I know anything I say will sound like an excuse. But it wasn't that simple."

"And the boy. It's my son, of course."

"Yes. Our son."

She stood, walked to the window and gazed out at the empty street. It seemed to shimmer in the heat. She felt an urge to break the glass pane with her fist. What would John Snow have said in this situation? He would never have gotten into this situation.

"I came here today to ask you to be my wife." Constable sounded strained, ready at any moment to choke.

She turned to look at him. An image of his head on a white pillow, next to hers, crept into her mind. With it came a dim memory of the pleasures she had felt with him. Now he looked like a man who would speak of Marital Duties. "I don't love you anymore, you know." She hadn't meant the words to sound as harsh as they did.

The corner of his mouth twitched once with pain; emotional or physical, she couldn't tell. She had assumed he would feel as cold as she, going through the motions of this mock courtship. If he still loved her, that unspoken certainty of his love she had felt so many years ago was entirely absent. He looked and sounded like a man talking to his solicitor.

"For the sake of the boy, at least," he said.

"Yes. The boy." The words meant nothing to her. She could just as well have said "the vase" or "the terrier."

"Perhaps you could learn to feel for me again, Lillian. It's not that there's someone else, is there?"

Lillian thought of John Snow. Even though he hadn't said it, she knew he loved her, perhaps in the way Philip used to. His hands and searching eyes already occupied a permanent niche in her mind, an area set aside for speculations and memories, with his name on the label. What was he doing now, at this very moment? The smell of his study came back to her, with the taste of the tea they drank, the taste of his mouth when he had kissed her.

Constable cleared his throat and coughed.

Lillian's mind felt unclear. She wanted to simply tell him, "I can never marry you." She picked up a pottery dog from

Olympia's bric-a-brac on the mantle and toyed with it as she spoke.

"I need time." Why did she say that? She'd never want to marry him. She turned her head sharply to Constable. "Does the boy know about me? What did you say to him?"

It struck her suddenly that if Constable were really responsible for Snow's attacks, and if it came to light, Constable would not be the only one disgraced. Her son, too, would be affected. But it seemed unreal to her, like a disastrous flood in a foreign country.

Constable looked at his gloved hands. "He thinks you're dead. As I did for so long." He ponderously rose from his seat and stepped over to her. Gripping both her shoulders, her looked into her face as though trying to see salvation. "Please. You don't know what's happened to me lately. I've made mistakes. If I had you to help . . ."

She still held the figurine and stood slack, passive, not meeting his eye. He pulled the tawdry thing from her and dropped it on the table where it shattered. With sad deliberation he began kissing her mouth, eyes, and neck.

She felt nothing; no desire, no fear, no inkling to resist. When alone with Snow, even with her eyes shut, she could feel the man's presence and sense the shape of his soul. But with Constable, it was as if he were invisible. She wondered if his was another kind of love, something she hadn't learned about. It felt like ashes.

A cologne was on his cheeks. His mustache pricked at her upper lip.

If I hadn't met John Snow, she thought, I would have made an effort to feel a quickening at this touch. It would have been like a hard stretch to reach something on too high a shelf. But I might have done it. As it was, she thought only of how Snow's kisses had felt, and how his hands had touched her.

He stopped and pulled away as suddenly as he had begun.

"I'm sorry. Please forgive me."

"It's all right. It's nothing." Some of her hair had been pulled loose but she made no attempt to brush it out of her face. He reached out to do it for her, but stopped midway, and turned to leave the room.

Just then the maid opened the door and brought in a note on a tray. Constable waited while Lillian read it to herself.

Can you come again tomorrow at ten in the morning? I need more help.

John Snow

An enormous weight lifted from Lillian's chest.

"Should Dr. Snow's messenger wait for an answer?" asked the maid.

Lillian snatched a scrap of paper from her writing desk and wrote, "Yes," then folded it and handed it to the girl, who went out.

Constable looked at her, breathing heavily. He put a hand on the arm of the sofa and sat down again. "You know John Snow?"

"Yes, that is—yes. I met him at Lady Tewksbury's." She decided to say nothing of Snow's suspicions.

"Lillian—you may hear things of me. I've made mistakes. I want to change, I want to go back."

She sat down cautiously, but not next to him. "What mistakes?"

"It's not that simple—I can't just tell you all—and I haven't been well." He put his head in his hands for a moment, then sat up. He looked around him, vaguely. "I must go."

She felt an echo of pity, but didn't ask him to stay. As his footsteps faded down the stairs, she remembered that she hadn't yet found out her son's name.

23

In Kensington Gardens Snow stepped over a fallen tree branch that blocked a path. Hyde Park was as neglected as a ruin. Weeds with thick stalks sprouted everywhere, and dry leaves floated on the Serpentine, along with a dead swan, loud with buzzing flies.

Under a huge old hydrangea lay what seemed to be a corpse, or maybe even two. They stank of decay and cholera. Snow passed by as quickly as he could.

He had started work at seven that morning, hunched over his desk trying to untangle all the information about the Southwark and Vauxhall water. He needed more to prove his point, but he wasn't sure what would help. Lillian was due at ten, and he planned to ask her to go through his notes with him once more, the way Caleb had.

Finally he couldn't think anymore, and went out for a short walk, leaving a note for Mrs. Jarrett to give to Lillian.

Heavy rain clouds hovered overhead. When he came to the duck pond he stood for some time staring at the brackish water, hardly hearing the quacking or the tearing that their beaks made as they pulled at the turf. Poplars and elms in full summer foliage blew in a wind, showing the white underside of their leaves.

He looked up from the ducks and saw her. She was too far for him to focus on her face, a white spot above a brown dress.

Mrs. Jarrett must have told her where he usually went; he

didn't think she'd follow him. She walked as fast as a man who's in a hurry but thinks running would be too extreme. In a moment she was beside him.

"Did you bring any crumbs for them?" Her words hung in the air after sounding, like bells suspended from the branches of trees. She took his arm and stood looking at the water.

"No. I didn't think." He felt in his pockets in an exaggerated gesture. Just lint.

"Here. I have half a bun." She dug into her bag and held out to him a raisin bun with two bites taken out of it.

He glanced down as he took it and saw her teeth marks in the bun. Her alignment was crooked. This one fact made him realize that until then he had seen her in a mythic light, as though she were perfect, with no past, born full grown from a seashell. His thumb stroked the crescent-shaped absences in the bread.

"I saw Sir Philip yesterday."

Snow's caution resurfaced, like a bad taste in his mouth. Her hold on his arm tightened.

"He says he has done something wrong. I'm beginning to wonder if you are right about him."

Snow burned to ask her again, "When did you know him? How well? What are you hiding?" But all he said was, "We should go back. It's not safe here. I could have been followed. Or even you."

He had been followed already, before Lillian caught up with him. Just inside the park, he had heard footsteps behind him, and turned to see the man he recognized as being so persistent in his digging the day of the riot. Close up he looked younger, with wide-set eyes and flushed cheeks.

"My name's Canty," the man had said. "I been trying to catch you, mister. I know you recognize me. I'm goin' straight now. Watch out. They're up to something. And there's more to tell."

Snow had been intensely curious, but he glanced at his watch. He had to get back to meet Lillian. "Will it take long?"

Canty turned, then, and looked through the trees behind him. "Best not here. Can we meet later?"

"What on earth—"

"You'll see. There's something you got to know about. But you'd better watch it. They're after you."

Snow had smiled, drily. "They haven't been too successful yet, have they?"

213

Then the man must have seen something that frightened him, for he looked back once and ran off. Snow saw nothing suspicious, so he kept on walking toward Kensington Gardens.

No, it wasn't safe for her to be here.

Even so, neither of them moved. It was a new pleasure for him to be totally alone with her, free of Mrs. Jarrett's constant knocks, and with no street crowd around. He pinched off a bit of the bun and threw it in, disturbing the algae. The ducks swarmed for it.

"No. You're quite right. We should go." She held out her hand for a piece of the bun and he gave her one, not looking at her. She rolled it between finger and thumb and threw it in, a good strong toss. The ducks quacked and flapped their wings. A white feather drifted loose and landed on the water, turning slowly.

Lillian looked up at him, and finally smiled. Without speaking she turned and slowly walked up a path that led farther into the park.

Snow put the bun in his pocket and followed her. A few drops of rain fell from the slate sky. When he caught up with her, moisture glistened in her hair. She had taken off her hat and was swinging it from its ribbon.

The rain fell harder, steadily. It was with pleasure that Snow felt it trickling down his neck, wetting his shirt.

"Perhaps you could put up your umbrella."

He felt stung that she could object to the rain. He hadn't; he was too much in love. But he obliged and raised the umbrella over the two of them.

Their walk had a flavor of truancy for him. He knew he should be back at his house, working hard. They ambled for an hour, walking in circles, going nowhere. She told him about Schumann. He told her about his childhood. Snow found himself unable to walk and talk at the same time so they stopped often. He hadn't talked about anything but cholera for ages.

The rain grew stronger until the sky poured solidly. His feet were soaked and Lillian's made squelching noises with every step. At a turn around a grove of dripping Norway spruce they almost walked into the park's Cricket Pavilion. The door was unlocked and Snow opened it. The wet door handle left a smell of pennies on his hand.

Once inside they both stood still, relishing the dry air and the

214

faint musty smell from a thatched roof. Snow's sense of truancy was still strong, and a schoolroom flavor to this space made it more so. Cricket bats stood in racks along the wall. Besides the thatch smell, there was a tang of sweat and playing shoes. Trophies glowed from dark corners of shelves. He felt that at any moment a school warden would catch them and send them back where they belonged. Rain drummed on the thatch.

Snow reached for his watch and was stopped, his hand halfway to his pocket, by her grip on his wrist. He looked stupidly at the soaking fabric of her cuff and the water on her skin over the carpal bones.

"I'm not like the others, you know. The women here. I can't hide things the way they do. There's no point in us waiting." Still holding his wrist like a wounded pigeon, and moving slowly, as if under water, she reached up with the other hand and pulled his head down to kiss her on the mouth, the way she had that first night.

He felt it again, that sense of communion with her, but this time it was expanded into an intense sexual longing that hadn't been there before.

He felt drugged, or as disoriented as if someone had changed all the furniture in his house while he slept. He wondered if he had a fever.

Her mouth was tight under his, and, at first, as resistant as someone in pain. She smelled of cinnamon this time, and curry. He pressed closer against her and felt the hard ridges of her crinoline against his knees and thighs.

"We must stop," he said, after a quick breath. He hardly recognized his own words, as if he had forgotten English.

She didn't answer, but pulled him to her. She kissed him again, her mouth open this time. Her hands pulled impatiently at his shirt under his jacket, and when she finally reached the bare skin of his lower back, she sighed.

It was then that he realized that her longing must be as strong as his. She loved him, and she desired him as well. It gave him an unbelievable sense of power; not power over her, but a power in himself. He felt like a giant, like a king of the earth. This goddess actually desired him. She wanted not just his sex, but his very being.

There was a pallet in a corner; perhaps for resting cricket

215

players. He stumbled over there, holding her hand and hardly able to walk, feeling that he was drowning in joy and desire.

She lifted her skirts; layers and layers of them, it seemed to him, and reached behind her waist, untying something. There was a slight rip, and then the crinoline understructure of her full dress fell loose at her feet. She stepped free from it and joined him on the bed.

A long time later Snow opened the door of the pavilion and Lillian left. It was almost dark and the rain had stopped.

"Please, won't you let me—"

"Absolutely not. I can manage. It's better this way. I must go, immediately." She walked off quickly, but not without looking back and giving him a long look that was better than any smile.

Snow put on his jacket and felt the bun in the pocket. After a while he took it out and ate it. He was exhausted and dazed, mostly with pleasure, but also with an observation that burned in his thoughts.

She hadn't been a virgin. He hadn't said anything about it, and neither had she.

24

1

The roast chicken was a small celebration Henry allowed himself. It used up the last of his funds.

The table's legs wobbled so that the motion of cutting the bird sent the wine bottle and glass shaking wildly. A mongoose in a cage behind him scrabbled at the wire, smelling the fowl. Henry's first bite was ready, the fork poised, when a jabbing pain stabbed through his abdomen.

Living as a fugitive had made him resourceful. When the cramp eased he calmly put down his cutlery, wiped sweat from his upper lip, and went to the door, tensing for another cramp, a protective hand over his stomach. He stuck his head out into the bright sun of the zoo courtyard. A pile of elephant droppings filled one corner. A street boy had wandered in and sat on the ground, looking stupefied by the cages and beasts. He held a straight stick and drew aimless patterns in the dust, humming a tune.

"Hey, you there!" Henry shouted.

The boy kept drawing circles. He swatted a fly from his ear.

"Boy! Get over here!"

Another cramp seized him. He grabbed at the door frame and bent double, breathing in loud gasps until it stopped.

The boy stood, curious, maybe sensing a chance for a handout. He didn't move as Henry began retching.

As soon as he could speak, Henry said, between gasps, "Listen. I'll give you money. Go find—" He was forced to stop for another bout of vomiting. When he finished he felt wetness seeping down his trouser legs and his strength seemed to have gushed out with it. He leaned weakly against the outer wall of the cottage.

The boy's mouth gaped but he didn't look as if he would run.

"Go find Greeley. Dr. Phineas Greeley. Eight Curzon Street, off Porter Square." Henry stopped again. His consciousness was drifting. "It's Bince. Bring him," was all he could manage before passing out.

The boy stood for a minute. He touched the toe of his boot, experimentally, to the puddle of vomit. Then he ran off.

In half an hour Henry stirred and managed to drag himself back indoors. He tried to make it onto the bed but that was beyond him. He fell against a large monkey cage, knocking the door open, and lay between it and the table leg, the fork he had dropped digging into his back. The monkey, a green-furred macaque, sniffed with hesitation at the open door, but didn't go anywhere at first.

Another gush of liquid escaped his guts. The cramps stopped but the vomiting grew worse. Even though he'd hardly eaten or drunk all morning the amount of fluid spewing from his mouth was copious and thin, like dirty water. He had trouble holding his eyes open.

A light touch brushed his mouth. It was the monkey. Its rough claws made a sandy sound as it tentatively pawed him. Suddenly it leapt over him and ran for the door.

There was a knock. Henry managed to groan as loudly as he could and the door opened a few inches.

Greeley stuck his head in and then pulled back quickly at the sight of the monkey, crouching like a gargoyle a foot away. The creature bolted through the gap and a short yelp came from Greeley.

Henry gathered his strength. "It's all right. Come in." It was only a whisper, but Greeley put his head in again and saw Henry, then stepped over the threshold. A green parrot flapped on its perch, sending feathers everywhere.

"Bince? Are you ill? I have what I agreed to bring you, but if now isn't the best time—" Greeley stepped closer.

"Never mind about that. Show me her things."

"We must get you to hospital." Greeley's hands hung at his sides. "I'm sure your mother—"

"Damn the bitch. Show me." A spasm gripped his throat and the vomiting began again. Greeley watched, keeping his distance. When Henry had finished, Greeley began carefully unpacking a satchel he carried, pulling from it an assortment of lace and silk camisoles, knickers, and petticoats. A vague, sweaty perfume began to mingle with the cholera smells. Then, with a delicate clinking, he drew out a sticky cup and saucer.

"See, just as I said. I can get more whenever you want. She used the teacup just this morning. And the laundress says the underwear is from yesterday. Now where are the letters?" Henry reached out with a shaking arm and picked up a sheer batiste camisole. "She never answered one of my letters. Not one."

Greeley turned his hands palm up, ready with a general response. "Women. I wouldn't expect much from them." He thought of Olympia as he had last seen her, lolling hugely on her sofa. Forget her complicated stepdaughter—the widow was the one to count on.

"You don't even know!" Henry shouted at Greeley. "What I offered her. I would have forgotten her past, forgiven her everything. We could have been perfect together." He paused for breath. "Listen. Forget the hospital. I know it's useless. That's not—"

"Don't talk nonsense. We could have you there in an hour."

"The letters are there. Take them." He waited, expectant, relishing the command a dying man can hold.

Greeley frowned, searched the table, and spotted the packet next to the chicken. Some of the grease had splashed from the bird and spotted the top one. The letters were frayed at the edges, tied with string.

Greeley pulled on a glove to pick them up. They were mottled and warped, as if they'd been wet and carefully dried. Some of the ink was smeared. He tested their weight, like a measure for an elixir, and looked sharply at Henry.

"And you swear these are all of them?"

219

Henry opened his mouth and tried to speak, gave up. He nodded.

The door creaked and Greeley jumped, jerking around. It was the macaque, pushing its way back in, eager for food. Suddenly bold, it sprang onto the table and began pulling at the chicken.

Greeley took out a handkerchief, wrapped the packet, and put it in an inner pocket of his coat.

"Let me get you out of here, Bince. We'll fix you up."

"Do what you like."

2

Greeley got back three hours later with two reluctant orderlies from Guy's Hospital. The macaque had crawled back in its cage. It crouched there in a corner where it gnawed the last of the chicken. Henry was dead, lying where Greeley had left him, the bundle of Lillian's underwear clutched to his chest like a child's toy bear.

25

1

The room was empty, the furniture gone. In daylight everything looked alien. To Snow, the only thing familiar was the dome of St. Paul's, jutting like a fat man's elbow above the landscape of rooftops. A bony woman in her forties scrubbed at the floorboards with a brush, and at bloodstains the size of farthings all over the wall behind where the bed had been.

"Where's Sophie?" asked Snow.

The woman jumped and gave a shout. She almost knocked over the bucket of suds, and steadied it as she answered.

"You should ha' made some noise coming in. Startle a body like that. Sophie. Was that her name? Died yesterday." She resumed her scrubbing.

Snow felt his temples go cool and lightly touched the right one, then the door frame. He left his hand on the flaking, splintery wood. "Was it cholera?"

The woman looked up again, as if surprised he was still there. "It were and it weren't."

"What do you mean?"

"She weren't taken so bad. It was the baby that did it. Losing the baby. All that blood."

221

Even through his shock Snow felt like a fool. He should have guessed it from the day he met her. Her breasts had grown over those few weeks. She had lost her appetite. And she had changed, internally, when they had sex. He flushed to remember it. Not his—

"I was here. I live downstairs." The woman held the scrub brush vertically and lightly tapped the floor.

"Tell me."

"It was the cholera cramps. They squeezed that mite out before its time."

"How much time?"

"Four months, I'd say. Maybe three. Yours?"

"No."

"Whatever you say." She returned to the scrubbing.

Cholera, even in milder forms, caused miscarriages. The disease sent some spasm through the uterus, squeezing with an iron push. What effect would it have on the fetus? Would the disease have gone into its system, too? Perhaps a dissection—Snow was too disgusted at his own thought to let it continue.

"You want something more?" The woman seemed to be unable to work with him there.

"Was she in much pain? Did she suffer?" He tried hard to keep a clinical note out of his voice but he knew it was still there.

"Hard to tell. She was a tough one about pain. Thing was, I think she done it on purpose."

"What do you mean?"

"I saw her just a few days ago, lookin' low as anything. Boilin' a pot of water over a fire." She gestured at the now empty grate. "She said, 'This is the last one I'll boil. Tomorrow I drink it straight.' *I* think she poisoned herself."

"Perhaps you're right." Yes, she probably did, but just with water. She would have known not to drink it unboiled. He had been careful to teach her.

He thought of asking for more details but it seemed pointless. He lumbered back down the stairwell and into the street.

He found that he could hardly remember Sophie's face or even the color of her hair. The song came to him, but not her eyes that first triggered it. Were they blue? As he stumbled along the empty street he passed first one corpse, then three. A cat ran from one of them.

He knew he could have saved her. If the scrub woman was

right, it was a simple matter of blood loss from incomplete parturition, and a quick, easy surgery, with a few doses of ergot, might have fixed it. Grief swelled in his chest, but he knew it was for one more failure on his list. Not for Sophie.

He kept walking, blindly, his shoulder weighed down by the heavy wood kit box. His chloroform set hadn't done much good that day.

He'd been called out to a surgery early in the morning for an emergency appendectomy. The note had surprised him. No one had asked for him for weeks, and he assumed all the surgeons were using another man. He needed the money, so he went. The cholera work was at a standstill, anyway.

The surgery theater at Guy's hadn't changed since his student days. A day-old bucket of blood stood in a corner next to a basin of God knew what body parts. The light was no better, slanting from skylights glazed over by soot and pigeon droppings.

He'd seen from his first entrance that the patient was bad off. It looked like peritonitis to him, and surgery would be useless.

Sure enough, once the man was unconscious and they opened his abdomen, the sweet stink of sepsis filled the room. The entire gut around the appendix was suppurating, and the appendix itself, usually the size of a short earthworm, was as black and swollen as a blood pudding.

The surgeon gave Snow a long look and Snow knew his thoughts exactly. Let's give a stronger dose of chloroform, he seemed to say. Let's make sure he doesn't wake up.

But Snow had done nothing. He felt that his task in life was complicated enough without deciding who should live and who should die. He had ignored the surgeon's glance, and cleaned and packed his anesthesia equipment. He wrote up careful instructions for the man's care when he woke from the drug, as if he would be fine and would need only nausea drops for an hour or two, liquid meals for the first few days. And he had left, feeling ashamed, even though he hadn't done the shameful thing.

Sophie's death, no more his fault than the peritonitis, shamed him too. He hardly noticed where he was walking until he broke into a sudden fit of violent choking.

A wall of smoke rolled over him from the front of a burning house, and he had breathed in the fumes without thinking. Screams came from upper floors, and two men ran by with a cholera patient on a stretcher. Snow found himself trotting the other way, then running, downhill, the wood case bouncing and bruising his ribs.

He felt as if demons were after him and the square corners of the box could have been their pinchers reaching out. Finally he slowed but kept walking, close to the river now, past warehouses and dockyards.

His failures rang in his head like church bells. Three months' work wasted, an entire practice of patients abandoned, an affair with a dead whore. He didn't know quite where in this litany to place his love for Lillian, but somehow it felt like another grievous error. He had seduced her, and he had nothing to offer her. Even if she married him, what life could she have with a failed, worthless doctor?

And then there was everything with Constable.

Snow had gone from the appendectomy at Guy's Hospital to see Sir Philip. Snow had waited two whole days after discovering Constable's name on the water company lists before talking to him, and all that time he had hoped to turn up something that would destroy the connection. He wanted so badly to believe in the man, and even now he didn't quite know why.

Constable kept him stewing in the airless corridor for almost an hour, with nothing to look at but the blank walls and the piles of water company notes he brought. When Snow finally went in, Constable had looked the quintessential politician behind an expanse of mahogany desk.

Snow stood nervously, feeling a ridiculous disappointment that Constable wasn't warmer to him. "If you have a few minutes, Sir Philip, there's a question or two I need to ask." To Snow his voice sounded hesitant and childish.

"By all means, Doctor. Feel free." Constable walked to the front of his desk and pulled a chair out for Snow.

"Perhaps if you could have a look at these figures." Snow spread the papers over the desk.

Constable bent, obedient, polite. "I'm afraid it doesn't make much sense to me," he said, still smiling.

"I'll explain, then."

And Snow told him all about the two water companies, the different houses, and carefully explained the salinity experiments.

When he was finished, Snow looked up. "If you know anything about this, Sir Philip, it's your duty to speak up."

224

Constable laughed with a sound Snow thought was relief. "I'm afraid you're on the wrong track, Snow."

"What do you mean by that?"

"The Public Health folks have been after Southwark and Vauxhall since the company started. But there's nothing to prove. They analyzed every bit of information, trying to show that the water wasn't pure."

Snow's doubts, always near the surface, clouded his mind. But he was determined not to show it. "Perhaps you didn't understand the meaning of the salinity tests."

"Oh, no, I understand them well enough. What I can't see is why you think they prove anything."

"It's absolutely conclusive—"

"That some of the water has a high salt content. Or that some of your storage vials were contaminated with salt. But I don't see anywhere here a proof that salt causes cholera."

Constable rifled through the papers as if genuinely searching.

"But it's a given—the water is salty because it comes from the Thames. The water was never filtered; it's polluted."

Constable gave a downward sweep with his hand, as if cutting off Snow's words. "Dr. Snow, if you want to amuse yourselves by this project, that's fine. But as I told you, the Board of Health has an inquiry going into the whole matter. Only Farr's official methods will be considered in the long run. There's no point in your pursuing it, especially if it results in accusations like this."

Snow looked closely at Sir Philip and saw that he was sweating and breathing heavily. He face had flushed darker since they arrived. He didn't look well.

"But that's absurd," said Snow. The Board of Health isn't investigating anything, they just threaten me, hire an insane dwarf—"

"And may I point out to you, Doctor," he went on, "the Board of Health would not look kindly on a doctor who frequents a whore in Seven Dials. Not good for the medical image."

Snow had been waiting for this, but dreading even more that somehow Constable would have found out about yesterday's secret hours with Lillian in the rainstorm. "You infernal bastard. I'd like to see what you might do in the same situation."

Sir Philip only looked away, still breathing heavily.

Snow bent over the desk and tried to gather all his papers with dignity. "Do what you like with the things you know about me.

I can see we have nothing further to talk about. Thank you for your time, Sir Philip."

Then Snow had left without looking at the man again. His first thought had been that Constable would tell Lillian about Sophie and that would be the end of anything with her.

Going to see Sophie right then was probably the stupidest thing he could have done; but thinking of Lillian in the darkness yesterday, with the rain pouring down on the bushes outside, left him flooded with nervous desire. Lillian wasn't a woman he could have on a moment's whim; for all he knew he'd never see her again after what happened yesterday. Feeling vile every step of the way, he'd headed for Seven Dials. As it turned out, his sexual need disappeared instantly when he heard what had happened to Sophie.

Snow guessed she had finally broken down and given the details to Mango, who had somehow gotten them back to Constable. One letter from Constable to *The Lancet* would do it. Or *The Times*. Caleb wouldn't be much help on this one. Probably the letter was out already, being read at that moment by every doctor in the Royal Society. With the anesthesia practice washed up, and nothing to show for all the cholera work, he might as well go back to mixing headache pills at a pharmacy. If they'd let him do that much.

By now it had been dark for half an hour. Snow was walking east, meandering in and out of the narrow ways along the river. He finally reached the huge basin of St. Catherine's Docks and, blocked by water, could go no farther. He leaned against a wall and stared at the ships swaying in the moonlight. Not much ship traffic these days. Everything out of London was quarantined for so long in the docks that it wasn't worth sending it. The boats were stuck there, inert, useless. He watched them for an hour before turning around to go home.

2

It was a long walk back. His feet were burning and a headache pounded his skull before he realized he was famished. He stopped in a lawyers' chop house off Chancery Lane. The clinking glasses and low talk sounded like life noises of a distant tribe from a far place, not his fellow Londoners. He craved a slow, wandering conversation with a clergyman or a banker. Perhaps they could mull over the weather, or the value of the pound.

He sat at one end of a long table at whose opposite sat the very type he was looking for. Fiftyish, bald, new black and white clothes. The man was finishing dinner and a small decanter of sherry.

He took one look at Snow and put down his glass, nodded curtly, and hurried off.

Snow's spirits sank. He glanced down at his rumpled clothes, his muddy shoes, felt at the untrimmed beard. When was the last time he had changed his linen? Not last night, he had worked until four. Was it the day before? Or before that?

Somehow the inability to remember was wonderfully soothing. He gave up trying. It was as if he had just been excused from an examination in neurological anatomy. He sighed with relief.

"What'll it be, sir?" The waiter stood with a white cloth over his arm.

"The same as that gentleman there just ate. Two chops and half a decanter of sack."

"Are you all right, sir?"

"Yes, perfectly. Why do you ask?"

"You look as if, well, as if you just stepped from a graveyard, if you'll pardon me." The man nodded and went off.

Snow glanced around the room for a mirror and spotted one over a fireplace. He went over and peered in.

He half expected that his hair would have turned white, or his face gone green. But there was nothing different. Just the usual exhausted pallor.

"Like he'd been in a graveyard." He remembered the last time he'd been in one. It was in Yorkshire, a few weeks ago. There had been a wind in the pines, and that little man with his notes and his chart of the graves. A box for dysentery, a box for childbirth.

And then, as if in a dream, an image came to Snow of Lillian, standing next to him where he had stood alone that windy day. She smiled with love and held out to him on the palm of her hand one more box, not a drawing but an actual golden cube, well cast and shaped as carefully as an Egyptian scarab.

A box for cholera.

Suddenly he had it. With openmouthed delight Snow watched the idea unfold in his mind like a peacock's tail.

227

The maps of London had been too big. The parishes had been too big. A map of one street was all he needed. And he knew which street it was.

That morning when he had left for Guy's Hospital and the surgery, he had passed through Golden Square, and then from Wardour Street through Broad Street. It had been the worst scene since the epidemic began. Bodies lay in rows in front of every door. He must have seen a hundred. Retching came from upper rooms where they had opened the windows to get a breeze. Nothing looked normal. The death count must have been atrocious.

He had kept on walking, too dazed to react, unable to think of anything useful to find out from this mess. And then, by the time he reached Little Windmill Street, things looked ordinary again. A maid leaned out of a window beating a carpet, and a canary cage hung from the front door. Granted, half the houses were empty, but the people who stayed on were not ill.

That was the street to map. Broad Street. Not populations, general figures, shaded-in areas. But each and every case on Broad Street and around it. Looking at all the deaths was easy, even counting them. But it proved nothing. Only a map would show it.

Snow was still standing by the empty grate in front of the mirror. He looked at his watch. It was eleven P.M. Lillian would be asleep, but he knew she wouldn't mind if he woke her. There was no one else he could trust.

The waiter appeared with the chops on a platter and Snow walked over and took one by the bone, reached into his pocket with the other hand, and laid a few coins on the table.

"Terribly sorry to rush off. I hope that will cover it."

With the chop in his hand, he ran out of the restaurant toward Lillian's house off Grosvenor Square, chewing the good, salty mutton.

3

On Brook Street the street lamps were all dark. Some failure in the gas lines, maybe. The row houses looked identical, with their spiked low fences and careful patches of front grass.

228

Luckily Snow remembered her address. Without hesitation he rang the bell. It was a long time before the door opened; it was Lillian. She was dressed but her hair was unpinned and hanging around her shoulders.

"The house staff has all gone to sleep. I thought it would be you," she said, smiling. But then she saw his tension. "What is it?"

"Can I ask for your help once more? I've figured something out; I'll explain it on the way."

"Yes. But I must put on some shoes. Come in; it will only be a moment."

"No. I'll wait here." He felt an impatient aversion to the warm lights of her house. He wanted to be off.

"All right." She went back inside and Snow ran down the steps to pace the sidewalk, too restless and excited to stand still. He couldn't believe he hadn't seen it before. The cause must be provable in the local, specific water; nothing as general as an entire city's water supply. He itched to get his hands on the records he could use to fill in the map, a map of Broad Street and the intersections around it.

A scuffling sound came from the foot of the front steps.

"Good," Snow called out. "Let's be off, then."

There was no answer. Someone ran past Snow, pushing him in a sudden blow just behind the left knee. Snow fell into a squat, his hands smashing the pavement. His head was yanked back by his hair, so tightly that the skin around his eyes felt stretched.

A knife glinted past his face before resting on his throat and pressing painfully against the skin.

"It was you who killed her, you bastard. She was fine until she took up with you. Our Constable won't be too sorry to see you go, either." The knife pressed harder, and a sting like a bee's stab spread across his neck.

This is it, was all Snow thought. I am about to die. In a short second, the smell of Lillian's hair drifted through his mind, and then a moment from thirty-five years ago, of sitting in a sunny window with his mother, eating fresh bread and laughing.

Suddenly the door opened and light fanned across the stairs. Whoever held Snow gasped and loosened the knife. Snow jerked his head violently and his hair was released. He staggered to his feet while running footsteps faded off into the darkness.

Lillian's voice came to him. "My God, are you all right?"

229

"It was damned lucky you came just then."

"I heard something. Then when I came out I saw him." She shuddered. "A dwarf. And I thought you'd imagined him before."

Snow swiped at the skin under his collar. His hand came away black with blood. "I can't understand why he didn't kill me. Someone like him wouldn't care who saw it."

Lillian wiped at his bleeding neck.

The cut on his throat began to burn.

"You're bleeding badly. We should go in and have a look."

"There's no time," said Snow. He stared off toward where the steps had gone. "Go back inside and get a dozen candles." She obeyed without a word. When she returned and closed the door behind her, he grabbed her hand and headed for Fleet Street.

4

An hour later the two of them sat, with bruised knuckles, at the same back office of *The Times* where they'd checked the water records. They'd broken in; an exploration of an alley behind Fleet Street turned up a low window. Snow broke the glass with his fist, opened the casement, climbed in and pulled Lillian in after him.

His heart was still racing. If he was found out here, his career would be over. But there was no other way. He doubted Caleb would help him, and every hour of delay was costing more lives. He wiped every now and then at his neck, where the blood still seeped.

"We need to find the entire collection of London death reports for the past ten days. Caleb said it was kept back here." Snow started leafing through piles of papers, and came across orphanage records, rates of cabbage shipments into London, a book of weather reports from Edinburgh. But nothing that looked like death records.

"Here," said Lillian, "what's this?" The folio was huge. It contained every cholera death in London for the past two weeks. Next to it was a similar one of the reported cholera victims who had recovered.

"That's it," said Snow. "You sit here, and read them. I'll start

230

the map." He ripped a huge piece of paper from the back of another volume (a listing of export rates for cotton cloth) and sketched out a rough map of Broad Street and the surrounding intersections. As he drew he felt a small yet growing fear that his idea would be wrong.

Lillian read off the name of each victim and his address. She had to go through deaths all over London, as the list wasn't separated by parish or in any way at all.

"Don't you think we should map them all?" Lillian asked.

"No, no. That's the whole point. By mapping them all we lose the focus, we get right back to where we were, looking at things in too large a view. I want you to read only the ones in the region bounded by Regent Street, Oxford Street, and Brewer Street.

Snow moved the sheet of paper to the floor. He marked every death in the neighborhood with a small dark stripe, a little wider at one end than the other. Like the boxes in the graveyard map. Like a coffin.

When they reached three hundred Snow was forced to change the scale and have a box represent ten deaths, not one. He had to go back and redo every mark, which took an hour. His fear of being wrong stayed with him, but lessened with each new mark on the map.

"Do you think this has anything to do with the water company?" She pointed to the growing stain of cases around the intersection on Snow's map, then went back to her lists.

"Probably, but it's impossible to tell. I can't know what water lines go through this area without seeing another map of them, a more detailed one than the one Caleb showed us. But it seems likely. Some source of contamination is causing these cases, that's a given."

"Then the Great Western Gravel Company would be implicated as well."

"I suppose, yes." Snow couldn't understand why she was interested in such a trivial detail.

"And what about Sir Philip?"

Snow tried to force himself to concentrate on the map, and not to wonder why she was worried about Constable's welfare. "As a member of their board, he would share the blame. But let's get on with the work."

Lillian resumed her reading. Her voice was less enthusiastic, though, and she had longer pauses between spotting the relevant addresses. She stopped again. "John—I—what will happen if this cholera isn't stopped?"

He began to feel impatient, but tried to answer her. "It will stop itself, eventually. All epidemics do, it's a law of nature." On a corner of the map he drew a small, bell-shaped curve. "If you think of the disease rate as following the shape of this curve, you can see that the rate falls, eventually." He drew a large "X" near the peak of the curve. "It may be that we've reached this point, and from here on the cases will slow down. There's no way to really know until it's all over."

He thought she was satisfied and would resume her search. But she went on. "Then why not just do nothing? If it will stop anyway?" Her voice sounded removed, as if she addressed a stranger. He couldn't understand what she was getting at.

"We could do nothing. But for every quarter-inch on this curve I've drawn, one or two hundred people will die. Don't you think it's worth trying to stop it earlier than nature might?

She was silent again, then finally began her reading.

At five in the morning, just as it was beginning to get light, they finished. Snow's knees were bruised from kneeling on the floor. The gash had stopped bleeding, but his neck ached terribly from both the attack and the strain of writing for so long. He gingerly lifted the map he had made and set it on the desk top.

There was no doubt. Black boxes scattered themselves over the neighborhood, clusters here and there, isolated cases on almost every street. But at the intersection of Broad and Cambridge the boxes stacked up, blotting out the street names, filling everything. The darkness in the center of the map was like the body of a spider, its legs stretching outward, made up of the occasional cases on the outer streets.

Lillian asked, "My God, what happened at that intersection?"

Snow was silent for a minute, then frowned and looked her. "And it's still happening, isn't it?" he said. "These lists are a day old. New ones will arrive when the office opens today. If we want to stop the curve, we haven't a moment to lose." He grabbed the map, rolled it and stuffed it in his pocket, then ran from the room. He used the front door this time. Lillian followed.

26

1

The curved handle of the old brass water pump stuck out like an absurdly long limb. Standing at the corner of Broad and Cambridge, it was worn smooth from a century of use. The dark metal around the handle had a barnacled look, as if it had spent time attached to the underside of a ship. But there was nothing unclean-looking about the thing.

In fact, on this hot morning, it was inviting. Drops of water glistened on the shiny curves, and damp spotted the earth around the pump, making the air at least five degrees cooler than a few steps away. It had a pleasant, spring-water smell, of new leaves and rust. A small puddle had formed at its base and the spout dripped, making a musical, trickling sound, as if it were a fountain in a monastery garden.

Snow had to resist an impulse to take a long, gasping drink, letting the water run over his face and his head, blinking it from his eyelashes, having the rising sun flash rainbows through it, soaking his shirt. As he stood and dripped sweat, with Lillian behind him, a wagon pulled up with three empty barrels. Horse smells filled the air.

"Scuse me, guvnor." A man who looked like a butler's assistant gently elbowed Snow aside and set a barrel down under the mouth. He began pumping to fill it.

Snow waited a full minute before asking, carefully, as if speaking to a child, "Where are you taking that water?"

"Mrs. Markham, St. John's Wood."

"Why?" St. John's Wood was nowhere near here.

The man didn't look up from pumping. "It's what she do ask for. Do she want local water? No. Water I could fetch in ten minutes? No. Broad Street only will do. Likes the taste. Bloody Hell."

Snow looked at Lillian, then back at the man.

"Would you mind telling me her address?"

The man eyed Snow's bloody clothes, his black-rimmed eyes.

"I don't care. Go rob her if you like. Beat her over the head. Make her drink local water. Five Appleton Lane. St. John's Wood."

"Thank you."

The man finished the first barrel and started on the second.

"How's her health?" asked Snow.

"Strong as a sow."

Snow came closer and peered over the edge of the barrel. The water looked pure and crystalline, like a mountain pool. It was so clear that the staves at the bottom of the barrel were outlined, rippling. A trout would look well in there, drifting through pure pebbles.

"If I give you five pounds will you stop pumping and drive me up there?"

The man stopped in mid-pump, looked at Snow without expression. "Ten."

Lillian, from behind, started to speak but Snow stopped her. "Done. Let's go." He turned around to Lillian. "Stay here. Don't let anyone take any water."

"That may not be easy," said Lillian. Already two women approached, buckets in hand. The man started loading the barrels back into the wagon, but Snow shouted, "Leave them, we haven't time." He grasped the full one with both hands and heaved it over, spilling the water into a street with a gush that soaked the hem of Lillian's dress. He knocked over the other barrel too, and jumped into the wagon.

2

The ride took only twenty minutes. Snow didn't speak a word, but stared straight ahead, his lips moving slightly. The driver looked at him sideways, cautiously, as if he had a dangerous orangutan as a passenger.

When they pulled up at Mrs. Markham's house Snow jumped down and ran up to the front door, found it unlocked, and jerked it open. A shocked housemaid stood inside, having just come down the stairs with a basin and a towel. Sounds of retching and moaning came from upstairs.

"Where's Dr. Philpott?" asked the girl. "She won't see no one but him."

"He—he'll be here shortly. I'm his—assistant. Is it cholera?"

The girl glanced down at the basin and moved it forward, showing him. The vomit was pale gray. Rice water.

Snow turned and ran back to the wagon where the confused driver still sat.

"Let's go back so you can fetch your barrels. And here's another five pounds to hurry. The sow seems to have weakened."

"What? That one's sick?"

"Cholera."

The man crossed himself and they set off. "Weren't it the right Mrs. Markham, then?"

"Oh, no—quite the right one. Tell me—does she drink only that water, the water you fetch from Broad Street?"

"Nothing but. Says it's the best."

"And what about the rest of you in the house?"

"Tap water's good enough for us. It's her private supply, that from the pump."

"Ah." Snow was silent for a few minutes. Then he asked, "Any other cholera on this street?

"Not a bit of it."

When they were still twenty yards from the pump Snow spotted Lillian being shoved and pushed by two women, as she held on to the pump handle. A third woman held her by her hair, which was falling in tangles around her shoulders. She was shouting at them. A small army of women with buckets circled around her. A few had already filled theirs and left, lugging them down the street.

"John!" she called out. "Thank God you're back. Tell them about the water." On seeing him, the women immediately let go of her.

Snow stood in his seat and looked down at the crowd. "The water from this pump is contaminated with cholera. It will kill you if you drink it."

They stirred like annoyed crows. "You're full of it! It's the best water in London! Ask anyone," shouted the woman closest. She'd already filled a two-gallon pottery jug and as she finished shouting she flung its contents straight at Snow, drenching him. The crowd shouted louder.

He shut his lips tightly and brushed the water from his eyes, drying his mouth with a handkerchief.

"Please, believe me. Get your water elsewhere."

"Easy for you to say. Most of the pumps around here stink of dead rats. It's hot enough out here to boil a kettle. We got to have water."

Snow looked over at the driver, who was now retrieving his barrels from a doorway. "That man there, he'll get you water. From the nearest fresh pump. There's an artesian well at Trafalgar Square." He knew that one was far deeper than this; it would have to be pure.

"Hey," shouted the driver. "I got no time for this nonsense." Snow pulled out another five-pound note. The man took it and clattered off, some of the crowd trailing behind him, some sitting on the back of the wagon, their legs dangling over the edge.

"Boil the water, just to be sure!" Snow shouted after them.

But a large group lingered on at the pump. Snow, off the

wagon now and at their own height, stood in front of it and eyed the hostile bunch.

A woman in front stooped for a stone and tossed it at him, almost in jest, but it caught him on the forehead and he staggered. He reached for support and his hand touched the handle.

The handle. That was the key. Remove the handle and no one could get the water.

"Lillian!" shouted Snow. "Come help me get this bloody thing off."

Lillian, who had been wrestling with another bucket-toting woman, hurried over and together they examined the bolt that attached it. It was an odd shape, a bolt no ordinary spanner would remove. Its wings spread out like the arms of a distorted star.

"The parish vestrymen. They'll know how to remove it," said Snow.

"How do we find them?"

"They meet on Thursday mornings. In St. Anne's Church."

"How on earth do you know that?" asked Lillian.

Snow smiled. "Parish news section of *The Times*. I read it when I can't concentrate on anything. It relaxes me; lost dogs and all that. And today is Thursday," said Snow. "Let's go."

4

Snow heard his voice as authoritative as a judge's when he shouted orders to Lillian and the driver, but he felt on the verge of a nervous ruin. He hadn't slept in two days. Or was it three? He knew he hadn't washed after the afternoon in the park with Lillian. His clothes felt as if they'd melted in with his skin. His nails were too long and even as he trotted toward St. Anne's Church he felt at the nails with his fingertips, annoyed, itching to have them shorter.

The spire of St. Anne's Church rose before him, piercing the muggy afternoon sky. Light came from its stained glass. By the time Snow panted up the steps Lillian had opened one of the huge doors and stood waiting for him.

The two entered. Thirty heads turned to stare, all sober parishioners at their weekly meeting for the good of the neighborhood. No one in there was under sixty. They looked apprehensive and aggressive at the same time; ready to fight this madman and his wild lady partner. Snow stepped forward and started to talk without thinking.

"Excuse me, please. I hardly want to interrupt. But there's—a problem to discuss."

A man at the front, older than the rest, his face dark and his eyes so hooded he could have been Greek or even Chinese, stood up. "All problems should be addressed in writing to the committee. Have you filled out the proper forms?"

"Forms?—No, I—"

"You'll find them next to the collection box behind the font."

Snow, dumbfounded and too dazed to resist, found the table and sure enough, there was a pile of blue forms with blank lines to be filled in. He reached into two jacket pockets before asking, "Has anyone a pencil I might borrow?"

A tiny woman in black, looking like the last survivor of the French Revolution, got up from her seat at the back and handed Snow a pencil from her black reticule.

He studied the form while the church waited, silent, lapping up their entertainment. Nature of difficulty? *Cholera*, he wrote. Specific request? *Remove pump handle at Broad Street*, was all he could think to write. There were other questions about funds, eleemosynary applications, the bishop's collections, but he left all those blank and walked up the center aisle to the three men in front. He handed his paper to the oriental-looking one, who took it without a word. The three heads bent together and read it, then stared at him as if waiting for more.

Snow felt light-headed, and went on with his explanation, though he found it harder, word by word, to make sense. "It's the water, you see. Mrs. Markham's barrels leave it settled. And the miscarriage—but no, you don't need to know—"

He trailed off as the dark man stood and went through a curtain into the vestry. He reappeared in a moment with a long wooden box, its corners bound in metal, an engraved plate on its lid.

They're going to shoot me, thought Snow. And Lillian, too. The man laid the box on the front pew and took from it a spanner, heavy and as long as Snow's arm. He handed it over.

"The water in that pump has been pure for years." He pronounced the words formally, as if reading a speech at a ceremony. "Only these godless times would affect something so innocent as water. If it is as you say, the water causing cholera, I believe it must be a judgment on the wicked people of Broad Street. They rarely turn up at this church. Do what you wish with their pump handle. But please return the spanner at the next meeting, which is two weeks from today."

At first Snow was confused by the man's lack of interest in his revelation. But then he thought, after all, Broad Street is a quarter mile from here. Few are sick here by the church. Why would the man be any more excited? Snow held the spanner cautiously, as if it could burn him. He turned to go.

"And be sure the proper forms accompany it. You'll find them on the same table." The man's voice was admonishing, hostile. He loves this job, thought Snow.

Carrying the spanner gingerly in his arm, like a congratulatory bouquet, he and Lillian left the church as sedately as a newly wedded couple, but the instant they were outside they started running.

When they reached the pump a solitary woman in bare feet pumped into a wooden bucket. Snow kicked it over and fitted the spanner to the bolt while her hands were still on the handle. She took one look at the two of them and ran.

The first turn took all his weight and for a moment he thought the thing was hopelessly rusted in place. Lillian pulled at it too. It wasn't until both of them had their feet off the ground that the handle began to give. After three turns it fell off suddenly and caught Snow's thumb against the spanner, scraping a flap of skin as it went. He and Lillian stared at the handle on the cobblestones, ignoring the slow drip of blood from his thumb.

"Done," said Snow.

"Now what?"

"Nothing. We watch. And count. I need some sleep. I expect you do, too. Got to keep counting." Snow picked up the handle and the spanner and leaned both against his shoulder like a mine worker with his picks. He walked her home, then went back to Sackville Street.

5

Snow was burning up in his dream. Brush fires raged all around the stone tower and he had to head uphill to get water. This was no problem, his legs were strong and made long strides. It was the downhill trip that did it. Wheezing, shaking, he spent his last strength in handing the bucket of water over to someone, then tumbled onto a stretcher. They carried him feet first up the tower stairs, with Lillian leading the way, telling them to protect his head. Questions hammered out of the air. What is your name? When were you born? He knew nothing.

Snow woke to the pain in his neck and his hand. Sleepily looking at the hand, he saw that it was stuck to the sheet with dried blood and was bleeding again. Blood streaked the sheet in wide strokes, like a whitewasher's trial marks on a stone wall.

He became aware of something else; people were in his room. He turned his head sharply. Two helmeted and embarrassed bobbies stood by his bed, Mrs. Jarrett behind them, looking delighted and panicked at the same time.

"What on earth—"

"Dr. John Snow?"

He sat up, pushing the hair out of his eyes with his unbloodied hand. "Yes, of course."

"Were you in the region of Broad Street and Cambridge Street last night at midnight?"

Snow looked from one to the other, trying to gather his thoughts. Then he remembered. "Yes, yes. The pump! Did it work? Have the cases stopped?" Even as he asked it he knew it was absurd; though he knew nothing of how long it would take to show results from removing the pump handle, a day was surely too soon to see anything.

"And was this object in your possession last night?" The bobby hoisted the pump handle.

"Yes. That's the pump handle. Have they changed their minds? Let me talk to—"

"Please come with us, Dr. Snow. You are under arrest for murder."

27

They sat across from each other at a table, Mango's hand stroking the stubble on his jaw and Bucks draining a glass of gin. As
soon as he put it down Bucks's hands started shaking again.

"This'd be the best place to hide. It'll only be for a couple of
days." Bucks's teeth were chattering, making his words fresh and
wintry. "You said once I could—"

"Damn what I said once. That was before. You can't stay here,
I say now. You want every copper in the docks on my small
arse?"

The rising sun streamed in through thick dust motes. Bucks
looked down at his hands. "Jesus! There's more!" He spit on his
fingers and frantically rubbed them against a rag from his pocket,
then flung the rag on the floor. "You talk as if you had nothing
to do with it."

"I wasn't even there, Bucks."

Bucks pulled in a deep ragged breath. "I don't believe this. It
was you and me together. If you hadn't been so damn late—"

The door to the pub opened and Bucks jerked around. His
shoulders sank when he saw it was just the owner with a broom
in her hand.

"You two still down here?" She hardly looked at them.

"What if we are?" said Mango. "I ain't heard of you closing
down. I pay my rent."

"Just askin." She began sweeping and approached their feet, stooped for the rag. "Filthy thing." She picked it up like a dead mouse, between thumb and forefinger, and tossed it into the stove.

She started washing glasses behind the bar, holding them up to the window, checking for streaks.

Mango resumed his whisper. "If I hadn't got there when I did, you would have just left him there. No use at all."

"And why'd we have to move him? To that pump? We could have been off by now if that hadn't took so long. The plan would still have worked. We could have made the boat."

"You still don't understand, do you? That he's trying to get Snow out of the way? There's no time to explain again. Like I said, you can't stay here."

"I'll go home then."

"They're watching your place already."

Bucks's lower lip quivered. "I can't put up with this, Mango. I keep seeing him. And the way his head sounded. Like breaking open a melon. How could I know there'd be so much blood? None of the others ever bled with the shovel like that. And I never had to do the job myself, not once. I can see him now, brains everywhere."

"Well close your eyes then. And shut up. I need to think."

Bucks's eyes dropped again to his hands and he began examining his fingernails carefully. He took out a pocket knife and started cleaning them, then stopped. "Do you think Canty really would have talked to Snow? Maybe we didn't have to do it."

"If you hadn't bungled the job with Snow you could have saved yourself trouble."

"I bungled it? Who's the one who was supposed to be scaring him off? Who's the one said he would cut his throat last night, put him out of the way? I'm surprised the man's still around. I think you must have slipped, yourself. Besides, if they're this cut up about a nobody like Canty, think what Snow—"

Mango looked like he wasn't listening. "I never saw a face like hers," he said, his voice low. "That's what stopped me. I never let myself think what my life would have been if I'd been big, *never*. But sometimes . . ." He shook his head. "I don't think I can kill him, not now. Not with her in the picture."

Bucks paid no attention, but kept on with his nagging. "We'd be well out of it now, you said. Off in France, living it up."

242

Mango, serious again, held out an impatient hand for silence. "Did you bring the charts Canty had?"

Bucks pulled a roll of paper as long as an umbrella from behind his chair.

"Let me see them."

Bucks obediently unrolled them. Sewer plans. Huge, they covered the top of the table and hung down over the sides. The stack of sheets was an inch deep. Mango studied the top one. Blue, black, and red lines crosshatched each other over and over. Countless pencil markings scrawled on top of everything. They were as vague as cave paintings and their only clue was an occasional street name or the round dark marking of a sewer outlet.

"And you say these were the only ones? No copy?"

"Right." Bucks rolled them up again.

The dwarf lit a match and held it out to Bucks, who hesitated a moment and then put the edge of the roll to the flame. There must have been some combustible chemical in the paper, for it burned like a torch. In two seconds he had to drop it on the floor.

"Hey! See here, you can't do that!" shouted the owner, but by the time she got over the flame was out. She kicked at the ashes with disgust and went to get her broom again.

"The sewer tunnels," whispered Mango. "That's where we'll take you. Right under their bloody noses." The dwarf hopped off his chair and headed for the door.

Bucks shook his head, his eyes shut. "I swore I'd never go back down there. My old grandad's ghost might be lurking somewhere, waitin' for me. That's where he died." His right hand started to shake again, and he held it steady with the left. "And what about you?"

"One of us has to stay above, to keep in touch. You're the one they're looking for, not me. It was you who wrote the note to the MP, wasn't it?"

"But you delivered it."

"That's not the way I remember it at all. We better get going."

Book III

28

1

They took Snow to the Coldbath Fields Prison for questioning, which puzzled him even through his shock. There were plenty of closer places. Scotland Yard itself was hardly a quarter mile away from his house.

The inside of the cab was hot. Old sweat rose from the two policemen's uniforms. Snow sat as passively as if they were his private coachmen.

Soon after leaving Golden Square he looked out the dirty window and saw how close they were to the pump. He turned to the policemen.

"Would you mind if we turned here, just for a moment? There's something I need to look at."

They studied Snow briefly, as if trying to fathom some plot. "Don't see why not." One banged on the ceiling with his night-stick. "Turn down Broad Street."

Snow pressed his face to the glass. The pump looked different. It had shed all its sinister aura and seemed only a jutting bit of old brass, amputated of its handle, useless. Three women and a man, all carrying buckets or jugs, stood by, arguing. One woman was poking with a stick into the hole left by the handle.

The cab kept going and within five yards Snow lost his view. He turned to face forward again, sighing with exasperation. No handle. No water. No cholera. Damn! He'd be in no position to find out anything.

If the cases stopped, or even slowed, it would probably happen in the next forty-eight hours. Up-to-the-minute reports were crucial. A week from now it would be close to impossible to make sure the case count was correct.

Even if removing the handle caused the cholera to slow, without accurate proof he might just as well have discovered nothing. And while he should have been at the Record Office, or even doing the rounds on Broad Street, doing the case count himself to be sure it was correct, here he was bundling away to some jail.

"Who am I supposed to have murdered, anyhow?" he asked listlessly.

The men looked surprised but apparently saw no reason not to answer. "Matt Canty," said one, not looking at Snow. "Assistant foreman to the Great Western street works. Head bashed in with that pump handle." It was clear that not even he suspected Snow. Just doing as he was told.

Matt Canty. The man who had tried to warn him. And he had said there was more to tell. Snow realized without any surprise, that what happened to Matt Canty might have been intended for him, too.

2

Snow crouched on his hard chair like a schoolboy kept late for cheating on Latin. It was the third hour. He still had his watch and checked it more and more often. An hour ago his stomach had begun to grind with hunger, loudly enough to hear it. No one had come to the door since they first brought him there. There was no window.

He was just thinking of shouting, kicking at the door, throwing the chair, anything to get some attention, when there was a loud rattling of keys and a young man entered.

"Now see here," began Snow, but the other interrupted him.

"I'm from Forms, sir. I'm afraid I can't answer any of your questions. That's for another department." Without looking up he pulled over a table and the other chair and laid out an inch-thick pile of papers and pen and ink.

Snow was too dazed to answer.

The young man wore glasses and a worn-out black suit, perhaps bought secondhand from a bank clerk. He had an ink blotch the size of a thumbprint on the side of his nose.

"Name of primary school?"

"What?" asked Snow. "Why in God's name do you need to know that?"

"Primary school?"

3

An hour later the man had recorded Snow's entire life on small blank spaces, including every single form of employment, the names of his tutors at university, how much he paid his house-keeper, and the exact scores in every examination he had ever taken, with a large, ominous "X" for any item Snow couldn't remember.

Halfway through it all Snow gave up asking questions about when he might be released, who he could talk to in charge, or why he was being held. He just answered the questions as they became more absurd and impossible.

Finally, the clerk asked, "Reason for committing act?"

"Act? What act?"

"Act for incarceration, sir."

"But I didn't commit anything. That's the whole point. I need to talk to someone in charge, immediately!" Snow heard a note of hysteria in his voice and took a few slow breaths.

"Yes, sir. I can't put you through the next step until we complete the forms. Reason for committing act?"

Suddenly there was a commotion in the corridor and the door burst open. A short man in a dusty black suit came in and at the sight of him the clerk jumped to his feet and stared straight ahead, his shoulders stiff. Snow recognized the man from somewhere but couldn't place him.

"Get this man released immediately." The older man's voice was full of annoyance; but it sounded as if that were his normal tone.

"Yes, Inspector."

That was it, thought Snow. Inspector McGowan, who was there when they found the murdered man in the ditch.

"I never heard of such a thing," said McGowan, half to Snow and half to the clerk. "Detained for three hours. No evidence whatsoever." He gave a short nod to Snow. "Good morning, Doctor. We never did find the man who did that shovel job last month. But one thing's certain: that's the man we want today."

Another man came in, behind the inspector. To Snow's complete surprise it was Sir Philip Constable. His cheeks were bluish-white and the purple marks under his eyes had deepened. To Snow he looked dangerously ill. Snow wondered that he had never noticed before the telltale signs of heart disease. He thought of the digitalis drops he always kept in his anesthesia case. But the case wasn't with him now.

Snow found himself wondering once again what exactly had happened between Lillian and this man. The questions, now unleashed, sprang out at him. What was she holding back? Why had she been so silent two nights ago, when the two of them were making the map? Distrust rose in him, unbidden.

Constable turned to Snow but didn't meet his eyes. "I'm terribly sorry this had to happen." He grabbed Snow's arm and almost pushed him from the cell. The three of them walked rapidly down the dank corridor, which stank of urine.

"This is Inspector McGowan," said Constable. "Such a series of mistakes, you wouldn't believe me if I told you."

"No, no, it's nothing. And I've already met the inspector." Snow wanted to scream at Constable, but years of polite routine held him tighter than chains. "I didn't mind, really. These things happen. Perhaps if I could just get a cab back to my house, or even better, to the Registrar General Office—" Even as he spoke he wondered if he really did want to be out on the street, unprotected.

They had reached the street and Constable, without answering Snow, hustled him into a waiting hansom. The inspector climbed in behind them.

"Scotland Yard," he shouted out the window. He pulled his head back into the cab and turned to Snow. "And we've got our man. Had a good lead on him this morning."

The inspector's eyes were bright, his cheeks set hard in anticipation. Constable stared out the window, silent and moody.

Snow tried to smile and found that he couldn't. "I'm happy to hear it, but I really must get back to—"

"Sir Philip and I want you to be in on the chase. We need your help."

Snow fidgeted in his seat. With this inspector around he might be safe. If there really were anything to be afraid of. He looked sideways at Constable.

"Really, I don't see how I could possibly—" he addressed this to Constable, but Sir Philip persisted in ignoring him, so Snow was forced to turn back to McGowan.

"Yes, it's a good thing you were there when I thought of it. I'm determined to grab him before the day is over," said McGowan. "We need you and your chloroform kit. He's a dangerous man."

29

1

Constable took a deep breath, getting mostly mildewed Scotland Yard dust, but there was a different smell in the air, asserting itself even through the layers and crusts of city brick and cobblestones. It was like the week before the monsoons started in India. Autumn was on its way, and rain with it.

It wasn't just the weather that had changed. From the time he'd woken, Constable had felt in his chest the old heaviness and constriction, but it had altered. The stabbing became more consistent and demanding, as if the sensations in his body were inseparable from a gloom descending thickly over him, closing down his vision and movements.

The pain was constant. It came and went in waves that affected his vision. A minute of sickening darkness in the periphery of his sight, with spasms that made him sweat, then five minutes of respite. Then a half hour later, like a faithful clock, the darkness would return.

The heaviness of the air in Scotland Yard did nothing to lessen his brooding. Today a stinking mist from the river spread through the buildings, as bad as anything rising from the Bombay harbor.

Damn McGowan. If Constable had known that anyone would pay the least attention to the murder of a ditch digger, he would have torn Bucks's note into pieces. But Bucks's suggestion to murder Canty had seemed the easiest thing, especially since no one could connect Constable with it. It was Bucks who would carry the guilt, if anyone. Then when Constable thought of the additional plan to keep Snow out of the way for a few days, the plan seemed perfect.

But this infernal inspector had sprung up out of nowhere. McGowan wouldn't let it drop. He had led the chase for this insignificant murder as if it had been a political assassination. Of course Snow was released right away, ruining that part of the plan. Constable was bewildered by the inspector's drive until the man had confided in him.

"My father dug ditches. His whole life, never got the red stain from his skin. I'll see this boy gets justice." And he had rubbed his hands together, as if to take a stain off his own skin, and stared straight ahead.

McGowan would get Bucks. Constable could see it. They'd already had a tip from a pickpocket in Coldbath Fields. Check with his ma, he'd said. Constable already guessed where Bucks would be, but there was no point in hurrying things. And then there was the incredible bad luck of McGowan getting the idea of using Snow's chloroform equipment. There had been a few recent cases of thieves using chloroform to subdue their victims. "Since we've got the chloroform expert right here, let's turn justice around," McGowan had said.

Even now, Constable thought, he could leave. No one knew anything yet. He could simply stand and leave the room like any other man, say that he couldn't spare the time to lead the search after all. He could take a cab to his banker's, or even go on foot, withdraw a large sum, and head for Brussels or Geneva. By the time they caught Bucks, Constable could be drinking coffee on a sunny terrace by Lake Como, listening to a nightingale. Lillian might have softened by then. With a flood of emotion, Constable decided to ask her to go with him. It was perfect. A terraced villa beside Lake Como. She could be reading a novel on the chair next to him, the boy playing Mozart inside.

But he didn't move.

Canty's body was on a slab in a room downstairs. As soon as they had arrived here with Snow, McGowan had corralled the doctor into examining the head wound, herding Constable along with them as if to some sideshow.

"Here we are, Doctor. You have no idea how happy I am to have you here; it looks like the same man did both jobs, doesn't it?"

Snow had touched the smashed skull with detached clinical interest. "Exactly the same kind of impact," he had said, lightly stroking the concave skull. "This time, though, they cut through the superficial temporal artery. That's why there was so much blood."

The body had must been saturated with spilled blood, for the clothes were black and stiff, and Canty's open green eyes, unharmed, peered out through what looked like a coal miner's grime.

Constable had felt sick and moved away as soon as he could, while Snow and McGowan conferred.

That was an hour ago. Now he looked across at Snow at a writing desk. The doctor hadn't spoken to him since they got into the cab outside Coldbath Fields. Did the man have any idea of the power he held? Constable didn't think so. Snow seemed to be stumbling blindly into his disastrous findings, without making any connections at all. There he huddled, scrawling frantically on a sheet of scrap paper, oblivious to the gloom and to the Scotland Yard stink.

Maybe McGowan's chloroform idea wasn't so bad. By getting Snow into the sewers at least he'd be delayed a day from finding out. Long enough for Constable to think of something, maybe. It was a slim hope.

By now Constable hated Snow, yet at the same time he yearned to talk to him, to tell him how it all had come about, especially about Lillian. Greeley couldn't have had any insight into such a delicate situation, but perhaps a younger man—

"Sir Philip?" The question broke through, sounding impatient, as if it were the third time the clerk had spoken.

"Eh? Yes, are we ready to be off?"

"They've arrived with Dr. Snow's anesthesia kit. And there's a message for you."

They had sent a messenger to Snow's house for the kit and the boy walked in now, handing the heavy box to Snow.

Snow hardly looked up, pen in hand, as if hoping he didn't

254

have to stop writing. "Thank you. Any news of those cholera lists I asked for?"

"No, sir. Not available yet."

Constable opened his note. It was from Greeley: "Must see you immediately. Important information." Constable crumpled the note into his pocket; Greeley seemed far away, like something out of his distant past.

"Well," said Snow to Constable, "we can't know anything about the new cholera rates for another twelve hours anyway. I'll just have to wait it out."

"Quite." Constable looked at his watch. "Shall we go, then?"

Snow stood, resigned, and stuffed the papers into his jacket.

Constable took a step toward the door and felt his heart give another skip with a sharp pulse of pain which ebbed slowly, like flowing oil. Nausea came and left, and a cold sweat soaked through his collar. Snow was still behind him.

"Sir Philip," asked Snow, "are you quite all right? I can offer you some digitalis. It might ease things."

Constable hadn't realized it was so apparent. "No, nothing. It's just a mild weakness I get from time to time. Old age." He tried to laugh it off.

"Whatever you say."

"Let's be off," said McGowan.

2

Nothing ever happened on this street. That was obvious from the crowd of children and dogs that gathered around the police wagon as it pulled up outside the house. Every house in the row looked exactly alike. Five steps to the door, an iron railing, no grass, no tree, no flowers in the windows. Most of the houses had the blinds down tight, as if it wouldn't be respectable to look out at anything on the street.

Bucks's mother's house was no different. It was far from middle class, but not exactly a slum. They knocked at the door and it was two full minutes before a woman in her seventies, dressed in shoddy black silk and cheap American lace, opened it.

"Mathilda Bucks?"

"Yes?" She looked gratified, as if expecting an award or special recognition from the parish council.

Behind them, on the street, half a dozen curious children hovered at the foot of the stairs.

"We need to ask you some questions about your son, Ralph Bucks."

The expectant look wavered. "Ralph? What's he done?" She touched the corner of her mouth with one finger.

They all went into the house and shut the door.

The edge of the old parlor sofa bristled with broken springs, and Constable squirmed. He almost wished the old lady weren't giving the answers so freely. It was as if she wanted to gain favor with the officers and would gladly do anything, even betray her son.

"Oh, that Ralph. He always said, 'If they ever are after me, Ma, I'll know where to go,' and I would say, 'Who? If who are after you?' and he would just wink." She lifted the grubby teapot and offered it once more to the one policeman who had been foolish enough to accept a cup. The others all shook their heads without smiling.

"Where did he say he might go, Mrs. Bucks?" McGowan asked this patiently, as if talking to a child.

Her answering smile made Constable cringe, but McGowan didn't seem to notice it.

"Why, the place he always knew best. That his pa taught him about. We weren't always in these grand digs." She gestured around at the faded flashy wallpaper and the dim windows. "Worked our ways up, you know. Toshers." She giggled. "Not me, that is. I met Joseph after he'd made his big find."

"It was a full tea service in sterling," she went on. "Lying right there in the tunnel." She took a sip of her tea, savoring the memory. "I tell you now 'cause it was so long ago, and Joseph is passed on. All bashed up it was, but silver is silver, and he got eighty pound for it."

"For God's sake, woman. We haven't much time." Inspector McGowan tapped his feet in impatience. "Tell us where you think he might be."

She set the cup noisily in the saucer and sat up straight. "Well, aren't I tellin' you all along? Down below, in the sewers. That's where a tosher works, finding what he can. My Joe knew them as well as any."

256

"In the sewers? But where? There are miles of them." McGowan looked dismayed.

She seemed troubled and vague. "I can't tell you exactly. But he knew the entrance by the Queenhithe Docks. That's where they used to work. And there's a man still there, named—what was it? I can't recall. Ask at The Drowning Man. They'll know."

Constable flinched at the name. He'd met Bucks there, once.

McGowan herded them all out the door, back to Snow who had insisted on waiting in the cab, still writing. He didn't even look up when the door opened and only stopped when the wagon was under way.

"Where are we headed now?" Snow asked the inspector, ignoring Constable.

"Under London. The sewers beyond the Queenhithe docks."

Snow narrowed his eyes, unbelieving. "But what about the cholera? The water is deadly."

"What," said McGowan, "and let the man go free?" He glared at Snow and Constable, as if accusing them of a crime too.

A younger policeman sat up. "And another thing, sir. There's the tides."

McGowan asked him, impatiently, "What about the tides? What does that matter?"

The young man cleared his throat. "Well, the water level'll go up when the tide comes in, you know? And it won't be just any tide today. Big storm coming."

"What the devil do you know about it?" asked McGowan.

" 'Is dad ran a 'erring boat out of Greenwich, sir. 'E's right," one of the other men said.

"And high tide today is at four P.M., sir."

Constable looked at his watch. It was noon.

257

30

1

They picked up the tosher right where Mrs. Bucks said he'd be, drinking his profits at The Drowning Man. The dark-haired woman behind the bar pointed to him silently when asked.

"Does I know the sewers?" he said, drunk, leaning sideways. "Like the wife's quim, sad to say. All too well. And I know Bucks, too." Then he sat up straighter, frowning, gathering his wits and narrowing his eyes at them. "You can't be thinkin' of going down now, not with this storm coming on."

For an answer the row of grim men simply stared at him while McGowan pulled out his Scotland Yard badge and held it up.

"You must be mad, if you'll forgive my sayin' it, sir. I've worked the sewers for years and nothin' would force me down there. You got the worse thing possible; storm comin', tide risin', autumn tide too."

McGowan folded his arms. "I'll be plain with you. You can take us down and then go straight to Millbank Prison. Or you can take us down and then go straight to the next deportation ship. Or you can take us down and then go home. It's up to you."

The tosher sighed, as if having been through it before, and picked up his shovel-shaped rubber hat, making for the door. "I always knew toshin' was against the law, but who ever thought you coppers would bother with the likes of us? We better get a move on then, that's all I can say."

Once outside the man, sober, sure of himself now, and professional, faced them like a judge. "The only way in, this time of day, is by the old doors."

"We're going in closer to the City," said McGowan. "I don't know anything about any doors."

"The Queenhithe Dock doors, sir," said the tosher, even though McGowan hadn't asked. "It's a bit of a walk once we get inside, at least two miles, but it's the surest way. Any other access would put us God knows where, might be miles of passages before I knew where I was. And things shift down there, there's no telling. But the Queenhithe doors, as long as the river's not too high already, that'd be the way."

McGowan glanced once at Sir Philip, as if asking for authority, and then nodded his head shortly.

The place was only a few streets from the pub, and they trotted in a tense parade down upper Thames Street, to a spot where they could descend steeply to the river by a flight of stairs. All the street noises were left behind. At the bottom step it was just the men and the river and the darkening sky.

The shoal of muddy pebbles under their feet seemed a flat watery world to itself. Gas works jutted up on the Southwark shore. Boats, moored along the river as far as the eye could see, were deserted and silent, their rigging and tackle not even clanking.

The low tide exposed twenty or thirty yards of slate-colored mud, sloping down to the lapping water. An embankment wall of decaying black bricks showed a green line where the tide would rise to, higher than the heads of any man in the group. The tops of the doors were so big that Constable wondered if the architect had ever envisioned some ghostly vessel sailing through. The iron gates could have allowed a sailboat with a thirty foot mast.

They weren't bolted open in any way, but a decade of tides had built up a pile of sand at the base of each that made it impossible for them to close. A continual trickle flowed from the center of the tunnel, down the middle of a channel gutted by

259

erosion. On either side of this foul brook were footprints, fresh since the high tide that morning. They were all sizes, both bare-foot and shod.

"Look!" cried Snow, finally taking an interest. "Someone's been in before us!"

The tosher laughed. "Laws, sir, of course. This tunnel is bread and butter for dozens. There's treasure glimmering in there, if you knows where to look, and if you ain't too picky about smells and rats and such. I had a mate found himself a gold coffee pot, solid through, and coins by the pound. Besides, the city works folks would have been digging in here. Rebuilding, they tell us."

McGowan cut off the man with his hand. "We have two hours before the next high tide. Allowing for forty minutes to get to the area under Golden Square and at least another forty to get back, we've got to go now if we do it at all."

They all looked at the sky, dark with clouds.

For a moment, as if in a dream, Constable saw huge mountains to the east, an Alp-high range he had never known before. It filled him with fleeting amazement, this previously unknown body of land so close to London, where before all had been flat and marshy. But then he realized that of course it was only a bank of thunderclouds rising above the river beyond Eastcheap.

A day in northern India came back to him. It was late after-noon, and since dawn he had been scouting along the plains near Jampur. A distant range of treeless hills had for a second seemed to him a bank of blessed, impossible rain clouds. Even when he had realized his mistake, the sensation of relief had lasted all day. It had been years since he'd remembered it.

These London clouds, though, were real enough. The tosher was right. In a few hours the tunnel could be flooded.

Constable was the first in. Within yards, the ceiling lowered, and he saw that his idea of a boat sailing in would have been impossible. In the same way the descent from the street to the beach hushed all city sounds, this crossing muffled all the river noises and all the light. He hadn't realized before how reassuring was the steady lapping of the waves and occasional gull's cry, even the rustle of light wind around his ears.

The time he had gone down with Bucks to see the sewer renovations, it had been far from the river, and much narrower. But the overall effect was the same as now; the tosher's torch and McGowan's lantern lit the brick walls with a highlighting which exposed all cracks and flaws and made the trickling stream in the center of the path look even slimier. The silence wasn't absolute. A constant dripping played a background to their gritty footsteps. And the squeaking of the rats rose and fell as the men passed unseen nests.

But more powerful than any sight or sound was the smell of human waste, almost giving a texture to the air; visible, caressing, and so strong that Constable had to fight to keep from retching. He was amazed that no one commented on it. I suppose Snow is used to this sort of thing from the places he goes, he thought.

"Better turn left here, gentlemen," said the tosher from the back of the line. "In fact, if you don't mind, I'd best lead from here on. It gets tricky in spots and I know what to expect."

By now McGowan seemed only too glad to let the man take over. They turned aside from the main tunnel, which had been high enough that the ceiling was lost in the darkness overhead, into a much smaller passageway, too narrow to allow for more than a single-file approach and low enough that Snow had to stoop.

Constable felt as if he were walking deeper and deeper into a land of coffins. He had never liked enclosed spaces.

They passed a pile of new brick and a clutter of abandoned pickaxes, shovels, and lengths of rope. Again, no one commented but Constable noticed it. In minutes there was another spot like it, and here the arch overhead had lost its bricks, even though they looked new.

As the last of the file passed under the spot there was a sudden tumble of sand and mud from the ceiling. The second policeman cried out and they all rushed forward.

"The damn tunnel is collapsing on us, Constable," shouted Snow.

"Nothing to worry about," called the tosher from the front of the line. "Happens all the time. Especially lately, with the new works."

Constable saw Snow glaring at him, and he tried to look straight ahead. It was his first sight of what happened when salty sand was used for construction. Holds up for long enough, Bucks had said. Constable assumed he meant a few years. Now he saw it was a few weeks. They might as well have used powdered sugar for mortar.

The water at their feet, a narrow trickle until now, deepened to a few inches. The brown stew soaked through Constable's shoes in seconds, working its way through his socks and between his toes. Again he fought his desire to vomit.

They came to a section so low that all had to bend to get through. Constable's panic rose and as he crouched he felt the tightness in his chest expand, clenching and gripping like a fist. He forced himself to keep walking. Sweat dripped from his brow and his breath came in gasps. In a few yards they could stand upright again and the movement of straightening sent a new course of pain through his chest, so violent that he groaned aloud. He paused, praying that it would pass.

McGowan heard. "We're making good time. Let's stop a moment."

"No, no, go on, quickly." said Constable. "I'm fine, just a little short of breath."

The pain faded, the sweat dried, and Constable felt stronger. He forced himself to breathe evenly and deeply, putting each wet foot before the other in a conscious act of forward motion.

Another ruined digging site opened up on their right. This one was much bigger. It looked as though an arch had already been completed when it collapsed, for there was a waist-high pile of brick rubble on top of sledge hammers and buckets. Through the debris the words "Great Western Gravel" showed on the buckets.

This time McGowan stopped. "What's been going on here?" he asked, indignant. "It looks like someone's been destroying the sewers."

Snow looked hard at Constable. "Perhaps Sir Philip could tell you."

Constable took a deep breath in panic, but McGowan's question must have been rhetorical, for he didn't respond to Snow's answer and just kept walking.

Constable went back to chewing over what he'd do when he found Bucks, how he'd get to him first, what he could say in five words that would convince Bucks to keep silent. It was as though the broad expanse of his consciousness had shrunk to three points; his pain, a place to talk to Snow, and how to silence Bucks. Nothing else got through. Least of all any thoughts on what he'd actually say to Snow, or the consequences of not silencing Bucks.

Lillian hadn't crossed his mind in an hour. He'd forgotten his son. His life was now a stream of dark wet brick, pain, forward motion, and repetition of a frantically imagined whispering. "Don't talk, I'll make it worth it. You'll be rich." The only other effort Constable allowed himself was an occasional attempt to get in front of the file again, in case they should come on Bucks unexpectedly.

The water was now splashing to their knees. Snow lifted his heavy case shoulder high, muttering in annoyance.

Suddenly the tunnel opened up and Constable felt he could breathe easier.

"This is it, sir," said the tosher. "We've reached Golden Square."

They were in a vaulted space like a small cathedral transept, with tunnels going off symmetrically in four directions. Smaller recesses and stairs in between the four main tunnels led to darker spaces. The noise of the rats was loud. The stink was abominable.

"What are we to do now?" said McGowan. "Have you any idea where in here he could be?"

"Well, those smaller places, each of them leads up to the street eventually. One of them, the north one I think, has a little space in it about halfway up, almost like a room. A place toshers from my father's day used for to hide out. That's the spot where I'll bet he be. But we've got to be quiet. If he hears us coming he can get out and up to the street and we've lost him."

McGowan fidgeted. "Why didn't we just come down from above?"

"It ain't that simple. The passage ain't direct. It goes down into a smaller sewer path before it comes up. Some of them have been blocked since I last was here. The best one is under water now. Only Bucks knew it well enough to use it like this."

As the man spoke, a rushing watery sound swooped behind them from the passage they'd just come up. It was the only warning they got of a thigh-high wave which drenched them and withdrew in seconds. Constable almost fell with the force of it.

"Damn," shouted Snow. "I've lost my case." He grabbed a torch from one of the bobbies and held it down to the water, groping with one hand. The light was useless, though. Only black reflections shimmered up at him. He could have been standing in oil, or thin tar.

The rest of them took a moment to catch their breath. Constable was the first to speak.

"We can't go back the way we came, that's clear. We'd better get up those stairs." He watched Snow, still kicking the water all around them, hoping to find the case.

"Snow, we've got to go on," shouted McGowan.

Snow looked up, an expression of loss on his face. "That was my best brass ether tube. I designed it myself. I used it on the queen."

"We'll just have to use force when we catch him," said McGowan, "it can't be helped."

Snow didn't bother to answer, but leaned over for one more look.

The tosher stamped his feet with nervousness. "Come on, guvnor, we got to get going. Maybe it'll turn up in my bag someday."

No one laughed. Suddenly, inches from where Snow had bent to grope one last time, a hansom-sized section of new concrete and brick vaulting crashed into the water. Snow covered his head with his arms and lurched forward. Constable stumbled to one knee with the shock.

When the dust cleared they all looked at the ceiling. On one side of the arch, a hole now gaped into the medieval carvings of some older vault, left from the time before the fire of London, or before the Plague. From it came a stench far worse than anything they'd smelled before, and in the dim light the working of some metal piping chugged and bubbled.

Snow stared up at it while he rubbed the back of his head, where a brick had glanced. He turned to the tosher.

"Did you say we're under Golden Square?"

"Well, not exactly, sir. A bit to the east, I think. Under Broad Street."

"Broad Street and Cambridge?"

"I expect so." He looked over his shoulder, not interested, just wanting to move. "Best be off. The whole place could come down."

They all followed. Except for Snow, who stared over his shoulder at the exposed pumping works until he had to run, splashing through the water, to catch up.

They silently filed into the smallest of the four tunnels. It immediately narrowed even further and turned into a winding staircase. It was so cramped that Snow, the tallest among them, was forced to bend over to get up.

"How far below the street are we?" Constable asked the tosher.

"Shh! About twenty feet when we get to the room. But don't talk. We're almost there."

Constable, at the head of the party, was the first to see a light ahead. He motioned to the others to stop and cover their lanterns, dampen their torches. They were left in a deep brown darkness. He groped his way toward an open door. A clear bar of yellow light came from behind it.

A soft slapping from the room sounded vaguely familiar to Constable. He couldn't quite place it. He inched his way up to the open door, secure in his darkness, and looked in, gesturing to those behind him to be silent.

Bucks sat at a rough table with his back to the door, playing solitaire with a deck of cards. He continually held his watch to the candle. Across the room another doorway opened onto darkness.

Constable had only a few seconds to decide. As he stood trying to catch his breath another spasm gripped him across the chest. A low moan burst out of him.

Bucks whipped around, scattering cards, his face rigid with fear and surprise.

"Don't—don't speak," gasped Constable in a whisper through his pain. "Rich—you'll be rich. Don't talk."

That was all he had time for. Just as the rest of the search party pushed up behind Constable into the room, Bucks hurled his chair at the men in the doorway, shoved over the table to further block their way, and rushed from the room out the opposite passage. The single candle fell to the floor and went out. In the confusion of sudden darkness Bucks's steps faded down the passageway.

2

By the time they managed to light the lanterns and torches several minutes had passed. They pressed forward.

The tosher was now in full stride, with no qualms about giving orders to everyone. "Got to go faster. He can't get far now, not if the tide continues the way it has. There's a place up ahead where the stairs go down again like I told you, and it's the only way out. I know that passage'll be underwater by now. Unless he's a water rat, that's where he'll be."

They were going down stairs even narrower than the ones they'd climbed. Constable's pain was continual now. His vision came and went. But now that he'd delivered his message to Bucks, that part of his mind was at rest and he felt enormously relieved, almost jubilant. He could focus on his body's direct orders to breathe, walk, breathe, walk.

Until he collided into the man in front of him he didn't realize he'd been staggering forward with his eyes shut. They'd stopped at the bottom of a flight of stairs.

The tosher was whispering, "When we turn the corner of this passage, that's where the flooded part'll be, along a channel, and that's where he'll be if I'm right." The man turned and headed up the last short passage. Constable followed blindly.

The tosher was right. As they turned the corner and went down three steps, Bucks was there, pacing on the brick embankment of a rushing underground stream. He saw them and made as if to jump in but stopped. He probably couldn't swim.

But even as the first man stepped forward they heard a gurgling roar from the darkness to the right, where the water flowed out of the tunnel. Before anyone could think, a wall of water poured out on them. It was neck high, but they held on to the bricks behind them and didn't fall. As soon as the wave receded enough to stop the pull against their legs the party retreated back up the stairs.

Constable shouted to Bucks, using what felt like the last air in his lungs. "For God's sake, man, get out of the way. Give yourself up, come to higher ground." Bucks's footing looked unsteady and the place where he stood was still two feet deep. Warnings of another swell spoke from the darkness to their right, and Constable reached a hand out to the man, shouting, "Grab it! This one will be bigger, let me pull you in!" Some mechanical reaction seemed to take over and he felt suddenly stronger. He knew his plea to Bucks in the room wouldn't be enough, or would even make things worse. Bucks had to be silenced.

Now was his chance. Constable felt for a firm footing and

made ready for the push he could give Bucks under cover of the rushing flood. The light of the torches was too dim for the others to see what was going on. But as icy froth swirled around him he looked at Bucks's face and saw in his eyes the dread of death. Constable knew that fear too well. It sang him to sleep at night with the ringing of the blood in his head.

The shock of realizing that he had something in common with the man was so great that he hesitated and lost his chance.

The wave receded but another came almost on top of it. This time Constable didn't think. He reached his arm out and shouted, "Grab it, you fool! It's your last chance!"

Bucks lurched toward the outstretched hand. He gripped fiercely in his panic. Constable no longer thought of pushing Bucks in. Suddenly, it seemed that the most important thing in his life was to rescue him. He was dimly aware of Snow, behind him, leaning out from the stairs and shouting something, grabbing his other hand.

But even before the water reached its highest level, another flood of pain washed over his chest. It was connected, like a tree root, to Bucks's grip on his right hand and the pulling of Snow on his left. Pain surged over his whole body, even down to his toes, and the dark spots that had filled his view earlier turned golden and brilliant.

He felt Bucks's tug on his right arm and he knew that the man, in his panic, was too strong to be rescued. He knew he would be pulled in along with him.

His last thought was a decision to pull his left hand free of Snow's, and he did it. A final wave of river water burst through the tunnel. As Constable's vision was overwhelmed with a wash of light, the stream lifted him off his feet, engulfed him, and sent him and Bucks into the tunnels beyond the foot of the stairs.

31

1

In a drenching rainstorm Snow arrived home. Even though he was soaked with the rain it wasn't enough to wash away the water from the tunnels. He stank like a corpse tossed up on a beach. There was a taste in his mouth of shit and rotten eggs, worse than anything left from too much bad wine. He felt as if he'd been poisoned.

He rushed up the stairs, stripping off his clothes as he went, and shouted down to Mrs. Jarrett for hot water.

Once Snow had treated a patient obsessed with cleanliness. Every three minutes the woman had looked at her fingers, rubbed them suspiciously, sniffed them, then gone to the nearest water to scrub them once more. Their skin was raw and cracked from so much abrasion. He had tried to keep her from doing it by locking her in a room without water and within an hour she was shrieking convulsively, writhing on the floor, wiping imaginary filth from her skin. In the end he gave up and told her family she should keep washing.

Today he knew exactly how she must have felt.

Mrs. Jarrett appeared at the door of his room with a can of

268

water, looking apprehensive and alarmed at his half-dress and his long absence, and obviously dying to ask what had happened with the police.

He grabbed the lukewarm water from her and shouted, "I don't want just a can of water. Bring up the tub. I need a bath."

"But, Doctor, today's only Friday and you usually don't—"

"I don't give a damn what I usually do. I want a bath this instant."

She hurried off.

"And throw these in the dustbin!" he shouted after her, hurling his sopping linen down the stairs. He poured the can of water over himself as if putting out a fire, not caring if the carpet was ruined.

She finally appeared with the tub and he stood, panting with impatience, until she had filled it.

Once in the steaming bath he felt calmer. The downpour continued outside and its hypnotic dripping soothed him into almost forgetting where he had been. But visions continued flashing before him, of Constable's last stretch toward Bucks, the surge after surge of water, and the crumbling rotten brick all around.

When it was clear that Constable and Bucks were beyond rescue, the rest of the party had rushed back the way they came. Even the brash, path-finding tosher seemed nervous. They all expected to find their way submerged or blocked by crumbled brick.

But the man stopped unexpectedly at a side tunnel, a way they hadn't gone before, and he had led them to a rickety ladder going straight up. Half of the rungs were rusted out. As Snow stood at the base, waiting for his turn to climb, he heard above him rungs snapping in the darkness. One of the policemen shouted in fear before catching himself.

Snow was the last to go up. It seemed that he climbed for an hour, though it was probably only five minutes. The aperture he ascended grew narrower. Holes appeared on either side with rats poking their snouts out, sniffing, annoyed. Finally the light at the top grew much stronger and Snow emerged onto the cobblestones of Jermyn Street, surrounded by expensive shops. He felt as stunned and disoriented as if he'd emerged into the middle of a bedouin camp.

The rest of the party had been waiting for him in the downpour. The early evening rush of cabs, carts, and omnibuses inched around the unexpected hole in the ground, which gaped before them with its grill pulled aside like the door of a liberated prison.

Snow stepped back to the edge and peered into the descending blackness. Although he never would have said that heights bothered him, this long look into the hole's darkness had an effect on him like a drug, so greatly did it change his consciousness and his sense of place. He must have swayed, for one of the policemen grabbed his arm.

"Steady, sir. You be needing an escort home?"

"I'm free to go, then?"

The man looked puzzled. "Go? Of course, sir, whatever you likes. The rest of us has to go on to Scotland Yard, but not you. You're sure, now, you don't want some help?"

2

After the bath Snow dressed and rushed to Lillian's house, dying to get rid of the feeling of distrust that had lingered with him ever since seeing Constable that morning. He would tell her that Constable was dead. He was sure she would finally explain everything to him. Then the two of them, together, could follow the course of the cholera cases to see if the pump handle changed things. By the time he reached Brook Street his mood was almost elated.

She was out, the maid told him. Olympia, too, but not with Lillian. Didn't know where either of them went.

He felt crushed. He was about to leave, but at the last minute wrote a note for her: "Send for me as soon as you return. We must try to find out if the cholera case rate changes."

He went back to his house and straight to his desk.

Snow thanked providence that the pages he'd already worked on that morning in the jail had been in his coat pocket and not in the chloroform case. They were warped and stained with damp, like some old church archive, and seemed more than just notes. Snow found himself unwilling to leaf through them, as if he might find things some spooky other voice had dictated.

A strange reluctance to begin working rose in him. There was

270

no reason for it; the pens lay ready, there was plenty of ink. No one would interrupt him tonight. He had only to start his strings of words and his entire project would be finished. And yet he sat staring at nothing for a full hour.

The stacks of notebooks which had seemed so cryptic and frustrating a week ago lay before him. Every figure in them, every jot and ink blot would fit into his solution like a piece in an ivory Chinese puzzle. They shrank in significance, almost visibly, before his eyes.

They weren't the only puzzle pieces. There were the loose bricks fifty feet under Broad Street, revealing that gaping hole into the lower works of the pump. He could hear again the oddly musical clink that the last few chunks of fired clay made as they fell, rhythmically, onto each other, and the bubbling of the water at the base of the pipe.

Finally, after ten at night, his thoughts were broken by a message from Lillian. Snow tore it open, hoping she would say she'd be there any minute.

> *New cholera cases in Broad Street down to eight by this*
> *afternoon. Urgent family matter has arisen; I will see you*
> *when I can.*

He crumpled the paper and threw it on the floor. His sense of disappointment was overwhelming. Not about the cases, of course; that was just as he expected, down to the exact hour. There would be a few cases still, from the various buckets and ewers people had filled in the last hours as he stood by the pump. But those supplies would have been drunk soon enough. He had estimated that the soonest a slowing of the epidemic would show would be in forty-eight hours.

But he had hoped Lillian could be at his side for this. He felt there was something deeply wrong. What did she mean by a family matter? She had no family.

He tried hard to put her out of his mind, and to feel triumphant, or at least clever, at finding his final proof. But he couldn't. It all seemed too easy, too obvious. Cholera was scattered all over London, spread by a variety of water sources. Even though he knew it, he still couldn't prove it. Not there, at least; his proof lay in the case concentration on Broad Street. Any idiot could have figured the Broad Street thing out. Stop the

Broad Street water supply and you stop the Broad Street cholera. *Quod erat demonstrandum.*

As far as laying the blame somewhere, Constable and Bucks were dead, and there was no one left to punish.

Snow would have sworn that Constable was showing classic symptoms of angina from heart failure, and must have been in terrible pain after all the exertion of the search. Snow dwelt on what his last moments must have been like. Constable didn't look the least bit afraid as the water bore down on him. The expression on his face had almost been one of ecstasy, as if a final understanding had broken over him.

Snow got up for one of his rare drinks of whiskey, and forced himself to return to his writing. The phrases started to flow in clear, detached prose, even though his mind was actually filled with sentences lurid enough for a street patterer's murder yarn.

It would make such a good story, he thought. When the ceiling fell in, a few bits of brick had actually hit him and his mouth had filled with dust. After the pain subsided the first thing he noticed was the taste. The dust was salty. As salty as the old stains on Constable's shoes and on the boots of that dead man so many weeks ago. Now he knew where it had come from.

It had probably not been Sir Philip who had started the short-cuts. But someone had helped him to it. Ralph Bucks. And Snow knew, as surely as if he'd been told, where they got the salty sand for these brick works.

Those sand beds, up the river beyond Teddington Weir, had to be replaced every ten weeks or so, and Snow knew now what they did with the old sand. Full of Thames salt and every particle of sewage that passed through the piping system, the sand was carted a mile or two into London and mixed with the mortar. Saved them heaps of money, he supposed.

It wouldn't have been so bad if it had just been dirty. The dirt itself probably wasn't enough to infect the water. But the salt, that was the weak ingredient. The salt could no more hold mortar together than could a mix of spit and flour. It weakened the structures and they collapsed.

Snow could see it before him now, the thin trickle of sewage burbling into the collapsed well over the rusted pipes. Sounding like a pastoral brook, or like the background murmur of a Schubert song. The sound of raw sewage going directly into the pump, straight up the seventy feet and into the water jugs of the

272

Broad Street housewives. There wasn't enough there to taste it or smell it. Just enough to breed cholera.

There was no way to prove whether the pump's water came from Southwark and Vauxhall. Even though the company's water was just as bad as river water, it seemed it was beyond Snow to prove that it invariably caused cholera. And, of course, the pump alone couldn't have caused the cholera all over London.

The city's cholera was from a combination of watery sources; an initial infection from some ship dumping its refuse into the river, the poor drainage all over the city, Southwark and Vauxhall's criminal evasion of the filtering, and the collapsing sewer works under the streets.

Even the people who got Southwark and Vauxhall water weren't all unlucky; some boiled their water, and some probably didn't drink much.

And Snow's final conclusion was that he didn't think he could prove any of it.

Except the case of the Broad Street pump and the map of cholera around it. Whatever happened elsewhere in the city, if you stopped the Broad Street water supply, you stopped cholera in Broad Street. It was so simple, so clear. *Quod erat demonstrandum.*

The map of Broad Street and its pump was the key. It showed that cholera was in the water, it came by water, it spread by water. That much Snow knew and could prove. If he could just publish his report and use it to get people to stop drinking city water, his job was done.

The map was on his desk. When he reached home he had spread the paper out flat on the floor until it dried, then carefully refolded it. He didn't want to lose contact with it, and kept his left hand flat on the crisp paper, which seemed to give off a heat of its own.

He took the pages he'd already written and straightened the edges. They made a weighty stack. He put them under a plaster bust of Hippocrates which Caleb had given to him when he got his medical degree, and pulled out a fresh sheet of paper. In the center he wrote the words, "On The Mode of Communication of Cholera." That would do for a title. It would look well in the clear Roman typesetting that *The Lancet* used.

32

Two medical students walked with Greeley as he left the lecture theater, each vying for the occasional luck to open a door for him or hear some choice words. There was always a chance of an unexpected lecture during the long walk to the commons room. Maybe a discourse on wound corruption and sepsis, or new surgical and amputation techniques.

But today Greeley was silent. He seemed barely to notice them trotting along. His face was rigid with self-absorption, as if he were on his way to a delicate and lifesaving surgery.

The students gave up and fell behind him, starting up their own conversation in low voices.

"We'd better hurry if you don't want to miss the guest lecturer in the hygiene class. Sir Philip Constable, the deputy minister of public health, is talking about cholera."

"Hardly likely, I would think," answered the other.

"What, have I got my schedule wrong?" He scrabbled nervously among his books and papers and pulled out a carefully drawn timetable.

"No, I suppose your bloody schedule is good. It's just that Sir Philip was drowned in the Queenhithe sewers yesterday. They still haven't found the body."

"No!" The student's papers were forgotten for a moment, but they both kept walking.

274

"He was apparently heading some sort of search party. So now we have to sit through two hours of the Saturday talk on poorhouse sanitation techniques. Damn."

The two turned a corner. Ten paces behind them Greeley stopped, his face suddenly flushed, his hands clenched tight around a case of papers. His breathing came in short gasps, loud enough that an anatomy lecturer stopped to see if Greeley needed help. The man backed off at Greeley's curt reply.

Greeley shivered, as if suddenly cold, and then left the hospital courtyard and hailed a cab.

33

Saturday morning came and went. The points of Snow's pens were so worn down that his writing left uncouth smears across the paper, but he couldn't be bothered to fix them. In another two hours or so he'd be finished with the first draft and he could get to work drawing the tables.

Through the squeak of his pen he heard a cab stop at his door and then the receding clatter of hooves on cobblestones. He tried to pretend he didn't care who it could be, and forced himself to keep writing. But his mind filled with Lillian and he smiled. His bell rang once, and again. He imagined her standing at the door, waiting, maybe tapping her foot.

Mrs. Jarrett seemed to be out so he went downstairs himself, trying to look unconcerned and indifferent.

It was the first time he had seen her in black. She brushed past him up the stairs, looking distracted, even angry at something.

When the two stood alone in his study there was a long silence. Snow felt himself physically drawn to her in a way that reminded him of standing at the edge of that pit in the street yesterday. When he approached her it was with the feeling that he could fall into a long, dark descent. But she pulled away from him and began to pace the room, taking short breaths and staring at her feet.

"What's all this about?" he asked.

She stopped walking and looked at him. Still distant. "As you already know, Sir Philip Constable died yesterday." She gave a harsh, short laugh that grated on his ears. "I'm a little surprised you didn't think to tell me."

Snow fought his irritation. After all, *she* was the one who had insisted there was nothing between her and the man. "I did try to see you, as a matter of fact. But you weren't exactly available. After that I was thinking only of the cholera cases, to see if they slowed. Your note said that they had."

She obviously didn't intend to tell him why she had refused to see him. "Yes. You were right about the pump. It doesn't surprise me. Congratulations." Her tone was flat, as if she were a stranger thanking him for a seat on a train. "But in the past twenty-four hours things have come to light. Remember when we saw Constable's name in connection with the Southwark and Vauxhall Water company, and The Great Western?"

"Of course." The image came to him of the buckets, shovels, and abandoned equipment in the tunnels, with "Great Western" proudly stamped all over them.

"His death brought it all out. The company was a fake. Constable set it up and pulled in a few big names to give it the stamp of approval, he connected it with the renovations, and took the investors' money." Her air of detachment didn't change while telling this story. She still talked as if to a stranger. "Constable's debts were apparently enormous, forcing him to do something like this sooner or later. If he had lived he would have been ruined. As it is, dozens of investors will lose their fortunes."

"And you? What does this have to do with you? Or us?" He tried to get Lillian to sit down, but she refused.

"Dr. Greeley persuaded Olympia to invest every penny she had. And to put an end to their chattering pressure on me, I put in a little too."

Snow had never once thought to wonder about her money. He assumed she had enough to live well; Brook Street wasn't cheap. But, except for the night of the ball, she dressed so modestly, with little jewelry. And she befriended him, a doctor dependent on his trade. "How much did you lose?" he asked, bluntly.

"Only five thousand pounds. A tenth of my fortune."

Snow breathed slowly, trying to take it in. His own income, until he had quit treating patients that summer, had been eight hundred pounds a year. This summer, except for the occasional

277

anesthesia job, it had been nothing. No one was paying him to tramp the streets in his cholera search. He was living on his savings.

"I had no idea—" He faltered. Forty-five thousand pounds. She still had more than most heiresses one read of in the society pages.

She finally smiled at him. "No, you had no idea. That's one of the things I loved about you." Her smile faded. "But I have terribly important business to attend to. I must go."

She left without kissing him, her manner still withdrawn. It wasn't until the door shut behind her that he remembered, with a chill, that she had said "loved" instead of "love."

Then he began to slowly realize that if he hadn't meddled with Sir Philip's doings, she'd still have every bit of her money. So would all the other investors. He tried to tell himself that the company would have crashed sooner or later, anyway. Investing in these doubtful, mushrooming companies carried its own risks and was disastrous for the economy. But he still felt guilty.

He sat for a few minutes, trying to summon his strength to continue writing. Finally he moved to his desk and began to work again.

34

All the black fabric made a dark periphery to Lillian's field of vision, a black ripple constantly in motion. She had changed from a black street dress into full mourning after coming home from Snow's, dragging the things out of a chest in the attic where all her mourning clothes had been for months. The wool stank of cedar and felt terribly hot after her cotton dresses. But it wasn't important how she felt.

She then left the house, quickly, before Olympia could hear her, and walked to a house in the Edgeware Road, ascending a short flight of steps. She'd spent the morning in Constable's office, persuading Lawes, his secretary, to let her dig through papers to find the address.

The Chopin Ballade in F major drifted from the upper story. The boy's playing it too fast, she thought. Even so, the music was played so well, and the melody so lovely, that tears came to her eyes, and she realized it was the first emotional reaction she'd had to anything since hearing, through Dr. Greeley, of Philip's death. She couldn't tell what the tears were for; surely not Philip. To say they were for her lost money would be ridiculous. Maybe they were for all the lost possibilities of her life. Or for the nine lost years that she could have spent with this boy.

A man in his seventies answered the bell. He, too, wore black, but it looked like an ordinary suit.

"You must be Mr. Romney."

"Yes, miss. How can I help you?" He looked puzzled only for an instant before a flash of knowledge crossed his face.

"I'm Miss Aynsworth. I've come to take Paul Constable."

Romney didn't answer, but Lillian thought that he smiled, actually a small tightening of the side of his mouth. He ushered her in and up the stairs.

"You haven't put the house in mourning?" Lillian asked.

Romney stopped on the stairs, two steps above her. Lillian noticed a small black band over the black wool of his jacket sleeve. "We weren't sure what would be best. Sir Philip always wanted to keep things quiet. It wasn't generally known who maintained the boy."

"Does the boy know?"

"I suppose we must be plain with each other," he said.

"Yes, please."

"Sir Philip decided long ago that he should know nothing. And I still haven't told him about the accident."

Lillian winced, as if a photographer's bright flare had burst before her.

"It would be easy to keep it so," continued Romney. "My wife and I are happy with him. We could keep him with us, break it to him gradually."

"No." Lillian ascended the next step, forcing the man to proceed.

The two entered the room where the boy played. He stopped mid-phrase and looked from Romney to Lillian. The one time she had seen him she hadn't noticed many details, and now she studied him with an intensity he probably found uncomfortable.

His shirt was a bit too short in the arms so that his wrists, no longer those of a little boy, stuck out. His face was absolutely grave as he cast his eyes down and then back to the music on the piano. He seemed to have grown in the intervening days since the concert.

His hair is cut too straight across his brow, she thought. It makes him look so serious, when actually there is a touch of whimsy in his expression. I can cut his hair differently, she thought. And it came to her in a delightful flood all the other things she could do differently. The two of them could have fun. Games. Laughter. That sort of thing. Anything was possible.

She looked straight at him, without smiling. "Paul, I am your mother. You will be coming to stay with me now. You must have some special toys and books you would like to pack up."

"My mother is dead." He said this not sullenly, but as if gently and shyly correcting a mistake a grownup had made.

All through the day she had been rehearsing the answer to this protest, the many possible answers, the complicated stories or lies. What she said was nothing she had practiced.

"They thought I was dead. But I am not, you see." She finally smiled at him but she knew it to be a false smile, rather a nervous grimace, and she quenched it immediately. She would start with no dishonesty this time. Friendliness wouldn't win over this child anyhow. He required something else.

"You sang the Schumann at the concert," he said. "If you are my mother then you'll know where I was born." This was put as a clever riddle, one he was confident she couldn't answer, like one an ogre might give to a goatherd in a fairy tale.

"You were born in Coimbatore in the Nilgiri Hills of southern India. On June 17, 1844." She smiled again, and this time she meant it, in a small glee at having caught him at his own trick.

He stared at her, not so much astonished as admiring. "That's true. And they always lied to me about it. But I knew. I remember the monkeys, you see. And there was an elephant. They don't have those here, except at the zoo." He eyed her differently now, with less skepticism, as if the bargain were already three quarters settled.

She found herself wondering what would happen to the boy with no father, no imagined uncle. Snow was out of the question; she took it for granted that he'd drop her the moment he found out about the boy. It was a fact of life to her, as inevitable as the June monsoons used to be. She clamped down her reaction to this and told herself she felt nothing.

The image of Henry came to mind. He was somewhere in London, waiting, maybe watching her. Somehow with the boy around her she felt safer. Now that Constable and Snow were out of her life, Henry had little he could use against her. The boy would know soon enough that his mother was a whore; Henry would make no difference.

"Shall I get his things ready, miss?" asked Romney. He put one hand on Paul's shoulder as he said this and clutched it hard. It must have hurt a little, for the boy's brows tightened, although he said nothing.

"Yes. Just a few things. We can send for the rest. And the piano."

The man coughed. "The piano belongs to me, miss."

Lillian flushed. "Of course. How silly of me. He can use mine, though it's probably not as good."

"And what about Uncle Phil?" The boy said this as if suddenly remembering. He had been listening intently to the exchange about the piano. "He's my father, isn't he?" His question was earnest; not hostile. He seemed to take it for granted that he would get truthful answers from Lillian now.

She hesitated for only an instant before replying, "You're right. We'll talk about that on the way to our house."

The boy's resemblance to her own father was as unsettling as the first time she saw him. She thought over once more how her father must have looked as he was giving the orders for the baby to be taken away. How did he do it? For all she knew, the day she left for the Nilgiri Hills, five months pregnant, he had taken some man aside and whispered in his ear, "Kill it." She pictured his face, his kind white mustache and tanned skin. Maybe he was even smiling as he gave the final instructions.

No, life without a father might be better for this boy.

She looked at Mr. Romney. "Perhaps you could order a cab."

During the ride to Brook Street she was still uncertain about trying any gesture of affection so she left her hands in her lap, the fingers tensely holding each other. But every time the cab jolted over a rut, she could feel the boy's warmth where he sat next to her on the slippery seat. He made no effort to pull away from her. She supposed she would learn about these things in time.

35

The Lancet office was closed. Disappointment swelled through Snow in a way he hadn't felt since he was a child and a promised trip to the sea was canceled. A green shade covered the window and a small, annoyingly neat printed sign read "Will Open Again For Business on The Fifteenth of September. Cholera death of many staff members."

Four days from now, he thought. Snow stood for a moment, at a loss for what to do next. The manuscript felt heavy and burdensome in his hand. He tapped it against his leg, feeling foolish, trying to think.

He could take it to another journal, but felt a shamefaced reluctance to do so. Nothing else really carried the same weight as The Lancet, not even the British Journal of Medicine, which had published his things before.

A newsboy pushed past him with a stack of Times, shouting as he went, "Plague Wanes! Plague Declines!"

Snow stopped the boy and bought one. The first line of the story read, "The sudden break in hot weather seems to be responsible for a dramatic decline in cholera deaths."

Snow grabbed the boy by the collar. "Who wrote this?" he shouted. When the boy didn't answer immediately he had to restrain himself from striking out.

"Don't know, guvnor. I just sells 'em." He didn't look at all afraid, just startled and amused. When Snow let go, the boy carefully patted his collar back into place. "Got no right to bend a fellow around like that," he muttered, looking annoyed and yet oddly pleased, as if this one insane toff had connected him closer to real news.

It was strange, thought Snow, that in all these years of knowing Caleb he had never seen his office. Shared office, that is. A tiny room. Another desk, its owner absent, was so close that it must have been difficult for the two men to move through the room at the same time. On Caleb's desk a cup of tea and a stale-looking half loaf took up the only clear spot amid stacks of proofs. Caleb turned a pencil around in his hands, pausing before answering Snow's question.

He finally said, "Snow, you've got to believe I have no control over these things."

"Then I suppose it's out of the question that you print this tomorrow?" Snow tossed over a one-page abstract of the pump story that he'd scratched out while waiting to see Caleb.

Caleb picked it up with a skepticism and read it quickly. "I can try," he said in a clipped voice. "But the chief editor doesn't want anything that might cause a panic. Contagion theories don't appeal to him. And if you want to know the truth, the public is getting tired of cholera."

"How do you know such nonsense as that?"

"Look, yesterday our three lead stories were on cholera and two other papers did the action on the Crimean front and a family murder in Manchester. And their sales were double ours."

"You can't be serious. We're talking about large numbers of deaths being prevented by this one bit of information."

"Snow, whatever the reason, the epidemic is over. It's old news now. Cholera's a summer plague, isn't it? It's September now. Summer's gone. Next week, ask any man on the street about cholera, and he'll say, 'Oh, that was ages ago.'"

"But, Beersdon, you've got to print something about the pump. You know it's true."

"I'll see what I can do," said his former friend. "What about The Lancet? I thought you were going to try there."

"They're closed for four days." Snow's voice sounded whining and petulant to his own ears but he didn't care.

Caleb shrugged, moved the pencil again. "I'll see what I can do."

36

1

The bells of St. Anne's were ringing again, for the first time in three days. They'd been silent since the bell puller died of cholera. They must have found a new man. It was five o'clock and Snow was just beginning to think of getting Mrs. Jarrett to bring up some tea.

Lillian had sent back his notes and apparently refused to see him. He'd called three times and was always told the same thing: "Not at home." He ached for her and was in complete confusion over why she would do this, but at the same time he felt removed from it, as if he were reading the trials of a romantic hero in a cheap novel.

He sat at his desk, carefully stacking up notes and papers and odd bits of writing. He felt restless and exhausted at the same time.

It was gradually dawning on him that he had nothing to do. His paper was finished. Until tomorrow morning, when *The Lancet* opened, he could take it nowhere. There was no more information to collect. His practice was so abandoned that not a single patient waited to see him. For the first time in weeks he could feel free to simply sit and look at his hands.

The bell rang. It was Phineas Greeley, shown in by Mrs. Jarrett.

What on earth was the man doing here? Snow hadn't seen him since that night at the party, and before that they hadn't spoken in years. There rose in Snow's mind a ripple of distrust. He found himself on guard. When the two sat down, Snow could feel his manuscript behind him on the desk with the sort of presence that only a human should possess. It weighed on his mind and he felt a strange protectiveness over it. He wished he had put it away. Suddenly Snow remembered that Greeley, too, had lost money in the Great Western crash. How much?

"Just a little social call, Snow. I like to keep up with my more gifted students." He looked around the disordered room. "Still not married, eh? No one to pick up the scientist's mess." Greeley blinked his pink-rimmed eyes rapidly and licked his lips. He gave a quick and obviously unthinking brush to the shoulders of his coat where dandruff lay like ashes.

"Well, Snow, I understand your theories about cholera are becoming more certain. Congratulations."

Snow felt his guard rising further. "Yes, I have a few small ideas. Nothing really."

"I would so like to hear about them."

"They're hardly in a final state," said Snow, almost stuttering.

"Just a few notes jotted down, eh?" Greeley's eyes focused on the pages behind Snow, and stayed there. "Do you happen to remember, Snow, that little talk we had at Lady Tewksbury's?"

"Yes, of course I remember talking with you."

"I mean specifically, what we talked about. About cholera."

"Why no, I can hardly recall the exact words." Other recollections flooded Snow's mind. Lillian dancing. And Lillian's first sight of Constable. "It's a terrible thing, Greeley, about Constable."

"Sir Philip. Yes." Greeley looked aside, his smile briefly fading.

There were a few moments of silence. Snow wondered how long the man would stay. He had been relishing his solitude. Just as he was thinking of a reason to have to go out himself (he could always come back in a few minutes), Greeley spoke, in a different tone of voice.

"I want my name on that paper, Snow."

Snow felt tongue-tied and yet not surprised, oddly gratified that he had been right about the man from the start. "What paper?" He knew it was just stalling.

"I know you've finished it, and it's sitting right there behind you. You can't deny that my ideas contributed."

Snow stretched to recall what they had talked of. Was Greeley fabricating this?

"If we discussed any theories, Doctor, it could only have been in the most trivial way." It came to him then; it was Greeley who first talked of two water supplies, separating their effects. And he had been right.

"I'll expose you, boy. You'll never be published again."

Snow stood up. "It's out of the question, Doctor. You can't imagine that I'll—"

"I have something here you may want to look at before you give me your answer." From an inner pocket of his coat Greeley pulled a rough envelope, now curved to fit the shape of his chest. He drew from it a few sheets of yellowed paper, peeled one off as if it were a layer of onion skin, and held it out toward Snow. His dry lips spread in an unpleasant smile.

"Go ahead. Look at it."

Snow took the paper and crossed the room to the window and began to read. The handwritten ink was blurred with age and the paper was almost transparent, but the writing was clear and strong, easy to read.

June 4, 1844

Dear Phil,

I write knowing this may never reach you. The birth should happen in a few days. You have answered no letters yet, but please, please, answer this one. Someone will try to get this to you. I am watched constantly.

Lillian

Even as he absorbed the contents with shock, he registered a small delight in this peek at her writing at an earlier age. It was girlish, with large loops to the "p" and "l." The one message she had written him had a spiky look to the hand that must have developed as she matured.

With a sense of nausea Snow remembered Constable's fungal nails. Of course it was him. It all made perfect sense.

"What a load of rubbish," he said. "I'm surprised you allow yourself to touch these obscene forgeries." As he spoke he crumpled the letter in his fist and stuffed it deep into his pants pocket.

Greeley didn't seem the least perturbed by his response. "Fine, fine, destroy that one. But I have many more. The lady was quite a letter writer. And she was not discreet in what she wrote."

Snow tried to look unconcerned, but he felt his heart pounding. The woman he thought he knew was changing shape before the eyes of his imagination into someone alien. And at the same time he wasn't completely surprised. He'd known she was no virgin. Even in the dim light of that cricket pavilion he had seen small signs and probably denied them to himself. The little marks below the navel, the faint separation of the abdominous rectus muscle. If only it hadn't been a man he knew.

"And that isn't all, Snow. Perhaps you didn't know she has a stepbrother? Had, I should say. No, he wasn't a specimen a family would talk about much. Well, you ask her sometime, just how close was her friendship with this stepbrother. Red hair. A handsome fellow, until cholera got him last week."

"Look here, Greeley." Every trace of madness and reptilian slime about this old man was coming to the surface. "I refuse to listen to this nonsense about Miss Aynsworth's family. Whether these letter are real or not, you can't mean to expose them."

Greeley said nothing.

"And why do you tell me about them?"

"Ah, but Snow, you fail to see my point. We can make a fair exchange. I am happy to see that you have all the letters. I'm sure the lady's secrets will be quite safe with you. I know that you have her, ah, interests, at heart."

Snow felt absolute mistrust but still talked as though it were a normal conversation about an everyday thing.

"Well, then. Give me the letters and I will see that they're destroyed."

"Exchange, I said. Exchange."

"Is it money you want then? You came to the wrong man if you wanted to turn a large profit, but I can give you something."

Greeley smiled, benevolent, his paternal grace almost return-

288

ing. "No, no, Keep your money." He turned to the manuscript. "Just a little change on the title page. We can keep your name on it somewhere, if you like. Technical Assistance, that sort of thing."

Snow was silent for a long time, and then without a word, reached behind him for the manuscript and handed it to Greeley.

Greeley left with the pages under his arm while Snow sat at his desk, leafing through the yellowed sheets he had gained in exchange.

2

At first he tried not to read them. He laid his hand flat on the stack and shut his eyes, reasoning that just because he had paid for them they were not his. He tried to make himself believe he didn't care. They could have been anyone's letters.

An image came to him from the day in Hyde Park, in the cricket pavilion. Throughout much of the afternoon a damp rose petal had adhered to the leather of Lillian's boot. The tip of the petal was a flushed pink and its oval shape was crossed with a translucent brown line where it had been crushed. During moments in that dark room, with the rain drumming outside, Snow had tried to listen to what Lillian was saying and found that he could only focus on that petal.

He finally gave in. The letters were so short that he could have read the batch in fifteen minutes, but it was over an hour before he put the last one down and rubbed his eyes, which were burning and raw, as if he had spent a day studying anatomy texts.

He attempted without success to keep the pictures from his mind, of Lillian, younger and remote, her bare skin chafed against a horsehair sofa in an abandoned colonial drawing room, palm fronds clattering a window and cockatoos hooting in the background. What had happened to the child?

A hot and unexpected anger surged through him. He couldn't tell at first who it was against. Certainly not Greeley. And Constable was dead. So it must be Lillian, he thought.

Snow's glance fell on the bare spot where the manuscript had sat. Now there was only the bust of the ancient Greek doctor,

289

pale in the remaining light from the window, looking at him with reproach. After all his talk that he was about to publish, and so sure finally of his idea, he would become a figure of absolute ridicule. What could he possibly say? I'm sorry, but I've decided to wait. It was wrong after all. Or, I've decided to pursue a different career.

A dull recognition broke through that Greeley had probably thought that out, and had already started on a plan to discredit anything connected with Snow, so that when the paper appeared no one would be surprised that it was Greeley's work and not Snow's.

He hadn't known it was possible to feel so humiliated and worthless.

Vaguely smiling, as cool as wine, Lillian's face appeared before him, so vivid that he almost reached out to push it away. What an infernal bitch she's been, he thought. Then he rose suddenly and left. He'd force his way in if necessary. He had to see her at once.

37

1

There was a hollow, unused sound to the bell at Lillian's door. Snow felt furtive, as if he should turn up his coat collar or make some other typical gesture of concealment.

It wasn't until a maid opened the door that he realized the knocker was tied with a small stiff black ribbon. The ribbon wasn't anywhere near big enough for a family member. Some servant, he thought. This time she let him in, and went off to get Lillian.

He had to wait in a stiff green parlor for twenty minutes, where he began leafing through an album of photographs of India, all large and mounted on gold-leaf paper. Most were colonial types, sitting stiffly beside men in turbans or atop an elephant. Then he was faced with a picture of a much younger Lillian, different from the way he'd imagined her an hour ago, standing with her stepmother and two women in saris, in front of a white veranda. She must have moved her hand as the photographer snapped his shutter, for instead of her right hand there was nothing but a white blur, looking like a dove's wing in flight.

"Ghastly, aren't they? I hate photograph portraits."

Snow jumped, startled and sheepish. Lillian had come in too quietly for him to hear. He hastily shut the book. He felt as if he had been meddling.

He looked up and felt a moment of physical shock on seeing her in full mourning. A quick electric pulse shot down his fingertips and left an alert tingling, while he took in the matte black dress, jet earrings, and the absurd widow's cap, which was too large for her. She must have borrowed her stepmother's.

Even though Snow had seen countless women in widow's weeds, the effect was as ghastly as if she were the first.

She looked older. There was a barely discernible graininess in the delicate skin under her eyes, which he hadn't noticed three days before. She was not less beautiful; just graver and sterner.

Behind her a dark thin boy emerged from the doorway, his eyes overly large for his face. At first Snow thought the child might be consumptive, but on a longer look he seemed to be one of those types of perversely healthy children who are never ill with so much as a cold, but whose ribs can always be counted and every line of cartilage marked on their faces.

The boy stepped closer to Lillian, looking questioningly at Snow, and reached out his hand to her as a much younger child might have.

She held him in front of her like a shield, her hands not on his narrow shoulders but farther down, meeting protectively across his chest. He was placid under her touch.

Snow was so thrown off by this unexpected third person that he didn't know where to begin. Then it came to him, in a blink of thought. Of course. Her child.

His first impulse was to look around, glance furtively out the window, and through the door to the hall. "Don't hold him like that," he whispered to Lillian. "People will suspect."

She gave a low, harsh laugh. "You make too much of my claims to virtue. You, of all people, should know better."

Snow found himself breathing quickly as his anger rose. The fat packet of letters in his inner pocket pressed against his chest like an examiner's hand feeling for palpitations.

"He doesn't look like you, except in the mouth," Snow said. Her mouth to him had always been so obviously sensuous, that he intended this as a barb, but it seemed to have no effect on her.

She glanced down at the top of the boy's head, and while still looking down, she said, "And his hands. His fingernails are shaped just like mine." She looked up and held one of her own hands out for demonstration. Paul kicked at the carpet, not in rebellion, but abstractly, passing the time until the grownups finished their talk.

Snow found himself drawn in, wanting to examine the hands for comparison, itching to step closer, near enough to touch her, to smell the soap she used.

Instead he pulled out the packet of letters and held them up. "These are yours." He tossed them on a side table with legs carved like dog feet. Cherubs entwined its rim.

Lillian stepped over, one arm still around the boy, and delicately fingered the packet. There was only a moment of confusion before she blushed deeply in a dark pink glow that started at her neck and moved upwards at the speed of blood. She left them there. "These don't matter now. I am done with secrets."

"I wish I had known that two hours ago." His anger showed only as a slight tightening of his voice, but she heard it and seemed to become alert for the first time.

"What do you mean? Where did you get these?"

"You had better send that boy upstairs, if you can bear to part with him for a moment."

"Yes, you're right. Paul, go upstairs to your room. I'll be along in a little while." The child turned obediently and left without looking at Snow.

It was a relief to see him go. Snow felt hostile toward him, with his uncanny silence and watching eyes.

As soon as the door clicked shut, Snow lost his control. "Do you realize what you have done?" His voice was shaking. "Greeley brought those letters to me this morning and said he'd expose you. And here I find you dressed like a crow, fondling the boy as if he were a pet spaniel. I suppose you intend to keep none of it a secret?"

She raised her chin. "There's no point. It's not a question of shame. I no longer feel things like that."

"You! What does it matter what you feel? What about the boy? Will he want it known that his father was a swindler?"

She didn't seem at all surprised that he knew who the letters were about. "Would you prefer that I raise the boy under the shadow of a constant lie, as his father did? He was a weak and vulgar man. I was one of his mistakes."

She went on. "Why do you concern yourself at all about it?

293

I hold you to no obligation as far as the two of us are concerned. That goes without saying."

Snow felt his anger soften. She looked so self-punishing. But it would have been too easy to let it drop. Too many things were unfinished. "Why didn't you tell me about any of this?" He tried not to sound self-righteous, without much success.

"Tell you what? About the boy? I only knew he was alive a few days ago."

"And what about Sir Philip? You could have said something, kept me from feeling like such a fool."

"I wouldn't have known that your pride was so sensitive."

"Don't sound so smug. It's not pride, nor is it jealousy, as you might like to think. Those letters cost me two years' work. I didn't get them for nothing." Snow was stung into telling her this, and he hadn't planned to.

"You said Greeley gave them to you."

"Don't you understand yet? He took my cholera manuscript. They were sold to me, not given. Your great family friend was fully prepared to publish them. He said he got them from some mad stepbrother before the fellow died of cholera." He saw her hard expression falter. "Someone you were supposed to have an . . . unnatural affection for." He knew it was spiteful but he said it anyway.

She stared at Snow, finally seeming to understand. "Henry— dead—" She sat down suddenly and put a hand to her forehead. Then she slowly began to stroke the inside of her forearm with one finger, a gesture that made no sense to Snow. She took a few deep breaths and went on. "It was foolish of you, as you can see, to give him anything." She blushed again, deeply. "I will repay you, of course."

She stood and walked to a small desk and opened a drawer. "Surely a manuscript like that has a specific value? For how much shall I write out the cheque?"

Snow was unable to answer the question, or even to speak. He felt as if his mind were frozen in confusion and dismay. Every word they had spoken to each other was hostile and distant, and for himself at least, the exact opposite of what he was trying to tell her. He wanted her more than ever. The boy meant nothing to him. For all he cared she could have a dozen illegitimate children.

"Lillian, please, I—"

She turned her face to him, the pen in her hand, her expression harsh and unforgiving. "The amount?" It sounded like an accusation, or a bitter insult.

There was a knock on the door and a maid stuck her head through. "If you please, miss, luncheon is served in the dining room." She raised her eyebrows on seeing Lillian's black dress, then looked at Snow. "Shall I set another place, miss?"

Snow picked up his hat and practically ran past the maid, down the stairs, and out the front door.

2

"They didn't want the bloody thing," shouted Greeley. He threw the pages on the floor of Snow's study where they fanned out like a big pack of cards, their edges now bent and smudged from so much handling.

At first Snow didn't believe him. Everything coming from Greeley was suspect now, even the most logical statements. He must have made some mistake, bungled it somehow.

"You aren't talking about *The Lancet*, are you?"

"What else could I mean? Did you think I'd take it to *Punch*?"

Snow wondered at his own disappointment. He should be pleased that Greeley's scheme had failed, but he felt only rejection. "What did they say, exactly?"

"They said the subject was stale. Too much on cholera already." Greeley absently checked his skull for the placement of a few strands of silver hair. "They said the proof wasn't strong enough, anyway."

"No," said Snow to himself. "They never have gone with the infection theories anyway. I should have known."

Greeley seemed to have recovered from his anger and bent to pick up the sheets of writing. "No matter," he said. "I'll just try *The British Journal of Medicine*."

Snow leaned forward and gripped the man's arm, more tightly than he had planned, and pulled him into an upright position. He saw him wince. For a moment Snow felt a rush of intense physical hatred, and had to strongly resist striking him in the face. He felt himself shaking with the effort.

"Get out of here," he said, and released his grip.

Greeley smiled horribly and rubbed the place on his arm. "You don't want to make a mistake like that, my boy. That girl's—"

"I don't give a bloody damn about the girl."

Greeley's grin became vague, his eyes grew less focused. "We could try a coauthorship. I'm willing to be fair. It wouldn't look half-bad, my—"

Snow lunged at him, just stopping himself from putting his hands around the pink throat, and instead grabbed both his shoulders and shoved him toward the door. The man became suddenly unresisting, and let himself be pushed out. He stumbled down the stairs with his shoulders stooping, not looking back.

As Snow stood at the top and watched him go, he felt a short rush of guilt and pity for Greeley. It faded almost before he noticed it.

He slowly gathered up his pages. During the scuffle he and Greeley had both tread on them, and they were scattered around, under the desk, a few over by the armchair. When he stood up with them clutched in a bunch in his hand, he found that he was sweating and his hands were shaking. He sat down for a few minutes, doing nothing, just staring into space.

It all seemed such a waste. He tried hard to think of the people he had saved by removing the pump handle. But it wasn't enough. Another pump could become contaminated tomorrow. Or right at this moment.

He had to try one more thing. Even if Caleb wouldn't help him print a part of the article, maybe they would take just a letter. He straightened out the pages, still in his lap, and went to lock them in a drawer of his desk. Then he left for *The Times*.

3

He could see Caleb through the glass door into his office, before Caleb could see him, and he watched Caleb's face while the clerk told him who was waiting. Caleb rubbed at his forehead, hard, and breathed out through his nose in a long, tired sigh before rising to meet Snow.

"Did *The Lancet* accept your paper?"

Snow wanted to tell someone the story about Greeley, but not Caleb. All he said was, "No. And I have another favor to ask you."

Caleb was immediately guarded.

"I understand what you said about printing a portion of the whole report. But what about a letter? Any one could have sent in a letter."

Caleb shook his head. "I'm sorry. The chief editor said no. Nothing on cholera being infectious."

"But that's absurd! You know—"

"It's the final stance of the paper. No infection theories. He says it'll cause a panic. No one will want to drink any water in the whole city. The water proof and the pump, especially, were frightening to him. He said it was out of the question."

Snow felt that a defense was beyond him. It all seemed an enormous joke. "But, Caleb, you worked on this with me, at least at the beginning. You understand exactly what all the findings mean. Can't you see how urgent it is that we publicize it?"

Caleb looked out the window, away from Snow. "Perhaps you should forget about it and go back to your anesthesiology work." He turned back to Snow. "There's no question there. Your ether and chloroform research has been brilliant."

For some reason Snow remembered the letters against him that had appeared. It was all too easy. Now that he thought of it, no other newspaper had nonsensical correspondence like that, at least not against *him*. "The paper paid you to do it, didn't they. *You* wrote those letters against me. And they're paying you to keep my writing unpublished."

Caleb didn't answer him. He just kept looking at Snow, not quite as distant as before, his brows knitted.

"Constable's dead, Caleb. He can't hold you to any bargain."

"I don't know what you're talking about."

"Was it Greeley, then? He can't have paid you much. The old man's on the edge of madness, did you know that? I wouldn't side with him if I were you."

"You need a rest, Snow. I can't understand why you imagine all these things. It's simply a matter of editorial priorities. *I* know your theory is true. But that doesn't mean I can use the paper as a broadcasting tool."

Snow started to protest again but Caleb interrupted him.

"Think about it for a moment. Cholera is dying down fast.

There were only thirty cases in the whole city yesterday. People are calming down, getting back to business, coming back from the long vacation. And then we publish your letter, or even the whole paper, saying that water carries the thing, that the city's pipes are polluted, that nothing is safe. It will start all over again!"

"Cholera won't start."

"No, but all the rest. Did you know that five shops on Oxford Street were looted last week, during the worst of it?"

Snow said nothing. He wasn't listening any longer. Caleb's face began to swim before him, strangely out of shape, as if they were both underwater. A loud humming, which must have started some time before, blotted out all the clattering office sounds, and through it came Caleb's voice, dim now, maybe from another room.

"Snow, what the devil—"

A sudden sickening pain had racked the small of his back, and to his wretched embarrassment he found that he was urinating in his pants. He couldn't stand and knew he'd fall any moment. He stumbled toward Caleb's chair, where he sat with his head in his hands, rocking like a blind man.

"Not cholera. Kidneys," he panted, and tried to ask for a glass of water. "Or the chloroform experiments," he muttered, but his tongue felt as thick as if he'd been sucking on ice. He could focus on Caleb better now, and guessed that *he* assumed it was cholera. His face showed no fear, though, and Snow felt grateful to him for that. It was the last thought he had before passing out.

38

"John, you've got to try."

When Snow opened his eyes he thought he must still be light headed. Lillian sat at the side of the bed, a spoon in her hand, jabbing it toward his mouth as though he were a reluctant infant. It held some pink viscous stuff which Snow batted away. She pulled the spoon back just in time to keep it from dripping over the sheets.

"You asked for this stuff yourself. Now take it."

"I did?" It was real. He could smell her there, her mix of sandalwood and strawberry. And his own urine too, on damp clothes. The scene came back to him. Had that look on Caleb's face been compassion, or just curiosity?

"How did I get home?" He was afraid to question why she was there. He just tried to enjoy it while it lasted. She was no longer wearing black, but the same gray dress she'd had on the day at Hyde Park.

The old bed curtains around his head seemed as comforting as broken-in flannel pajamas. He touched the fabric lightly with his fingertips.

"Caleb brought you in a cab."

Snow rubbed one eye. He remembered now; not coming home, but being here, on the bed, shouting out to some blurry figure for his elderberry elixir. "Can I talk to him?"

"He left as soon as you were on the bed." She made another jab with the spoon. "What is this mess you wanted, anyway?"

"Elderberry syrup. For my kidneys."

Snow struggled to sit, but the sudden jab of pain in his lower back made him grunt and he gave up.

"It started with my father, too, at about my age." Snow took another spoonful with effort. "You get used to it, he told me." New waves of agony came and faded and Snow took a deep breath. Snow opened his mouth and once more felt the spoon slide in over his tongue.

When he was done with the bottle he lay quiet and stared at the lump his feet made under the cover, afraid to look at Lillian.

"I came to say I was all wrong," she said. "I'm sorry. I should have told you about it from the beginning. You were right to be angry."

Snow waited, afraid that any interruption would stop her story.

"Philip Constable was my lover. You know that now, of course. Since I'm keeping his son now, my son, that is, I understand why you can't see me. It's all right. That's what I came here to tell you. I'll go as soon as you want."

Relief washed over Snow, making him feel even weaker. He had to take a few breaths before speaking; he was afraid his voice might shake. "Is that all? All you were angry about? I can learn to live with your son. If you had only let me finish, this morning, you would have known that. I just wish you had told me." He felt, finally, that accepting her past was like accepting any other flaw that came with the package; bad handwriting, perhaps, or a tendency to snore.

She leaned over to embrace him. Though he felt so foul, he welcomed it.

Finally she stood up. "There's a letter from your father. It came an hour ago, marked 'urgent.' Do you feel up to reading it?"

Snow opened it. His vision was still blurry but if he squinted he could make out his father's cramped, angry writing.

John—

The money's all gone. Don't try to tell me it was a fool's thing to do. The Great Western shares tripled in two

300

weeks, until they fell. We lost the house and the farm. Don't ask me to come live with you; I can do better than that with my last days. I just wish you had let me know, since you were in with Constable from the beginning. Didn't I tell you I bought the shares? All I can say is I'm not surprised that loyalty would come last with someone like you.

Snow started laughing. His hoots sounded hysterical and he stifled them as quickly as he could.

"What is it?" asked Lillian.

"He was right. I did forget all about his investment. My father's joined the club of the Great Western crashers." He started laughing again.

"Oh, no. How terrible for you."

He forced himself to stop again. "No, really. The farm was dwindling in value every year. Bad soil, a crumbling house. It makes no difference to me." He tossed her the letter. "It's his accusations that hurt. You know what he's like." He fell silent, staring at the wall. "You know, I don't think I ever loved him," he said quietly.

She read the letter in silence, then took Snow's hand and held it. "I forget who, in the Bible, said 'Honor thy Father.' They didn't have a father like yours. Or mine."

He didn't ask her to explain. He hoped there would be plenty of time for that later.

"Did Caleb say anything before he left?" asked Snow.

"About the cab fare, you mean? He paid that."

"No, no, about—" Snow found he didn't know how to put it.

"Not much. He said you were ill at his office. Oh, yes, I almost forgot. He gave me this." Lillian pulled a note from her pocket and handed it over.

Snow unfolded it eagerly but was disappointed. All it said was,."Try publishing privately. I've written a note to Jackson's in Golden Square. They may give you a good rate."

Snow's first instinct was to feel insulted. He squirmed in the bedclothes, suddenly restless and hot. Only amateurs published privately. It would be the beginning of the end of his career. Caleb must have known that.

"What did he say that made you so quiet?" asked Lillian.

Two carts rattled by on the street. Snow listened to them,

feeling removed from everything around him, and wondered what to tell her. She didn't know of his failure at *The Lancet*.

"I had asked him to help publish my conclusions about that pump."

She tensed, and asked, quietly, "So you got the manuscript back from Dr. Greeley after seeing me?"

"Yes. Don't worry about it."

Suddenly she started laughing. "No, I won't worry about anything Dr. Greeley might do. I almost forgot to tell you. You won't believe what happened. This morning when I went down for breakfast Olympia was gone. She wrote me a note. She and Dr. Greeley left for France together. She said I was too wild for her. Said she knew she would never get used to having Paul in the house, playing all that serious music."

This broke their tension. Snow, too, began to laugh. "You've got to be joking. Was he after her money?"

"What money? She lost it all, and so did Greeley as far as I know. I still can't believe she really did it. He always reminded me of the lizards that lived on the ceilings at home."

Greeley's pink-rimmed eyes, as the man clutched Lillian's letters, came back to Snow. He tried to suppress an image of his pink, wrinkled frame laboring atop Olympia in some French hotel room.

"And what about Caleb? Didn't he publish it?" asked Lillian. Her voice was serious again.

"No, as a matter of fact. Said it would cause a panic."

"What about that medical journal you were talking about?

"*The Lancet?* They wouldn't have it either. They said cholera's written about too often. They don't like the theory of contagion. So far no one has read about the pump, if you can believe it. Caleb suggests that I publish the work myself. Privately." He waved the note.

"How many pages is it?"

"What does that matter?"

Lillian said patiently, as if to a child, "Because the printer would probably charge by the page. And that's the only way I can know if I have enough liquid funds to do it."

Snow's face flushed with surprise, embarrassment, and plea-sure. "I have funds. That's not the issue here," said Snow. Even as he spoke, he realized it wasn't true. He had about fifty pounds to his name right now. He didn't know how he'd pay Mrs. Jarrett at the end of the quarter. He thought with regret of the five-pound notes he'd flung at the man driving that wagon of water barrels.

"I'd like to do this thing for you. I know you haven't got much saved, if you spent the summer working on cholera instead of earning money."

"I can't let you do it, Lillian." Snow swung his legs over to the edge of the bed. Dizziness rocked him for half a minute and a surge of nausea passed over him like a wind.

"You shouldn't get up yet." She put a restraining hand on Snow's shoulder. "Wait a day."

"There's too much to do." Snow stood and pulled at the bell. His trousers were still damp. He felt as filthy as a man who has slept on the street for a month.

Mrs. Jarrett arrived and gave a short bend of her head to Lillian.

"I want this room stripped and cleaned," said Snow. "I'll sleep in the study until it's done. The bed curtains, the window drapes, everything. Send it out if you can't get it done here." He didn't look at her as he spoke, but started pulling his shirt off.

Half-dressed, he limped to the window and raised it as high as he could. A cool evening breeze, carrying smells of horse dung and autumn leaves, stirred his hair. The summer was over.

He turned to Lillian. "All right. You can pay for it, whatever it costs. On one condition."

She looked nervous, and asked, "What's that?"

"That you burn every page of those damned letters. I want to see the ashes." He remembered he still had one, crumpled deep in the pocket of his wet trousers. He pulled it out, unfolded it, and tossed it to her. "You see, they could end up anywhere." She caught the damp piece of paper without a word. They both started to laugh again.

39

London, January 1855

Snow stood next to Lillian in the metallic din of the print shop. An icy draft blew from under the front door, but he didn't care. The smell of fresh ink filled his senses as he flipped through a copy of his cholera paper.

He had printed it as a pamphlet, with a red cover of the most expensive paper Lillian could afford. His secret dread had been that it would look like a methodist tract, or some swindling investment proposal. But it was all right; it had a distinctly medical air.

He handed one to Lillian and she, too, flipped through it, then handed it back to him. "I hardly need to read it. Don't I already know every word? But I can tell you want to. Go ahead. I'll wait." She smiled and turned away.

She was right. He wanted to pore over every page. His heart raced with a nervousness he couldn't explain. While he scanned the first section, absorbed, she seemed to be busy with her hands at the printer's worktable. He looked up and saw that she had taken a blank sheet of foolscap paper and folded it into a perfect white bird with outstretched wings. With a small overhand toss, like tossing a pebble into a brook, she sent the thing flying. It swooped gracefully across the room until it crashed into a bookshelf.

The printer's apprentice, a boy of about ten, looked at Lillian with admiration.

"Coo, miss, where'd you learn that?"

"In India. Here, I'll show you. It's like a little kite."

She took another piece of paper and bent over it with the boy while Snow went on reading. After half a minute he realized he hadn't read much of it; he was just too excited to concentrate. He put three copies under his arm and turned toward the door.

"Lillian, I can't think in here. Let's go for a walk. What time do we have to be back at your house?" Lillian had left Brook Street and had bought a small house in Bloomsbury Square, near the British Museum.

She looked up from her paper lesson. "Paul will be through practicing at two. We'll have lunch then." She held up another model of a bird, this one with a sweeping tail, and let it fly. The apprentice murmured with delight and ran to retrieve his prize.

Snow looked at the wall clock. Eleven. "Come on, then. I need some air."

Lillian buttoned her coat and showed the boy for a third time an important fold in the bird's wing, then followed Snow out the door.

There was a heavy gray sky and the wind cut right through the seams of their coats. It had been a mild autumn and Christmas, but it seemed that winter was really here now.

Snow thought of the stacks of pamphlets in the office behind them. "Lillian, when the distributors start selling the pamphlet, I'll have a little more money. Won't you reconsider?"

She kept walking, looking up at the dark sky instead of at him. "Do you think it will snow?" When he didn't answer, she went on. "No. I won't marry you, not yet." She put her arm through his. "Can't you understand it? I want to try doing things a new way. I can't see that marriage helps anybody. I'm afraid it would destroy what we have. My other offer is still open."

Flakes started drifting from the sky and Snow thought over her offer, once more. To live with him, sleep with him, have children with him if he wished it. But she wouldn't sign the papers or go to a church. He looked over at her. Her eyes were wide with delight at the snowfall, and yet the concern for hurting him still showed on her face.

"I love you more than I did in those first days, if you can believe it," he said to her.

She smiled at him; a few snowflakes stuck to her hair. "Oh, I believe it. I think I can tell. Now you can trust me, at least."

305

"Yes." But he wasn't telling the complete truth. He knew there was a part of her that would always be hidden from him. She was not secretive, but she was private. He had grown used to it by now. The unknown parts of her made her seem larger in his presence, as if she actually took up a few extra inches of space outside the outlines of her body. It made her seem like some secret goddess, and he loved her no less for it.

The snow thickened. Their shoulders grew white with it. They were almost to Regent's Park and on a whim they decided to go in, even though the snow was worsening.

At least the wind was dying down. The place was deserted, of course. Yellow stalks of unmown grass, the last from the summer, stuck up through the thin white snow. The ducks on the pond seemed to ignore the snow, and bobbed for freezing algae, their curly tail feathers catching flakes for a minute before they melted.

They both stood for a long time at the edge of the water and watched.

And then she kissed him, holding his face in cold hands. It was a kiss one early Christian might have bestowed on another, full of charity and good will, with a trace of mysticism. Her cheeks were cold, but her lips were warm.

"All right," he finally said. "I'll agree to your plan." He turned from the pond, holding her hand now, and kept walking, kicking the snow in front of him. "I don't know what it will do to my practice, though. If the income from my practice stays steady I insist on sharing expenses. Your fortune—"

"Good." Her voice was so soft he barely heard. She gazed at the sky; he thought she was absorbed by profound introspection until she said, "I'll come to your house; there's more room. Mrs. Jarrett might quit, you know, but I think I can win her over. And Paul can have the upstairs maids' room—but where will we put his piano?" She dropped his hand and turned to him. "You keep walking, I've got to get back and start packing immediately." She buttoned the top button of his overcoat, kissed him again, and turned around to hurry down the white path.

Snow watched her go. As she passed a small tree she must have startled a flock of pigeons, for suddenly about forty of them burst up into the sky over her head, veering in unison to the left, before heading for another part of the park. The sky, even though snow was falling heavily, was so bright it was hard to look at the birds.

He was at the zoo now, the snow falling so thickly it was difficult to see the brick gates. Surprisingly, they were open, and he found himself going in.

Most of the animals were holed up inside, too wise to stand out in the snow and wind when they had the option of a hutch or shed. All but the elephant. The snow apparently didn't bother him. His feet were planted firmly on the packed ground as he munched hay from a manger. He used his trunk to pull the pale strands out from under the snow with complete indifference to the weather.

A keeper emerged from the brick interior. The man, an Indian, stooped to fork more hay up to the top of the manger. He was dressed only in a thin shirt and pants and was barefoot. His arms shook as he tried to straighten the pile of hay. When he noticed Snow he was so startled that he dropped the fork.

The elephant stirred at the metallic thunk the fork made against the earth.

"I'm sorry," called out Snow. "I didn't mean to frighten you."

The man said nothing, just stared at Snow. Snow stared back, until he saw the fellow give an involuntary shiver and clutch his arms to his chest.

Carefully, without any hurry, Snow took off his overcoat and folded it. He raised the coat over the railings and offered it up.

The Indian shook his head, motioning with his hand that he didn't want it. But Snow persisted, pushing the coat at him over the fence as far as he could without actually dropping it on the other side into the litter of straw and droppings.

Snow had a vision of taking off his shoes, his shirt, even his wool trousers, and offering them up. He didn't. But he could see so clearly in his mind the pink stripe he'd make against the white ground, walking naked out of the park.

Finally he left his coat draped over the railing and turned to go. There wasn't enough wind to blow the coat off. He shivered, though nothing like the Indian man had done, and turned to go. At the first tree he stood behind the trunk and turned back to look.

The man was stepping lightly over to the fence, picking his way carefully. He snatched up the coat, shook it once, and put

307

it on. It was much too big for him, and covered his hands beyond the fingertips. Even though he couldn't have seen Snow, he made one short bow, his hands together, toward the trees. Then, opening his arms wide, he pivoted toward the elephant, his head back, moving with a dancer's energy Snow wouldn't have thought him capable of. He executed a few steps of some folk dance with his hands high, gyrating in a circle around the placid beast, until he disappeared behind the elephant.

Snow felt like an eavesdropper and stopped watching. His feet were wet. A light wind sprang up, chilling him instantly, and he almost regretted his gift. Hunching his shoulders together, moving in a trot to keep warm, he headed down the path out of the park.

Afterword

John Snow died on June 17, 1858, of a stroke brought on by kidney disease, and perhaps by self-experimentation with anesthesia. He was forty-four years old and unmarried.

His theories on the communication of cholera were never fully accepted by the scientific community in his lifetime. But since then, he has been fully credited as being the discoverer of the cause of cholera, and the first modern epidemiologist.